The Rome Affair

Karen Swan was previously a fashion editor and lives
in East Sussex with her husband and three children.

Visit Karen's website at www.karenswan.com, or
you can find her author page on Facebook
or follow her on Twitter @KarenSwan1.

Also by Karen Swan

The
ROME
AFFAIR

KAREN SWAN

PAN BOOKS

First published 2017 by Macmillan

This paperback edition published 2017 by Pan Books
an imprint of Pan Macmillan
20 New Wharf Road, London N1 9RR
Associated companies throughout the world
www.panmacmillan.com

ISBN 978-1-5098-3801-1

1 3 5 7 9 8 6 4 2

A CIP catalogue record for this book is available from the British Library.

Typeset by Ellipsis Digital Limited, Glasgow
Printed and bound by CPI Group (UK) Ltd, Croydon, CR0 4YY

For Wol
Who wrote this book, really.

Prologue

Rome, November 1989

'Darling?'

He knocked at the door, his ear straining to pick up the usual sounds of his wife in her suite – running water from the bath, the soft 'tock' of the wardrobe doors opening and closing, her gentle humming as she dressed. 'Elena?'

He waited another moment before letting himself in. The curtains were open, the sidelights on, and a small indent on the bed showed where she had been lying, the pillows still slightly crushed from her earlier nap.

He smiled to himself as he went to close the door again – but his eye caught on an object which had been designed expressly to be noticed and, instead of leaving, he walked over to the dressing table and picked it up. The ring was still warm from the heat of her body. He rubbed the stones with his thumb, then brought them to his lips and kissed them lightly. She must have forgotten to put it on after her bath, he thought, slipping it into his pocket and thinking to check the library next.

She must be—

The little white slip was, in and of itself, hidden from view beneath a ring dish. Ordinarily, he never would have

1

seen it, but the thick crystal had a magnifying effect and he would have known that handwriting anywhere. He tore the note from its hiding place, his breathing ragged as he read and saw and understood.

And then he ran.

Chapter One

Rome, July 2017

'"*The amber light and sparrows,*" that was what she wrote,' Matteo said, putting his phone back down on the table.

'*That's* what you like best about this city?' Alessandra asked in disbelief.

'And it's had more likes than almost any other post!' Cesca laughed, her palms splayed towards the stars. 'What can I tell you?'

'I know *I* can tell *you* that most people would say the Colosseum, or the Forum, or the Pantheon,' Alé replied wryly. 'Even the hawkers selling roses at the Spanish Steps are in with a chance, not the little brown birds that scavenge off the plates.'

'Ah, but most people have no imagination. I refuse to be a cliché. Perhaps that's why they enjoy my little blog so much.'

'Less of the little,' Matteo said. 'Your following is growing so fast, you'll have advertisers knocking on your door soon and that is where the big money is.'

'Yeah? Well, if they could hurry up about it . . .' Cesca quipped.

Yet it was true that The Rome Affair – her online homage

to the home of the Ancient World, pecorino and *la dolce vita* – had hit some sort of collective nerve; she was both thrilled and amazed by its growing popularity. Since putting out a first tentative blog post seven months ago, she had found her voice, musing on everything from the locally made honeycombs in Aventine Hill to her favourite vintage stores, as well as sharing anecdotes from the tours she guided as her day job.

Guido cracked a grin, his tanned pate gleaming under the golden, glowing lanterns. 'Well, I guess at least it is clear why you could not have carried on as you were. Anyone for whom Rome is defined by its light could not be expected to work in a world as dry as the British law courts.'

'Thank you, Guido,' Cesca said, raising her glass to him. 'I'll drink to that.'

Everyone joined her, draining the grappa and sitting back in their seats with relaxed smiles. It was the tail end of another beautiful night, the hot air drooping like sleepy eyelids, the scent of jasmine like a powder that dusted the sky. They had feasted well on courses of pasta and fish, every table in the courtyard restaurant occupied; it was after ten but that was early still for Rome; early, usually, for her too these days.

'So what now? Shall we go to Zizi?' Alé asked, leaning back in her chair and pulling her black hair up into a ponytail, her slim bare arms on display in her khaki vest. 'They've got that band playing tonight. You know, the one we saw at Rock in Roma in June?'

'With the hot lead singer?' Matteo asked, looking interested – as he always was when an attractive woman was involved.

'Well, *I* thought he was hot,' Alé laughed, letting her hair tumble down to her shoulders. 'But I'll be honest, I didn't think beards were your thing.'

Everyone chuckled, Matteo dropping his head as a couple of napkins were thrown his way. 'I thought you were talking about—'

'I know, those three sisters.'

'I'm up for Zizi,' Guido said. Beards *were* his thing.

'Well, you'll have to count me out, I'm afraid,' Cesca said, reaching down for her bag by her feet. 'I've got a group booked for six so it's up at five for me.'

'But that's so boring.' Alé frowned, watching as Cesca took the bill from the saucer and calculated her share, her lips moving in silence.

'Tell me about it,' Cesca said a moment later with a roll of her eyes. 'Unfortunately, though, that rent's not going to pay itself.'

Alé tutted. 'I can't believe they don't pay you to live in your flat!' she quipped, giving a lazy, half-flirtatious smile to the waiter as he came back with another round of digestifs.

'Thanks for that. *I* happen to think it's charming. You should see what the equivalent rent would get you in London. At least here everything's—' Cesca frowned. 'How do you say "quaint"? You know, like small and cute and old?'

They all translated for her in unison.

'Right, so *that*.' She nodded, rifling through her purse while wishing her Italian could be half as good as their collective English. Perhaps if she had insisted on their speaking only Italian to her, she might have progressed further, but she suspected they wouldn't laugh so often or have half as much fun.

'But you said a cockroach ran over your face in your sleep,' Alé reminded her with a shudder.

'Only the once. And that was in the very first week. I think I've scared them away now.'

'And the lights flicker when you walk across the room,' Matteo added. 'And your TV must be the only black-and-white still in operation in the whole of the country.'

'The whole of Europe,' Guido corrected.

Matteo looked across at him. 'Exactly.'

'Plus, it smells of *horse*,' Alé said, wrinkling her nose.

'Nothing a scented candle can't fix and I'll have you know everyone thinks my black-and-white telly is a design statement – like Guido's craft beer and hipster beard,' she added with a grin, before brushing her hand against said beard affectionately, as if Guido was an Irish terrier. She'd never known him without it, couldn't imagine him clean-shaven. It would be like seeing him naked. 'Besides, it's got a bath in it—'

'Ugh!' Matteo grimaced. 'What is this English obsession with lying in your own dirty water?'

'It's comforting! I'd like to see you survive an English winter. At uni, taking a bath was sometimes the only way to get warm.' She took a deep breath as she saw their grinning faces watching her, enjoying making her dance. 'Besides, it's not like any of you are living in penthouses, anyway,' she pouted, as they collapsed into laughter.

'Stay. At least for one more drink,' Alé implored.

'I really can't,' Cesca said, bending down to kiss them all. 'I've pushed my luck too many times recently and you know what I'm like in the mornings.'

'I *wish* I did,' Matteo chuckled, stretching his arms up and back to show off his impressive muscles.

'You're incorrigible.' She grinned. 'But I need this job. I've got holes in my shoes from all the walking and I can't afford a new pair.' To prove the point, she lifted her foot to show them the worn-through canvas of her yellow Converse.

'But you can afford wine with your dinner, obviously,' Guido said, tipping the nearest empty wine bottle.

'Obviously. Priorities, baby,' she joked.

'I thought your shoes were supposed to be like that,' Matteo said, eyeing them. 'Everything else you wear is falling apart.'

'Hey! Just because *you* haven't got an eye for vintage,' Alé riposted in solidarity. 'You think that if it isn't box-fresh Gucci, it must be trash.'

Matteo's gaze pointedly fell to the hole in the side of Cesca's white cotton Edwardian camisole. She covered it with her hand. 'It's just loved, that's all,' she laughed, retrieving her (admittedly somewhat donkey-nibbled) panama from the back of her seat. She put it on, blowing kisses to them all. 'So long, amigos. You're the best. Call me!' She smiled, waving as she began to walk away, her friends' voices already bubbling above the low hum of the rest of the restaurant as they resumed their conversation about the club.

It wasn't a long walk home. Nowhere was particularly far from anywhere in Rome. She crossed the Piazza San Cosimato, where the market stalls were stacked and chained ready for the next morning's trading, stepping into the maze of winding narrow streets, the buildings steadily disappearing beneath bushy facades of jasmine and ivy. There were crowds everywhere, tables pushed against walls to allow the airport limos to get past, scooters arranged in precariously dense lines like dominoes, music curling from every open window.

Her apartment in the Centro Storico, hidden in the warren of meandering streets between Piazza Navona and Campo de' Fiori, may not have been a fashionable address like her friends' trendy Trastevere places – where artists, designers and hipsters hung out at late-night bars and pop-up restaurants – and she might have been single-handedly responsible for bringing down the average residents' age by forty years, but it *was* centrally located, making it handy for work. She walked so much for a living these days, the last thing she wanted was another hike just to get home.

Besides, she'd never been one for following the crowd; dressing top-to-toe in vintage was the least of it. As a teenager, she'd listened to Patti Smith and Carly Simon when everyone else was crying over McFly; she had accepted early on that her frizzy strawberry blonde (okay, ginger) mane was never going to respond to hair straighteners; and at five foot ten, she was too tall to hide in the crowd. So, yes, her apartment may have had cockroaches and dodgy electrics, but it also had original 1960s turquoise tiles in the kitchen and a tin bath. Its tiny roof terrace – barely bigger than her table – looked out onto a vista of rooftops with no fewer than seven church towers (she loved to watch the bells swing out of time with one another on Sunday mornings). Perhaps best of all, it was positioned on one side of a particularly small and quiet square which led off from the bustling Piazza Angelica and which had everything she needed in it: a dark osteria in one corner, a pizzeria opposite that and Rome's best bakery right next door to her flat. There was a bushy fig tree in the osteria's corner and smack bang in the centre of the square was an ancient olive tree whose branches swayed in the breeze like hula dancers. It had felt like home the first time she'd set eyes upon it.

Occasional piazzas opened up the narrow linear spaces as she walked, letting the sky stretch out in cut rectangles overhead, silvered moonlight dressing the sleeping streets. Her feet, shod in their tatty Converse, were silent on the cobbles, her head full of tomorrow's tour and the stories she'd need at hand if she was to do her job well. It was still something of a novelty that she was here, doing all this. Her old life felt like a distant dream, like a story she'd been told by someone else rather than something once belonging to her, concerning her, defining her.

She turned into her little square, Piazzetta Palombella, and passed Osteria Antico, which was always full, even though they didn't accept reservations, had no specials and no menu – you were simply served whatever Signor Accardo had cooked and his wife brought out to you. As she strolled by, Cesca raised a hand in greeting to Signora Accardo, who was wearing her traditional long black apron and carrying plates back to the kitchen.

On the opposite side of the square, Franco's Pizzeria had the usual line of people queuing out the door, the loud chatter and whoops and calls of the waiting crowd pitching and diving as the dough was tossed with acrobatic flourishes and the flames of the wood-fired oven threw a gladiatorial light onto the street. Owned by Franco Luciano, himself a third-generation *pizzaiolo*, it was now run by his six sons and they were as much a part of the draw as the famous Luciano dough. It was so hard to tell them apart in the kitchens – they all had mops of dark hair, white teeth, brown eyes and olive skin, and dressed identically, shouting and gesticulating wildly as they jostled, wove and waltzed around one another – that Cesca had decided she would master the Italian language before she'd learnt all their names. They worked by instinct, handling the ten-foot oven paddles with deft experience. She had never realized pizza-making was such a virtuoso skill until she'd come out here and seen how they kneaded and tossed and turned and flipped the bases with an artisanal skill, their biceps bulging as they did so in tight white t-shirts.

Ricci, Franco's eldest son, caught sight of her as he took out one of the bins and hailed her; she waved in return, feeling grateful for her new neighbours' welcoming sense of community.

She climbed the side-on stairs which led up to the front of her apartment, having to step carefully around the many potted geraniums arranged on each step by her landlady, Signora Dutti, a widow who lived downstairs. For the past seven months now, Cesca had awoken to the sound of her sweeping those steps every morning on the dot of seven-forty, the pick-up and put-down of the flowerpots the Italian equivalent of the tinkle of breakfast china.

It was cool and dark inside her flat, the vintage hand-worked lace curtains hanging limp and still in the window: she opened the shutters to let the breeze rustle up and disturb the day's stagnant air. The terracotta-tiled floor felt good underfoot as she slid her feet out of her Converse trainers and padded across the open-plan sitting/dining area to the dark, minuscule kitchen at the back, pouring herself a glass of water and cutting a peach straight onto a saucer. Flicking the TV on, she channel-hopped until she found an old rerun of a Detective Montalbano series, then went through to the bathroom and began running a bath – her nightly ritual, irrespective of her friends' mockeries.

She ate the peach slowly, sitting on the edge of the sofa and watching a shootout in silence as, in the background, the sound of the water hitting the tin bath became a deeper splash. She could judge by ear just when it was at the perfect depth and when it reached that point she turned off the taps.

The peach stone now the sole item on the saucer, she took it back through to the kitchen, rinsed the plate and bagged up the rubbish. Lifting it carefully, aware that yesterday's cereal bowl had had rather more milk left in it than she'd realized before scraping out the leftovers, she hurried to the front door, her slim bicep straining to hold the bag up off the ground. As she slid her shoes on again, standing on the backs so as not to have to untie the laces, she turned and – sure enough – saw large white milk drops on the tiles behind her. With a tut, she hobbled down the stairs as fast as she could, cursing as she clipped one of the flowerpots with the bottom of the bag and sent it toppling sideways, soil sprinkling the step.

She turned left into the tiny alley between their building and the bakery, and lifted the top of the large covered bin, her holding arm ready to swing the bag up and into it, automatically holding her breath as she did so – the stench was always overwhelming.

But she frowned as she caught sight of something on top of the other bin bags. Dropping her own by her feet, she reached in and pulled out a handbag. It looked brand-new and expensive. Powder-grey leather, it was a clutch style with stiff sides and a whip-stitch detail over the seams. Cesca was no fashion maven, but even she could tell from the bamboo-styled clasp that it was a Gucci (in her old chambers, a power bag from the holy trinity – Gucci, Prada or Céline – had been one of the defining characteristics of the more senior barristers, a way of communicating success when any other indicator such as a watch, suit or fortnightly Hersheson highlights were obscured by the wig and gown). She rubbed her thumb across the leather – it was supple and pliable; lambskin, too. It didn't look like a fake; didn't smell like one either, she thought, sniffing and savouring the rich aroma of leather. What on earth was it doing in here?

She realized why instantly.

Forgetting all about the large, leaking bin bag by her feet, she opened the handbag. Unlike her own, which contained a panoply of clutter, this was almost disappointing in its restraint – a hairbrush (with not a single hair on it), a Chanel Les Beiges compact, an Annick Goutal miniature perfume bottle, various business cards held in place by a silver money clip . . . But what was notable was what *wasn't* there – neither a purse nor phone. The thief would have just grabbed the bag, taken what he needed and thrown this at the first possible opportunity; it would have been incriminating evidence if he'd been stopped.

Still, even without the value of cash or credit cards, this had to be a 1,000-euro bag, yet without any identifying documents, there was no way to return it to its owner. What next? she wondered. Would the police be able to do anything or was it finders keepers? Not that she'd ever really carry something like this herself. It looked as though it should belong to a woman who had a daily blow-dry, considered manicures as one of the pillars of civilization and wore diamonds at breakfast. Perhaps she should sell it? She needed the money and—

A sudden thought struck her – might there be a serial

number inside the bag, much as you might find on a Rolex or a car, something that could be traced back to the owner? One of the partners at the chambers where she'd worked had owned a Hermès Birkin and that had had a small card with various authentication numbers on it. If there was something similar for this bag, she'd be able to return it: a solution that sat with her better than benefitting from someone else's misfortune.

She unzipped the side pocket. It appeared empty from the outside but there was something in there. She pulled out a small, unopened blue envelope, the edges badly rubbed and scuffed, and on the front, in an elegant hand, was written a woman's name: '*Elena.*'

Cesca bit her lip. Now was that the name of the woman the bag belonged to, or the person to whom she had written?

'*Buona notte*, Cesca.'

She looked up to see Signora Dutti watering the profusion of flowerpots outside her door, giving the plants a drink now that the day's heat no longer scorched the leaves. She was wearing the navy housecoat she always wore, her feet pushed into a pair of old Scholl sandals, a hairnet keeping her small curlers in place ready for tomorrow.

'*Buona notte*, Signora,' Cesca smiled, inadvertently waving the handbag at her. She saw it catch her landlady's eye – the quality and implicit value evident even from a distance and to an elderly woman with 10/10 vision. 'Oh.' She skipped quickly over to her. 'I just found this in the bin.'

Signora Dutti shook her head and tutted. 'Thieves.' She put down the watering can and took the bag as Cesca held it out to her, the smooth, pale leather in stark contrast to the landlady's wrinkled, stippled skin.

13

'Yes, unfortunately they've taken all the valuables inside – purse, phone . . . But the bag looks pretty expensive; someone must be missing it. And I found this.' She held up the letter.

Signora Dutti's expression changed as she saw the name on it.

'I don't suppose you have any idea who Elena might be?' Cesca wrinkled her nose. 'I mean, I realize that's like—' She stopped as she saw the look on the older woman's face: satisfaction. 'You do?'

Signora Dutti nodded and very slowly raised an arm, one finger outstretched, pointing towards the pale-blue palazzo on the opposite side of the square. Its shutters were painted in a pale-oatmeal colour and there had to be twenty-four windows – six on each of the four levels – just on this aspect alone. The palazzo didn't actually front onto this little piazzetta, but rather its right side faced them here, the front door being situated on the Piazza Angelica around the corner. In the seven months that she'd lived there, Cesca had never seen anyone come or go from the building. The shutters – on this side at least – always remained shut.

'She lives in there?'

Signora Dutti nodded, an inscrutable expression in her dark eyes. 'She lives in there.'

Chapter Two

Behind her, Piazza Angelica was dimpled with light, rows upon rows of scooters lined up in military formations, the young Romans all clustering around the fountain in the centre as though it was a centre of gravity, pulling on them hard.

Cesca stood on the front steps of the palazzo and listened as the bell echoed deep inside the fortified building. Standing here in its shadow, her face only feet from its walls, it felt imposing and grand, far too ridiculously large to be a single private residence and not one of the many government buildings which usually occupied palaces of this scale. *Who* lived in a place like this these days? It could probably house a hundred families – or be converted into a school or a hospital. Something worthwhile, something useful.

She gripped the bag tighter in her hand, looking up at the very top edge of the five-metre door, where she spotted a security camera trained upon her. She looked away again, feeling exposed without her trademark panama on – she rarely went anywhere without it in this city's heat. In her peripheral vision, she could see Signora Dutti standing by the fig tree in the corner of the square, wiping her hands on her housecoat as she watched. Her curiosity made Cesca feel even more nervous. What was so interesting about knocking on this door and returning a stolen handbag?

Ready to give up, she turned towards her elderly neighbour and gave a shrug as if to say 'well, I tried', when the door opened and she found herself face to face with a middle-aged man in black trousers and a short white housecoat, rather like a chef might wear. He was sporting tortoiseshell-rimmed glasses and no smile, his improbably smooth face set like a death mask.

'Yes?' He looked at Cesca enquiringly, his keen eyes catching on the small hole in her top, the scuff of her yellow canvas shoes and noting how she was still standing on the backs of them . . . He grew an inch. 'It is late. What is it?' he asked in an unfriendly tone when she didn't reply absolutely immediately.

'Yes. I'm sorry about that,' she replied, realizing he was right – it must be after eleven by now; she needed to get to bed for she was due up again in just over five hours. 'But I thought you'd want this back sooner rather than later.' She held up the Gucci bag.

The man looked startled, then angry. In the next instant he had snatched the bag from her hands, making her gasp as he grabbed her by the elbow. 'You have no idea what you have done. Are you one of them?' He stepped out onto the top step, looking around the immediate vicinity of the steps with a fierce stare.

'O-one of who?' she stammered, taken aback and trying to wrest her arm free. Who was he looking for?

'The gang.' He looked back at her again, scrutinizing her with contempt and outright hostility, squeezing harder on her arm. 'The gang who stole this bag. Because if you think we'd be so stupid as to pay you a reward for what you stole in the first place—'

'What? No!' Cesca surprised herself as much as him with the force of her tone as her indignation caught up with her shock. He thought she was the thief? He mistook her vintage shabby-chic look for genuine vagrancy? 'How dare you! I live around the corner and found this in my *bin*,' she snapped, snatching her arm away. 'My landlady Signora Dutti told me someone called Elena lives here and I came over to return it, that is all,' she continued, furious now. 'I was doing you a favour, but hey – don't feel like you have to thank me. It was my pleasure!' Bitterly, she turned away and stomped back down the steps.

She'd barely walked five paces when he called after her. 'Wait!'

She turned to find him halfway down the steps, the bag – open – in his hands. 'Please follow me.'

What? What for? Where was he going? If he thought she was going to go into that house after the way he'd just—

Hang on, where had he gone?

She ran back up the steps and stared into the dark cavity of the hall. The man was nowhere to be seen.

'Hello?' she called, and when no one answered, stepped over the threshold and called again. The corridor extended in a straight line for sixty metres to the left and right. Cesca felt the temperature drop a clean five degrees as the thick stone walls encircled her, the sticky city heat stopped at the door and allowed no further. She glanced behind her at the party still going on in the square, all the cool kids sitting on the edges of the fountain, faces uplit by the shimmering aquatic light, their nights at least still sticking to the script.

Not far off, she could hear the click of shoes moving

17

quickly on the floor and she hurried after the sound, finding herself jogging down a long gallery as she just caught sight of the man before he turned a corner.

Her eyes took in the barest of details as she ran: there was far too much to process in those few seconds, but her 'tour guide' eyes clocked the ceiling frescoes, the baroque gildings and the staggering ranks of Renaissance artworks grouped on wires along the walls.

She reached a stone staircase around the corner and ran up it, two at a time, her breath beginning to come more heavily as the steps rose away from her, floor after floor, the light dim in spite of a magnificent chandelier hanging overhead. With her eyes down to keep from tripping, she didn't see the tips of the shiny black shoes until she was almost upon them.

'Oh!' she gasped, launching backwards instead and feeling her balance desert her. A white-sleeved arm shot out and a hand caught her for the second time in five minutes – but this time with very different intent. The man's face was impassive as she righted herself.

'It's this way.'

He had the handbag tucked under his arm as he walked and Cesca – although bewildered by the turn of events – had to suppress a smirk at the absurd image.

She followed him through yet more galleries, one after another, each a long, narrow salon with its shutters closed to the world in the square beyond. She saw paintings she knew were museum-standard – Caravaggio, Raphael, Velázquez, Titian; she trod over rugs spun from the finest silk. The colours of the walls were heavy and jewel-like: garnet red, peridot, malachite green . . . It wasn't her style, nothing like, but she couldn't help but be impressed. The palazzo was even more sumptuous inside and belied its muted, rather sober exterior.

If there was everything to see, there was nothing to hear – the raucous shouts and laughter of the piazza were as diminished by the fortress-like stone walls as the heat – but gradually her ears strained to pick up notes of music, drifting gently in snippets down the long corridors like fish on a river's tide. Was that . . . was that *La traviata*?

The man – butler? Cesca supposed – stopped outside a pair of closed doors. He turned to look at her. 'Wait here.'

Cesca blinked, feeling bemused as he disappeared through them, the bag still under his arm. A slice of falsetto escaped at full volume for a brief moment as the door was opened and then closed.

Cesca turned on the spot, head nodding in time to the faint music as she surveyed this 'holding chamber' – it was what could only be described as absinthe green, with a large portrait of a cardinal on one wall, some marble busts set upon pillars against another and a grouping of ruby velvet gilded chairs. It was too much, the colours oppressive and claustrophobic. Everything was so heavy. Where was the light? The lightness? Oh, for some cotton instead of these silks; some linen in place of the flocked velvet. She felt weighted down, as though the palazzo's history was a physical presence that had to be borne.

She closed her eyes, continuing to nod in time to the music – only to realize it had stopped. She turned and found the doors were now open, the butler standing in the doorway watching her.

She stopped nodding.

'The Principessa will see you now.'

. . . *Principessa?*

He stepped aside, clearly her cue to enter, and after a moment her feet obeyed. She walked in and stopped again. In contrast to the almost garish richness of the other salons, this room – three metres high and surely ten metres squared – was shocking in its simplicity. It was almost brutally minimal, with a pair of white linen sofas in the middle of the room, a shaggy deep-piled ivory sheepskin Berber rug like a landed cloud in the middle of the floor, and three utterly enormous canvases – of something abstract and modern with lots of black on them – on the walls. Everything was overscaled: not just the sofas, which could surely seat eight people each, but also the fireplace at two metres high, which was hewn from marble with an intricately carved *trumeau* that reached to the ceiling. In addition, a stunning collection of giant white hard corals – some self-enclosed and shaped like the heads of calla lilies, others flat like fans, their lace fretwork stretched as though on a loom – was set out on wooden stands and placed on display tables, beautifully punctuating the run of floor-to-ceiling windows on both sides of the room.

Cesca was aware that her mouth was hanging open but she couldn't quite recover herself to close it yet. Walking into this, after the heady opulence of the rest of the palace, was like diving into the cool sea after a hot bath.

'I feel exactly the same, my dear.' The voice – American, as soft as a powder puff – made her turn and she saw a woman, who must previously have been standing by the far window, walking towards her. 'I have to wear my sunglasses just to walk through the gold gallery or I come out in hives, don't I, Alberto?'

The butler nodded his acquiescence but Cesca ignored him: she couldn't take her eyes off the woman coming towards her. Dressed in ivory silk pyjamas and an olive silk Japanese kimono, and relying on the support of a hand-carved cane, she was tiny and bird-like, with bobbed and coiffed grey hair, and a discreet pair of spectacles perched at the very end of her nose. Her bone structure was feather-light, as though she'd been handblown from glass, with high, appled cheekbones, an aquiline nose – with the faint-est flare at the nostril, giving an impression of haughty displeasure – and a beautiful, still-tight jawline. But it was her eyes that entranced Cesca and kept her rooted to the spot – not blue, not green, they were a pure celadon colour, like the untouched waters of a Philippine lake.

She came barely to Cesca's shoulder, the hems of her silk pyjamas silent as they trailed over the sumptuous rug. She held out her hand in such a fashion that Cesca wasn't sure whether to shake or kiss it but, taking the conservative option and shaking it, she was surprised when the woman – princess! – covered Cesca's hand with her other one. 'How ever can I thank you?' she asked warmly.

Cesca remembered to close her mouth. The bag. She meant the bag, she prompted herself. 'It was nothing, really.'

The woman smiled. 'It was not nothing. You have done something far greater than you can realize. I have been dis-traught all day. The contents of my bag were valuable beyond measure.'

Cesca frowned. Hadn't the butler told her that the purse and any money in it were missing? 'But I . . . I'm afraid the contents have been stolen. You know your money, credit cards—'

The woman smiled, tossing the caution away as though money itself had no value. 'Come. Let's sit. I want to know you better. Are you thirsty?' And before Cesca could reply: 'Alberto, bellinis.'

The quiet click of the door behind her told Cesca he had gone as she and the princess walked the half mile – or so it felt – to the sofas.

'Tell me your name,' the princess said, sinking onto the cushions. With a sweeping hand motion, she gestured for Cesca to do the same.

'Francesca Hackett,' Cesca said, wondering why the room smelled so good. There were no flowers that she could see, no candles. 'But everyone calls me Cesca, sometimes Chess.'

'I am Viscontessa Elena dei Damiani Pignatelli della Mirandola, but everyone calls me Elena. Sometimes Laney.' She laughed and the sound was every bit as surprising as this very room in this palazzo. A husky, low laugh, it sounded like it should have come from a woman twice her size, half her age, who feasted on cigars.

'Viscontessa? But your butler said you were a princess.'

'Did he?' she sighed. 'Oh, how I wish he would stop doing that. You must have got him on the back foot somehow; Alberto can become a little prickly if not handled correctly. He's far grander than me. I much prefer Viscontessa. So much more friendly and approachable, don't you think?'

Cesca's eyebrows shot up. 'So, you're a princess *and* a viscountess?'

'Double princess, actually, plus two dukedoms, five marquessates . . .' She rolled her eyes dramatically. 'Oh God, it goes on. Like a shopping list. I think there are eleven titles in all.'

Cesca realized she was staring at her and that her mouth

was hanging open again – it was suddenly strikingly clear now why Signora Dutti had been so fascinated by the prospect of her coming into this building and meeting this woman. A Gucci bag was small fry in this arena. 'But you're American.'

'That's right. I married into the Roman aristocracy. Love makes you do crazy things, doesn't it?' Her voice was informal and inclusive.

Cesca didn't know what to say; she'd never been in love. She sat back a little on the sofa, her eyes freely roaming the room again. Now that she was sitting, she took in details she hadn't noticed earlier – the small side tables either side of the sofas, which were carved from wonderfully twisted chunks of wood and inset with glittering semi-precious crystals; a white alpaca-fur throw over a seat cushion; a potted blossom tree in one corner.

'But let's not talk about me. I'm far more interested in you.' Her eyes narrowed thoughtfully. 'Because you, I think, are the girl in the hat.'

Cesca looked back to find Elena watching her with interest. 'I'm sorry?'

'You usually wear a hat.'

'I do, usually, yes,' she said in surprise.

As if reading her mind, the Viscontessa continued. 'I'm not as mobile as I once was; I spend a lot of time at the windows. I enjoy watching the comings and goings of the square.' She smiled. 'I often see you hurrying past in your hat and I wondered what you must look like. I have only ever seen your hair clearly.'

Cesca rubbed her bare, freckled arms self-consciously, still scarcely more tanned than she'd been when she'd arrived here just over seven months ago in rainy November.

'I have to wear a hat because of my colouring. I burn to a crisp otherwise.'

'It's worth it. You are so distinctive – like a flame. I can see you when you turn into the piazza from the far corner.'

Cesca smiled shyly. 'That's what my groups say too. It has its benefits, definitely.'

'Your groups?'

'I'm a tour guide.'

'Oh, I see.' She looked at Cesca with curious eyes. 'I wouldn't have guessed that. Do you enjoy it?'

Cesca shrugged. 'It pays the rent, I guess. And I meet some pretty interesting people sometimes. But I write a blog, too. I guess that's my real interest.'

'A blog,' the Viscontessa echoed, looking blank.

'It's a bit like an online diary or journal. It's called The Rome Affair. I write posts about beautiful things I see in the city or which attract my attention. This city is so full of history and intrigue.'

'Indeed it is. Why, just look around us here,' she said, indicating the Renaissance building they were in right now. 'Do you have many readers?'

'Forty-three thousand.'

'Heavens! And do they all contact you every time you write something?'

'Thankfully not!' Cesca guffawed. 'But that really isn't a huge number. The very biggest blogs have readerships in the millions.'

'Do they really?' the Viscontessa breathed, looking fascinated. 'And how often do you write something?'

'Some people post daily, so that they appear higher in search engine results, but I prefer to do it weekly. I don't want it to become too pressured, worrying about having enough content. The point is it's a celebration of everything I love about this city. I don't want to *have* to post for the sake of it. I think my readers appreciate that there's an authenticity to what I do – they know I only write about something if I really love it.'

'So then, really, you are a writer.'

Cesca considered it for a moment. 'Umm . . . I guess you could say that.'

Elena nodded, just as Alberto came back in with the two drinks, holding them aloft on a silver tray. Cesca flickered her eyes towards him as he set hers down on the quartz side table beside her, first wiping the immaculate surface with a silk cloth. 'And what made you come to Rome?'

Cesca felt her heart catch, as it always did when she was asked this question. 'It's just always been my favourite place in the world. I think I probably first fell in love with it watching *Roman Holiday* when I was a little girl and then, when I came here, it was exactly as I had hoped it would be.'

The Viscontessa smiled and nodded as she talked, looking over at her with those extraordinary eyes, her gaze roaming Cesca's unmade-up face, her wild, unbrushed hair pulled back ready for her bath, her vintage clothes.

'Do you work?' Cesca asked politely, feeling the chill of the glass in her palm.

'Me?' The Viscontessa paused for a moment as though having to consider it. 'I suppose you would say, these days, I paint.'

'Oh? What type of thing?' she asked, sipping on the bellini and wondering how she had gone from dinner with friends in Trastevere to drinks with a princess in under an hour.

'Landscapes, mainly,' the Viscontessa replied, her eyes trained inquisitively on her guest. 'Occasionally portraits too. You would be wonderful to paint. That glorious hair of yours.'

'Oh . . .' Cesca demurred, shaking her head modestly. She couldn't think of anything worse. 'Are . . . are these yours?' she asked, motioning towards the giant canvases on the walls.

'Sadly not. Would that I were so talented. No, I'm afraid I'm just a silly old woman with delusions of skill.'

She was smiling, her self-deprecation charming and deployed – Cesca sensed – to put her at her ease, but she wondered how old the Viscontessa really was. Her skin was beautiful and no doubt the result of an intensive and expensive skincare regime begun in adolescence. Perhaps she was in her early seventies?

The Viscontessa's hand tremored suddenly, so that the bellini splashed perilously close to the top of the glass. Alberto rushed over and took the glass from her grasp as Cesca held her breath; to spill anything on these sofas or rugs seemed unthinkable.

'Oh, for heaven's sake,' Elena tutted under her breath as Alberto fussed.

Cesca quickly rose to standing, not wishing to prolong the Viscontessa's embarrassment. 'I should get back. It's late and I've already imposed on your time as it is.'

'Nonsense.' She smiled, but rose, shakily, too. 'I wish I could have offered you greater hospitality than a mere drink. If it were earlier, I would have invited you to stay for dinner.'

'You're very kind but I assure you, that's not at all necessary. I'm just sorry your bag was stolen at all. I take it you've cancelled your credit cards?'

The Viscontessa waved away the enquiry with another of her dismissive shakes of her head. 'The only thing of any value in it was still there. It contains a letter from my dear late husband, which he wrote on his deathbed. For fifteen years, I have taken it everywhere with me.'

'Fifteen—' Cesca frowned, faltering, confused. 'Forgive me, I'm sorry. I wasn't prying – I was looking for identifying details and I saw the letter, it had your name on it. But it hadn't been opened.'

'Oh, no, I haven't read it yet,' the Viscontessa said in a tone that suggested to do so would be rash. 'Fifteen years I've been holding it close to me, waiting for just the right moment. It sounds silly, I know, but I fear that . . . to open it would end the conversation somehow. This way, there's still something left to say between us. It gives me a reason to get up each morning. Every day I wonder if today will be the day I finally open it.'

Cesca didn't know what to say. Fifteen years carrying around a love letter? 'Maybe today really is the day then,' she shrugged. 'It so easily could have been lost forever and you would never have known his last words to you.'

The Viscontessa nodded. 'Perhaps you are right. I am in your debt, Miss Hackett.'

'Please. You really aren't.'

'Well, I am pleased, at least, to be able to offer you the reward. Alberto?' Her eyes flickered towards him in the corner behind Cesca and she looked over to see the butler holding out a thickly wadded envelope towards her.

There was a reward? Cesca shook her head even as her

eyes widened at the sight of it. It was so thick! 'That isn't necessary, really.'

'I should like to.'

Cesca should have liked to, too. 'But it's the principle of it. I don't believe you should have to pay people to return something that's rightfully yours.'

The Viscontessa looked flabbergasted. 'But it is five thousand euros. Surely it would be helpful for you?'

Cesca swallowed. It was months of rent but she knew she could never accept it; she simply wasn't made that way. 'Thank you, but no.'

The Viscontessa's expression perceptibly changed. 'I don't often meet people with principles.'

Cesca held out her hand. Unlike when her host had done the same earlier that evening, it was a straightforward proposition with the palm side on. Everyone knew where they stood with her handshake. 'It's been a pleasure meeting you, Viscontessa.'

'Please, you must call me Elena,' she replied, looking at her with what appeared to be both bafflement and intrigue.

'You have a beautiful home,' Cesca added.

Elena laughed at the gross understatement, the throaty sound still as surprising as it had been on the first occasion. 'It is pretty, isn't it?' she replied with even greater underestimation. 'Well, I must say, I'm very pleased to have met you at last.'

Alberto opened the door, ready to escort her out through the interconnecting salons, the gaudy gold trims and absinthe-green walls stretching out before them like the physical manifestation of a headache. Cesca took a deep breath, not wanting to step into it again. In here, the space was calming, reflective, expansive. But beyond those doors

– what was it? She had a feeling of needing to galvanize herself just to walk through it, a sense of inescapable history trapped in the walls; of a past that still ruled the present; of a world that had been built on secrets and lies.

Chapter Three

The gasp was like a scream, a bullet, a punch – shocking and violent, wresting her from her sleep like a soul being ripped from its body. She was sitting up in bed, the sheet twisted around her hips, her muscles trembling from the sudden shock of oblivion to consciousness, her heartbeat as panicky as a trapped bird.

She stared at the stubby shadows without seeing them, trying not to see instead the images that were burnt in her mind, tattoos that would never fade no matter how she clawed or rubbed or scratched at them. They had become a part of her now, another shadow stitched to her heels and trailing her through the sunlight and the snow, coming alive every night when the moon rose and her eyes closed.

She rolled back down to the mattress, pulling the sheet up over her shoulders, her body curled into a comma – but there would never be a pause from this. She closed her eyes and tried to fall back to sleep, knowing it would come again, knowing it was only right that it should.

This was her just deserts for what she had done.

She deserved everything she got.

The sound of the steps being swept, of the toppled geraniums being righted again, was more effective than any alarm clock and Cesca sat up in bed with a sudden gasp. She didn't need to check her phone to know the time would be seven-forty, but she did it anyway, giving a little scream as she saw that the 'alarm ignore' icon was on the screen.

'Oh no! No, no, no,' she whimpered, throwing back the sheet and clambering into the clothes she'd discarded last night – Edwardian camisole, check; long daisy-print skirt, check; destroyed yellow Converse, check. There wasn't time to brush her teeth or her hair. Grabbing her panama from the pine table as she sped past, she was out of the apartment in under ninety seconds from when she'd first opened her eyes.

'*Buongiorno!*' she cried to Signora Dutti as she scrambled down the steps awkwardly, trying to avoid the sweeping brush.

Signora Dutti straightened up with an expectant look and Cesca could tell at a glance that she wanted to have a conversation about her meeting with the Viscontessa last night. 'I'm so sorry, can't stop. I'm really late. Really, badly late,' she cried over her shoulder.

She flew across the tiny, slumbering Piazzetta Palombella, the steel shutters to the pizzeria still down, the tables and chairs still stacked in the osteria opposite, although delicious smells were already wafting from the vents of the bakery. With one hand holding her hat onto her head, she sprinted across the Piazza Angelica without even a glance at the imposing pale-blue palace she had visited last night. A few beer bottles on the rim of the fountain were all that remained of the carousing partygoers, but unlike in her tiny pocket of Rome a few hundred metres away, where the piazzetta remained quiet at this time, here the day had already well and truly begun. A bin man was pushing his

31

cart over the cobbles, while two *carabinieri* were walking slowly around the cordons which pedestrianized the central section of the square. Busiest of all, in the centre of it, were the stall-holders setting up their stalls, arranging buckets of flowers in dense tiers, displaying stripy coloured ribbon and bow pastas in open boxes, and hanging clusters of chillies and smoked sausages from the gazebo struts.

When she had first moved here, she had fallen in love with this market. It had become a normal sight to her now, but in those early days its colours and shouts and smells (some good, some not) had been all the proof she'd needed that she had been right to do the unthinkable and leave her old life – for here, everything was bold and chaotic, fresh and unformed, too big to press into a box. It gave her exactly the freedom she'd needed, the chance to escape and start afresh as someone new. Someone better.

She ran through the intermittent shadows – already hard-edged and black even at this early hour – jumping over low-slung chain railings, weaving between scooters, her long pale limbs flashing like switchblades. She passed from square to narrow street, short alley to narrow street again, the rumble of traffic on the Via del Corso like thunder as she emerged, panting, into the swarm of commuters. Dodging and ducking, she weaved her way to the front of the crowds, sprinting through the stationary cars when the lights turned red before diving into the back streets again. She outpaced a Mercedes airport limo trying to navigate a road with no more than thirty centimetres' clearance and ran through the middle of a group of Chinese tourists, all wearing red caps as they followed their guide. She was running up the middle of the street, legs pumping, when a scooter suddenly rounded the corner at terrifying speed.

Cesca gasped as it headed straight for her. With a parked car to her right, she was forced to jump left, but she hadn't seen the low-slung spiked chains looped between bollards and they tripped her. As she fell in a tangle of limbs towards the shiny cobbles, she got a good look at the driver – mid-thirties; athletic; dressed in navy cargo shorts and a once-white polo shirt, with his biceps bulging at the tight sleeves; and straight, brown, longish hair that peeked out past his helmet. Most striking of all were his arrogant eyes – as though he expected nothing less than for her to fall onto spikes to let him pass.

'Hey! You bloody hooligan!' she shouted after him in furious, native English – her Italian wasn't strong enough yet to be truly effective at hurling insults – as he continued on without stopping. 'Seriously?' she asked aloud as he turned out of sight without so much as a backwards glance.

For a moment, she sat there on the ground, the cobbles chilling her skin through the cotton of her skirt, before she suddenly remembered what she'd been doing before the fall and why she'd been running. Her knee was bleeding but there was no time to worry about it, clean it or even feel it, for she had to pick herself up and carry on.

She sprinted again, trying to ignore the throb in her knee as well as the stitch in her side, but she knew it didn't matter how fast she ran – she was two *hours* late. She would be getting there just as she was supposed to be finishing the tour. A few seconds, a minute wasn't going to make any difference at this point; they'd have called someone else in ages ago.

She rounded the corner into Piazza di Trevi, the torrents from the magnificent, justly famous fountain as loud as a waterfall but, for once, the square itself was quiet. That was the point of the Sunrise Tour, after all – grabbing the opportunity to see the great Roman landmarks free from the hordes, hawkers and street-sellers that blighted the daytime trips. She sprinted past the steps, past the great statue of Neptune, and on to the tiny building around the corner, which thousands passed every day without noticing. There was no time for beauty right now, though, no time for culture, for—

Sonia, the girl in the ticket office, was sitting in a small kiosk by the door and jerked her head towards the inside of the building as Cesca careered through the doorway. 'He is in the office,' she said, with a sympathetic look.

'Thanks, Sonia,' Cesca gasped, still keeping up a jog past the little cinema – whose construction had been the reason this wonder had been discovered in the first place – and down the metal staircase into the Città dell'Acqua, as the subterranean space was known. It was well lit, the smooth foundations of the modern buildings sitting within metres of the rough stone of earlier dwellings – dwellings which existed, even now, under Rome's streets. Most Romans, much less tourists, had no idea that so much of the ancient architecture that had shaped this city still stood partially intact below its streets. Trickling through the cavern was an ancient aqueduct, too: the Acqua Vergine, first built by the Roman statesman Marcus Agrippa in 19 BC, had been delivering pure drinking water to the city for over 2,000 years, and scarcely any of the millions of visitors to the impressive Trevi Fountain round the corner knew that it was fed by this very water source. But she did. She loved this city and knew it inside out and underground.

Cesca ran lightly past the narrow stepped alleys – ancient roads that now led to nowhere – for once not looking at the thin, hand-made bricks that had once formed basilicas and stadia but now stood as half-formed arches. Instead, she had her eyes fixed only on her boss's office. The door was open, as though he'd been waiting for her to arrive.

'Giovanni, I'm *so* sorry,' she panted as soon as she reached it, hanging onto the doorframe and taking off her hat so he could see her eyes, which were wild with apology.

He glanced up at her with the hangdog look of the long-suffering, the expression in his round eyes even sorrier than hers. 'Francesca. Look at the time. Look,' he said, stretching out the last word to at least four syllables as he tapped his watch.

'I know. And I'm so sorry, but it wasn't my fault. Honestly,' she said, the words mere disembodied breath as she struggled into the tiny room, wounded and exhausted. 'Let me pick up the next tour. Who covered for me? I'll do their shift.'

He shook his head. 'Fran—'

'No, scrap that,' she panted, almost collapsing onto a folding chair. 'I'll do *two* of their shifts to make up for it. It's only fair.'

'Is too late, Francesca.'

'I know and I'm *so* sorry. But I'm here now. I'll make it up to you. Tell me how I can help.'

'You were supposed to be here two hours ago.'

Cesca felt a tremor of anxiety. Giovanni wasn't usually difficult to placate. Although he'd been married since he was eighteen and loved (and was also quite scared of) his wife, Cesca knew he had a crush on her. It was the hair. She was as rare as an arctic fox around these parts. 'I know, but you see, my landlady . . . she tripped,' she said, flipping her hair over her shoulder.

'For two hours?' he asked, watching it arc through the air as though in slow motion.

'Yes, I . . . I had to take her to hospital.'

He looked back at her again. 'And in all that time, you couldn't call?'

Cesca smacked her hand to her chest. 'I couldn't *speak*, Giovanni. It was terrible. There was . . . so much blood.'

Giovanni raised a sceptical eyebrow. 'But I suppose she make a fantastic recovery? Just like after the fire?'

Cesca swallowed. 'Well, that was only a little fire . . .'

'You said the whole building could have been destroyed.'

'*Could* being the operative word. Luckily, I . . . I saw the candle smoking and was able to smother it before it went out of control.'

Poor Signora Dutti: if only she knew how colourfully her life was portrayed on this side of the Via del Corso. The truth was, she was as sturdy as the Pantheon, rarely ever left the square except to go to the market, and the high point of her day was sitting on her chair in the late afternoon with Signora Accardo and watching the tourists go by.

Giovanni sighed. 'Cesca—'

'Giovanni, please,' Cesca cried, panicking now that she appeared to be making no headway. Yes, she'd been pushing her luck for the past few weeks – forgetting to charge her phone or not saying no to that last limoncello were hardly helpful when her nights were already so sabotaged. And yes, perhaps the blog's growing success meant her mind had been less on her day job than it should have been, but she still needed it. The equation was simple: no tours meant no rent meant no blog. No more Rome Affair. No more Rome.

'Cesca, it is the third time this month.'

'I know, but it really wasn't my fault.'

'It never is. Your poor landlady has almost died three times in three weeks: the landlady and the scented candle; the landlady and the almost fatal collision with the pizza van; and now the landlady and the . . .' He arched an eyebrow. 'How did she trip?'

'On a geranium.'

'The landlady and the geranium,' he repeated in a monosyllabic tone. 'I cannot decide if she is the luckiest woman in Roma or the most unlucky.' He tutted, looking sad. 'You are one of my best guides. Your history, knowledge? Amazing! And the tourists, they love you. But if *you* are not here when *they* are here, it does not matter how good you are. I need someone I can depend on.'

She slapped a hand over her heart. 'And from now on, I *promise*, you can depend on me,' she said, as earnestly as if she was about to launch into 'God Save the Queen'.

'Today, Astrid had to do the tour for you.'

'Astrid?' Cesca's hand dropped, indignantly. 'But she barely even speaks Italian!'

Giovanni arched his eyebrows. 'I know.'

'And she always confuses Augustus with Nero.'

'Exactly. A disaster. But I had no choice. She was the only person available.'

Cesca felt her chest tighten as she realized she'd backed herself into a corner. 'Okay, look, I'll be straight with you – I slept through the alarm,' she said quickly. 'I don't sleep that well and—'

'Cesca, I am sorry. It is the third strike. You know our company policy.'

She swallowed, hardly able to believe this was happening. Third strike? What was this – Borstal? 'You mean, I'm

37

out?' she whispered, feeling the blood drain from her flushed face. She had precisely two hundred and eighty-six euros in her bank account. Her rent – due next week – was nine hundred and ninety euros but she'd had eleven tours booked in between now and then. Earning eighty euros per tour, she would have just made it. Dinner, last night – to celebrate Guido's twenty-fifth birthday – had been factored in to her weekly outgoings for weeks. Oh God, why hadn't she taken that reward last night? Five thousand euros for returning a bag! She could have been here, sitting pretty. How could she afford to be principled when she couldn't afford to eat?

'I don't suppose it would make any difference if I told you I was almost run over on the way over here?' she tried.

Giovanni arched an eyebrow that indicated he was done with her stories.

'Look at my knee!' she said, rucking up her long skirt and showing him.

'Cesca, *please*,' he pleaded, his eyes drooping like a blood-hound's. 'There is nothing more I can do for you.'

'But you're the boss!'

'I know. I am sorry it must end this way.'

He was adamant. She sat there for a moment, trying to think of another way to change things, but she had tried it all: outrageous stories, a frank confession, honesty, plead-ing, begging . . . What else was there? She had overslept one time too many.

'*Ciao*, Francesca,' Giovanni said, as solemnly as a judge in a black cap. 'Sonia will settle up with you on the way out.'

Cesca sighed, pulling herself to standing and walking out slowly, her knee beginning to throb. She added in a limp, hoping he'd take pity and call her back, but her rubber soles on the metal walkways were the only sound as she walked out, back towards the light.

Sonia had the envelope all ready as she approached. 'Sorry, Cesca,' she grimaced, handing it over.

'No, it's my fault. I've only got myself to blame,' Cesca sighed, feeling last night's exhaustion creep upon her as the adrenaline ebbed away. And she stepped back out into the light to where the shadows were still hard-edged and black, to where the crowds were beginning to gather and the day was already pulling away without her.

Chapter Four

Rhode Island, June 1961

The lights from the pool outside flickered around the silk walls and ceiling of the peach bedroom: the only movement in the room. Laney sat on the bed listening to the hubbub of the crowd, to all those people waiting for her, the baby-pink tulle skirt of her dress fanned out around her, as though arranged by the famed Norman Parkinson himself, ready for the shot.

She could see her reflection in the full-length mirror from where she sat. Her skin, not yet buffed by the sun, looked milky in the dim light, her shoulders, neck and arms extending elegantly from the raspberry velvet bodice that seemed almost heart-shaped to her now it was on. Her brown hair – not dark enough, always too limp – had been back-combed, sprayed and coiffed so that the ends kicked out at the nape, the front section quiffed and held in place with a satin band, highlighting the large pearl globes at her ears that her mother had presented to her at dinner the night before. Laney would have preferred something smaller, something that suited sixteen, but understatement wasn't a concept that her family either understood or observed.

Her face, though ... She had never worn make-up before, and the powder felt thick on her skin, her lips too distracting in this vibrant cherry shade that overpowered even the dramatic sweep of kohl at her eyes. She couldn't stop staring at herself: part-doll, part-geisha, part-Hollywood siren. She wasn't quite sure who she was supposed to be, looking like this, but there was no doubt in her mind that she was going to have to act the part; she would only disappoint otherwise.

A woman's shrill laugh – not her mother's – pierced the night and Laney broke away from her reflection. They would be waiting for her. She rose, hearing how the skirts swished and rustled with the movement. The feel of them was slightly rough against her nylon-clad legs. The bodice skimmed tight against her ribs and she tugged at it slightly, feeling another urge to gulp down breaths as she had a few minutes ago.

Opening the bedroom door and crossing the large landing, she stood at the balustrades and looked down for a moment at the greyed – occasionally balding – heads: satin lapels upon ivory jackets for the men, stiff silks and sapphires for the ladies. Her mother, she knew, was wearing the new Schiaparelli gown that had arrived tissue-wrapped and boxed from Paris three days earlier: cut in silver lamé plissé, its fluidity and minimal, strapless form would have all the other women clucking like hens – it struck such a contrast to the fussy gathers and tucks of their own dresses. Which was precisely the point. But would she have accessorized it with the rubies Laney's father had given to her at Christmas, or the Larchford emeralds inherited from her paternal grandmother? All week it had been one of the more pressing questions, along with whether to dye the swans pink on the lake to match Laney's Sweet Sixteen dress (they had), and whether or not it was *'de trop'* to place a pearl in each open oyster at the seafood bar (apparently not).

Someone saw her and the gasp that followed led to an almost biblical parting of the crowd, coos and sighs at her appearance breaking into applause as she descended the stairs. She felt embarrassed and overwhelmed, wanting to scurry instead to her governess Winnie's rooms and sit on the couch, eating popcorn and watching *The Ed Sullivan Show*.

'Darling, you're a vision.'

It was her father, his salted blond hair and moustache toplighting his yachting tan. He looked so handsome in his evening jacket. Mother had had the hand-stitching redone in gold thread especially for the occasion and for once Laney agreed it looked just the thing – discreet and yet lending an opulent shimmer.

He kissed her on the cheek and reached to take a couple of glasses of vintage champagne from the waiter hovering by his elbow. She quickly took a sip – admiring the pale biscuit colour, liking the way the bubbles fizzed on her tongue – feeling herself calm under his protective gaze. 'Come, there are so many people who want to say hello to you.'

Laney wished it could have been just the two of them there. They could have walked down to the shore together, taken off their shoes and talked about their favourite things – what to name the new boat (even though she couldn't swim and was terrified of water); his plans for the stud now that the black stallion was settling in. They could have sat with their feet in the pool and – with napkins tucked in at their necks – eaten with their bare hands the lobster she'd watched the kitchen staff preparing earlier. She could have danced the Viennese Waltz with him and shown him how hard she'd been working in her lessons to make him proud. She was sixteen now, after all, a young woman, as he kept telling – reminding, instructing – her: no longer was she the little girl she'd hoped desperately to remain, no more the child hidden from view and protected behind security-patrolled gates. As everyone kept telling her now, there was a whole world waiting to meet, or at least catch a glimpse of, America's little heiress.

'Charles and Miranda Stowcroft, may I present my daughter Elaine?'

'How do you do?' Laney nodded politely.

'Enchanted,' the tall man replied, taking her hand and kissing the back of it.

'How do you do?' Miranda said. Her grey hair was set into small stiff curls, her blue eyes bright against her rouged cheeks and mustard-yellow gown. 'You look exquisite, my dear. Why, those pearls must be the size of golf balls!'

Laney smiled her thanks before her father gently took her by the elbow and presented her to the next person waiting in line. With a sinking heart, Laney realized that almost the entire party had formed a sort of queue, all of them wanting to shake her hand or kiss it.

Almost the entire party – but not quite. Beyond the doors that led onto the terrace, she heard the ribbon of familiar, delighted laughter that had curled through the night air on so many of these occasions at their home before – her parents simply loved throwing parties – and she would know that amused trill anywhere. As a child, she had lain in bed listening to it with the windows open, hearing the hushed whispers that usually followed, sometimes ending with a shout or a curse or the smash of crystal. Now though, she could just make out the shimmer of liquid silver couture through the old glass, the dots of cardinal red rubies, that sweep of raven-dark hair.

As they listened to that laughter, her father's hand gripped tighter on her elbow; he had seemingly forgotten all about the couple standing in front of them with frozen smiles, awaiting their official introduction.

'. . . Sorry, forgive me,' he said, remembering himself in time and rescuing them all with one of his famous, dazzling smiles. The papers always said he'd built his fortune with that smile, even though they knew perfectly well he'd inherited a billion-dollar highways engineering empire from his father. 'Larry and Dinah Stanford, my daughter, Elaine.'

'A pleasure to meet you,' Laney smiled, falling back into her role. Business resumed.

The man took her hand and kissed the back of it. 'The pleasure is all mine.'

'You look perfectly lovely tonight, Elaine,' Dinah added with a small, inhibited smile. 'Aren't you just the luckiest girl in the world to have such a swell Sweet Sixteen party?'

'Oh, Daddy's just the best!' She smiled, clutching his arm tighter, even though she'd never wanted this party at all, much less to invite four hundred people when she could barely identify fifty faces here. But suddenly that didn't matter because now that she anticipated how the evening was going to play out, with her on her father's arm, it didn't matter at all how many strangers she had to meet. It was quite apparent too that no one actually wanted to talk to *her* anyway – they simply wanted to be seen by her father, and be seen being seen by her father.

Six couples had glided past them, saying the same thing

six different ways, before the laugh came again like a mockingbird's echo, a taunt that the real party was happening
elsewhere. Her father's gaze automatically fell beyond the
doors again, his eyes squinting at the glass every few
moments, as conversation faltered and names were forgotten.

He looked back at them all and she saw the clouds
behind his eyes. Laney felt herself loosen, as though the
stays binding her together were being gradually unpicked,
one by one . . .

'I'm sorry, won't you excuse me?' he asked tonelessly.
'There's . . . something I have to attend to. Laney, look after
our guests?'

'But Daddy—'

He left and, in the sudden vacuum created in his wake,
the people that had been clamouring to meet her moments
before now sank back into the body of the crowd, the
receiving line closing into private clusters that left Laney
standing alone in the room, watching her father's retreating
back, his hair bright beneath the chandeliers as he headed
for the terrace. For all his charisma and intelligence, his
kindness and insight, there was one truth that George Valentine, as a father, a husband and a man, would never grasp
– that they had all the money in the world, but never
enough time.

'You look sad.'

Laney jumped. The voice, in the dark, had come from the
left side of her, by the beech tree. Behind her, the house
looked to be dripping with light like liquid gold, a celestial
haze rising above the estate like a nimbus. She thought she
had found refuge here in the crepuscular nooks of the

sunken garden, the music from the live band distant, as though caught in a box, and this intrusion on her privacy alarmed her.

'Who's there?' she asked, detesting the tremor that shook her voice and betrayed her fright, hating even more that someone had seen the truth. She'd thought she was alone here.

A shape emerged from the shadows – broad-shouldered, long-legged, the glowing tip of a cigarette like a firefly in the night sky. 'The question is, what could *you* possibly have to be sad about? You're the luckiest girl in the world, aren't you?'

She blinked. Even without seeing his face, she could detect the faint sneer in his voice. Money made you bullet-proof, right? 'So they keep telling me.'

'You must feel pretty special. It's a hell of a party. Your folks know how to throw a bash, that's for sure.'

'And were you invited or did you just manage to scale the walls?' If there was one thing she'd learnt from her mother, it was the art of the waspish put-down.

She heard him chuckle, and followed the cigarette end as it arced up to his mouth, stayed there for a moment – glowing even brighter – before dropping down again, the grey smoke that curled from his mouth seconds later looking white in the darkness. 'With those dogs you've got on patrol? You've got to be kidding me. No girl's pretty enough to risk those teeth. Not even you.'

She didn't know what to say – not sure whether she'd just been insulted or complimented. Or both. She raised herself up to her full height – all five feet two of it – and asked in her most imperious voice (the one that made her cringe whenever she heard her mother using it), 'Do I know you?'

'Not yet.' He made no effort to move or introduce himself.

'Who are you? I insist you tell me or I'll call for those dogs. I've got an alarm in my pocket,' she lied. 'They'll be here in under thirty seconds, wherever they are on the estate. You'd never outrun them.'

'I don't doubt it.' She heard his smile in the dark and knew he didn't believe a word of it. 'Tell you what – I'll tell you my name if you tell me why you're running out on your own party.'

'I'm not running out.'

'No? You always socialize half a mile from your guests?'

A small laugh escaped her at the wisecrack, surprising her in the same moment.

'Now there's a pretty sound.'

She hesitated, then took a step closer, wanting to see his face, wanting to appear bolder than she felt. 'Tell me your name.'

'Tell me why you're sad.'

'I'm not sad.'

'On the contrary – you're the sorriest-looking sight I've seen since my dog got caught in the rain. Aren't you happy to be sixteen?' He walked around her, still out of sight, like a cat circling an injured bird.

'It's fine. It's just a number.'

'Oh, I don't think so, Miss Valentine. Not looking like that.'

The compliment – unveiled this time – took her bravado from her like a thieving wind. 'I should get back.' She turned to leave.

'Why?' He stepped out of the shadows now, the pale

light of the half-moon falling across him like a satin sheet. His blond hair, closely cropped at the back and sides, swept across a broad forehead, his blue eyes a colour-pop against his tan, his nose straight and his chin strong with a slight cleft. He looked just like the movie star Tab Hunter, her most fervent crush; her mother had met him a few times at some Hollywood parties and promised to introduce them but Laney didn't hold out much hope. Her mother's promises were notably lax.

'I can't stay.'

Flicking the cigarette to the ground and grinding out the little light with his shoe, he walked over to her, stopping just a few feet away. 'Has anyone even noticed you're gone?'

She swallowed. She had never been alone with a boy before, much less alone in the dark with a boy who looked like him. 'They will do.'

'No, they won't, and do you know why?' He looked down at her, his eyes seeming to blaze with an anger she couldn't comprehend. 'Because they're damned fools, too busy lining up to kiss your dad's ass.' He reached an arm out to her, tipping up her chin with a crooked index finger, his eyes raking over her face like fingers. 'It's your Sweet Sixteenth but it's not about you. Nothing ever is, is it? They don't even notice that the beautiful girl with every earthly gift also has the saddest eyes.'

She looked away, trying to hide, but his grip was firm and his eyes found hers again easily. 'But I do.' He paused and with every silent second that passed, she felt he was drawing the breath from her as though it was golden thread on a spool. 'And what's more, I know exactly what to do about it.'

Chapter Five

Rome, July 2017

It was an extravagance she couldn't afford. Coffee on the Piazza Angelica came at a premium the tourists were prepared to pay for the views of the bustling market, but for a local – as she was, at least temporarily – it was madness. Rather, they all went to Luca's for their morning espresso, standing at the bar behind the window and chatting briefly, loudly, with their neighbours before heading off for the day. Alé had taken her there in her first fortnight of arriving here but it had taken Cesca another month before she had built up the nerve – and linguistic confidence – to go there on her own and shoot the breeze.

But today she had needed to sit. Having walked for hours, she had needed to sit and stare at nothing and make a plan because without a plan, she would be back in England within three weeks. Her coffee had been finished in three gulps, at a cost of one euro eighty per gulp, but she continued to stir the spoon in the empty cup meditatively for another good hour or so.

As far as she could see, she had several options. She could set up on her own and do her own tours. But that meant getting a website and some brochures printed and she didn't have the money for any of that; and anyway, the city was already overrun with walking groups trekking between the public sites of the Forum and the Pantheon, the Spanish Steps and the Colosseum.

She could teach English – there were numerous language schools in the city and she was already experienced in dealing with the public. Or she could be a waitress. Perhaps Signora Accardo needed help; she always seemed rushed off her feet whenever Cesca passed.

As for what she would have loved more than anything – writing her blog full-time – that was still a pipe dream. In spite of Matteo's sweet support, if she was to have any chance of attracting advertisers and some sort of proper revenue through it, she would first need at least half a million subscribers.

The waiter came over and removed her empty cup from her hands with a knowing, rather unapologetic nod. Time out. It was her cue to move on. They needed the table.

She got up and began walking again, not noticing the flower stall with its buckets of cascading peonies and tulips and lisianthus; she didn't see the group of idling tourists, their rucksacks worn – in common agreement – back-to-front on their chests like baby papooses: it wasn't a fashion trend, more some sort of declaration of war against the pickpockets. But she *did* hear the scooter buzz around the periphery and she recognized Ricci – Franco's eldest son – with no helmet on, heading to open up the pizzeria.

How much had changed for them both in those few hours since she'd waved to him last night, she reflected. For him, a batch of dough had simply proved overnight, whilst for her, her very future here was now in jeopardy.

She slowed her walk, feeling rootless, her gaze flickering

towards the grand palazzo that fronted the entire width of the far end of the square, its creamy shutters still latched shut over the many windows, keeping out the heat (and perhaps prying eyes), its simple, plain, ice-blue facade a bare-faced denial of the baroque extravagance on the other side of the walls. She remembered again the excesses of the galleried rooms and how they had seemed to pulse with a latent energy, as though vestiges of the many lives spent amongst them hovered still beneath the rugs and behind the paintings, and she gave a shiver, feeling pity for the tiny bird-like woman who seemed to share the space with them now, alone in that white room.

'Damned principles,' she muttered to herself, wondering whether to check the bins again. Could she be so lucky? As if.

She rounded the corner into the piazzetta. It was not so different to how she had left it in her haste earlier, except that the fig tree was now in the sun: the angled edge of light was steadily pulling back the shadows over the pizzeria, the cobbles, the olive tree in the centre, her apartment and the already-swept steps. It would continue its path until finally the osteria would be bathed in an amber glow, ready for the lunchtime trade.

Cesca jogged up the steps lightly, not wanting to run into Signora Dutti, who still wanted to know what had happened last night with the grand neighbour, and who would now want to know why she was back so early and could she pay her ren—?

'Oh!'

She stopped dead on the small tiled area at the top of the steps, seeing that her front door was wide open. Dust motes

whirled in the air in the triangular wedge of sunlight spilling into the flat.

Elena Damiani, regal in the dim light, slowly rose from
the narrow-backed chair by the small square table as though
she were the host. 'I hope you don't mind.'

'. . . Not at all,' Cesca replied, quickly recovering herself
and setting her bag down on the floor, wishing she wasn't
still in yesterday's clothes. Elena, naturally, had changed
from her languid pyjamas and kimono into a crisp shirt and
ankle-grazing narrow trousers and looked so chic, Cesca felt
sure she must be en route to lunch with the Pope (who
would also, no doubt, feel distinctly shabbily dressed by
comparison).

'It's a *charming* apartment you have here, you must be so
thrilled to have secured it.'

'Um . . .' Cesca automatically surveyed the small, shady
space in response, noticing with fresh eyes what her friends
saw: the dated décor, the sparse furniture, the bloom of
damp on the ceiling from a dislodged roof tile. It probably
looked like one of the broom cupboards in the palazzo.

'I always wondered what it must be like in here and it's
even better than I imagined. So authentic,' Elena said, delicately pointing a ballerina-pump-shod toe at the floor tiles.

Cesca didn't reply. She was wondering how long this
woman had been sitting here, and how long she intended to
stay. What if Cesca had made her tour in time and managed
not to get the sack? She would have been out for the rest of
the day with her other bookings. Would the Viscontessa
have sat here and simply waited all that time? She resolved
to have a word with her landlady about keeping strangers
out of her home in her absence. 'Can I get you a drink? A
cup of tea? Some water?'

'That would have been delightful but sadly I must be getting on. I have a lunch appointment at one. Terribly dull, but needs must.' She gave a small bored sigh, and Cesca wondered whether she was indeed lunching with the pontiff.

'Then . . . how may I help you?' Cesca asked, cutting to the chase with a polite smile.

'I saw you sitting at the cafe in Piazza Angelica. You looked terribly upset.'

'Oh. Well, it's been a bit of a morning,' Cesca said with forced understatement, this time wondering from which of the many windows Elena had spied her.

'Yes, I gathered. You looked as though your world had ended . . .' When Cesca didn't offer up any explanation, she added, 'So I thought I might be able to help out.'

Cesca looked up. The reward? That five thousand euros would be the buffer she needed until she could find something new. To hell with principles! A girl's gotta eat!

'It was funny seeing you again so soon, actually; I'd been thinking about our meeting last night.' Her cool eyes settled on Cesca with a surgeon's clarity. 'I like you.'

'Uh . . . thank you,' Cesca replied, stretching the words out, feeling on guard.

'I think we could become great friends, you and I.'

Cesca worked very hard not to allow her right eyebrow to hitch up to her hairline. What exactly did she have in common with a seventy-something socialite princess? 'Okay. I . . . I mean, yes. Thank you. Of course, me too.'

'You are a terrible liar!' Elena laughed, that distinctive sound filling the room. 'Don't worry, I appreciate this may seem a stretch of the imagination but, inside, I am your age, twenty-seven years old and yet to meet the love of my life;

in my head, my life is still ahead of me: it's only the mirror telling me otherwise. So when I look at you and see a confident, principled, intelligent young woman, I see someone I instinctively feel is a kindred spirit, regardless of the age gap between us.'

'Thank you.'

'To get to the point, I have come with a proposition for you.'

'A proposition?'

'Yes, I would like us to work together.'

Cesca could see Elena watching her closely, reading the fractional twitches of her features as her words landed. No easy money then? No handover of the five thousand she had already 'earned'?

'It crossed my mind to ask you last night but you said you had a job, so . . .' She arched a plucked eyebrow, clearly waiting for some sort of confirmation from Cesca.

Cesca's shoulders sagged. 'Well, amazingly, between then and now I've managed to lose it.'

'How absolutely wonderful! I rather hoped as much!' Elena trilled, clapping her hands together. 'Then their loss is my gain—'

Cesca looked at her sceptically.

'—Because, you see, I need a writer and you are a writer.'

'Well, I'm a blogger. I wouldn't say I'm a writer *per se*.'

'Nonsense. You write your posts and people read them. They engage with them. Forty-three thousand people engage with them.'

'I guess . . .' Cesca said slowly. 'But what is it you want written?' Cesca's mind began to race. A blog for the palace? A website?

'I've got an old publisher friend who's been on at me for

some time to do a book about my life. He's been asking for years, in truth. I tried putting him off and onto some of my friends who would just *die* for this kind of thing, but he's so awfully insistent they want me and, really, as he put it to me: what else have I to do with my days?'

'That was hardly diplomatic of him.'

'Well, to be honest, he has a point. Lately I've been coming around to the idea of getting my house in order. At some point, I have to start paying attention to what the mirror's telling me, whether I like it or not.'

'You're a very striking woman,' Cesca said politely, taking care to omit the 'still'.

Elena smiled, but she knew when she was being flattered. 'Well, I wasn't sure about it until we met last night. It's a very intimate process, you see. It would mean going through my personal photographs, talking about my life in great detail . . . I'm sure you can appreciate that is a daunting prospect for me. I would need to be able to trust the person I was working with and you, Francesca, have already proved yourself to be *highly* trustworthy.'

'So you want me to write your biography?' Cesca asked, wanting to clarify things completely.

'It is not necessarily as overwhelming a proposition as it may first sound, as some of the preliminary work has already been done,' Elena said reassuringly, seeing the alarm on Cesca's face. 'A few months back, I employed an archivist to go through my photographs and arrange them chronologically as much as was possible. But after that, well, I'm afraid I rather ran out of steam. I didn't like any of the people the publishers proposed and I had no idea how to find a writer myself.' She shrugged. 'At least, I didn't until you turned up on the doorstep last night. I looked at your blog after you left.' She smiled. 'You now have forty-three thousand *and one* followers.'

Cesca chuckled, flattered. 'Thank you.'

Elena handed over a small piece of folded ivory paper. 'That's what the publisher says they'll pay but if it's not enough, let me know and I'll make a call. They're not going to lose the project on account of something like that.'

Cesca's mouth dropped open in astonishment as she read the figure. *That* was a year's rent, with enough left over to buy a second-hand scooter. It was more than she had made in her first year at the Bar.

'They want it done by the beginning of September, so it would mean coming to work with me full-time for the next couple of months. The remit is to present "the woman behind the enigma".' Elena shot Cesca a wry look. 'Their words, not mine. What do you think?'

Cesca stared back at the immaculate woman. Cartier watch, navy Valentino trousers, globe pearls, a very discreet facelift – she was her opposite in every possible way: rich where Cesca was poor, old where she was young, tidy where she was scruffy. And yet there was a recognition of sorts between them. Whether it was shared intellect or a rather weary world view, she didn't know, but Elena was right: she felt certain they could work together.

'I'd be interested on one condition,' Cesca said slowly, glimpsing an opportunity for the long game, something that would benefit her beyond this project and that pay-cheque.

Elena arched an eyebrow. 'Oh?'

'You grant me an exclusive for my blog.'

'An exclusive what? An interview? Because I've never spoken to a journalist in my life.'

'I'm not a journalist,' Cesca replied calmly. 'And you would have full veto.'

Elena looked sceptical. 'What would it be about?'

'I don't know yet. I know nothing about you but there must be something in your wonderful palazzo that I could show my readers. It could be whatever you felt comfortable sharing, just so long as it was something no one has seen before. It would have to be something that would get a buzz going, and bring people to the site.'

'Oh, I see.' Elena gave her a long, appraising look – clearly conflicted by the counter-proposition – before nodding slowly. 'Well, I'm sure there must be something we could find that would be of use to you.'

Cesca beamed. 'Fantastic,' she replied, holding out her hand. 'When do we start?'

'You're like a cat, you know that?' Alé gasped in amazement as Cesca raised her glass for a toast.

'On account of my long tail, you mean?'

'You always land on your feet!' she laughed.

'Well, I'm never usually *this* lucky. I've certainly never lost one job and landed another in a day before.'

'For triple the money!' Matteo said, shaking his head in disbelief. He'd not had a pay rise in three years.

'I assume, from the fact that this is the sixth time you've mentioned it, that you're expecting me to pick up the tab tonight?'

'Aw, would you?' Alé winked. As a newly qualified teacher, she only just made her rent and was having to supplement her income by working as a private tutor through the holidays; Matteo, though well-dressed, earned a pittance as a manager at a pricey menswear boutique on Via

Condotti; and Guido was a graphic designer at one of the city's big firms, with big dreams but pockets too small for breaking away and setting up on his own.

'To think this time yesterday you were running away from us on the pretence of protecting your job—' Matteo said.

'I *was* protecting my job. I needed an early night.'

'And instead you ended up sipping bellinis at midnight with one of our city's most enigmatic socialites.'

'And now I'm working for her. It's all very strange,' she shrugged.

'Some might say fated,' Guido said, with dramatically furrowed eyebrows and a deeply ironic tone.

'So what's she like then?' Alé asked. 'My mother is going to go nuts when I tell her. She thinks the Viscontessa is the most stylish woman in Rome.'

'Uh, well yes, she's very chic. She's got that *rich* manner about her, you know? Everyone's "Dahling, kiss, kiss!", everything's easy and breezy.'

'That's because she never has to get her hands dirty. She has people like us to do it for her,' Matteo said.

'Plus she's *unbelievably* tiny. I don't think she can have eaten since 1987. She makes me feel like a giant. I swear I could fit her in my coat pocket.'

'She would fall out of the holes at the bottom,' Matteo quipped, pulling a 'sad' face.

Cesca stuck her tongue out at him.

'Just being serious for a minute, though,' Guido interrupted. 'I mean, I know the timing is good and the money's great, but aren't you worried this is a bit of a comedown?' he asked, getting to the point as ever. 'You're so clever,

Chess. You're capable of so much more than transcribing the recollections of a rich old woman.'

It was a compliment – of sorts – but still Cesca bridled. 'Well, it's no worse than trekking tourists from one monument to the next in the blazing midday sun, is it? Besides, you're working on the assumption that just because I was a barrister, I was a good one.'

'Oh, I know you were,' he replied. 'You can't hide clever.'

Just then, Signora Accardo came over with the *primi*, setting down plates expertly balanced from wrist to elbow. She picked up the bottle to replenish their glasses and was amazed to find it empty.

'Already? You drink like fishes!' she chided, in spite of the fact this meant more profit for her.

'We're celebrating, Signora. I got a new job today.'

'Yes?' Signora Accardo's black eyes brightened. 'What you do now?'

'I'm going to be working at the Palazzo Mirandola for the Viscontessa.'

The older woman's expression seemed to freeze. 'What doing?'

'I'm writing her biography. I'm a proper bona fide writer now.'

'All she will tell you is lies,' Signora Accardo said, in a voice so low it was almost a growl. 'She is the devil woman.'

'I'm sorry?' Cesca wasn't sure if she had misheard.

'You must keep away from her, Francesca.'

'But I can't. I need the job. I don't understand, what's made you—?'

'She is a bad woman. Wicked things happen from her.' Signora Accardo shook her head, reprimand in her eyes already – as though Cesca was tainted by association. 'You

59

must stay away. I know what I'm saying about.' And she stalked off, her doughy hands pulled into fists, the empty bottle still left on the table.

'What was all that?' Cesca whispered to the stunned table. 'She makes her sound like The Godmother!'

Guido and Matteo shrugged, both looking baffled.

'Well, the Viscontessa was married, like, seven times before she settled here,' Alé said knowledgeably – *Mail Online* was her bible. 'And the circles she moves in are very conservative, very Catholic. I bet it's a snobbery thing – she's in the club, but not really, you know? She just married her way in. She's looked down upon by the oldest families.'

Guido arched an eyebrow. 'So Signora Accardo, the notably high-born osteria-owner's wife, is making it her cause because . . . ?' Irony dripped from his every word.

Alé held her breath as she thought about it for a moment. 'No, I've no idea,' she shrugged finally.

'Well, snobbery be damned then,' Cesca said, pushing it from her mind and picking up her cutlery. 'She seems decent enough to me, plus she's paying me a king's ransom for the cushiest job of my life.' She smiled at her friends. 'As far as I'm concerned, she's the blinking fairy godmother.'

Chapter Six

Alberto set down the jasmine tea, the morning light shining through the white of the bone china. 'Her Grace will be with you shortly.'

'Thank you.'

She had been taken to a room which, given the left turn they'd taken at the front door, was on the opposite side of the palazzo to Elena's monochromatic apartment. Situated on the ground floor, its ceilings were vaulted and decorated with flying cherubim and pink clouds, the walls clad with pastel-coloured marble marquetry, occasionally dimpling inwards with statue-decorated niches. Compared to the other lavishly gilded galleries they had passed through to get here, though, this one felt sedate and Cesca was grateful for the reprieve, her head throbbing both from lack of sleep (again) and last night's wine (again – when would she learn?).

Set against one wall was a large desk and a chair, which were both so dwarfed by the vast proportions of the room that they appeared like dolls' furniture; piles of boxes were arranged in stubby towers around them. It was a strangely makeshift office in such a grand room and she wondered as to its original intended use. Ballroom dancing? Indoor bowls? Whatever, it didn't easily or graciously accommodate its new guise as a modern workspace and she didn't even like to think of how slow the wifi connection must be, having to get past those marble walls.

She sipped the fragrant tea, taking her cup over to the window and looking out, her eyes automatically lifting up to where the other side of the palazzo loomed as she tried to identify the white apartment three floors up, but the rows of windows were unblinking, giving away nothing. Looking away, back down again, she stared out into a large garden tucked tight outside the windows. She had expected to see a stone courtyard, but although a colonnade ran along the opposite side of the palazzo, between the two wings was a pebble-mosaic parterre planted with orange and lemon trees, leading – she craned her neck left to see better – to steps and a wall and seemingly, given the neat groupings of cypresses falling away from sight, more land beyond. It was almost impossible to believe they were still in the heart of this ancient city, where the buildings nearly tumbled upon one another along tiny streets, and not in the open land-scapes of Tuscany.

'Exquisite, isn't it? Whenever my friends ask why I con-tinue to live alone in such an absurdly large house, I simply show them the garden.'

Cesca turned to find Elena standing in the middle of the room. Cesca was surprised not to have heard her come in, particularly given her hostess was using her walking cane again. She was wearing a khaki linen shift with an African-style horn necklace and stacked bangles which only served to highlight the slenderness of her arms. Her skin was pale and lightly freckled and her complexion boasted a radiance that Cesca's – at forty years her junior – couldn't muster this morning, on only six hours' sleep. As ever, her past had woken her with a punch.

'It's such a lovely surprise. I was expecting to see . . . I don't know, the back of your neighbours' building or a courtyard? It's remarkable you've got so much land, right here in the capital.'

'Well, we have my late husband's father to thank for that. He was instrumental in keeping the estate intact when Mussolini appropriated it during the war.' She smiled warmly. 'And I hope Alberto greeted you with better grace than the other night?'

'Yes, he was charm personified,' Cesca replied, even though he had greeted her with even more suspicion than when he'd thought she was running a scam. She walked back to the middle of the room and returned her tea cup to the tray on the table.

'Good. He's becoming quite grand in his old age. I fear soon *I'll* be bringing *his* coffee.'

Cesca smiled but she couldn't imagine a world in which that would ever be a possibility. Elena possessed an innate regal grace; there would always be people to wait on her. 'So is all this material for the book?' She indicated the boxes.

'Hmm?' Elena glanced down. 'Oh yes, those are the photographs the archivist worked on. My life in pictures, as it were. Everything should be in date order – both in the boxes and on the backs of the images themselves. Heaven knows how he managed to be so precise, but then I guess that's what he was paid for. He considered himself a historian, you know. He would use details from the photographs such as the fashion of the clothes and hairstyles, or he would magnify the cover of a magazine on a table to identify the date.'

'Wow,' Cesca murmured, counting fourteen boxes in total whilst thinking how she'd been trained to do the same with case photographs.

'Everything should be there – from my childhood at Graystones to now, and everything in between.'

'Graystones is in America?'

'Yes. It's my parents' compound in Rhode Island.'

'Oh.' Compound, she thought. It wasn't often people had cause to use that word. 'And how long have you lived in Rome for?'

'It will be thirty-seven years in August, can you believe it?'

'Gosh. You really are an honorary Roman then.'

'I'm not sure they ever truly accept you, to be honest, but heaven knows I've tried leaving here and failed miserably.'

Cesca nodded, recalling Alé's gossipy conjecture at dinner the night before.

'When my darling Vito died, I didn't think I could bear to stay. We are so terribly lucky, we have so many places we get to call home: Tuscany, London, Aspen, New York, Bel Air. I tried them all – I even lived in Marrakech for a while; I thought the colours and bustle would cheer me up – but somehow I can never settle anywhere but here. I feel this city claimed my heart as much as the man did.'

'Well, I can relate to that – the city, I mean, not the man.'

'When did you first come to Rome?' Elena asked, looking interested, and Cesca noted that she had a way of gazing at her as she talked that suggested she was not only the most interesting person in the room (which was just as well, given they were alone), but possibly the most interesting person she'd ever met. She struck Cesca as a good listener, a confidante to many.

'The December when I was nine. My parents brought me and my brother to see the snow falling through the oculus in the Pantheon.'

Elena's eyes softened. 'The oculus. I have always thought it is the most romantic spot in the city.'

'Well, it certainly made me fall in love. When my friends talked about going to live in Paris or New York, it was always here that I wanted to come. I meant to come back before now but you know how it is – life got in the way. School, uni, law school . . . There was never enough time or money.'

'Law school?' Elena was like a hawk, spotting the single mouse in the field of hay.

Cesca blanched, realizing her slip. 'Oh . . . yes . . . I'm a trained barrister. But I knew very quickly that it wasn't for me,' she said hurriedly, closing down the topic before it could be opened up. 'Once I realized I'd made a mistake following law, I figured I needed to shape my life to the way I wanted it to be and that meant living here.'

'All that work, though, the years of exams, hours of studying . . .'

Cesca shrugged, already regretting opening her mouth. It was always the same; people could never believe she had turned her back on something she had strived so hard to reach. 'Well, it led me here so I don't regret it. I can't. It's a step on my path.'

'And your parents are supportive?' Elena asked, watching her closely as if detecting, somehow, something more.

'They want me to be happy.'

Elena nodded. 'Ah yes, well, as a parent, I can understand that very well.'

'Do you have children?' They were back on safe ground
again.

'One. A son, Giotto. He lives in London with his wife and
three children. We are very close.'

'How lovely.' Cesca looked back at the boxes again,
remembering that she had to turn this small talk into a
product. She was here to work after all. 'Well, I'm afraid I
haven't done any background research on you, yet. But—'

'Background research?'

'Yes. A few hours on the internet and I should be pretty
much up to speed on the broad strokes of your life, and
then you and I can go into finer detail face to face.'

'No.'

Cesca tripped over her own thoughts. 'I'm sorry, what?'

Elena looked pained. 'I would rather you did not *google*
me, if that's what you mean. At least, not to begin with.'

'But—'

'Francesca, many lies have been written about me over
the years; my wealth has made me a target from the day I
was born, but this is *my* biography. I want to tell my life
story but I can only do it through you and if you were
to read those malicious, downright slanderous stories, I
would become a cartoon character to you – something that
would almost certainly translate onto the page.'

Cesca swallowed down a sigh. It was true she knew practically nothing about her subject: mother of one, grandmother
to three, American-born but settled in Rome for thirty-seven
years, widowed for fifteen, a big property portfolio with a
spectrum of taste that ran from the baroque to the brutally
minimal. If it was a blank slate Elena wanted, she had

found it in Cesca. 'Okay, so then I won't go near Google,' she acquiesced. 'I'll start with the first box – go through it, select what appear to be the most pertinent photographs and then I can come to you with any questions I have and we can kick off from there. Does that sound okay? That way it's more of a conversation than an interrogation.'

Elena smiled, looking mollified. 'What a marvellous idea. It all sounds so simple when you put it like that.'

It took all of ten photos to establish that Elena came from money. Proper money. The Graystones box was the first she opened and it positively frothed with black-and-white kodaks of the rich at play – showjumping, shooting, yachting, water-skiing, even acting in glorious statue-filled garden theatres . . .

Elena had been a plump child, her light-brown hair kept at shoulder length and pinned back with a satin ribbon band. Throughout her childhood, it appeared she was dressed in Mary Janes and white socks, often with gloves and a bonnet or boater too; her coats were tweed with velvet pan collars. The smocking on her dresses was impossible to miss.

To Cesca it all looked incredibly uptight – and she noticed that in very few of the images was Elena ever smiling. That was no doubt due in part to the fact that she was almost always surrounded by adults, the only child in the group, but Cesca wondered as well about how close the child was to the incredibly glamorous parents flanking or holding her in some of the shots.

The mother was like a blade – narrow and sharply angled in the best couture – with blue-black dyed hair set in stylized waves, her distinctive almond-shaped eyes giving her a sensual, feline quality. With small bones and no bosom, she looked great in a bias cut and was more often found in eveningwear than anything else. (Although Cesca made a mental note that it was these 'high day and holiday' occasions that were more likely to be recorded with a photograph, than those regular 'nothing doing' days.) There was a lot of fur, a lot of satin, and she was often photographed alongside lots of men in penguin suits with oiled hair.

The most handsome of them appeared to be Elena's father. Even now, seventy years later, his looks – frozen through the lens – transcended his era, marking him out as a timelessly stunning man. He was the physical opposite of his petite wife: sunshine-blond curls, a deeply polished tan, pale-grey eyes and a strapping, athletic physique. Judging from all the photographs, he rowed, sailed, rode (hunting and polo), skied (both water and snow) and boxed. Cesca could see Elena had inherited his pale eyes and aristocratic slim nose; from her mother, she had gained her petite frame and that radiant smile which cut through the otherwise icy hauteur of those good bones.

Cesca felt a thread of envy ripple against her skin. Elena's spoon hadn't been silver but gold: not only had she won the gene-pool lottery but she had been born into unimaginable privilege. The house – Graystones, she had to assume – was like a scaled-up White House with porticos and balconies, except it had a shimmering weathered shingle roof. One particular shot, an aerial view, showed the entirety of the estate with its grand stables, polo field, tennis court, pool, lake and formal French garden carved into the swathe of fields and woodlands that ran down, on one side, to the sea. Suddenly, Elena's gracious elegance made sense. She hadn't needed to marry a prince to become a princess; she already was one in all but title.

Cesca stopped at one photograph in particular. It showed the little family of three at yet another party: Elena's mother in a light-coloured pleated silk dress, her father in a white silk DJ. Though the photo was black-and-white, Elena looked especially radiant in a velvet dress with a heart-shaped bodice. She looked different in this image – more sophisticated, somehow – and Cesca realized it was because she was wearing make-up.

The three of them were standing on a terrace. Behind them were hundreds of people all looking up at them; there were pretty lights strung up between the trees and a halo of brightness just coming into the bottom of the shot. A birth-day cake, perhaps? They were all laughing at something, mouths parted spontaneously and eyes dancing, her parents gazing upon her devotedly.

Cesca sighed and wondered whether she had the stomach for so much unremitting perfection. Elena really had been the luckiest girl in the world.

Chapter Seven

Rhode Island, August 1961

'Do you like it, Mother?'

The seamstress stepped back to allow Whitney Valentine an unimpeded view of her daughter.

Whitney's steepled fingers pressed against her lips. 'Darling, it's simply divine. Grace of Monaco has nothing on you. We were absolutely correct to go for the silk tulle, don't you agree, John?'

The couturier nodded. 'You were right as ever, Mrs Valentine. The zibeline would have been too stiff.'

'Exactly.' Whitney clapped her hands once, like a judge's gavel bringing down sentence. It was official, then. The zibeline would have been too stiff; they had been right to choose the silk tulle. 'It needs to be fluid, easy, weightless. Laney needs to float down the aisle like a feather on the wind.' Whitney's own slim hand twirled in the air expressively. 'She is, after all, a thoroughly modern girl.'

She was an It Girl to those who read the society pages. Since her coming out at her Sweet Sixteenth a couple of months earlier, Laney had become the most in-demand guest at every party, even though she was already no longer eligible.

The sixteen-year-old bride stared at her reflection in the mirror. The dress was a dream – albeit her mother's dream – with a crossover silk tulle bodice, shaped over the hips and then fanning out dramatically to a full tulle skirt over-laid with downy white feathers, which shimmied with every move. Long white gloves and an extravagant veil completed the look. *This* was the dress in which she would become Mrs Jack Montgomery.

'Do you think he'll like it?'

'Kitten, he adores you, how could he not?'

Her parents had rejoiced at her engagement – it meant hosting another of their famous 'occasions', for one thing – with her mother immediately swinging into action and procuring the services of Mr John Galano's atelier. The stiff ivory wedding invitations had become the most sought-after accessory of the season; not making the cut as one of the 400 guests at Graystones on the afternoon of Thursday 16 August was akin to social exile for the Manhattan elite.

Some eyebrows had been raised as to the speed of the engagement, yet more as to the relative poverty of the groom – the wealth of his family's modest but rapidly expanding timber business in Vermont was as nothing compared to the colossal Valentine fortune – but that was only to be ex-pected. They were bigots and snobs, stuck in the past. Her mother was right: she was a modern girl, marrying not for fortune or influence, but love, and these past seven weeks she had never known such happiness. Jack had showed her another, freer world beyond the strict confines of the Gray-stones compound and she loved nothing more than sitting on the rocks as he fly-fished for stripers, watching him skip-per down Block Island Sound (Jack had promised to teach her how to swim so that she wouldn't be so nervous around boats), bringing him luck and kissing the die on his black-jack nights.

He was invigorating to be around, a breezy gust in the otherwise still air of her circle, charming her friends, who all agreed he was a dream and 'the absolute spit' of Tab Hunter. In fact, he had bowled over everyone apart from Winnie, her beloved governess – but she, by her own admission, didn't believe anyone could ever be good enough for Laney, so that didn't count.

Every day, Laney gave thanks that their paths should have crossed. Her instincts had been correct – he *had* crashed the party, although he'd been cleverer than to scale the walls. His roommate at Brown, the son of a valued client of her father's, had been invited but was struck down with a bout of gastroenteritis the morning of the party. In spite of the security at the gates and the patrol dogs, mere presentation of the stiff invitation had been enough to get in and Jack had spent the night glad-handing her father's guests, waiting for the moment when she would make her appearance. Her reputation as a beauty had preceded her, he'd said, and he'd wanted to see with his own eyes the creature throwing his generation's finest into raptures – even though he'd always gone for blondes; even though, as far as he was concerned, heiresses were more trouble than they were worth. A seduction had seemed like fun, he'd teased, but he hadn't counted on losing his heart.

He was bold and confrontational, unpredictable. A wild card. Unlike the acolytes in her parents' circle, he was fearless. And when Laney's furtive relationship with him had been discovered by her parents and he had been invited for lunch (with the express intention of intimidating him away), he had flirted with her mother, coolly thrashed her father at backgammon and then promptly asked for her hand. Most grown men fawned in her father's company, but even George Valentine had to admit that at the tender age of twenty-one, Jack Montgomery was already not most men.

The church bells still jangled in her ears, the memory fixing in her mind of the stretched faces in the congregation, so hazy behind her veil. Her dress was draped on the chair opposite, looking more like a storm-battered swan's wing now that several feathers had detached from the skirt. The tulle was hanging limply (would the zibeline have been better after all?), the torn veil rolled up in a ball on the dressing table.

She stretched in the bed, grateful to be out of the corset, her body soft and heavy in the drip-dry sheets, wondering when she would finally get to be alone with her new husband. She was excited and nervous at the same time. Whenever his hands had wandered before, in the back of his car or down at the lake house, she had had to move them away, even when she hadn't wanted to, his urgency a breathless pleading in her ear. But now they were married, husband and wife, they could do whatever they wanted, whenever they wanted. She couldn't quite believe he was putting off this moment longer than necessary; how many times had he begged her these past few weeks, reminding her they were engaged, 'all but married anyway'? And now he was the one keeping her waiting, his craps game still in play on the other side of the door, his friends – so courteous earlier in their blazers and flannels – now growing rowdy and drunk, their jackets off, shirt-sleeves rolled up.

She pulled the sheet tighter around her as a voice approached the dividing door, sounding close – too close.

There was laughter, then some shouts. More laughter. And then the voice faded away again, silence dominating as the dice were thrown.

Her eyes never left the door. It didn't do to look too closely at the 'hotel' he had brought her to for the first night of their honeymoon. They were not two miles from home and she hadn't been able to hide her surprise at the flickering road sign or the rattling windows, the plastic flowers in the vase at reception, but she didn't think to complain; she didn't want to. He was giving her what she'd told him she had always wanted – a real life in the real world, no longer kept behind the glass like a doll in a house. It was also his way of making a statement, a way of showing the world – and the press that had clamoured at the church steps – that he didn't care about money, hers or anyone's. They loved each other, plain and simple. He was no gold digger and she loved him for it. She didn't care where they slept or how they lived. She was Mrs Jack Montgomery, sixteen years old and married to the handsomest man she had ever seen.

Besides, it wasn't the décor that had disconcerted her most, but the adjustment to getting ready for bed without Winnie to help her. Tonight had been the first time ever and though the tiny silk buttons on the dress had been tricky, as had the stays on the corset, she had managed it and lay here now, expectant in blush satin, her hair down and brushed to a midnight gleam.

She changed her position, bending the right leg over the left to maximize the undulations of her still-developing curves, her newly dyed blue-black hair fanned over the pillows. She wondered whether the party was continuing without them at Graystones and whether everyone was still having a good time; whether anyone was wondering if *she* was. The send-off had been jubilant, rose petals showered on them like a scented rain as they ran, hand in hand, towards the new Bentley her father had presented to them as a wedding gift, her honeymoon trousseau already packed in the trunk. She closed her eyes and conjured visions of couples still twirling in their summer colours, straining to hear through the open windows the echoes of the big band sounds drifting down the water here to Newport and out to sea.

Was it the hand that woke her first? Or his breath? Both were hot and hard against her skin as he grappled with the slippery nightgown that was now twisted around her, the sheet thrown to the floor, one knee between her legs.

'Jack—?'

She went to lift her head, to look over her shoulder, but instead she was pushed face-first into the pillow, the stale odour telling her too much in one breath about the hygiene of the motel, his hand pressing her cheek down to the mattress and keeping her there.

'Quiet!' His voice was a hiss, his breath rank with bourbon, the full length of his body pressed against hers, the full weight of it squeezing the air from her lungs as he fumbled with his fly, the cold leather of his shoes pressing against the bare soles of her feet, forcing them apart.

She struggled, panicking, trying to breathe, trying to get out from under him, to get away. She freed her head from his grasp, lifting it up for air and glimpsing the room in snatched gasps – the pink fringed bedside lamp, the crack of light through the curtains, her forlorn dress ghostly on the chair, the wire hangers like silver ribs through the open door of the wardrobe. But though he was drunk, he was too strong and as his palm spread around the back of her head, pushing her down again, she was as pinned as an entomologist's butterfly.

'No—'

She knew what was coming. Instinct and the brief talk from her mother that morning – 'Just try to relax and hold still' – told her. Hot tears, with nowhere to go, puddled and pooled in her eyes as she felt him tear into her. Her face twisted and contorted with pain, her mouth open to scream, but any sound that came was muffled in the pillow as white hot flashes streaked behind her eyelids.

This couldn't be happening. It wasn't how it was supposed to be. They loved each other. They were married. She was his. What had she done wrong?

He moved faster, her own blood a lubricant, abetting him. She stopped fighting – it only made it worse – and he grunted, sensing her surrender, pushing deeper, harder, faster. She willed herself to be still, to survive this.

Three minutes was all it took. With a final guttural groan that boomed and swirled in her ear, he pulled out and collapsed on his back on the bed beside her. Silence blanketed the room, shame permeating her as surely as the blood staining the sheets. She didn't stir, she couldn't move at all through the shock and terror, forced instead to listen to the sound of his breathing become regular again, watching him through the blur of tears as though she was at the bottom of a pool, looking up to the sky. He stared unseeing at the ceiling, not noticing the spider cracks in the plaster, before rolling his head to the side and looking at her, the whites of his eyes pinked, his lips and cheeks ruby with drink, his blond hair like a stray shaft of sunlight on the pillow.

Drowsily, with sleep already rolling up his body like a wave, he lifted his hand and dropped it heavily on her bare ass. He patted it.

'Goodnight, Mrs Montgomery.'

Chapter Eight

Rome, July 2017

Cloud pines dotted the sky, pigeons sporadically darting across her frame of vision. The grass felt cool beneath Cesca's bare arms, the spongy mat sticky with sweat between her shoulder blades. A short distance away, she could hear the splash of oars cutting through the boating lake, the babble of tourists' chatter as they exited the Villa Borghese and explored the park.

Beside her, Alessandra began to snore.

'Stop it,' Cesca giggled, walloping her lightly on the stomach with her nearest arm.

Alessandra cracked up, rolling onto her side and resting her head in one hand. 'You know this bit bores me.'

'You're supposed to be centring yourself. Connect with your breath.'

'I'd rather connect with that guy from Zizi the other night.' Her voice was low, her laugh dirty. 'You really missed a good time.'

'Yes, well . . . I was *trying* to be a responsible adult for once.'

'And look what happened there. You got fired. I hope you have learned your lesson.' Alé grinned and collapsed onto her back, staring up at the sky, a red bra strap peeking out from beneath her khaki ribbed vest, the orange nail polish on her toes chipped and missing from some nails altogether. They always said theirs was a pop-up friendship, like one of those camping tents you could pack in a bag and throw open wherever you stopped. From the first time they'd met at Glastonbury, there had been an immediate recognition, an understanding between them. It had helped that they were both drunk at the time, but Alé was certain they were both old souls reconnecting from another life. Whatever, Cesca was just grateful they'd been in the queue for the toilets at the same time. It was Alessandra who had talked her into following her dream and coming out here when Cesca had tearily told her she'd quit her job and had no idea what her future looked like any more; Alé who had helped her with her Italian when her audio course had her speaking like a courtier; Alé who had opened the doors for her to this life in Rome, introducing her to her 'brothers' – the boys she'd befriended in childhood, Matteo and Guido – and helping her secure the apartment, Signora Dutti being a friend of her grandmother.

Cesca closed her eyes again, her body heavy with fatigue after another night of broken sleep and an intense day's work. She had left the palazzo at five, after eight hours of sorting through thousands of small black-and-white photographs. It had been a dizzying introduction to a life lived at the very highest level of privilege. She half felt she had experienced Elena's childhood in real time – almost every moment had been captured because almost every moment had been special. How could it not be when ponies and rabbits and puppies were as plentiful as toys, and some of the finest real estate on the Eastern Seaboard was her playground?

As Alberto brought through trays of tea and cakes at two-hourly intervals, she had begun by pulling out one or two images from different times in Elena's childhood, starting with all the obvious baby and pram shots, through the toddler years and moving through childhood towards Elena's adolescence; she had finished the day with Elena at fifteen or sixteen, which she considered to be pretty good going for one day's work. She had then gone through them again, writing down the questions that each image posited – who's that woman in almost all the photos? What was the name of that horse?

Elena had told her the publishers wanted a 300-page book with a preliminary cut of 250 images which, given there had been over 1,000 photographs in the first box alone, meant they were going to need to be ruthless with the edits. Cesca could see why Elena had wanted someone objective working on the project. Whittling down a seventy-plus-year life to a set number of images, of moments, was harder than it looked. But Cesca was unfazed; as a barrister, she had had to work through boxes, several kilograms heavy, full of documents and evidence and testimonies, and cut through to the singular artery that defined every case. Because there always was one, and Elena's life would be no different.

'So how did today go with the devil woman?' Alé asked with a dramatic tone.

Cesca grinned. 'I barely saw her, to be honest. I've had my nose in a box of photographs all day, trying to get up to speed. Honestly, her life is unbelievable. I swear, her boating pond had a model boat on it that you could race in the America's Cup!'

Alé tutted.

'And they had peacocks! No scrawny pigeons for them.'

'I guess that's just how it is when you're born a Valentine.'

'*Valentine?*' Cesca asked in surprise. The name had immediate resonance – like Oppenheimer or Rockefeller or Rothschild, the Valentines were wealthy beyond measure.

'Sole surviving heir, my mother said,' Alé remarked, looking surprised. 'You didn't know that?'

'Only the name. I didn't know *she* was one.'

'Oh, so you are taking your research seriously then,' Alé teased with a wry smile.

'I'll have you know Elena has specifically asked that I *don't* do any background research to begin with. She wants me to hear her life story in her words, without prejudice.'

Alé considered this for a moment. 'I guess that is understandable. The tabloids love her. If she thought you believed everything they said about her, she could not act the principessa, could she?'

Cesca made no comment. She couldn't reconcile the frail, elegant lady she knew with the supposed notoriety of her public image – tabloid fodder, devil woman . . . What on earth had she done to warrant a reputation which seemed so at odds with the image she presented now?

'Tell me, what is it like inside the palazzo?' Alé asked, fidgety as usual and flipping over onto her stomach and assuming the plank position. She preferred their Monday evening HIIT classes to this yoga session in the park, but then, she didn't need to work on her tan.

Cesca gave a shudder. 'Ugh. Not my gig at all – all those long galleries and empty rooms. Gold everywhere.'

'What? You don't like it? It's one of the best addresses in the city.'

'And I can see why, architecturally, but to *live* in? The whole thing's like a mausoleum, not a home. I don't understand why she wants to live there – and on her own too! I mean, the garden's great and I appreciate the super-rich can't be expected to live in a two-up, two-down like the rest of us—'

'A two what?' Alé puffed, her cheeks beginning to flush.

'It's just a term for an average house,' Cesca said dismissively. 'Maybe this is what comes of all their jet-setting and living in hotels? That's what they know – marble floors and hard, dainty perching chairs. No toast crumbs in the kitchen for them, no saggy Ikea sofas or dog hairs blowing into the corners.'

'Is that what your home is like?'

Cesca realized it was, although Slipper, their border terrier, was so old now he was practically as bald as her grandfather, so there were fewer dog hairs these days. 'Pretty much, actually.'

'Sounds nice. I bet you have carpets too, yes?'

'Of course.' She knew Alé was teasing her Britishness.

Alé chuckled from under her mop of hair hanging forwards. 'You're so funny.'

'Thanks.'

There was a beat of silence. 'Do you miss it?'

'What? England?'

With a pant of effort, Alé rolled onto her side, her hands resting on her ribcage as she looked across at her. 'Home.'

Cesca resolutely kept her eyes closed. 'No. Because this is my home now.'

'But your family . . . your career. You've turned your back on everything you knew.'

'I haven't turned my back on anything. My parents were out here last month.'

'You know what I mean. Why do you never talk about it?'

Cesca felt Alé's hand on her arm.

'I know something bad happened.'

Cesca sat up, and in so doing dislodged Alé's hand. She pulled her legs in to her chest, her arms flopping over her knees. She kept her eyes on a young woman pushing a pram, a toddler walking alongside and licking an ice cream. 'Nothing bad happened, Alé. It was just a poor career choice. I'm not cut out for it. I don't have the disposition. It takes a certain type to thrive in that environment. A perfectionist; a stickler for detail.'

Alé arched an eyebrow. 'You read the terms and conditions of everything you buy online.'

'Everyone should do that,' Cesca said solemnly.

'Proving my point: you are the barrister type.'

'I'm not. There's not another barrister in the land who wears vintage bloomers unironically.'

Alé laughed.

'Besides, I'm happy here. I've got my friends, my deluxe apartment—' Alé laughed harder '—I'm living in the city I dreamed of living in as a little girl. I feel free here.' She looked around at the bright cloud-shaped shadows on the ground beneath the trees, at the short upright blades of grass resisting the unremitting heat like lines of brave soldiers, at a group of shirtless teenagers playing football on that grass on the other side of the path. Every sense was spoilt in Rome: the scent of jasmine wandered the air while the hum of scooters zipping round the perimeter roads was as calming as the buzz of bees. She inhaled and exhaled deeply, trying to prove the point.

'Are you sure it's freedom?'

'What else could it be?'

Alé shrugged. 'Escape?'

Cesca looked away, pretending to examine the freckles popping up on her pale skin like daisies. 'I'm afraid my life isn't anywhere near as fascinating as you give it credit for,' she murmured, rolling back down and laying her arms flat on the grass, palms upstretched, closing her eyes and trying to connect with her breath again. But it was a diversionary tactic, something to throw her friend off the scent and stop the questions from coming – because she knew those questions would lead to only one answer: that she had blood on her hands.

It was almost a carpet. The silk rug stretched to each wall with barely an inch gap all around. The wicker-framed sofas, meanwhile, were so soft and squashy-looking that Cesca half thought she would need a winch to get her back up again. Every side table had a lamp on it and a full-skirted bullion-fringed cloth, and the green-on-cream lattice-printed curtains – curtains, not shutters – matched the wallpaper. It was busy and fussy, an homage to the Eighties, but Cesca was overjoyed: there was no marble in here, nor any statues; there were no angels on the ceiling (just a delicate lacy plasterwork that she could live with) and not one pointless perching chair. Finally, in this palace of almost a thousand rooms – as Alberto had told her while marching her through the galleries earlier – they had found one that felt homely.

They were sitting in the garden room on the ground floor of the west wing. Elena was sitting opposite, her ankles crossed in Fendi ballerinas, small sun blemishes on her shins betraying a lifetime of summering on yachts. She was wearing a cornflower-blue shirt dress cinched with a leather belt, and tortoiseshell spectacles were perched delicately at the end of her nose. One eyebrow was arched as she leaned forward to scan the assembly of images Cesca had brought here, not necessarily for inclusion in the book but to get the conversation flowing about Elena's life.

To her right, Cesca had her voice recorder poised, ready to begin. They were waiting for Alberto to finish setting down the teacups – Lapsang Souchong, this time – and Cesca was idly watching a hatted and aproned gardener working on some rosebushes beyond the arched doors, the snip of his secateurs just audible through the glass.

'Will that be all, your Grace?'

'Yes, thank you, Alberto.'

He bowed his head. 'And just a reminder that the car will be ready for you in an hour. You have a lunch appointment with—'

'Christina, yes, yes, as if I could forget. Thank you, Alberto.'

He bowed his head again and left the room.

'Honestly,' Elena said, her voice barely more than a breath as she picked at a thread on the cushion nearest her hand. 'This gala. You'd think she was organizing a coronation.' When she saw Cesca's quizzical expression, she added, 'My husband's foundation has just completed a five-year restoration project of the ruins at Massimo's Forum and there's a charity gala at the beginning of September in his honour. He did so many great charitable works for his beloved Rome.'

'And Christina is . . . ?'

'Oh, an old friend. She grew up with Vito and his brother;

she rather sees herself as their honorary sister. She's my co-chair at the foundation, this gala's all her idea.'

'Oh.' Cesca thought for a moment. 'Well, perhaps I should speak to her for the book then?'

Elena frowned. 'Why?'

'It could be good to get in some colour about your philanthropic work. It would provide good balance,' she said, not wanting to elucidate that a non-stop barrage of luck and in-your-face privilege would also turn off most readers.

Elena considered the suggestion. 'Yes, I see,' she said slowly. 'Well, I don't see why not. I'll put it to her today and she can set something up. Although, to be frank, I don't think you'll get much from her; she won't be a particularly forthcoming interviewee.'

'Why not?'

'Well, as one of the Black families, she's not—' Elena looked at her, noticing Cesca's baffled expression. 'You've heard of the Black Nobility, obviously?'

There was nothing obvious about it. Cesca had never heard of any such thing. 'Uh . . .'

'Oh, I see,' Elena said, looking surprised. 'Well, the Black Nobility is used to describe those families who were given their titles by the popes, as opposed to the later White Nobility, who gained theirs from the state. I suppose you might say the Blacks are the ultimate "old money". Deeply conservative, traditional and very low-key. No scandals. No *fun*.' Cesca saw the glimmer of mischief in Elena's eyes. 'So if it's a press release on worthy causes you're after, then Christina will be your woman. But that will be the sum of it.'

'I see.' Cesca nodded with a smile, understanding now.

Discreetly, she started her recording device, knowing they were off. 'But from what I've seen of your childhood so far, it strikes me that you hail from whatever America calls its aristocracy.'

Elena sat back in her chair. 'Well, it's true we were rich, absurdly so, but we were only second-generation wealthy. We were what they would call "new money". My father inherited a billion-dollar fortune and doubled it in his life-time. He was an intensely charismatic man and business was easy for him. He was good-looking, intelligent, delight-ful company – people were just drawn to him; they honestly couldn't help themselves. My mother used to laugh that they gave him their money, just to have an excuse to be close to him.'

'Your mother was very beautiful too.'

'Oh yes, she was considered one of the great beauties of her generation. And her beauty combined with my father's star power meant they were highly sought after. I suppose you might say they were a power couple, long before such a thing was in the tabloid domain.'

'Was it a happy marriage?'

Elena paused. 'It was a *passionate* marriage. That is not always the most peaceful kind. But there is no doubt they loved each other intensely, some might say to the exclusion of all else.'

Cesca thought she sensed an unspoken point: *to the exclu-sion of her.* Or was she just being a barrister, still looking for a deeper narrative: a victim, a motive, a plot? 'Were you an only child? I didn't see any photographs of other children in the collection.' As if to prove the point, she scanned the assorted images again, looking for a playmate or compan-ion in the baby shots, but knowing there was none. She never missed the details, having been trained to read crime photos with a forensic eye.

'Yes, my mother had a difficult history. She had miscarried multiple times before falling pregnant with me and she was forced to take five months' bedrest before I was born. She said it may have saved me, but it almost did for her. She was a sprite, my mother, you see, always darting from one thing to the next, and such confinement wasn't good for her spirit. She said she couldn't bear to go through it all again. My father, I know, yearned for more, but my mother's happiness came above all else for him.'

'It must have been very hard for them,' Cesca sympathized.

'Indeed.'

'Was it hard for you?'

Elena looked surprised. 'I'm sorry?'

'Being the only child in such a big house? Did you ever wish you had brothers or sisters to play with?'

'Well, of course, which only child doesn't? But I was never alone. I had Winnie, my beloved nanny, and she came everywhere with me. I couldn't be parted from her. I would cry and call for her terribly any time she left the room.'

'Is this Winnie?' Cesca asked, leaning forward and pulling out a black-and-white snapshot of a baby – Elena – in a grand carriage pram. She was wearing a velvet bonnet and coat, a lace coverlet over her legs. A sturdy woman was standing beside her in black boots, a black dress, a tweed coat and matching cloche hat.

'Darling Winnie!' Elena cried, taking the photograph from her and bringing it closer to her eyes in order to see better the woman's doughy features. She smiled, nodding at it affectionately. 'Yes, that's exactly as I remember her.

Stern as a scaffolder, she hardly ever smiled – I think only for me – but her voice was like water tumbling over rocks in a river. She was Irish, from the south; near Waterford, I believe. Oh, it was just the most beautiful accent. Even now, if I hear it, I stop in my tracks and close my eyes and it's like being transported back to my childhood.'

'It sounds like you loved her very much.'

'I did, I truly did. She was the centre of my world.'

'Did your mother ever feel jealous of your relationship with her?'

'Heavens, no! My mother was just pleased I wasn't squawking, I expect. You have to understand, my parents were very busy. Ours wasn't a normal family. My father often entertained important people and with Graystones being such a big house to run, my mother was always overseeing the staff or dealing with the flowers or checking on the horses – she was a very keen horsewoman, you see. So Winnie and I were left to our own devices most of the time. It suited us very well. My rooms occupied the top floor of the house and Winnie's was beside my bedroom, so we had plenty of space.'

Cesca nodded. 'Did Winnie have her own family?'

Elena shook her head. 'No. Although I understand from my mother that she was once proposed to by the head groundsman. They had been courting and he came to ask my parents if he could take her hand in marriage.' Her eyes sparkled as though the delight was still fresh.

'He asked your parents for her hand? But surely it was a private matter?'

'Oh no, not when her role was so pivotal to the running of our family. Winnie never would have done anything that would have disrupted arrangements.'

Cesca was taken aback. 'What did your parents say?'

'My mother had to refuse.' Elena shrugged, replacing the photograph in the box and sitting back again. 'I was little more than a toddler and very attached to Winnie by then. They couldn't afford to lose her.'

'But would her getting married have meant you would have lost her?'

'Well, of course. No doubt they would have started a family of their own and then, at best, her attention would be split; at worst, I could have lost her altogether.'

Cesca double-blinked as she always did when she was shocked. 'What happened to her?'

'Winnie? Oh, she moved on when I left home at sixteen. There was nothing more for her to do, really, once I had gone.'

'And how old was she when she left?' Cesca couldn't help asking the question; it was her barrister's brain, wanting the complete picture, to see every side of the story.

Elena considered. 'Mid-forties, I should think? It's hard to tell. Everyone past thirty looks old when you're young, don't they?'

'And do you know where she went next? Did you keep in touch?'

Elena shook her head sadly. 'No, and it is something I regret very much. I'm sorry to say I was at that most selfish of ages – sixteen years old. All I cared about was getting on with the rest of my life. I wanted to be an adult, in control of my own future. I was desperate to get away from Graystones and I suppose to some extent Winnie was the emblem of my life there. Once I left Graystones, I never saw her again.' She glanced at her hands – tiny, pale, with grey-blue veins lacing the skin. 'Well, not until her funeral, anyway,' she added, as though that was something notable. 'She died in 1978. Tuberculosis.'

Cesca nodded, seeing what Elena seemingly did not – that Winnie had forsaken her (possibly only, certainly last) chance to have a family of her own to look after someone else's child – only to be dismissed when she was past her own child-bearing years, only to be forgotten by the child she had loved as her own, only to die alone.

'Sometimes I feel very sad about it, but I have to take comfort in the fact that my mother assured me that when she left our service, she wrote a most warm reference.'

Cesca nodded, words failing her. And this was only the first photograph.

Chapter Nine

Rhode Island, January 1962

'Well, I'm sorry to say you've made your bed and now you must lie in it.' Whitney Valentine continued pouring the tea, her hand steady as the tears stood poised in her daughter's eyes. 'No man is what he first appears to be. Why, your father would have had me believe he was curing cancer when we first started stepping out together! That's just what they do.' She looked up at her daughter from beneath lashes thickly laden with mascara. 'You must remember, dear, that beauty is every man's greatest weakness – they'll say and do anything to catch you. So Jack exaggerated his family's interests a little? You never would have looked at him otherwise. You could have had your pick of every bachelor in America and he knew it. Besides, it's hardly relevant, is it? It's not like he could ever match your inheritance. No, it's Jack's resourcefulness and independence that are the very things your father most admires about him.' She set down the teapot and handed Laney the cup and saucer.

Laney took it with a trembling hand. 'But Mother, it's not just the lies. I think I could live with that; I could understand why he felt he had to pretend he was . . . more. But the gambling—'

'Yes, yes – cards, bourbon and no doubt other women too.' Whitney sighed impatiently. 'You need to grow up, Laney. You're not an innocent any more. You're a married woman and soon, no doubt, you'll be a mother too. You need to open your eyes and see the world as it really is. Life isn't like the movies. No man is perfect and you aren't either. It's about making the best of things and putting on a good show.' She paused, lowering her voice a fraction. 'And besides, there's nothing to stop you pursuing your own interests in private if that's what you want, just so long as you're discreet.'

Whitney arched an eyebrow as she sipped the tea. She looked resplendent in a mustard silk dress with teal belt and matching turban, which highlighted the severe curve of her cheekbones.

'You're right, of course, Mother,' Laney said after a moment, staring at the tea trembling in her hands. 'I think I'm just tired and let it all get to me. We've been travelling such a lot recently.'

But finding comfort in another man's arms couldn't have been farther from Laney's mind, not when her financial situation with Jack was so precarious. The Bentley was long gone; the pearls her father had given her the night of her Sweet Sixteenth also a distant dream. She had been forced to sell the diamond lattice bracelet bequeathed to her by her grandmother and she was genuinely terrified of what might happen if those men came back again. They would hurt Jack this time, she was sure of it. But how was she supposed to get her hands on $120,000? Jack – knowing just how to play her father and secure her hand in marriage – had insisted to her parents that they would live off his salary when they married, implying that he was a man of means, of integrity and of pride. But that was before he had learnt she didn't come into her trust until her twenty-first birthday. Now, with bailiffs – and worse – knocking on their door, they didn't have anything like that sort of time. His clever swagger had boxed them into a corner: they were surrounded by money, but couldn't access any of it.

She set down the tea on the table and clasped her hands tightly together to stop them from shaking. 'Talking of discretion,' she began. 'There's something I wanted to ask you.'

'Mmm?'

'Jack's birthday is coming up soon – he'll be twenty-two – and I thought it would be fun to surprise him with a new boat.'

'What a fabulous idea. Your father still adores *Andante*, even after all these years. She's been quite his favourite vessel, even though she's really beginning to look quite tired these days.'

'Well, I wasn't thinking of anything on quite that scale. Not yet, anyway. Perhaps an eighty-footer.'

'Good grief, that's rather meagre, isn't it?'

'Well, he much prefers to skipper himself.'

Whitney shrugged, baffled by the idea of sailing a boat without crew. 'I'm not sure our broker, Tony Beresford, deals in that class but I suppose we could ask—'

'That wouldn't be necessary,' Laney said quickly. 'I-I've already seen one. In Boston.'

'Boston?'

'Yes. Jack and I went a few weeks back. He had an important business meeting and took me along to meet his client's wife. We all had dinner and then I saw the boat when we took a walk along the harbour afterwards. Jack admired it

94

so I went back the next morning and enquired after it. The owner said it wasn't for sale but when I made him an offer . . .' She shrugged, hoping her mother couldn't read the lie in her eyes.

'Well, I hope you got a good price,' Whitney said, looking both surprised and impressed. 'Did he know who you were? Because you know as soon as they realize you're a Valentine, you can add a zero to the price.'

Laney shook her head. 'No, I don't think he knew.'

'No, of course. I suppose being a Montgomery now means you can move a little more incognito.'

'Yes.' Laney swallowed, wringing her hands together so that the skin blanched. 'The thing is, obviously I don't come into my inheritance for another four and a half years, but if I buy it through Jack's bank, the surprise will be ruined. And really, what's the point of buying him a boat if it's not going to be a marvellous surprise?'

'Quite.'

'I just have such visions of walking him down to the water and watching his expression when he sees the boat he admired sixty miles away, docked here and waiting for him.'

Her mother smiled. 'It's a simply wonderful idea, darling. What do you need?'

Laney swallowed, feeling a wave of relief so powerful, she thought she might throw up. 'One twenty.'

Whitney picked up the telephone on the table beside her and spoke into the mouthpiece, issuing an order for the transfer to be wired into her daughter's account.

In the next moment, the teacup was back in her hand. 'Now we must discuss Palm Beach,' her mother said. 'We're going to throw a party and we're thinking of theming it. Tell me, what do you think of Carnivale . . . ?'

April 1962

Laney sat in the front seat of the car, which Jack had deliberately parked in the farthest corner of the parking lot, but from where the babble of chatter from the town hall's single small room could still be heard. Disembodied cameo-black heads drifted past the high-set windows as everyone greeted each other and chatted animatedly, before gradually taking their seats and dropping out of sight.

She took a deep breath, willing herself to go through with this.

'This is stupid,' Jack muttered, watching as she readied herself to go, checking her appearance in the mirror one last time. They would be waiting for her. 'What's going in there going to do for you?'

'I must make an effort to be sociable, Jack. We need to build up our circle of acquaintances. Don't you want us to entertain?'

'Not them,' he sneered, his eyes on the profile of a particularly toothy lady with her hair in a demure chignon, who was laughing at something said by someone out of sight.

Laney stared straight ahead, a sob stuck in her throat that he didn't see the irony of their situation. Stranded by his own pride, he now felt either unwilling or unable to accept what he considered her father's charity – money they desperately needed. On the other hand, he considered as beneath him anyone of his own financial standing; none of whom dared approach them anyway, intimidated by the great Valentine name. The result was that they were set apart, isolated. Her old friends – unmarried and eligible and still going to balls and parties all year long – had fallen away, scared off by the rumours of Jack's drinking and his troubles with the casino bosses. She knew they gossiped about her, holding her up as the parable for an unwise, rushed marriage.

'Don't be such a snob,' she said, as lightly as she could. 'I'm sure they're perfectly nice. And besides, they do such good works for the community and raise so much for charity. It's only right I should get involved and give back.'

'They'll never accept you. You're just a freak show to them, a zoo animal. They only want to stare at you and see whether you cry tears of solid gold.'

'You're wrong. I'm just like them now.'

He grabbed her wrist, suddenly infuriated. Challenged. 'What? Impoverished?'

'I didn't mean that.'

'No? What did you mean?'

'You know what. I just want to live a normal life, Jack. As your wife. I don't want to be shut away like I'm made of glass. I want normal things – a husband, a home, friends.'

He gave a snort of derision, but didn't stop her as she opened the car door and moved to get out. 'I'll be waiting here.'

'You don't need to. I can walk—'

'I'll be right here,' he reiterated firmly.

She nodded, seeing the threat in his eyes, and he let her go. She took out the covered coat from the back seat and walked towards the noisy hall, feeling his eyes on her back the whole way to the door, then eyes on her face on the other side of it, as she stepped in and fifty-four women turned towards her. Mary-Beth Erskine, the leader of the Newport Ladies' Guild and she of the toothy profile, looked relieved to see her.

The room fell silent.

'Ah, Mrs Montgomery,' she beamed. Mary-Beth stood at the front of the room; there was a fashion mannequin with one arm bent and a hand poised in a conversational manner standing nude behind her. 'We were just about to begin.'

'I'm sorry if I'm late,' Laney said, seeing in one scan of the room that she was younger than everyone by at least four years. The Young Wives division of the Ladies' Guild clearly didn't mean *that* young.

'Not at all. We were just remarking how pleased we are by tonight's turnout. Almost a full register!'

Laney felt her heart rate quicken. Was it diligence for the club or sheer curiosity to ogle her that had driven them out in such numbers tonight? She felt heat in her cheeks as she walked to the front; felt, too, the keen-eyed gazes assessing the cut of her skirt, the silk of her blouse, how she had rouged her cheeks, the size of the diamond on her finger – and she knew she had her answer. Jack had been right: everyone wanted to see the billionaire's daughter who was mingling with the masses.

Keeping her face turned away, summoning courage, she took out the coat she was carrying and draped it carefully over the silent moulded figure.

'Ladies, we're so lucky to have our newest member, Mrs Elaine Montgomery, talking to us tonight,' Mary-Beth said, addressing the expectant room. 'Elaine has agreed to share her expertise on storing your furs for the summer months. Elaine?'

'Thank you, Mary-Beth.' Laney stared out at the sea of faces, the mink that had been a sixteenth birthday present from her paternal grandmother like a ghost at her shoulder as she faced what she hoped would be her new future, her new friends. 'It's very kind of you all to come tonight. I hope I can be helpful to you.'

'Sorry, could you speak up?' a voice from the back called.

Laney flushed and cleared her throat. 'So . . . uh, obviously, with summer coming, this is the time to prepare our coats for storage and the first thing is to ensure they're cleaned thoroughly beforehand. If dust permeates the fur and is trapped there, it can mix with the natural oils in the hair shafts, acting like a sponge – soaking up the natural moisture and leading to cracking of the hide, so cleaning it first is a really important part of the process. Then—'

A hand rose in the audience.

'Yes?'

A woman at the back rose to stand. 'So how do you clean the fur?'

Laney blinked. Winnie did it. Or rather, Winnie took it to the person who did it. 'Well, you, uh . . . shake it out, first of all. And then . . . gently beat it with a small paddle.' She had come across one of the maids doing just that to her mother's lynx coat, when she'd been much younger.

'Should I apply water?' the woman asked.

In a flash, Laney remembered her mother's horror at once coming across a sable that had been left damp in a cupboard, proclaiming water 'the devil!' 'No. No water.'

The woman nodded, satisfied, and sat back down again.

Laney, her heart pounding now that the interrogation was over, swallowed and resumed her talk. 'If your fur has an odour – perfume, cigar smoke or the like – zip it into a garment bag and add ground coffee beans at the bottom, stirring them every day. After a few days, the odour will have been absorbed.'

Another hand. 'But surely the fur would then smell of coffee?'

'Yes. But if you hang the coat somewhere dry and cool for a day or two, the coffee aroma will disappear from the coat too.'

Another nod; an impressed look.

'I always store my furs in silk bags, but you can use cotton too. Just no synthetic materials, that's the important thing.'

A hand went up. A different one.

'Yes?'

'Exactly how many furs do you have?'

Laney felt her mind blank again. What did that have to do with anything? 'Um . . . I'm not sure.'

'You're not sure?' the woman – an attractive brunette – echoed. 'Gosh. It really must be a number then.'

'*How* old is she?' someone whispered not so quietly at the front.

'Seventeen?' someone else replied, guessing.

'Looks younger.'

'It's eight. I have eight,' Laney said decisively, talking over them, shutting down the buzz that was beginning to stir like a colony of disturbed bees. 'Anyway, um . . .' She tried to remember where she'd been in her speech. 'The ideal temperature for storage should be between forty to fifty degrees Fahrenheit, with fifty per cent humidity. The worst thing would be if the hide were to dry out and crack because then the coat would tear at the slightest movement. Keep it somewhere dark, away from both sunlight and light bulbs. And make sure to hang it on a large padded hanger with a clearance of three to four inches from other clothing, else the fur will be crushed.'

A hand. 'What about moths? Can I use cedar sachets?'

'Well, the problem with cedar is that the odour is so pungent and it would be absorbed straight into the fur. I personally steer clear of it. Cleaning it before storing it in the garment bag should be sufficient.'

A hand. 'Just going back to your eight furs again, what exactly are they?'

Laney was quiet for a moment, able to see the dark interest in the women's eyes, all of them craving this detail, as though to know what hung in her closet was to know what her life was really like, what it was like to be her. 'I would have to check,' she mumbled, her eyes darting towards the window and the dark parking lot beyond. She couldn't see Jack, sitting in the car, but he could see her, she knew, back-lit in this room of gingham-clad hyenas.

'Roughly, though,' the woman persisted. 'I mean, you must have a general idea – mink? Sable?'

Laney swallowed again, feeling herself shrink, wishing Winnie were here. 'Well, this is a mink,' she said quietly, holding its arm as if for moral support.

'Your newest?' someone asked.

She nodded. The silence that followed was expectant, pregnant with awe and envy and judgement. 'And there's a lynx, a gold fox, a white fox, a sable, chinchilla—'

'She's barely more than a child,' a woman at the front tutted to her friend.

'Terribly overindulged. What does a girl of her age need all those furs for? Why, it's more than one for every day of the week.'

Another tut. 'With their money, they probably work on a monthly schedule.'

A titter rippled through the front rows.

Laney looked down, feeling her composure desert her. It had been a mistake coming here, thinking she could do this. She had thought this would help make her one of them, not mark her out even further.

'You're so lucky,' one of the younger women in the room said, half-standing with a kind smile.

Laney shook her head, feeling tears gathering like storm clouds, ready to break. 'No—'

'Oh, but you are. It must be so wonderful being you.' She began to clap, a few others joining in too.

Laney kept shaking her head, wanting them to stop. It was everything she didn't want; everything Jack had said would happen. She would never be accepted. She would always be on the outside. Always alone. 'Please, don't—' But as their claps grew, the storm inside her broke and everyone craned to see the tears fall: was she flesh and blood, or something more – rarer, more precious? All of them envying an idea, a mirage.

'Oh, don't cry,' one called. 'Why are you crying? You're just the luckiest girl in the world.'

Chapter Ten

Rome, July 2017

'I really was the luckiest girl in the world,' Elena said, from the same chair in which she had sat the other day, her eyes moving back and forth over the small selection of images Cesca wanted to discuss today. It was late afternoon and the sun had moved round to the windows on Cesca's left, throwing down a dazzling flare of light across the papers on her lap, bleaching out the questions she had been compiling all day as she sorted through the photographs – who was that man? What was the name of that dog? Where was this house? Already, her job of a week ago, tramping through the heat with a gaggle of tourists behind her, felt like a distant dream. In the space of just four days, she had become fully immersed in Elena's life and was gaining a rhythm for editing the images as the shock of the Valentines' colossal wealth began to recede and their lifestyle began to seem normal. Not just that, but she was now beginning to be grateful for the palazzo's 100-foot-long rooms, of which her 'office' was just one, for she had begun to lay out her edited selection of images in long lines along the marble floor; Alberto now had to tread carefully when he brought her tea. 'It was a truly golden childhood.'

'When we last spoke, we discussed in some detail your relationship with Winnie, your nanny.'

'Yes.'

'Today I'd like to get some more detail about your relationship with your parents.'

Elena tipped her head interestedly, a benign smile on her face. 'What would you like to know?'

'Well, you said your father inherited his wealth, that he was born into money, but what about your mother?' She pressed 'record' on the digital recorder beside her.

Elena crossed her ankles. 'My mother was born in Connecticut to second-generation Portuguese immigrants. She was the third of six children and her father worked at the Ford factory. They weren't poor, but there was never anything extra – no second helpings at dinner, one present at Christmas, clothes that were recycled from her siblings. But my grandfather was a very proud man; he worked hard and had climbed his way up to the rank of foreman before his sudden death.'

'Oh? What happened to him?'

'He got his arm trapped in the machinery. It was torn clean off and he bled out before the paramedics could get to him,' she said with grim matter-of-factness.

'Good lord.'

Elena nodded and sighed. 'Apparently, my grandmother never really recovered from the shock.'

'No. I can imagine.'

'She'd never been of a strong disposition anyway and although my mother was only fifteen at the time, she said she realized immediately that she had to save the family. Her eldest sister was already married and had moved away to Indiana; the eldest boy had learning difficulties, which meant he could never provide financially. So it was up to Mother to bring the money in.'

'What did she do?'

'Modelling. She began as a house model for a local dress-maker, then she was noticed by a photographer who began using her for a magazine called *Ladies' Home Journal*, and that opened the door to more magazine work. When my father first set eyes on her, it was in an advertisement in *Vogue* magazine.'

'So your father fell in love with her image?'

'Yes. I'm not sure whether it comes across so much in the black-and-white photographs but my mother had striking looks – very dark hair and olive skin, but with light, bright-green eyes. It was the Portuguese genes. My father had never seen anyone like her before.'

'Wow. So how did he go about meeting her?'

'He made an appointment with the dressmaker in whose advert she had starred, on the condition that she – my mother – modelled the collection. He bought every single piece and then gave them all to her, taking her out for dinner that very night. They were engaged within the month.'

'So it was truly love at first sight, then?'

'Yes. They were infatuated with one another until my father's death in 1979. He fell from his horse,' she added, as though anticipating Cesca would ask.

Cesca found herself taken aback by the unemotional way in which Elena recounted her life – the losses told in the same tone as the joys and triumphs, as though she had rehearsed the words so many times in her head they ceased to have any meaning as she now recited them by heart. 'And how did your mother cope, being widowed quite young too?'

'Oh, in her own way. She wasn't like my grandmother; she remarried within the year – Artie Shaffer, the Hollywood film producer.'

'I see,' Cesca said in surprise. The name was familiar but she couldn't conjure a face. 'What was he like?'

'I don't know; I never met the man. I was informed of the marriage by telegram. I was living in New York by then and obviously they didn't want to make a fuss.' Elena gave a wry smile before adding, 'Which, translated, meant my mother didn't want the press writing headlines about her.'

'So she moved to California?'

'Yes, Pacific Palisades.' Elena gave a light sniff. 'I never visited – not my sort of climate. So arid.'

Cesca hesitated, musing on the tension this development brought to what she knew of the family so far: a passionate marriage in which even their only child was sidelined, yet the mother remarried within a year of her husband's death. The one negated the other, surely? She thought about the family's stiff body language in the photographs, Elena's unsmiling face as she gripped her nanny's hand. Was Whitney Valentine's concern about press headlines anything to do with the speed of the marriage? Cesca wondered. And if so, did that imply some sort of relationship – nay, affair – before the death of Elena's father? Did passion trump love at Graystones? Did they actually feel anything quiet and true, these people, or was their sentiment all for show too, along with the well-bred ponies and gleaming cars? Because the principal feeling Cesca had been getting as she immersed herself in their past, was that for all their material good fortune, the family had seemed ... *unglued* somehow, as though they'd all been living under the same roof without ever really seeing each other. 'Would you say that you and your mother moved apart after your father's death?'

Elena hesitated, her smile becoming fixed. 'No, I wouldn't say that. But neither did we move any closer. I suppose you might say we were like the fixed points of a compass, never moving further apart, nor ever closer, just pivoting around each other in circles.'

'"As stiffe twin compasses are two / Thy soule, the fixt foot, makes no show / To move, but doth, if the'other doe."' Cesca smiled.

Elena raised an eyebrow, impressed. 'John Donne. "A Valediction: Forbidding Mourning" if I remember correctly. One of my favourite poets. You are very well read, Cesca.'

Cesca decided not to remind her new employer that she had a degree, post-graduate qualification and three years' pupillage to her name. It wasn't education she was short on – not that she wanted to reopen *that* conversation – but as her gaze fell back to her notes, her barristerial instincts were kicking in regardless. She was practised in interviewing people – defendants, witnesses – and she knew when she was being told lies; and if not lies, then at least not the whole truth. What was the whole truth here, when there were fewer than ten photographs of a young Elena with her mother in the entire box of almost a thousand? In practically all the images, Elena was shot with Winnie, on occasion her father too. Cesca suspected that the two women had always been emotionally distant from one another. Had her mother somehow viewed Elena as a rival for George Valentine's affections?

The sun had moved around a little, the shade edging across her lap, and she now caught sight of her favourite photograph of George Valentine, Elena's father, arranged on the tray on the low table between her and Elena. It was upside-down from where she was sitting, but no less impressive: he was sitting astride a magnificent horse in tan jodhpurs and a tweed hacking jacket, a cream silk cravat at his neck. He had been caught side-on by the photographer, the moment snatched from a casual glance to the camera. His hair was swept back, his cheeks deeply flushed, and his lips were parted either in speech or by the onset of laughter.

'Let's talk a bit more about your father. The impression I'm getting is that you were a daddy's girl. Would that be a fair assessment?'

Elena preened like a cat in the sun. 'Most definitely. We were the world to each other. He used to call me his little lamb.'

'That's so sweet.'

'He truly was the sweetest man.'

'This is my favourite image of him so far.' Cesca reached forward and tapped the photograph to which she was referring. 'I think it's definitely a strong option for the first edit.'

Slowly Elena leaned forward and picked up the photograph. 'I've always loved this one of Daddy. He looks especially golden, don't you think?'

'I think "golden" is a very apt description of him.'

'Of course, sunburns were all the rage back then. They didn't call them suntans, you understand, and Daddy couldn't be doing with anything as fussy as tanning lotion. It wasn't a question of vanity; he was just always such an outdoorsy person. Of course, everyone else would be desperately frying themselves in a bid to look good whilst Daddy would be larking about on the polo field or playing golf.'

'Do you think he knew how good-looking he was?'

'Oh, I'm sure he must have done, but he wore it very lightly.'

'Did the ladies love him?'

'Well, if they did, it was from afar,' Elena replied crisply.

'I'm sorry, I didn't mean to imply—' Cesca's voice trailed off. It had been too forthright a question, she realized, her tone too direct. She reminded herself that Elena was not one of her defendants: she was not a police suspect with a rap sheet and no alibi. There was no ulterior story here beyond the facts as Elena presented them, but old habits die hard. She softened her stance: 'So he was born into a dynasty?'

'Yes. Tobacco and coffee originally, which had been diversified into print media and telecoms by the time my father was born. As the first son, he inherited the business and the lion's share of the family portfolio; something for which I'm not sure my aunt ever really forgave him.'

'I guess that's sort of understandable, really,' Cesca said without thinking. When she caught sight of Elena's frozen expression, she added, 'I mean, from the perspective of this day and age.'

There was another icy pause. 'Well, these laws have stood for generations for good reason,' Elena said quietly. 'I'm all for equality, but things are quite different when you get to estates and fortunes of this scale.'

Cesca's mouth parted in immediate, hot disagreement. Was Elena seriously suggesting women couldn't be *trusted* with vast sums of money? And what if Elena herself had had a little brother and he had inherited the lot from under her? Would she think it quite so fair then, or were her judgements rooted in the safety that comes from being the only child, the sole heir? But there was ice in Elena's eyes and Cesca held fire, sensing her new employer wouldn't respond well to an intellectual debate on the topic. In fact, she was getting the distinct impression Elena didn't like to be challenged at all. Ever.

Elena visibly relaxed, like a cobra recoiling from an aborted strike, as Cesca bit her tongue. 'Besides, it wasn't my father's fault that that was how things were,' Elena continued stalwartly. 'He was a product of that age and was brought up in the expectation of heading the family trust from birth; he knew nothing else and he made sure my aunt was well provided for. My father was generous to a fault.'

Cesca nodded, trying to muster her reserves of diplomacy. She remembered how 'generous' the Valentines had been when compensating Winnie for her abrupt termination of employment and estrangement from the child she had loved as her own, and had even put *before* having her own: *a good reference*. 'Yes, I'm sure,' she murmured.

'Are you?' Elena asked, her voice bristling. 'You sound unconvinced as to my father's good character.'

'No, it's not that.'

'What, then?'

Cesca bit her lip, wondering how hard she could press this button without getting fired. 'It's just that, well, to be honest, I'm struggling to get a handle on your relationship with your parents, full stop. On the one hand, it seems like they had eyes only for each other, to the exclusion even of you. But then, I sense a . . . distance between you and your mother which I wondered might be down to your closeness with your father, so that perhaps she felt the odd one out? But then that doesn't seem likely given she remarried within a year of his death. I can't seem to find a continuum.' Cesca's voice quietened to a mumble as she saw the flint in

Elena's eyes. 'Added to which, your parents feature in hardly any of the photos of you as a baby or young child.'

Elena blinked. 'Well, I should imagine my father was the person who took most of the photographs.'

'But wouldn't it have been more usual for Winnie to take the photographs? Why would your parents want so many snapshots of their child and her nanny? I mean, I'm not trying to imply anything, but I just don't . . . understand yet. I'm trying to get an insight into the dynamics of your family setup, that's all.'

There was a long silence. Elena's face had set into a frozen mask. Inanimate. Lifeless. *Mortified.* 'My parents adored me. I wanted for nothing.'

Cesca nodded, even though that hadn't been what she'd asked.

'Did you see the photos of my horses? Miss Midnight, there—' Elena pointed to the selected photo of herself in full show-jumping kit, standing beside a young black mare, a rosette on its bridle. '—Was sired by a three-time Olympic champion. It was like riding a rainbow, sitting on her back. I was only eleven.'

'Goodness. How lucky,' Cesca murmured, looking down at the photo as Elena clearly desired her to do. But perhaps the set of her expression wasn't pleasing enough, for in the next moment Elena stood up.

'That's quite enough for now. I'm tired,' she said abruptly. As she straightened up, the photograph of her father on the horse fluttered from her lap to the floor. She let it lie there. No doubt, someone else would pick it up. 'I need to rest. I have plans for later.'

'Oh, yes, of course,' Cesca said, staring up at her, knowing that – in spite of her best intentions – she'd still gone too far. She'd been too frank, her questions too searching. 'I'll keep going through the boxes. Perhaps we can meet again in a few days.'

'Yes. Perhaps,' Elena said enigmatically, gliding towards the door. 'I'll send Alberto in with some fresh tea.'

'Oh really, that's not—'

'Good evening.'

Even after she'd gone, Cesca continued to watch the space Elena had left behind her, adrenaline coursing through her veins at the subtle contretemps. She looked back down at the photographs on the floor – George Valentine, dashing on horseback; eleven-year-old Elena standing proudly beside her rosette-clad mare – wondering why Elena, who until now had been understated to the point of diffidence, had resorted to bragging. Did she think Cesca's head would be so turned by the horse's Olympic pedigree that she would forget the thread of what they had been discussing: her father's love?

Stop it, Cesca told herself as she picked up the photographs and shuffled them back into the pile of preliminary edits. Why couldn't she just see what Elena was telling her about those images? That she had loved her parents and they had loved her. She'd been the luckiest little girl in America.

But Cesca couldn't help it: she couldn't take off her barrister's hat. She knew when she was being fed an angle.

'Honestly, it was the weirdest thing. She just stormed off.'

She and Guido were sitting on the small, square, flat area at the top of the steps outside her front door, a beer in their hands and the sun on their faces. A jazz trio on bass, sax and acoustic guitar was playing under the ancient olive tree in the middle of the little square. Free entertainment for the night.

Cesca stared at the shuttered side end of the palazzo as she drank. She still felt deeply unsettled by Elena's tantrum. She wasn't sure how they could work together if this was going to be Elena's attitude. Elena had talked about needing to trust her, but it cut both ways. How could she do her job if a gently expressed enquiry could escalate to Elena cutting short the interview and leaving the room?

'I don't get it. What's her problem?' Guido asked. 'I thought that was the point of employing you – a brilliant brainbox, completely over-qualified to be writing the memoirs of a silly old socialite.'

'Stop it, you've made your point,' she said, slapping his arm lightly. 'And anyway, she didn't know I was a barrister when she hired me. She thought I was a writer.'

'Well, you're clearly far more than she bargained for,' Guido said with a grin. 'These socialites are all the same – self-absorbed, selfish, entitled. They don't think about anything beyond the edges of their own shadows because they've never had to. She's not used to having her opinion questioned.'

'You should have seen her face when I questioned the issue of primogeniture. She probably thinks I'm some militant feminist now.'

'She's the sort who thinks anyone who misses a leg wax is a raging feminist.'

Cesca half-laughed, half-groaned. 'Oh God, it's not good. That was only our second interview for the first chapter.'

'How many chapters do there have to be?'

Cesca shrugged. 'Judging by the number of boxes of

photos still to go through? Five hundred? I swear there's not an hour of that woman's life that hasn't been documented.' Guido squeezed her leg as she dropped her head in her hands despairingly. 'Guido, I can't lose two jobs in one week. I just can't.'

'You're not going to lose your job,' he consoled her.

'Aren't I? How can I interview her if I'm stepping on eggshells all the time? If she flies off the handle at something like that, how will I know what's going to set her off next time?'

'She's just sensitive. Maybe she felt you were judging her.'

'I was trying to be honest about what I felt was contradictory information. It's supposed to be a collaboration, after all. I'm on her side!'

'Yes, but I suppose it cannot be easy to hear your own life being examined like that. What if her father really did love the ladies? Or her mother married him for the money?' He shrugged. 'Perhaps it is more hard than she thought, having to do this.'

Cesca nodded. 'I guess.'

'*I* would certainly not want to be under your scrutiny.'

'There are no skeletons in your closet, surely, Guido?' she teased.

'We all know I smashed down *my* closet years ago,' he laughed.

'That's true!'

'Just, whatever you do, do not get fired before you see her jewels.'

Cesca frowned. 'I *really* hope that's not a euphemism,' she quipped, putting the beer bottle to her lips and swigging again.

He laughed. 'No. She's got one of the most important collections in the world. Rumour has it that she was the anonymous buyer of most of Elizabeth Taylor's collection when it was auctioned after her death.'

'Really?' Cesca made a mental note. That would make for a great chapter in the book – or possibly the exclusive on the blog that she was angling for.

'Yes. One of the necklaces alone was worth $18 million.'

To their right, she watched Signora Accardo bustle amongst the tables, plates balanced on each arm. Her white hair was pinned back with a green-and-orange printed headscarf, her navy-blue dress covered up by the long apron that fell almost to her ankles. As plump as an apple, she walked with a pronounced limp – a legacy of contracting polio as a child – but it never seemed to affect her ability to balance several full plates down the length of her forearms; and there was certainly nothing wrong with her voice, which often echoed around the square as she scolded her husband for one thing or another.

'So, what's Matteo up to tonight?' she asked, changing the subject.

'He's got a date,' Guido replied.

'Of course he has.'

'No, this is a *third* date.'

'Good God. It must be serious,' Cesca deadpanned.

'And Alé?'

'Off with her mystery man again. The one she keeps pretending doesn't exist.'

'How do you know he does?'

'Because she jumped a mile when she got a text from him while we were having dinner the other night. She practically threw her phone in the gazpacho to stop me from seeing the name on the screen.'

'Which probably means he's married,' Guido said with a tut.

Cesca sighed sympathetically, remembering that Guido had experienced his own bruising entanglement with a married man a few months earlier. 'How about you? Have you seen that Swedish film guy again? You really liked him.'

'Hans? He was the second grip in the unit . . . Oh, and what a grip he had!' He winked, before his face fell. 'Tragically, no, he cruelly used me and then left me, never to be heard from again.'

'Oh, shame.' Cesca pulled an exaggerated sad face.

'It's not like I wasn't expecting it. They were moving on to Tunisia for the next location. Still, a few more days would have been nice.'

'You never know, he might finish filming in Tunisia and come back here looking for you . . .'

Guido laughed as though the very idea was incredible. 'I don't think so. He got what he came for. Why go back?'

Cesca winced dramatically. 'Oooh! Such cynicism in one so young!'

He patted her hand. 'We cannot all be romantics like you.'

'Me? A romantic? Are you kidding?'

'Cesca, you are the definition of a romantic. Look at you, with your vintage petticoats and tea dresses and camisoles, your wild flowing hair, that poor, *poor* hat . . .'

'Listen, don't be fooled,' she laughed, protectively stroking the hat resting on her knees. 'I wore nothing but men's clothes for eighteen months at the height of my Patti Smith phase, and I spent three years wearing a wig and gown at work. Clothes are disguise, not identity.'

'So what are you hiding from then, dressing as Lady Chatterley in her wilderness years?' Guido asked.

Cesca pulled an indignant expression. 'How very dare you. I object!'

He laughed and Cesca dropped her head back against the umber-coloured wall. She felt happy, sitting here in the amber light of a long summer's evening, hanging with a friend as cheeky brown-capped sparrows hopped at her feet, pecking for crumbs from their crisps. It was all a long way from the grey rain of Hackney and the blue lights whirling in her face, the static of radios in her ears and the sight of that zipped-up body bag being wheeled out of the house, feet first.

In moments like these, she could almost believe that it was someone else's story, someone else's fault.

In moments like these, she could almost pretend it had never happened at all.

Chapter Eleven

She had heard it. Felt it too. Deep in her sleep, the vibration had echoed through her body, but not enough to wake her. While eating breakfast on her small roof terrace, she had dismissed the melee of voices, echoing from just out of sight in the Piazza Angelica, as a coachload of tourists. But then she had rounded the corner by the jasmine hedge and seen all the small vans parked on the pedestrianized section of the square outside the palazzo, the *carabinieri* patrolling with stern expressions. Unusually, the front door of the palazzo was wide open, people standing by curiously and peering in as officials (of what organization, she didn't yet know) hurried up and down the steps in hard hats and hi-vis vests. Alberto, who was watching proceedings from the top step and looking stressed, had been pleased to see her for once and had bustled her past the police into the building, much to the fascination of the gathering bystanders.

'Alberto, what's happened? Is it Elena? Is she okay?' she asked breathlessly as he strode, always half a step ahead of her, through the long galleries, past the priceless artworks on the walls which she had already started not to notice, and past her office too.

'The Viscontessa,' he said pointedly, 'is very well, if a little shocked. It's a miracle no one was killed.'

'Killed?'

But he wouldn't elaborate and she had to wait until they reached the garden room, where Cesca had so unsuccessfully conducted the second interview yesterday. One set of the garden doors on the far side was already open, a gentle breeze wafting through, and straight ahead was a large group of people, all gathered around a staked-out length of yellow tape.

'Sinkhole.'

Cesca looked at Alberto in astonishment, before looking back out at the garden again. Sure enough, beyond their legs, she could see the sudden yawning chasm in the middle of the garden – several of the orange trees had disappeared altogether, the elaborate parterre in ruins. A shudder ran through her. It was the exact spot she had seen the gardener working in just the other day. The thought of the ground opening up beneath him . . . She shivered again.

'How deep is it?'

'Twenty metres.'

'My God.' She pressed her hands to her lips, watching as a man lying on his stomach wriggled to the edge of the hole and spoke into it. Elena was standing to the side, listening intently to something a man in a boilersuit and hard hat was saying to her, one arm folded calmly at her waist, the other on her cane. She was wearing a pale-blue belted dressing gown over white linen pyjamas, her spectacles on, her feet shod in flat white leather mules, yet still, somehow, she managed to look more formally attired than her companion. 'Was anyone hurt?'

'No. But they easily could have been. We were lucky it happened just after six this morning; the garden was empty.'

'Did you hear it?' she asked.

'I am surprised you did not,' he said simply. 'You are not so very far away.'

'Well, actually, I'm wondering if I may have done.' She wrinkled her nose. 'But I'm not sure. I was sleeping. I think I did but I incorporated it into my dream.'

He raised an eyebrow but said nothing – thankfully, for she really didn't want to share her dreams with Alberto. They both went back to looking at the activity in the garden again.

'Elena must be very upset. Her beautiful garden, ruined.'

'Yes. Although I believe at the moment she is just grateful no one was hurt.'

It appeared that someone – or several people – had already been lowered into the sinkhole, as there was a sudden flurry of activity and of ropes being hauled.

The bell at the front door rang loudly and Alberto tutted. 'More press, no doubt,' he muttered savagely, stalking away.

Cesca didn't watch him go. She stepped out through the doors and into the still-shaded garden, curiosity getting the better of her. What did a depth of twenty metres look like? Quietly, not wanting to bring attention to herself, she skirted the group, moving in the opposite direction from where Elena was talking with the boilersuited man.

She found a quiet, unoccupied corner of the taped-off square and peered over the edge as far as she dared, staring down into the bottomless black. Except it wasn't bottomless – huge heaps of earth, paving slabs and mangled trees were tossed together like a cake mix, some of it reaching up to only a few metres from ground level. 'Goodness—'

'Hey! How did you get in here? You can't be here!'

She looked up in alarm to find the man in the boilersuit

and hard hat striding angrily towards her, and she felt her stomach muscles contract as she realized that she recognized him. In fact, she would have known him anywhere.

'This is a restricted area!' he exclaimed, clearly not recognizing *her* as he bore down upon her. 'Get back from there! Do you have permission to be here?'

'You again!' she exclaimed, feeling a rush of heat. 'What are *you* doing here?'

The man looked perplexed. 'What?'

'Francesca!'

She looked up to find Elena walking towards her. 'Can you believe it?' Elena asked in a tone approaching excitement.

'Uh, well—' Cesca began, but she was stunned into silence by Elena kissing her warmly on both cheeks. As though they were friends. As though yesterday had never happened.

'Another ten feet to the right and the east wing of the building would have slipped into the earth. I could have been buried alive in my sleep!'

Cesca thought she, personally, would have been a lot less excited and lot more upset to wake up to find a chunk of her garden swallowed up. But that was just her.

'That would have been unlikely, Viscontessa,' the man said gruffly, his hostility towards Cesca abated, somewhat, following Elena's effusive greeting. 'But it is true it could have caused real damage to such an historic building. I'm afraid until we have finished our checks, we cannot be sure this sinkhole has not already caused trouble to the foundations of the building, nor can we discount the possibility that another sinkhole may open up nearby.'

Elena's grey eyes widened. 'Should we evacuate?'

'At this point, no, but we will keep you informed, naturally.'

Elena looked across at Cesca again, seeing the confounded expression on her face. 'I'm sorry, Cesca, have you met Signor Cantarelli? He is the Soprintendenza Archaelogica di Roma. Signor Cantarelli, this is Francesca Hackett, my biographer.'

Cesca was a little taken aback to hear such a grand title bestowed on her stop-gap job.

'Signorina.' He held out a hand, not in the least fazed that only moments before he had been shouting in her face and about to throw her out.

Cesca stared at it. Did he seriously think she was going to shake his hand when he – *he* – had almost run her down? He had drawn blood. She had a scab! But Elena was there, Elena was watching, Elena was her boss.

Slowly, she shook his hand. 'Actually, we've met before,' Cesca said evenly, her eyes flinty.

'Yes?' he frowned. 'No. I think I would remember. Your hair is very bright.'

Bright? Was he trying to be offensive? She swallowed, refusing to be ruffled. 'Last week, near to the Trevi? You almost ran me over on your scooter?'

He continued to look at her blankly, his dark-brown eyes clear and steady, not a flicker of emotion on his face. 'You have confused me with someone else.'

Cesca raised herself to her full height. How could he not remember? He'd looked straight at her! 'On the contrary, I would nev—'

'Excuse me.' He walked off, leaving Cesca staring after him, open-mouthed. He had got to be kidding! She couldn't believe he had just done that! Disrespecting her. *Again.* She watched as he joined the man who had just been hauled from the hole and was stepping out of a harness, the flashlight on his head torch still switched on.

'It's funny – his mother is a friend, although I haven't really seen him since he was a child. But I must say, he seems highly capable,' Elena said, watching as the two men began talking together intently.

He seems arrogant and rude, Cesca thought, glowering, but she didn't say the words out loud. She watched as Cantarelli and the other man walked over to where a laptop had been set up, both examining whatever was on the screen attentively.

'You can imagine my fright,' Elena went on.

Cesca turned to face her. 'Yes. It must have been terrible.'

Elena nodded, her eyes still bright. 'At first, I thought it might be an earthquake. I couldn't understand what my eyes were showing me. We had no idea whether it was going to keep growing, you see. Alberto was just fabulous, of course. He took charge, calling the authorities, and they were here within minutes. Obviously they understood the historical importance of the palace.'

'I'm sure,' Cesca mumbled, her eyes drawn back to Cantarelli again.

'It was almost as though he had some sort of contingency plan already in place. Alberto, I mean: he started evacuating the most precious treasures from the galleries; he called in all the gardening teams and they helped him to move anything of importance, in case the building should become unstable.'

'Good thinking. Where is it all now?'

'In the north wing. It's the furthest point from this courtyard, so it seemed the safest.'

Cesca raised her eyes skywards. Elena's private apartment was four floors up at the very end of the east wing, looking straight down on this. If the ground floor should crumble, the upper storeys would come down too. Her pristine white home . . .

'My thoughts exactly,' Elena said with a shudder, looking towards the top floor. 'Anyway, there's nothing more we can do at this stage. We must let the authorities conduct their tests and explorations. The sooner they've ticked all the boxes, the sooner they can close this gaping hole up again and I can get my beautiful garden back.'

'And how do they do that? Close it up, I mean?'

'Mortar, I believe. It's quick, stable and eradicates any future risk of something like this happening again.'

'Ah.'

'Anyway, I need to go and get dressed. I look an utter fright. I cannot quite believe I'm standing in my garden in my pyjamas in front of all these strangers.' She cocked her head. 'When did we say we were meeting up next?'

Cesca blinked, wondering whether Elena really *had* forgotten the manner in which she had abruptly terminated their interview yesterday afternoon. 'Uh . . . we hadn't.'

This seemed to surprise her. 'Well, how's four o'clock this afternoon?'

Cesca nodded. 'Yes, wonderful. I'll get everything ready.'

'I'll see you then, then. You're doing a great job, Francesca.'

'Th-thank you.' Baffled by the sudden about-turn, she watched Elena walk – regal in her pyjamas – towards the French doors in the east wing, which exactly mirrored those of the garden room. The men glanced up as she passed before returning their attention to the screen.

Cesca turned and walked back into the garden room in the west wing, passing through the long, grand galleries towards her office, already exhausted by her working day before it had even begun.

The blond man was significant. Clearly neither Elena's father nor a brother, he nonetheless shared the same unassailable self-confidence and matinee-idol looks of a Valentine. In almost every shot, he was a man of action. In one photograph, he swung out from a yacht's rigging, wearing white shorts and a navy jumper, the sleeves pushed up to reveal muscular, tanned forearms, his smile revealing a straight set of brighter-than-white teeth. In another, he was standing by a propeller-engined plane in dark slacks and a chunky cream polo-neck jumper, his eyes hidden behind reflective aviator sunglasses. He had a commanding presence even in black-and-white. He could well have been an actor, Cesca mused: he clearly loved the limelight, with Elena barely in any shots with him. Cesca wondered whether she had been the one taking the photos, like her father.

The wedding photographs were visually gripping. The church was surprisingly humble – just a single-storey, white weatherboarded affair – but the flowers more than compensated, with Casablanca lilies cascading from Elena's bouquet and mop-headed white roses braided round the door. Her parents looked like they were dressed for a regatta – George in a dark blazer and ivory flannels, Whitney in a pale dress with knife-pleated skirt and white fox stole. Elena looked stunning in a magnificent sort of 'Swan Lake' dress with downy feathers on the skirt, her eyes bright behind a plumed veil, her youthful plumpness shaped into waspishness by a tight corset. In almost all of them, she was openly laughing, her body language so much more expansive than in the photos of her childhood. Those, Cesca realized – now that she had a direct comparison – had been muted and stiff with Elena staring at the camera warily, Winnie standing devotedly at her side, the two of them grouped as though arranged by the photographer. But in these, standing beside her handsome new husband, Elena looked radiantly happy. And incredibly young.

Cesca frowned, staring closer at the image, trying to gauge her age – eighteen? Nineteen, perhaps? It was hard to tell when, back then, everyone looked forty by the age of twenty-eight. Whatever. She was evidently madly in love, with her whole life stretching ahead of her. It was clear the all-American dream was rolling on.

Chapter Twelve

Boston, September 1962

Laney stirred the silver spoon slowly. She never usually took sugar in her coffee but Winnie always used to put sweetener into her drinks to help with shock whenever she fell as a child – and she was shocked now.

'Mr Charles, do you mean to say that unless I tell the world the intimate details of my marriage, I cannot divorce Jack?'

The lawyer looked back at her over his heavy-rimmed glasses, the tinkle of china and titters of laughter around them as inappropriate to the gravity of their conversation as a can-can dancer high-kicking on their table.

'I'm afraid, Laney dear, we have to cite *something* and the classic grounds for divorce are cruelty – be it physical or mental – desertion and adultery. Legally, we have an obligation to show why you are justified in becoming exempt from the assumption of marital permanence.'

'But Mr Charles,' she began. 'Once the press gets wind of this divorce, it will become a front-page story and any one of those reasons will be a red rag. They won't stop until they get the truth. Desertion is my opposite problem. He'll never leave and he'd happily tell that to the press. Adultery? Well, that would be nothing less than an invitation to start digging around any woman unlucky enough to be seen with him, be she his sister or accountant or secretary. And as for cruelty—' Her voice caught and she looked away quickly, watching the girl at the coat-check taking a man's jacket from him. It was windy outside and it had started raining, too, judging from the way he took a comb from his suit pocket and raked his hair back slickly.

Mr Charles leaned a little closer, so that she could see the shine of the pomade in his grey hair, even detect his cologne. He lowered his voice. 'It would be helpful if you could provide me with some insight as to why you cannot continue with the marriage. I assure you, everything you tell me is kept in the strictest confidence.'

Laney sat back, glancing around at the bustling room. There were diners at every table, waiters gliding between the round tables with matching trays, dispensing cocktails. She looked back at him. Stanley Charles, the Valentine family's lawyer, had been in her life from the day she'd been born. She had grown up with him walking the grounds with her father, playing backgammon with her mother, knowing him as her family's benevolent guardian, the man they always turned to for help. So familiar to her was he that she saw him almost as a grandfather figure – which was precisely why she couldn't go into the intimate realities of her marriage with him. If he knew, if anyone did . . .

'I can't carry on, Mr Charles,' was all she said briskly. 'You'll just have to think of something.'

He looked at her for a long moment and she held his gaze, determined now. No one could see by looking at her how Jack hurt her, but last night had been the worst yet; last night had been the last time. She wouldn't endure it again.

Whether Mr Charles recognized any of this in her eyes she didn't know, but from the way he nodded, she knew he was finally seeing her as something more than the seventeen-year-old daughter of his client.

'Well, we can do it, but it'll be costly. Not to mention the public scrutiny. I'm afraid that is quite unavoidable. People will talk, no matter what reason we ascribe.'

She looked away, knowing perfectly well how the shame of this divorce was going to play out, not just amongst the press but her own set. Her parents would express a thin-lipped disappointment that she couldn't keep up appearances; from the few girls she still kept in touch with there would be invitations to lunch but not dinner, offers to partner at tennis but not dances. A divorcee was the most dangerous of women. 'Then let them.'

He nodded again. 'I propose we offer a lump sum, a one-time-only offer to get him to leave, and then we can go for desertion; it's humiliating for you, but potentially the least flammable choice.' He caught his breath for a moment, looking at her with very still, concerned eyes. 'If things are as bad for you as I think they might be, then he's not going to want the truth to come out any more than you.'

She blinked, feeling a rush of heat to her cheeks, pressure behind her eyes. 'What if he says he doesn't care about the truth coming out?' she asked, a tremor in her voice even though she was determined not to betray herself. 'He might want more money. He could even blackmail us.'

Mr Charles gave her a look so gentle it almost made her break down there and then. 'Laney, has . . . has he done anything to you that could – *if* you reported it – result in criminal charges being brought against him?'

Laney was quiet for a long moment before she nodded. 'I . . . I'm not sure . . . possibly, yes.'

He looked pained but he patted her hand. 'Then we use that. Though it galls me that he should get anything at all, it would be better for you to simply get him gone. The threat of an allegation should be enough for him to take the money and run. Hopefully, though, we won't even need to go that far – he'll be sensible and see he's getting a good deal.'

'Well, given that he came into the marriage with practically nothing . . .' she mumbled bitterly.

Mr Charles squeezed her hand. 'The important thing now is that he leaves, and with minimal fuss.'

She inhaled deeply. 'You're right. I just—'

'Stan!'

They both looked up to find a man standing by their table. It was the man she had seen a few moments earlier checking his coat.

Mr Charles sat back in his chair, looking happy to see their visitor. 'Leo Znowski, well, I'll be damned. I thought you were strictly West Coast these days.'

'I am. I'm back for my nephew's bar mitzvah.' He tilted his head. 'And maybe a *little* business . . .'

'Why am I not surprised?' Mr Charles laughed. 'Leo, I want you to meet someone very special to me: Laney Mont—'

'Laney Valentine,' she said forthrightly, offering her hand.

Leo took her hand – but rather than shaking it, he kissed it instead, the way she had seen men do to her mother's hand. 'A pleasure, Miss Valentine.'

He held onto her hand for a moment longer than was necessary, before allowing her to sit back in her chair. He was older than she'd thought from a distance. Late thirties, early forties, perhaps? His hair was raven-black and he had a neatly clipped beard that made a feature of his teeth when he laughed. His nose looked like it had been broken on more than one occasion and beneath his three-piece suit he was stockily built, looking more like a wrestler than the sailor type she was used to with Jack.

'Leo here is the finest sports agent I ever met,' said Mr Charles.

'Oh?' She arched an eyebrow, appraising him openly. He had an affability that was reassuring – ready to smile, with eyes that seemed to *see* and not just look. Her maiden name hadn't seemed to provoke any reaction either.

'I'm the *only* sports agent he ever met,' Leo quipped.

'True,' Mr Charles laughed. 'But he represents eight of the top ten players in the NBA and he signed them all in college. There's a reason they show this man loyalty.'

'Yeah, it's called a no-break clause in their contracts,' Leo quipped again, his eyes coming back each time to Laney. 'Do you like basketball, Miss Valentine?'

'. . . Why, yes,' she said, deciding on the spot that she did.

'Who do you follow?'

'Boston Celtics.' She had heard of them.

He looked pleased. 'They're having a very good season. I think they could go all the way.'

'Do you represent any of them?'

'Sam Jones.'

'How wonderful,' she smiled. 'He's my favourite player.'

'Well, if you'd like to meet him, I could arrange something. Dinner perhaps . . . ?'

There was a pause and Laney was vaguely aware of Mr Charles looking between the two of them. She blinked.

Looking into Leo's eyes, she had a feeling of being caught in a new current, of an undertow carrying her back to shore, back to safety. 'How kind. I'd like that very much,' she replied, keeping her voice as neutral as she could.

'I'll get your number from Stan and set it up then,' he said, taking a step away from the table and preparing to leave. She managed not to stare after him as he shook Mr Charles's hand and walked away, studying instead the menu that had lain untouched on the table since they had arrived.

Mr Charles cleared his throat. 'Laney, listen, Leo's a good man but he's much older tha—'

'Shall we order now, Mr Charles?' she interrupted, feeling suddenly brighter than she had done for months. 'I'm simply ravenous. I'm afraid I've been letting the day run away from me. Now, Mother always says the shrimp salad here is to die for. Have you tried it?'

Chapter Thirteen

Rome, July 2017

'You were married at *sixteen*?' Cesca couldn't keep the shock from her voice as she looked back at the wedding photograph. Unlike all the others which had prompted a wistful nostalgia, Elena had barely glanced at it, leaving it lying on the table between them.

'It seems so young now, I know, we were just babies.'

'But surely your parents—' She silenced herself before she offended Elena again. It hadn't gone down well the last time she'd questioned her over her parents. But, surely, even Elena could see this begged the question: what on earth had they been thinking, letting their sixteen-year-old only child wed at such a young age?

'It was a different time back then and I wasn't really expected to do much else anyway, beyond finding a husband and having children,' Elena said, as if reading her mind. 'Certainly it never crossed anyone's mind that I might "go out to work". What for, after all? We had more money than we could spend in a hundred lifetimes.' She sighed, her eyes resting on a Caravaggio behind Cesca's left ear. 'Besides, my childhood was so out of the ordinary – we had President Eisenhower to dinner, we spent part of every summer at Ari's villa – that, really, I was sixteen going on forty.'

Cesca nodded, assuming Ari was Aristotle Onassis; she had seen with her own eyes the pictures of little Elena clutching her fur-robed mother's hand at film premieres, jumping off the side of a full-sailed yacht with her armbands on, sitting in a scaled-down Bugatti buggy car. It had indeed been no ordinary childhood.

'What was the President like?'

'Very sweet. I remember he wanted to know my doll's name. He and my father would play golf together at Graystones.'

A golf course in the back garden? With a president playing the fourth hole? But of course, Cesca mused, unable to stop herself from drawing a parallel with how excited and awe-struck she'd been when her parents had merely bought a trampoline for her and her two brothers, even though it had taken up almost half of their narrow suburban garden. There was no comparison.

And it was beside the point, she told herself, forcing herself back on track. There was a different definition of normal within these thick palace walls. 'So tell me about him, then. What made you fall in love with Jack Montgomery?'

Elena sighed. 'Oh, darling Jack. Such a sweet boy. So sweet – although far too handsome for his own good,' she added with a wry smile.

'He was incredibly handsome,' Cesca agreed. 'Was it love at first sight?'

'Good lord, no. I absolutely hated him for the first five minutes.'

'The first five minutes?' Cesca grinned. 'But *then* it was love?'

'Oh yes. He was a wonderful kisser.' She sighed. 'He just adored me and I him.'

'How did the two of you meet?'

Elena inhaled deeply, thinking back. 'He gatecrashed my Sweet Sixteen party – which was no mean feat, let me assure you. My father lived in perpetual fear that I would be kidnapped for ransom, so the security was off the scale.'

'So how did he get in?'

'Oh, he used someone else's invitation, I think. I can't quite remember the details. But once he was in, he just behaved like he belonged there. No one thought to question him at all. It didn't cross their minds that anyone who was there hadn't been invited.'

Cesca was impressed by his daring – not just for getting in, but staying there. He would have had to behave as an equal to the great and the good, which given their usual roster of house guests . . . The cockiness of youth, she supposed. 'So he blagged his way in. What then?'

'We met for the first time down by the lake. I was feeling a little overwhelmed by all the attention: everyone wanted to talk to me, I'd been dancing all night and I just needed a few minutes to regroup. To this day I don't know whether it was coincidence that we both happened to go down there, or whether he somehow knew I'd make a beeline for it. The boathouse was always my place of refuge. I was scared of the water as a child, so no one ever thought to look for me down there if I was upset. They assumed it was the very last place I'd want to go.'

She shrugged. 'Regardless, he spent the first few minutes wildly insulting me and then, just when I thought he was going to kiss me, he grabbed my hand and pulled me into the lake with him. I couldn't even swim but he made me feel safe, towing me to the side. Oh, but my beautiful dress! My hair! It was so utterly thrilling. He made me feel free,' she enthused, as Cesca gasped and laughed in surprise. 'I honestly believe my life changed that night. I glimpsed another world, somewhere that wasn't ruled by etiquette and reputation. After that, I became obsessed with him, sneaking off as much as I could to meet up with him in secret. We only managed a few dates before Winnie rumbled me. I never could keep anything from her.' She smiled and shook her head. 'Oh, I was so *furious* when she told my parents; I saw it as such a betrayal. She and I had always been a team till then – us against the world or, at least, my parents.'

'What did your parents do?'

'What they always did when they wanted to get rid of someone – they invited him for dinner.'

Cesca gave another surprised laugh. 'Why?'

'To intimidate him. My father was very protective of us. He vetted everyone in my life. Father was such an excellent judge of character that he could tell immediately if someone was getting close for the wrong reasons.'

'But Jack passed?'

'With flying colours! He refused to be beaten by my father at backgammon – in contrast to most people, who would allow themselves to be beaten in order to be invited back – and flirted outrageously with my mother. He'd asked for my hand, and been given it, by the time dessert was served.'

'Crikey!'

Elena threw her head back and laughed at Cesca's very British turn of phrase. '"Crikey." I like that . . . Yes, my parents adored him. I think, in some way, they saw him as the son they'd never had. He was like a miniature vision of my father – athletic and competitive. They were both avid sailors and regularly went hunting together.'

'It sounds like a very happy time.'

'Oh, it was. I was a very lucky girl to land him. Very lucky indeed.' She nodded, smiling brightly.

'It helps when parents are on board with a relationship.'

'Yes. It was a funny thing, really: I would almost say he helped to bring me closer – *even* closer, I mean – to my parents. Once I was married, Mother became more of a friend, which suited her much better. I think the maternal role had always made her rather uneasy.'

'Uh huh,' Cesca agreed, keeping her face impassive whilst thinking how sad that sounded. 'And did you and Jack live at Graystones?'

'Heavens, no! Part of the point was to get away from there,' Elena said quickly.

Cesca looked up in surprise. 'The point of marrying him?'

'I mean, I loved him, obviously. Of course I did. But as you've just pointed out, I was very young too, barely sixteen. I was just in such a rush, you see, to start living my life, and I suppose at some level, I realized getting married meant that could happen. The last thing I wanted was to stay put. I needed to get out into the world.'

Cesca could see how claustrophobic life at Graystones must have been. Hidden away from the curious gaze of America – not to mention mercenary kidnappers – Elena would nonetheless have been painfully visible within the compound, her movements observed at all times by the watchful gaze of teams of staff. There would have been no privacy, no freedom, no spontaneity; Cesca wondered whether all the land and toys and glamorous parties were worth it. 'So what happened?'

'Happened?'

'Well, when you've mentioned your husband up till now, you've called him Vito. And Jack is . . . well, Jack, surely? I'm assuming they're not the same man? That the marriage ended?'

Elena stared at her for a moment. 'You really haven't googled me, have you?'

'Well, no, you asked me not to.' Cesca swallowed, wondering if she'd just failed some sort of test. 'Should I have?'

'No.' Elena shook her head. 'I am just always so surprised when I meet a person I can actually trust. Such terrible things have been printed about me over the years, practically none of it true. I would hate for you to form an opinion of me based upon that.' Elena glanced out at the yellow-bibbed teams working on the sinkhole in the garden beyond the French doors. 'The truth is, Jack and I loved each other very much, but we were far too young. He was the first boy I ever kissed. He should have been my boyfriend, not my husband.'

'Can you tell me a little about your married life together?'

Elena sighed, glancing at her hands briefly, and Cesca noticed she was gripping them together tightly, the knuckles blanched. 'Well, we moved to Newport, only thirteen miles from Graystones. It was a tiny house, just darling,' Elena said, eyes bright, a smile on her mouth, a small vein protruding on her forehead which Cesca hadn't noticed before now. 'Jack refused to take a cent from Father, he said he wanted to provide for me himself, like any other husband, and Father respected that.'

Cesca chose her words carefully. 'But wasn't your father

worried about your security? You just said he was worried about the kidnap risk—'

'Yes, and I should have known better at the time. I thought I'd got away, scot-free, but of course I should have realized . . .' She sighed, the sound weary and heavy. 'Unbeknownst to either of us, Father had bought the houses on all sides of ours and installed people from his security team – undercover, of course. Jack never knew a thing about it. I didn't either until I happened to see one of them talking to Davis, Father's personal bodyguard.'

'Were you angry about that?'

'Yes, but a part of me understood it too. It was what I had grown up with. I suppose it was naive to think I could just move into town and become a regular person.'

'*Did* you become a regular person?'

'I think I did. I certainly tried my best. I took such pride in keeping our home clean and tidy, and having Jack's meals ready. It was an enormous learning curve, of course. I had to learn to cook and clean and darn, and do all those things which give you your independence and which others take for granted. My whole life, everything had always been done for me, but it left me yearning to be mistress of my own home. I can't tell you how thrilled I was to learn how to iron a shirt and see him wear it the next day. It was the first time I'd ever been allowed to do anything like that. It was like an adventure to me. It felt just wonderful to be able to look after him in that way.'

Cesca tried to imagine the sheltered sixteen-year-old bride playing housewife. It was the kind of game Cesca herself had played as a toddler – and promptly outgrown by the time she'd started school. 'So you had to learn to do the laundry? Cooking?'

Elena nodded.

'Did Winnie teach you?'

'Lord, no! She thought it was beneath me to do those things. I think she was very disappointed by the marriage.'

'And yet your parents weren't . . .'

'Well, they too had married for love. Whereas Winnie thought only a prince would be good enough for me.' She laughed suddenly. 'And it turned out she was right, as she always was!' she smiled, gesticulating to indicate the lavish palazzo in which they were sitting. 'No, I can see now that my life with Jack was just a fantasy – and me being the housewife was just one part of it. Naturally, I wasn't remotely equipped for it all; I had no idea what I was letting myself in for.'

'Can you give me an example?'

'Oh, well, I just completely threw myself in at the deep end, trying to cook the dishes we'd had at home, for example, even though I'd never so much as boiled water.' She laughed again. 'I once made duck à l'orange – it was nothing like duck à l'orange by the time I'd finished with it, I can assure you! But I did my very best and when, after hours in the kitchen, I set it down in front of Jack . . . I realized I had no idea how to carve it!'

Cesca grinned at the image. 'What did you do?'

'We had to eat it straight off the serving plate, cutting the meat off the bone like cavemen in a huddle. It was so terrible and so funny all at once. I kept thinking about my parents' faces if they could only have seen us. And Winnie. Poor Winnie. All those years teaching me how to eat properly and there I was, eating like a savage.' She chuckled again at the memory.

'It sounds like a liberating time for you.'

'Oh, it was. I made many great friends in the town. I joined the Ladies' Guild and we would meet fortnightly.'

'Did they know who you were? That you were a Valentine, I mean.'

Elena hesitated. 'I'm not sure, but if they did then they were terribly discreet, which I appreciated. They never let it make a difference. To them, I was just one of the girls.'

Cesca nodded. 'So when did things start to go downhill with Jack . . . ?'

'Oh, who could pinpoint it exactly?' Elena replied vaguely. 'I suppose it was just a sad, steady disenchantment.'

'Who . . .' Cesca faltered, not quite sure how to phrase this. 'Who left who?'

Elena stilled. 'He left me. Desertion.'

'I'm so sorry . . . Can I ask why? Was there someone else?'

'Nothing like that. Jack just didn't know when he was beaten, that was all. He was a fiendishly good card player; he and my father would play late into the night. But when his luck failed, he didn't slow down, he played more, raising the stakes each time, certain that his losing streak was about to end.'

'And instead the debts grew exponentially?' Cesca sympathized.

'You've had experience with gamblers too then?'

'It's not quite the same – my dad got a bit hooked on lottery tickets for a while. He was spending up to forty pounds a week at his worst.'

Elena looked baffled. 'Gracious.' There was a short silence as she drifted through the dim corridors of her past. 'On our wedding night, he lost the lovely Bentley my father had given us as a wedding gift. He was terribly upset about it.' Her voice was quiet and hollow, her eyes fixed, unseeing again, on the Caravaggio.

'Anyway, I guess I should have seen the signs,' she said finally, rallying. 'But I thought I could help him, you see. I was just like every other sixteen-year-old girl, believing love was the answer. I wanted to save him from his demons. I thought I was invincible; money had always shielded me from ugly realities, so what a terrible irony it was that penury should be our downfall. But eventually he got into trouble with the casinos and, really, there was no coming back from that.'

'Surely your parents could have bailed him out?'

'Of course – if they'd known about it, but Jack wouldn't hear of it. He was very proud like that. My father's good opinion of him was very important to him.'

'So . . . what? When you say he deserted you . . . he just disappeared?'

'Mm hmm. Drove into Newport one day and never came back.'

'But that's terrible.'

'Yes. It is.'

'Did you ever see him again?'

'Once. At a basketball game. I had remarried by then and Jack was on the far side of the court, sitting with a dark-haired woman. I remember thinking she looked a little like me . . .' She tailed off, shrugging her shoulders.

'How long did the marriage last for?'

'Seventeen months in total. Married at sixteen. Divorced by seventeen,' Elena said wryly. 'It certainly wasn't how I'd envisaged my new grown-up life to be.'

Cesca slumped back in her chair, feeing saddened. 'No.

Life never is,' she remarked, thinking about her own grown-up life and how unlikely it was that she should be sitting in an Italian palazzo with an American princess, drinking tea and digging up the past, with a giant sinkhole outside the door. She never could have foreseen this as a teenager sitting on her bed in High Wycombe. Even this time last year, she hadn't seen any of it coming.

Chapter Fourteen

Malibu, August 1968

The ocean broke at her feet, smashing like glass as it ran up the white sand before bubbling into evanescence and trickling away. Laney flicked her hair back, the shortboard tucked under one arm as she waded through the shallows, her eyes fixed on Leo's pacing figure on the deck. He was early. She hadn't been expecting him for another two days.

Her breath was coming fast, her thighs feeling weak from the sunset exercise as she jogged lightly up the cambered beach towards him. This was her daily routine but it always felt different when he was home – watching her from the house, so proud of the way she was able to twist and turn with such ease on the water, making her feel talented, clever, sexy. She had come a long way from those early tentative swimming sessions in the ocean when they'd first married and moved out here. Leo had been the one to teach her to swim, and not Jack, after all – that had been just another of his broken promises.

She raised her arm and waved; he waved back but the phone – that goddam phone – was in his other hand, as it always was, and she knew he was only half-seeing her, his concentration elsewhere.

Another surfer was coming towards her. 'You're not givin' up so soon, Laney?' he asked, stopping in front of her and jabbing the nose of his longboard into the beach. It meant he wanted to talk, to linger.

'I wish I could stay,' she shrugged. 'But Leo's back.'

'Thought he wasn't back till the weekend?'

'Me neither,' she said happily. 'I'll see you, Cliff.'

'Yeah,' he said, watching her jog up the beach to the steps that led to their deck.

Leo watched her lean her board against the railings, jerking his head down towards the sand and wordlessly asking about the guy on the beach. She threw her hands out in a 'nothing' gesture, running over to him and throwing her arms around his waist and resting her head on his chest, her eyes closed in happiness. It felt like such a luxury to be able to do this and she listened to the steady thump of his heart beneath his navy terry-cloth top.

He pulled away after a few moments, his shoulders high, a frown on his face, as he saw the wet marks from her hair on his chest and he rolled his eyes at her, gesturing to them in case she hadn't noticed. She shrugged happily – what did it matter? – and playfully reached up to take the phone from his hand, but he jerked away irritably and stepped through the sliding glass doors into their vast living room.

Laney sighed. He was always tetchy when he was on a call, but then again he was always on a call and it was always important. She followed him in, feeling the chill of the ceiling fans whirring overhead. Without breaking his conversation, Leo pointedly pulled his damp top over his head and balled it into a corner of the room, glancing across at her. Laney looked at it, knowing he was annoyed.

But she knew how to remedy that. She wriggled the straps of her swimsuit off her shoulders and shimmied out of it, balling that into the same corner as his top.

Arching an eyebrow, she stood before him, dripping wet and naked. He stopped talking, his eyes wide as she stared straight at him, waiting. Her tan lines were deep from a summer spent in the surf and she knew they turned him on, that he liked how they emphasized the dazzling whiteness of her breasts, the pinkness of her nipples. He liked that what was hidden inside the tan lines was strictly for him alone.

She smiled, still waiting, and his mouth parted as he went to tell his caller – another player? A club owner? – that he couldn't talk right now, that he'd get back to him.

But then he raised his hand, the index finger pointed in a 'wait' gesture. To her! He turned away to concentrate and continued the conversation, his voice low and urgent and frustrated.

For a few seconds, Laney stared at his back, trying to believe what she was seeing. He had turned her down? For a phone call? Humiliated, she ran from the room and into the bathroom, locking the door behind her. It was another fifteen minutes before he came to knock.

Chapter Fifteen

Rome, July 2017

In spite of the fact that Cesca had been working in a palace for over a week, walking into the courtyard of the swanky Hotel de Russie still took some nerve. It didn't help that the clipped and primped style of the establishment was the polar opposite to her personal taste. Abandoning her beloved yellow Converse for once, she was wearing a pair of tan leather ankle-lace sandals, teamed with a long 1960s yellow cotton dress with a scooped neck and short tight sleeves. She had her battered hat on too, of course. She never went anywhere in the midday sun without that, but she had taken it off and held it since getting to the hotel, hiding the worst of the fraying with her hands.

She followed behind the maitre d' as he walked her to her table, where her lunch date was already waiting for her. Christina, Elena's friend, was tall and slim with broad shoulders and narrow hips, her silver hair worn in a shoulder-length, expensively layered cut. She was wearing a perfect melange of taupes – a gauzy linen knit cardigan over a silk ribbed vest, narrow 7/8ths trousers and Ferragamo pumps – and looked so perfectly understated and discreet, Cesca could almost believe she didn't want to be seen.

'Miss Hackett,' she smiled, rising from her chair and holding out a slim, manicured hand.

'A pleasure to meet you,' Cesca smiled back, shaking her hand firmly.

'Come, sit,' Christina ordered, making eye contact with the maitre d'. 'A bottle of my usual, please, Renato.' She looked across at her guest as Cesca settled herself in the chair. 'Wait, you're not one of those ghastly people who don't drink at lunch, are you?'

'Absolutely not,' Cesca replied, relaxing somewhat at the unexpected appearance of a sense of humour from that intimidatingly polished veneer.

'Excellent. And chill the glasses, please,' she added to the maitre d', before looking back at Cesca, fanning herself lightly. 'I can't quite believe I'm still here in July.'

'It's certainly a scorcher today.' It was forecast to hit thirty-six degrees that afternoon.

'Do you find it difficult, coping with these temperatures? You're so very fair,' Christina asked, openly taking in Cesca's lily-pale complexion and freckles, her flame-red hair.

'Well, put it this way, I always walk on the shaded side of the street these days.'

Christina smiled. 'Very wise.'

Cesca glanced at a waiter as he came over and filled her water glass. 'How are things progressing with the gala?'

'Oh, slowly.' Christina gave a wry look. 'The caterers are having trouble sourcing enough truffles for the *primi piatti* so we may have to rethink on that, which in turn affects the wine and potentially what we were planning for the *secondi* . . . And half of the venue is still covered in scaffolding following the conservation work, so that needs to come down before we can get the consultants in for the lights.' She sighed. 'It's all minutiae, of course, or "first world problems" as my son would tell me, but we women know that perfection is in the details.'

'Elena must be so grateful to you for organizing this. It sounds like it's going to be a wonderful tribute to her husband.'

'Well, I hope so. It has taken a great deal of work to see the restoration project followed through, and this is a just celebration of all those efforts. Besides, everyone loves a party and September always feels like such a fresh month. The worst of the heat is over, everyone's back in the city again. Life gets back to normal.'

Cesca wondered what 'normal' looked like for this woman. Did she live in a palazzo too? Did she own necklaces worth millions? 'So, you and Elena are old friends?'

'Oh, yes, we've known one another for far longer than I am sure either one of us would want to admit to.' Christina smiled. 'I think it was 1979 when we first met? We connected immediately. There was always a primal recognition between us. Do you know what I mean when I say that?'

Cesca nodded. 'Yes. I do.'

'We just understood each other. We didn't need a bank of memories and shared experiences to know exactly who the other one was; you don't often get that with people in this life.'

'I agree,' Cesca murmured. It was how she felt about Alé.

'But, of course, I knew her husband far longer. I grew up with Vito. And his brother Aurelio, too,' she added.

'Oh, really? You were childhood friends?'

'We are very distant cousins. Five times removed, I think? Something like that. I didn't have any siblings so I spent almost as much time in that palazzo as they did. We used to tear about the place. It was such fun. I still think of those days, you know.'

'I'm sure. They sound like treasured memories.'

'But, tell me, how did *you* come to meet Elena?' Christina asked, looking genuinely interested.

'Well, it was a strange thing, really – I returned a stolen bag of hers which had been dumped in my bin. It turns out I live just around the corner from her.'

'I see. And so . . .' Christina still looked confused. 'You came to start working with her on this project . . . ?'

'She invited me to stay for a drink and we got chatting about things and I mentioned to her about my blog—'

'Blog?' Christina looked as blank as Elena had.

'Yes, it's just an online journal, really, about all the different things I love and discover in Rome.'

'How fascinating. I must try to find it. What is it called?'

'The Rome Affair.'

'What an exciting title! I shall be sure to look it up.'

'Thank you.'

'So, go on. You told Elena about your blog . . .'

'Yes. Anyway, the next day I only went and lost my job! I was working as a tour guide and I overslept.' Cesca sighed, rolling her eyes. 'I don't sleep very well. Anyway, as luck would have it, when I got home, Elena was waiting for me with the proposal of doing this.'

Christina placed one hand on the table, an emerald-cut aquamarine almost entirely covering one half of her index finger. 'Wait – so you're telling me, you lost your job the very next day after meeting Elena, and then she was waiting for you at home, to offer you a new job?'

'Yes! It was just the most extraordinary stroke of luck. That kind of thing usually doesn't happen to me.'

'What a coincidence,' Christina said with a steady gaze. She took her napkin off the plate and draped it over her lap with deliberate care, her words still hanging in the air.

Cesca picked up on the intimation that the coincidence was almost too much to believe, but Cesca knew it had been her fault and her fault alone that she had overslept – not for the first time – and got the sack.

'And so, tell me, how are you getting on with her?'

'Very well. I think she's one of the most fascinating people I've ever met.'

'It's an extraordinary life she's led, isn't it? I must say I was exceptionally surprised when I first heard about the book. She's always been so private; she hardly ever refers to her life from before she moved to Rome.'

'Oh really? She seems secretive on the matter? Even with friends?'

'Well, I wouldn't say she's secretive about it, more . . . elusive. I think perhaps she's a little embarrassed about her "wild youth", shall we say?' Christina commented drily, sitting back in her chair and calmly placing her elbows on the armrests, fingers interlaced. At that moment the maitre d' came back with a frosted silver bucket on a stand, a gold-foil-capped bottle of Bollinger and two glasses so cold they almost steamed, as though with liquid ice.

Cesca sat back too and looked around them as Renato expertly popped the cork and began to pour. Below, in the Stravinsky Bar, a thin woman in a body-con dress did a fine job of navigating the cobbled parterre in high heels, her shadow like a reed as compared to those of the bosky dwarf orange trees dotting the courtyard. The entire area was enclosed by sugar-pink walls that split and divided at the far end, with balustraded steps leading up to this level, lollipop box balls in planters at intervals all the way around. The open-air restaurant was characterized by groomed gravel pathways and round white-cloth-blanketed tables, with puddles of shade thrown down from the open parasols. But it was the uppermost level that really delighted her – cascading terraces densely planted with cypress, plane, eucalyptus and monkey trees, ivy fringing the walls, jasmine bushes as thick as buses. It was so unapologetically verdant and dense, not so much an oasis as a jungle, and all the more shocking for being found in the very centre of a city. Much like Elena's garden.

Renato left them, tears of condensation already tracking down their crystal flutes.

'Did you know much about her before this project?' Christina asked, picking up the conversation again and angling her glass in an elegant toast.

'Honestly? Nothing,' Cesca said, mirroring the action.

'Nothing? Really?' She seemed as flabbergasted as Alé had been, as though the very notion were ridiculous.

'I mean, I'd heard of the Valentines. Like the Vanderbilts and Rockefellers, I just knew they were this rich American family – but of Elena specifically?' She shook her head.

'Well, of course, you're that much younger, I suppose, an entirely new generation,' Christina mused. 'But, forty years ago, she was one of the most famous women in America. She has either been married to, or rubbed shoulders with, almost every famous name of the second half of the twentieth century, be they power brokers on Wall Street, Hollywood actors, rock stars . . . She was the keeper of secrets; the confidante to the rich and famous. Her entire life has been about being seen and being watched.'

Again, Cesca detected an edge. 'Did that change when

she came to Rome? I understand things are different here,' she said lightly. If the Black Nobility families were as conservative as Elena had suggested, surely there would be friction between them? Each woman had painted the other's life in polar-opposite terms.

Christina angled her head slightly. 'I would say so, yes. But then, that's true love for you, isn't it? It has the most transformative powers. Elena has grown into a worthy matriarch for the Damiani family. She has become a *Romana di Roma*. A Roman's Roman.'

'*Romana di Roma*,' Cesca repeated. It sounded like a compliment of the highest order. 'And you work closely together on the foundation's charitable projects?'

'Oh yes. But then, I keep close to Elena on everything.'

Christina smiled at her and Cesca smiled back, but she felt a shiver ripple up her spine. In any other setting, with any other person . . . that would have sounded distinctly like a threat.

Chapter Sixteen

Malibu, November 1969

'Jay!' She opened the door a little wider in surprise. 'How lovely!'

'How are you, Laney?' he asked, leaning forward to kiss her once on the cheek. He stepped in and she moved out of the way to let him in, looking on in bafflement at the bottle of wine in his hand.

'Uh . . .'

She smiled as he turned back to face her. 'It's very quiet in there. Don't say I'm the first to arrive?'

'Well, yes,' she said. 'Dinner's tomorrow.'

There was a pause. 'What?'

'Dinner's tomorrow night. Leo's still in Chicago.'

Jay dropped his head into his hands. 'Oh my God. I can't believe—'

'But hey, it's fine,' she laughed. 'It's no problem.'

He pulled an apologetic grimace. 'Really?'

'No, of course not!' she demurred, and then, catching sight of his face, she realized he thought— 'I mean, I *would* rustle something up for you now but I've got dinner plans later, so . . .'

'Of course you do, of course you do,' he repeated, looking awkward. 'God, I'm such an idiot.'

'Honestly, it's fine!'

There was a short silence.

'Well . . . at the very least, shall we have a glass of this in the interests of letting it breathe? I mean, I'm here now, so . . .' He shrugged.

Laney hesitated for a moment. Leo could be possessive of her – he didn't like her talking to the other surfers on the beach – and she knew it was because the age gap made him insecure. But Jay was his friend, his age; they had been at Stanford together; to do anything less than host his friend would be rude.

'Absolutely.' She shut the front door and led him through to the open-plan living area.

'So, where did you say Leo is?'

'Chicago. Walt Bellamy's out of form; they're having crisis talks.' She rolled her eyes as she got them both a wine glass and set them down on the counter, passing Jay the bottle opener. 'I don't know. There's always someone having a crisis. Sometimes I think Leo isn't so much an agent as a counsellor.'

Jay raised an eyebrow sympathetically as he poured the merlot. 'Away a lot, is he?'

'Always, or so it feels,' she sighed, raising her glass and clinking it with his.

'Why don't you travel with him, then?' Jay asked, following her over to the white leather sofas, which were arranged in a U-shape to look out over the sea, although the black of night meant there was nothing to see other than their own reflections looking back at them.

Laney shook her head as she tucked her knees up under

her body, angling herself towards him. 'I used to, but I think, really, I just get in the way. It's work, after all, so Leo's either at a game or at the training sessions, and at the dinner afterwards, I just can't keep up with all the sport talk. I mean, I like basketball but—'

Jay chuckled. 'I hear you. There's more to life than basketball and deals.'

'I keep trying to tell him that!' she laughed, grateful someone understood. She sipped some more of the wine; it was a good vintage. 'Anyway, enough about him. How are things in the world of academia?'

'Oh, you know . . . dusty.'

She smiled. 'And Barbara? I haven't seen her in a while.'

'Dusty too.'

She laughed. 'Poor Barbara!'

He grinned. 'She's in Pasadena at the moment. Has been for the past few months, actually; she's looking after her mother after she took a fall.'

'I'm sorry to hear that. Is she recovering well?'

'A little too well, by all accounts. Barbara's been run off her feet.'

'Poor thing. Have you been over to visit?'

'My schedule barely accounts for sleep, much less tending to the mother-in-law.'

'Well, on the bright side, I guess at least you've got job security. Leo always acts like his clients are going to desert him if he doesn't satisfy their every whim.'

Jay looked at her, putting down his glass. 'Look at us. What a pair we are, huh? Both of us abandoned by our other halves; home alone; lonely . . .' He stared at her with a sudden, bold directness, a silence lengthening between them as – in the pit of her stomach – Laney felt a splash of bile rear up, nausea gripping her throat. She tried to smile and pass off the intimation, even though she realized with perfect clarity, now, that he had made no mistake in coming here tonight.

'Well, I wouldn't say I'm lonely, Jay—' she said, still smiling, not letting the mask slip. If there was one thing she had learnt from her mother, it was to keep up appearances.

But subtlety wasn't on his radar. Nor defeat.

'It could be the perfect remedy, don't you think? Something fun, harmless . . .' he said, his eyes on their reflections in the vast glass windows.

Laney put down her glass, the smile sliding off her face. 'I don't think so, Jay.' Her voice sounded funny – smaller, somehow. She wanted him to leave.

He looked at her now. 'Why not? It's not the age difference, after all; you clearly like them older.' He shrugged, implying with a single look that he was the other half to her equation: that he 'liked them young'.

'Because I love Leo.'

'I love Barbara. But it doesn't change the fact that we're both alone and lonely.' He moved his hand off his thigh and onto her own.

She tried to lift it off but the more she tried, the harder his fingers gripped her knee.

'Please, Jay, don't,' she said in a quiet, pleading voice that had never worked with Jack, either. Knowing that to fight him was to escalate the situation, she let go of his hand.

'Laney, Laney,' he shushed, his hand beginning to move in sweeping strokes, as though she was a dog he could pet. 'I never would have taken you for a prude. Not a free-living girl like you, always flirting with Leo's friends—'

'I don't flirt with anyone.'

'Let's not pretend you're the innocent,' he smiled, but his eyes were cold, the evening's earlier pretence already cast aside; they both knew how this was going to end. She was alone here, the nearest neighbours several hundred metres away; the sound of the sea would drown out her shouts. 'No one's buying it. You've been leading me on from the moment we met. You know perfectly well this was the date you gave me. You lured me here and now you're trying to pretend you don't want it?'

Laney felt something deep inside her begin to close down as he shuffled over to her, breaching the gap between their bodies. She could see the reflection of them in the large glass door, Jay's body leaning towards her—

It was another moment before she saw Leo standing there too, spectral in the glass, his face ghostly, his bag gripped loosely in his hand, a coat thrown over his free arm. Was it really him? Leo? The man who had saved her from her old life – was he really back? Or was her mind playing tricks, willing it to be true, to make this stop?

His reflected eyes met hers in the windows and for just a moment, time hung suspended; she saw them all like the toys on one of those baby mobiles, spinning silently in the air.

And then they were real again. Jay knew nothing before the moment Leo's fist connected with his jaw and he knew very little afterwards – of the way his feet dragged, tripping over themselves, as Leo hauled him to the door by the back of his jacket and threw him through it.

'Oh Leo!' Laney sobbed, throwing herself into his arms as he returned. 'I couldn't stop him. He wouldn't listen.' It was over. Thank God it was over.

Leo said nothing, his body stiff, and she pulled back to look at him.

'Leo?'

One look at his face and she knew it wasn't over.

'Why are you lying to me?' he roared. 'I've known him since college! He's my friend. He wouldn't do this . . .' He glared at her, his chest heaving, the top buttons of his shirt undone, his tie thrown on the ground somewhere between the front door and here. 'What did you do, Laney? You must have done something to make him think—'

'I didn't!'

'Don't give me that! I've seen you with those guys on the beach. Do you think I'm blind?'

'Leo, they're just friends,' she cried, exasperated. 'I have to talk to people when you're not here. You're never here! I'd go out of my mind! But I have *never* been unfaithful to you. There's no one but you, you *know* that!'

He shook his head, his hands on his hips. 'No, you led him on. You flirted like you always do and you went too far.'

Like she always did? The comment was like a slap. 'This isn't my fault,' she said, more quietly, still pleading.

But he wasn't buying it. He couldn't hear her. 'What did you do?' he repeated, eyebrows arched as though sceptical that she would ever tell him the truth.

'I offered him a drink to be polite. Because he's your friend and I knew you would want me to. Because I wanted to make you proud.'

'Proud?' he scoffed. 'You think I'm proud of having a wife who entertains other men while I'm away? Who thinks that her money makes her unaccountable? You're my wife!

159

Mine!' He walked towards her, grabbing her by the wrist. 'Tell me what you did!'

She stared back at him, the words as stoppered in her throat as if he'd rammed down a cork. He wasn't going to believe her, because he never did. It was always the same conversation, the same old fight. This wasn't new, but it wasn't yet old.

The feeling that had tingled on the sofa when she'd seen Leo watching them in the window bloomed again – shimmering like a mirage, growing in colour and strength. Life felt interrupted from its linear flow as though it was being forced into another lane, a train switching tracks, the actors on the stage suddenly picking up new scripts and playing fresh roles. This was who they were now.

It was over.

Chapter Seventeen

Rome, July 2017

Everyone had gone for the day when the ground rumbled and shifted again, shaking up through Cesca's bones and making her cup rattle on its saucer. All the specialists in their hard hats and hi-vis vests had packed up; she had heard their cheery farewell shouts a short while ago as they departed, leaving the hole in the ground just as they had found it a few days earlier. It was still big, still there, and Elena's initial 'laissez faire' demeanour was becoming more strained. It was an 'eyesore!', she exclaimed, fretting that all the exploratory digging work gave her headaches; she said she was tired of these 'workers' milling about her garden 'like ants'.

Cesca had been watching them all week from her office too, wandering over to the windows during her tea breaks and observing as they sent people down into the hole and then back up again. She wondered exactly how they were supposed to fill in something of that size. Was it a matter of simply trucking in replacement soil? Elena had mentioned they would fill it with mortar, but the sheer volume that would be required was staggering.

Not that they appeared to be in a rush to close it up

again. And was this why? Had they known it wasn't done yet, that there would be aftershocks? Might it continue to grow? She held her breath, not daring to move anything other than her eyes, which were darting around the vaulted ceiling looking for cracks and falling plaster, and skimming the ground searching for fissures in the floor or any signs that the sinkhole had encroached too close to the palazzo after all, the building now made unstable and unsaveable. Should she turn and run?

But everything was still again. The rumble had been only a few seconds long, not so much an earthquake as an earth-quiver. Moving hesitantly, she stepped towards the French doors and looked out. Perversely, everything looked un-changed – the sinkhole seemingly no bigger to her eye than it had been before. Deeper, then? Did the earth just continu-ally fall away, layer by layer?

She waited, but nothing else happened. No rumbling. No vibrations. She could almost think she'd imagined it.

Curiosity got the better of her. No one was around – Elena was at a wedding in Florence for the weekend and, without his boss around, even starchy Alberto was taking things down a notch in this oppressive city heat. The week-end beckoned – Cesca's own promised reward of Friday night drinks with Alé and the guys was only a tantalizing hour away now and she had been looking forward to it all day. It had been a long week, what with the vagaries of Elena's unpredictable mood swings, the somewhat unset-tling lunch with Christina, and the weariness that came from sifting a life story from photographs. Not to mention the time-consuming process of diligently following up on the facts that Elena had given her so far, a task that was as wide-ranging as putting in a request for a copy of her subject's wedding certificate to checking the pedigree of the Olympic stallion that had sired her prize mare, Miss Midnight. She was being unnecessarily thorough, doubtless, but whether she was writing a coffee-table book or a legal paper, professional pride meant Cesca would never leave a stone unturned in her presentation of the truth.

Though a wedge of sunlight still spilled into the furthest reach of the garden room, the courtyard was completely in shadow as she stepped outside and crept over to the edge of the sinkhole. Ducking below the tape, she peered in again. Her stomach dropped at the vision before her: crushed pipework and steel, snapped trees, layers of stone and earth and concrete tumbled together as if weightless, neon ropes dangling in the dusk and pooling at the bottom. There was something apocalyptic about the scene – it really could have been the aftermath of an earthquake or a war, a scar in this beautiful garden, a brutal reminder that nature couldn't ever be tamed.

She took a step back. It didn't seem much different from when she'd seen it the other day and she didn't want to linger on this wholly unnatural sight, like an open wound on an animal's flank. It had a primordial menace to it. Elena was right – the sooner it was filled in, the better.

She turned away, done for the day. It was time to meet her friends—

'Hello?'

She froze. The voice was distant. So far away, it could have been coming from the street on the far side of the thick palace walls. But that wasn't possible. Because the voice had come from below her.

'Is anyone there?'

She ran back to the edge and peered over again, looking

frantically beyond the big chunks of broken earth and con-crete slabs, scanning for detail – a face, a boot, a hard hat; something human to put with the voice. Instead, she saw the tiniest movement of earth, as though a mole was about to break through and nose the air.

She watched it, her heart pounding wildly, with no idea what to expect. If a fire-breathing dragon suddenly emerged, she wasn't sure she would be surprised. Instead, it was a finger – dusty, muddy, the pink fingernail caked in red soil – wiggling the earth loose and making a small hole.

'Oh my God!' she gasped. There was someone down there, buried beneath a two-metre heap of earth. Unlike most of the soil, which was pale and dried out from the week's exposure to the sun, this was darker, as though freshly dislodged. She realized now what she had heard – there had been a landslip.

She couldn't jump down there. It was too far, for one thing, and the ground was unstable; her weight could end up making the sinkhole deteriorate further. 'Oh my God! Help!' she shouted as the adrenaline hit, jumping to her feet and looking every which way for *something*, someone.

Nothing.

Not a damned—

She saw a harness on the floor, laid out on the grass like a sunbather, the contraption connected to the rope by a carabiner-clip, ready to go to work on Monday morning. She looked down at the length of rope – it reached to the bottom of the sinkhole.

There wasn't time to think about it. She stepped into the harness, having to bunch up her long skirt into her knickers so that it looked ridiculously like a nappy. Snapping shut the clips, she pulled on the rope, checking it would hold.

The rope quivered tightly, and she lowered herself off backwards. She didn't know if she was doing it right, it was just the way she'd seen mountain climbers do it in films – weight back, feet flat – but it seemed to work. The rope had a sort of ratchet attached that kept her stable and even though the walls of the sinkhole curved away – inwards – almost immediately, leaving her dangling in open air, she didn't fall.

Hands trembling with panic – how much air did that person have? – she lowered herself slowly, almost flinching when her feet gently touched the soil a few moments later. Unclipping the harness from the rope – it was quicker than getting out of the harness – she stumbled over to where she had seen, or thought she'd seen, the finger. But where was it? Everything looked different down here; from this perspective one heap of mangled mess looked much like every other. Exposed wires, jagged-edged clay pipes, twisted metal rods thrust and jabbed at her and up close she saw the debris of centuries of Roman life – broken pots, carrier bags . . . And the smell – of seeping sewage, of fetid earth. She felt herself gag and heave but she couldn't stop, couldn't turn away.

She heard something and turned to see tiny rivulets of earth and pebbles falling down a solid mass of earth. The one wiggling finger had now become four.

'I'm here, I'm here!' she cried in panicky Italian, running over, having to climb over the upended trunk of one of the orange trees, the branches scratching her bare legs. 'Can you hear me?' she cried, reaching the fingers and grasping them. They grasped back and, for a moment, all was still, their two hands touching. She squeezed harder, then released her grip. 'I'm going to get you out of here,' she shouted, hoping the person could hear.

Apparently they did, because they formed their hand into a thumbs-up sign before withdrawing it from sight.

Scrabbling her hands like a squirrel hiding a nut, she managed to dislodge and move the top layer of earth quickly – but it had slumped atop a heap of rubble, like a mudslide above a building site. 'Oh God,' she whispered, looking at the huge slabs, some of them bigger than her. Without the extra depth of the soil, the arm – surprisingly muscular – could push through an irregular crack between rough concrete boulders almost to the elbow, but the body it was attached to was stuck behind this perilous wall, as though entombed.

'Don't worry, I'm coming,' she said again, trying to sound braver than she felt. She ought to have gone for help first. Or called Guido or Matteo; they didn't work far from here. She looked back up – only the uppermost level of the palace walls was visible from this depth, the sky a blushing peach, occasionally dotted by stray pigeons heading home to roost. How was she even supposed to get up from here herself, anyway?

Quickly, she texted her friends, asking them to get here as quickly as they could, before she turned back to the arm. 'Can you breathe okay? Have you got enough air?'

'Yes.' The voice, though still distant, was certainly closer now. It was masculine – and it came back in English.

'There are some big boulders here so it might take a while, but I won't leave, I promise you. Help's coming,' she fibbed.

'It is fine. There is room here to move.'

Scrambling up the rocks at the side – fearful of sending

the whole lot collapsing down on the man – she got her arms around one of the higher boulders and, with a grunt, managed to heave it off the top of the mudslip. It scraped the skin of her inner arms when she didn't manage to move them out of the way quite fast enough, and sent a thick plume of dust into the air as it landed on the rubble, bouncing erratically on the rough surface.

One down, she thought with satisfaction, looking back at the pile still to clear.

She went again, using her full body weight, rocking and pushing the jagged slabs – anything to topple them – sometimes getting out of the way in time, at other times not quite. Within a few minutes, her legs were grazed and her skin coated in a grey dust shroud, but gradually the rock pile began to crumble, the debris falling to the new bottom of the hole, allowing air and light to peek through small pockets into the tomb. She glimpsed dark curls, now white with dust; proud eyes, now humbled; a t-shirt, now torn; strong muscles, now trapped and inert.

'We're nearly there,' she said as cheerily as she could, hoping to sound optimistic as she scrambled back down the rubble. 'There's just this last bit to move.'

But the worst had been saved till last. This final remaining slab was unlike the rest of the rockfall. Smooth on one side, it was a large section of the paved parterre which had fallen down into the sinkhole, slamming shut on the man like a door, rigid as a wall. She put her shoulder to the side of it, pushing hard, using all her weight, but the pile of debris and soil at the foot of it meant it didn't budge. She tried again. Nothing. And again.

'Oh God,' she panted finally, bloodied hands on her scraped knees. She had been digging for twenty minutes now and was exhausted, but still this man was trapped. She couldn't do it on her own. 'I can't . . . I can't move it. I've got to go and get help.'

'Wait!' The man's voice was much closer now. Stronger.

She straightened up at his tone. He didn't sound scared, but authoritative, decisive. 'There is a small gap here.' She looked and saw his hand again, the fingers wiggling through a narrow channel between the rocks. 'Is there anything you can use as a puller – a lever?'

'A . . . a lever?' she echoed, looking around frantically at the mess surrounding her. There were broken pipes, but they were made of clay; tree trunks, but they were far too long and heavy to move. But a few metres away she saw a metal rod, of the type that builders used as strengtheners. One end of it was sharp and lethal-looking, the very top of the other gloved in the remains of a concrete cylinder.

She scrabbled over to it, the clips on the harness jangling prettily as she stumbled over the rocks. 'There's this,' she panted, bringing it back and holding it up to the narrow gap.

The eyes blinked. 'Try it.'

She slid the rod through the gap. It fitted.

'Okay. Stand behind the bar and pull it backwards,' he said. 'Pull as hard as you can.'

Cesca heaved. Nothing happened. Her hands, slick with blood, slipped on the metal. 'I'll try the other way. Pushing's easier,' she said, ducking under the bar and beginning to push against it instead. For a moment, nothing happened again, her feet treading the ground, gaining no distance. And then suddenly—

The lever switched back and she fell face first into the rubble heap. The sound of the slab crashing forwards came a second or two later, a huge muffled *thwump* that made the hole shake again, yet more rocks falling, soil sliding. A mushroom cloud of dust filled the cavity and Cesca coughed, choking on the solid concrete-flecked air.

She felt hands on her back. 'Are you okay?'

But she couldn't stop coughing, grit in her lungs and eyes. Her cheek stung and she put a hand to it, feeling the shallow groove of fresh scrapes on her skin. She looked up and saw the ghost-man. Her first thought was to wonder whether she was as white-looking as he was. Her second—

'You!' She couldn't believe it. She got to her feet in an ungainly fashion, the harness clips jangling noisily as she tried to balance on the unstable ground. 'If I'd known it was you—' she panted, glaring at him.

'What?' The whites of Cantarelli's eyes looked super-bright against his dulled skin, his lips extra pink, his eyes ultra dark, trying to catch up with her rage.

But she couldn't finish the sentence; angry though she was, it wasn't true. She wouldn't have left anyone down there.

'You are—' He put his hand to his own cheek and wiped it gently. She echoed the movement on herself, her fingers coming back red. It stung. 'We should get that cleaned up.'

'*I'm* fine,' she replied indignantly, refusing to allow him the opportunity to take control of this situation, to reverse the roles as though she was the victim in this. '*I'm* not the one who needed rescuing.'

She saw the way his eyes flashed at her words, highlighting his momentary vulnerability. He looked back at her with that unsettlingly direct look of his. 'Thank you—'

It was like forcing a toddler to hand back an ice cream.

'—But I would have been fine.'

Cesca's mouth dropped open. '*Excuse* me?'

'You did not need to trouble yourself. I would have been able to get out.'

'Oh! You think so, do you?' she asked sarcastically, gesturing to the fresh heap of newly dislodged earth and rock, to the giant slab of parterre at their feet. 'I guess that's why you were calling to see if someone was there, then?'

He didn't reply but his displeased expression pleased her. He was in her debt and they both knew it.

'What were you even doing in there on your own anyway? Aren't there rules against that?'

'I knew what I was doing.'

'Yeah. It looked like it.' She put her hands on her hips. 'You realize everyone else has gone? Alberto would never have heard you from inside. Elena's away. You were lucky I was around.'

He arched an eyebrow. 'Was I?'

Cesca gasped in full-blown indignation. 'You could have died!'

'No.'

'. . . What?'

'I would not have died. There was another way out.' He gestured to the cavity where he'd been trapped – the space behind it was regular and smooth.

Open-mouthed, Cesca walked towards it and stared in. The passage extended back towards the west wing to her right and the east wing to her left. Small niches, carved into the walls at regular intervals, were blackened with scorch marks, indicating where candles had once sat, lighting the way. Presumably, there would be a door or entrance of some kind at either end, back into the palazzo.

She looked back at him, feeling her anger rise again. She

170

had put herself in danger for him; hurt herself because of him. She glanced down at her bare and bleeding legs, her bunched-up skirt now ruined. And he wasn't grateful. It hadn't even been necessary. 'So then, what the hell were you doing, trying to get out this way?'

'I cannot tell you that. It is confidential.'

Cesca's jaw dropped. She was so frustrated she wanted to scream. She wanted to slap him, kick him, knock ten bells out of him. How dare he behave like this when she had tried to help him? *'That's* all you have to say after I just moved that crap to get you out? I thought you were suffocating! I thought you were going to die! And you can't tell me why I bothered because it's "confidential"?'

He saw the stress in her face and how her eyes were red-rimmed, her lips trembling, her knees bleeding, her knuckles scraped. She noticed him close his right hand. 'And I thank—'

'What's that?' She pointed at his fist.

'Again, that is confidential.'

'Is that the reason why you just endangered your life *and* potentially mine?'

'No one was going to die.'

She straightened up. She'd had enough of this. Of him and his jobsworth pettiness. 'Show it to me. Show me or I'm going to report this entire charade to your bosses. I don't care what you say. There's no way your health-and-safety people would allow you down there alone.'

He glowered at her, still so shrouded in the dust he could have been a stone statue, only the anger in his eyes animating him. Slowly, and with visible resentment, he raised his arm and opened his fist.

Cesca looked down at the tiny fragment of a tile in his palm. 'That's *it*?'

He shrugged, his mouth set in a grim line.

'Hey!'

They both looked up to see three faces peering down at them: Alberto, Guido and Matteo.

'What is going on here?' Alberto demanded, looking furious.

'Is this a private party or can anyone join in?' Matteo asked, grinning wildly, the smile sliding off his face as he took in her expression. 'Hey, baby, what's happened?'

'You okay, Chess?' Guido asked, immediately protective.

She shook her head, feeling tears suddenly threaten at the sight of her lovely friends. She'd had enough of this man. Not only was he ungrateful, he was consistently rude and arrogant. *And* he'd drawn blood again. She was going to have yet more scabs on his account!

'Just get me out of here,' she said, stumbling over the rubble and towards the rope, hands shaking as she tried to fasten the carabiners to the harness again, Cantarelli's eyes like bullets in her back.

Chapter Eighteen

New York, December 1977

The lights strobed, picking out her silver dress – the one that reminded her of one of her mother's, half a lifetime ago – her tanned bare arms above her head, dark crimped hair swaying down her back. Steve was sitting in the booth with Andy, both of them watching something – someone – other than her, Steve's deep-set eyes hooded, one arm slung across the back of the banquette, a cigarette dangling carelessly between his fingers. Laney swayed to Donna Summer, feeling the love as she stared at her man. He even looked like a movie star in the dark, his top three shirt buttons undone, dark hair flopping forwards every few minutes and needing to be raked back – all the better for showing off the dramatic bone structure that made him such a dream onscreen. His new movie had just opened and was blitzing the box office, overtaking the new John Travolta picture, and creating a buzz around him that sometimes made her wake in the middle of the night and stare at the ceiling until the sun came up. Wasn't their life crazy enough already?

Being married to him was like harnessing the sun. Everyone was equal in here – once you got past the ropes – but some were more equal than others: wasn't that how the saying went? Mick was here with his new model girlfriend, Jerry Hall, Liza was already on the dance floor, she'd seen Elsa too, head bent in conversation with Halston and Truman, and the not-yet-teen sensation Brooke Shields, whose soon-to-be-released film *Pretty Baby* already had industry buzz, popping in briefly with her mother. Nevertheless, it was Steve who was the centre of gravity in the room, women in tight pants stopping at his table to talk, to laugh, to let the straps of their camisoles slide off their shoulders as they tossed their hair . . .

She watched as one – blonde, tall, a model type – slid into the booth beside him, her blue strapless dress clinging tightly to her narrow torso, shiny shoulders on display. They seemed to know each other: Steve extended himself to pour her a glass of champagne – not everyone received that courtesy – their white teeth matching as they smiled and clinked glasses.

Laney turned on the spot, shaking her hair, shaking them out of her head, shaking her hips harder as the song segued into 'Staying Alive'. Someone took her hands and danced with her, turning her, spinning her. Laney felt her heart racing. It was so hot in here, in spite of the thick snow outside, and she dabbed her nose again – a habit now, almost a tic – checking her fingers for any telltale trace of white powder.

The man ebbed from sight and unfamiliar people swam in front of her, the crowd a heaving mass that kept changing – too many new faces in here tonight – so that her friends, her clique, sporadically fell away from her, leaving her alone and exposed amidst strangers: a public she had been conditioned to fear. She turned back to Steve, looking for familiarity, an anchor.

The blonde had her hand on his thigh and he was leaning in towards her, his mouth inches from her ear. The woman's long golden hair was swept aside provocatively to expose her neck and the beautiful, almost sculptural sweep down to her bare shoulders. Andy, beside them, was staring into the crowd with his usual nonplussed expression, eyes blinking slowly behind those thick-rimmed glasses, his white-blonde hair shocking under the lights.

Laney couldn't take her eyes off her husband. He was hers, in spite of what that little blonde might think. He would never leave her – her name opened too many doors, her money throwing shade over even his earnings. Together they were dynamite. A power couple. Greater than the sum of their parts. They needed each other.

She kept watching him but she kept dancing too; she wanted to go over and throw that girl to the floor, to put his hands on *her* body instead, but her silver sandals were rooted to the spot. She was somehow caught in this game they had fallen into playing. It had been going on so long now, she couldn't remember how it had first started, or where. She couldn't remember a lot of things – like when they had started being happier apart than when they were together. Was it when they'd become a family? Because that didn't make sense to her; they were supposed to be closer now. Why weren't they?

She closed her eyes, feeling the music carry her, knowing that all these things she could see, she should also be able to feel. But she didn't. She was numb. Bullet-proof.

She felt hands on her hips, hands that slowed down her movements and brought them into time with another body.

She let it happen. She felt good; she felt so far away. The man came closer, turning her to him. She recognized the face but his name eluded her. She frowned, before relaxing into a languid smile. What did it matter anyway? Details, names, were irrelevant. There was nothing beyond this moment. Tonight.

'I need champagne!' she shouted to the guy over the music. And before he could answer, she took him by the hand and towed him behind her to the booth. The model pulled away, fractionally, from Laney's husband as she reached across the full width of the table for her champagne glass. 'Hey baby. Having fun?' she asked, swaying slightly from the suddenness of not dancing.

'You don't mind, do you, Laney?' he asked, squeezing the model's skinny thigh. 'You look happily occupied yourself.'

'I am,' she shrugged, looking back at her dance partner and wondering if she should know his name. They had met before, she was certain. Ugh, but there were too many people. It was hard to remember. Everyone laughing and dancing, shouting above the music, all moving so fast . . .

She winced, feeling suddenly weary. Exhausted. A chink of another world – another life – suddenly burst through into this one, too strong, too bright. The colours were beginning to glare, hurting her eyes. She sank one buttock onto the table and downed her glass. Steve was saying something in a low voice to the blonde. She smiled a private smile in this most public of spaces and they both rose, her husband grabbing his jacket and slinging it over one shoulder. 'See you tomorrow, babe,' he murmured, stopping in front of Laney to kiss her on the mouth, his eyes locking onto hers for a moment. Another private moment, publicly shared.

She nodded, watching them leave, her husband's hand on some other woman's bony ass, the crowd parting for them as they headed for the door.

Her dance partner – almost forgotten – took a step closer to her, refilling her glass quickly and taking a slug of it himself, before putting it to her lips, the liquid spilling out of the sides of her mouth. He leaned down and kissed it off and somewhere deep inside she registered a feeling of distaste. No, more than that – disgust. But it was a theoretical recognition, she couldn't actually *feel* it right now. She couldn't feel anything real in here, like this. She couldn't feel the horror she knew she ought to feel that her husband had left with another woman. She closed her eyes: she felt good; she felt far away. She was in with the in crowd. Always one of the lucky ones.

Chapter Nineteen

Rome, July 2017

Even by day, the brightness in the white apartment was unexpected. The room seemed to glow with reinforced serenity, defying the day's unseasonably overcast skies and blithely ignoring the despoiled garden four floors below. Elena was still in the bedroom, getting dressed, but Alberto had directed her up here for the interview, saying the Principessa – they were back to formalities again after Friday's transgression when she'd been 'caught' in the garden – was tired from her weekend of travelling and preferred not to be so close to the noise and disturbances from outside.

Cesca stood at the window, tugging gently on her plait, which was thrown over one shoulder, and staring down at the activity. From here, she had a bird's-eye view, able to see straight down into the hole, which was noticeably bigger than it had been when the workers had left on Friday evening. She had seen the first of them arrive and peer in, looking puzzled, then alarmed, getting out their lasers and measuring equipment and mapping out the new shape and dimensions. When Cantarelli arrived shortly after, two fingers strapped up and a nasty-looking cut on his arm, there had been a flurry of concern – of head-shaking and shoulder-patting, arms thrust out questioningly – and she knew they were asking the same question she herself had asked: what had happened? She wondered if he was admitting to having gone down there alone. She wondered when he had broken his fingers – during the rockfall? Or the escape? He had said nothing about it at the time and not done anything to indicate he was in pain; then again, she'd barely given him much of a chance. The guys had teased her all Friday night about it, recounting how funny it had been to peer over the top of the monstrous hole and find the two of them at the bottom of it, arguing like an old married couple. She'd practically shinned her way back up the rope, they'd said, her skirt still bunched up like a nappy.

She sighed, trying to banish the undignified image from her mind as she watched him striding around down there as if he owned the place. That man was not her problem. Next time, he could dig himself out. Or take the damned back door—

'Good morning, Francesca.' Elena's voice was almost singsong in its quality. 'Sorry to keep you. I trust you had an enjoya—' She gasped. 'Oh my goodness, whatever happened to you?'

'I'm sorry?' Cesca asked, before noticing Elena's gaze was fixed upon her cheek. 'Oh.' Her hand flew up to it defensively. 'I fell.'

'Down what? A *cliff*?' Elena asked, although there was levity in her tone.

Cesca gave a small laugh, brushing it off, wanting to move the topic on, glancing as she did so out of the window one last time. To her surprise, Cantarelli was standing in the garden staring up at her. The laughter died on her lips.

She moved away quickly, out of sight, back into the white

radiance of the room. 'So, how was the wedding?' she asked, skirting round the sofa she'd sat upon that first night – only twelve days ago now, yet seeming more like months.

'Oh, pure heaven. I do adore Florence. I always stay at the Medici. They're so sweet and always give me my old suite whenever I stay.'

'Who was getting married?'

'One of Vito's goddaughters. He'd known her parents since childhood. I do what I can to keep the connection going; I know it's what he'd want. In fact, I arranged for her to visit the Valentino atelier for her dress. It was my wedding gift to her. I'm a special client so they are most accommodating. Of course, she looked absolutely beautiful.' She noticed Cesca was still standing. 'Please sit, sit. Has Alberto gone to fetch tea?'

'Yes. He said jasmine?'

'Good. I find it a little lighter for times like these—'

Cesca watched as Elena settled herself into the chair opposite. She looked paler today, somehow more frail, the blue of her veins dark against her papery skin.

'It was a magnificent time, of course, but, my goodness, all those faces and names to put together, all the old stories being dredged up, so much chatter . . . I feel quite drained.'

Cesca nodded, wondering how well she would fare today, then, having to plumb the depths of her own past. She stretched forward and fanned out the small selection of photographs she had chosen for today's interview. A stocky, bearded, dark-haired man dominated them. He wasn't conventionally handsome to Cesca's eye, but he had an evident charm, with intense lively eyes and a seemingly ready smile. In most of the photos she had seen of the two of them together, Elena seemed to hang off him, her arms draped around his neck, curling up on his lap, piggybacking him or sitting on his shoulders . . .

'I thought we could start today by talking about this man?' she said, pointing to him and sitting back on the sofa, her digital recorder on.

Elena leaned forward to look at the images. She was quiet for a long time, nodding slowly, one finger pressed rhythmically to her lips like a pulse. 'Darling Leo. Such a good man.' She looked up at Cesca. 'He was my second husband. We met through a mutual friend in Boston.'

'And when was this?'

'Just after Jack had left me, actually.'

'So you were . . . seventeen?'

'Thereabouts.'

'He looks a lot older than you,' Cesca said diplomatically.

Elena shrugged. 'Yes. It caused quite a stir. My parents weren't anywhere near as pleased about this marriage. They never quite got over Jack.'

'But didn't you explain to them about his gambling problem?'

'Of course.' She sighed. 'But Mother had made up her mind about him and that was that. He was a good egg and so the blame must be mine. *I* had been a poor wife. *I* had let him down in some way—'

Alberto walked in with the tea tray.

'That's unfair.'

'It was easier to just let them carry on believing what they wanted to believe whilst I got on with my life. I had grown up a lot during my marriage to Jack. Leo was exactly what I needed and I understood it, even if they couldn't.'

Cesca's eyes fell to the photographs again, lingering on

one of Elena piggybacking Leo on a beach. 'Was he a father substitute, do you think?'

'Well, I would not have phrased it in such an *overt* term at the time, of course, but I recognized he was safety.'

Cesca's antennae pricked up at the word – a hangover from her previous career, her previous life. 'Why did you need safety?'

Elena seemed to still, like an animal hiding in the bushes, hoping not to be seen. 'I was brought up to fear the world, Francesca. I wasn't like other people. My family's wealth set me apart and made me a target. I learnt early on how to read people and who to distrust, which also meant I recognized when I had found someone I could trust. Like Leo. And you.'

Cesca blushed, startled to find herself drawn into the topic, the inner circle. 'S-so, you saw him as a protector?'

'Exactly. He was already wildly successful in his own right – he didn't need my money and he had nothing to prove.'

A sudden shout outside – followed by several others – made them both jump and look towards the windows. Cesca wanted to run over and see what was happening, but Elena showed no such curiosity and she felt obliged to remain where she was. 'Another bone hairpin, no doubt,' Elena sighed, bored.

Cesca nodded and tried to remember what they'd been talking about.

'Did your parents invite *him* to dinner then?' she eventually asked.

Elena laughed. 'No! I think they knew it wouldn't work on him. We just slipped off to Santa Barbara, quietly got married and made a phone call after the event.'

'I haven't come across any of the wedding photographs.'

'I'm not sure there are any. After all the fuss of my wedding to Jack, the last thing I wanted was another big splashy affair. We asked two people off the street to be our witnesses and afterwards we drove up to Big Sur and celebrated with hot dogs and champagne. It was perfect.' She smiled as she looked down at the images again and Cesca saw a marked difference in her expression from when they'd been talking about her first marriage. With Jack, though Elena had used words like 'sweet' and 'charming' and 'freedom', her eyes had fogged, her voice hollow, as though the memories had detached from her body and were now purely theoretical reminiscences. But with Leo, she still seemed to glow with remembered affection, embers of their love still stoking her from within.

'What was the best thing about your relationship with him?'

'Oh, the lack of pretentiousness, certainly. We lived a largely normal life. We bought a condo on the beach in Malibu and had no staff other than a housekeeper who lived off the premises. We'd have barbecues and friends over. We'd go surfing . . . well, I would.'

'So you overcame your fear of water, then?'

'Yes, Leo taught me, even though he was no water baby himself. I took to it like the proverbial duck to water – I couldn't believe I'd waited so long – and he preferred to watch. He'd pick out the waves for me to catch.' She chortled. 'If I didn't like the look of one, I'd simply let it go by and pretend I hadn't heard him.'

Cesca smiled. 'Please don't take this the wrong way, but I really can't imagine you surfing.'

'No, I'm sure not. I hardly look like a beach babe now, do

I? This hair—' She pointed to her sleek, blow-dried bob. 'Skin that's been slathered with sunscreen for the past thirty years . . .'

It was true: her immaculate poise was at odds with the beachy, tousled hair and salted-skin look Cesca imagined for surfers.

'No, I've changed a lot since then,' she sighed. 'But then, so has the world! This was the end of the 1960s. Malibu was the place to be back then – we had the Beach Boys, that wonderful film *The Endless Summer* had come out. Oh, it was just glorious. You know, I think I may still have my favourite dress from back then. Leo always loved it. I should fish it out and show it to you.'

'I'd love to see it. Is Leo still alive?'

'No, not for years. He died in a helicopter crash with one of his players outside Chicago in 1982. I was devastated. Just devastated.' Her eyes were watery, one hand pressed to her bony chest. 'Even now, I miss him.'

'So you were widowed, then?'

Elena shook her head. 'Heavens, no. We had divorced in 1975, a few years earlier.'

Cesca tried to keep up. 'But it's clear you still care very deeply for him, even now, after all these years. What happened between you?'

'Oh, it was the saddest thing and for the worst of all reasons, just so pointless.' She shook her head sadly. 'Jealousy. He just couldn't believe that I wouldn't look at another man. He travelled a lot for work and he . . . tormented himself with exotic scenarios that simply weren't true. They existed purely in his mind, but he'd get home and do silly things, crazy things.'

'Like what?'

'Like checking to see if there were two wine glasses on the drainer instead of one; or smelling the sheets for traces of aftershave; going through the laundry to see if I'd worn a sexy dress or lingerie. It was so . . . demeaning,' she said tightly. 'I couldn't bear to see him cutting himself down into smaller and smaller versions of himself, becoming petty and ridiculous.'

'So you left him?'

'I had to, for both our sakes. He wasn't getting any younger so the problem wasn't going to go away. It was the only option open to me.'

'Did he ever remarry?'

'No.' Her mouth became very small. 'We remained friends – well, as best we could, anyway; we would write occasionally, a card at Christmas. But there was no getting away from the fact I broke his heart. It's a terrible cross to bear.'

Cesca blinked and looked away. She knew exactly what it was like to destroy somebody. 'I'd love to talk some more about—'

A sudden knock at the door made them both turn. A short, wiry, dusty-looking man in a hard hat and steel-capped boots looked in on them, appearing more startled to see them than they were to see him. Cesca watched the way his eyes rolled over the minimal space, its blankness shocking compared to the riot of colour, pattern and texture preceding it in the long galleries.

'Yes?' Elena asked, a small polite smile on her mouth but her eyes cool.

'Apologies, Principessa,' the man said, taking off his hat and holding it in front of himself in a supplicatory manner. 'But there is something you must see.'

'*Must* I?' Elena echoed, clearly disliking his impudent use of the imperative.

He bowed his head apologetically, eyes still rolling around the room in awe. 'Signor Cantarelli requests it.'

Elena sighed. 'Well, then I suppose if Signor Cantarelli requests our presence, we must oblige.' She rose, as regal as if she'd been in ermine. 'Francesca, shall we?'

Cesca blinked. 'You want me to go too?'

'I am not so steady on my feet as I once was. I should appreciate your arm, just in case.'

'Oh yes, of course.'

The dusty man ran on ahead, almost sending Alberto into paroxysms of indignation as mud flaked off his boots with each step. With Elena resting her hand lightly on Cesca's arm, they walked slowly through the vaulted galleries of scarlet and emerald, magenta and turquoise, past the unseeing eyes of a thousand marble statues, past vast gilded mirrors bigger than most doors, which were hung at heights too high for them to see into.

The slow click of Elena's shoes on the marble floor was the only sound of life as Cesca drifted beside her in silent ease – her height meant she could take one stride to Elena's two – her brown-and-blue 1970s prairie skirt billowing behind as the breeze gusted in through the open windows.

'Why is that chair turned to the wall?' Cesca asked as they walked through a particularly ornate room, pointing to a gold chair with heavily flocked brocade.

'This is the Papal Suite and that is the papal throne. It is only ever turned around to face the room when the Pope visits.'

'Oh,' Cesca murmured, staring at it. How odd it looked,

with its back turned to the room like that. 'And when did the Pope last visit?'

'1873,' Elena laughed, throwing her head back in glorious amusement, almost as though she'd been hoping Cesca would ask. 'For a hundred and forty-four years that chair's been facing the wrong way! It drives me out of my mind! These damn traditions, I always said they'd be the end of me.'

They glided down the magnificent staircase, the builders' cacophony increasingly audible as they descended, while the open windows at each level brought in raucous shouts from the square, too. Rabble on one side, rubble on the other, Cesca mused, following Elena and Alberto through the ground-floor galleries of the east wing and out into the garden.

Cantarelli was dominating the space as usual, his customary frown spoiling everyone's day as he pointed at people and waved others away. Was it any wonder he'd been so ungracious at being saved? The man was a complete control freak. It must have galled him to be the recipient of her charity.

Crossing her arms over her chest, Cesca settled her features into a scowl too, watching as he put his manners on for the princess and led her towards a ladder that had been propped into the sinkhole.

'You want *me* to go down there?' Elena asked in astonishment before firmly shaking her head and taking a step back. 'No.'

'But Signora—'

'Signor Cantarelli, as you can see, I have needed assistance just to come down here. My navigating a ladder shall not be happening. Whatever it is, surely you can just tell me. Or bring it to me.'

'It is not something I can bring here, Signora. It is a significant discovery. You really should see it.'

Elena arched her eyebrows, before looking back at Cesca suddenly. 'Then show *her*.'

Cesca's arms dropped away. 'Huh?'

'Francesca can be my eyes. I trust her implicitly.'

Cantarelli didn't look very happy at the suggestion either, but he shrugged and motioned for Cesca to join him by the ladder. With a frustrated sigh, she walked over and peered into the sinkhole again, getting goosebumps at the sharp drop as she remembered digging at the earth with her bare hands, straining to move rocks and lumps of concrete – for no good reason.

Handing her a hard hat with a torch, Cantarelli at least had the grace to look away as she accusingly met his eyes before stepping onto the top rung. 'It's not another one of those little tiles, is it?' she asked. 'Because if—'

'Oh, that dratted map,' Elena muttered. 'I sincerely hope it's not. It's fast becoming the bane of my life.'

Cesca didn't know what Elena was on about but, given she was standing perched at the top of a very long ladder, it wasn't the time to ask. Tentatively, she began to climb down.

'For God's sake,' she muttered under her breath once Elena was out of sight. How had she moved from a barrister's wig to a builder's hard hat? But she knew exactly how, pushing the question straight back out of her mind again.

Cantarelli followed quickly after her, scrambling down the long ladder like a fireman before jumping the last few rungs and jerking his head in the direction of a short makeshift tunnel propped up by scaffolding poles and wooden boards, which had been dug out of the side of the sinkhole. It was in the exact same area from which she'd rescued him.

'It is this way.'

The going was rough and uneven for the first few steps, with large concrete blocks to scramble over in parts, the walls damp and cloying and the roof of the structure erratically low and worryingly crumbly. In which universe did he think Elena would ever have come down here? Cesca wondered to herself as she followed the bouncing beam from his flashlight.

But no sooner was the thought free in her mind than the landscape changed, tapping into a traversing artery and becoming suddenly tamed and smooth: a human construction. It was the underground tunnel she had glimpsed on Friday when saving his sorry arse.

The space was narrow enough to make her want to hold her breath; she could easily span it with outstretched arms, the walls rounding up to six-foot-high barrelled ceilings. Intermittent candle niches were set at regular intervals, scorch marks still blackening the walls and small puddles of wax still pooled on the floor.

'Wow,' Cesca whispered – because, somehow, an underground tunnel called for furtive voices; it reeked of secrets. It was straight out of Enid Blyton, Dan Brown . . .

Cantarelli offered a hand to pull her through and she took it, forgetting to scowl. 'Here. You will need to turn this on,' he said, reaching over and switching on her head torch.

Cesca, trying not to flinch, went very still instead, keeping her eyes on a space to the left of his head. It was bad enough having to occupy the same space as this man, much less the dark.

'Surely this isn't what you wanted to show her? You found this the other day,' she said tartly.

'No. She knows about this,' he said, ignoring her needling tone. 'This is just the service tunnel that runs between the east and west wings. But the Principessa says it has not been used for many years now. It was blocked up due to damp.'

'Oh! It's blocked up, you say?' she questioned, delighted now as she immediately latched onto the detail – the discrepancy – for this was the same tunnel he had been exploring before the landslide on Friday evening. So then, there *wasn't* a back door he could have used? It had been blocked up! He *had* needed her to rescue him.

She didn't need to say the words aloud to know he was reading her mind, for he scowled again. 'Come. It is this way.'

Cantarelli turned left towards the east wing and led the way down the service tunnel. Many of the niches were now lit with candles – 'Partly for the light, but mainly it is an easy way for us to make sure we have enough oxygen whilst we are working down here and the exits are blocked up,' he said over his shoulder.

'Makes sense,' she muttered, thinking she wouldn't want any canaries sacrificed on *his* account.

She followed after him, listening to the sound of his footsteps and breath, having to resist trailing her hands along the rough stone walls. After a minute or so, he stopped suddenly and Cesca had to keep from walking into the back of him.

'What? What is it?' she asked.

'This.' He pointed to the ground by his feet and scuffed it lightly. They had been walking on the service tunnel's dusty, roughly mixed concrete floor but, just at the very edge of the path, she saw the rounded edges of ancient cobbles ingress from behind the wall. 'We noticed these.'

Cesca felt a bubble of excitement in the pit of her stomach as she examined them more closely, squatting down to get the beam of her head torch upon them. 'You think there's something behind there?'

His eyes met hers: steady, self-assured. 'We know there is. We've been in there.'

Cesca stared, dumbfounded, at the wall, trying to imagine the T-junction he was telling her existed here. 'But . . . how?' She knocked it, wondering if it would sound hollow with a tunnel hidden behind it, but her bare knuckles made almost no sound on the stone wall. She pressed against it, looking for a line, a cut, a seam, an Agatha Christie-type lever that would make the entire thing fall away and reveal a hidden library with Colonel Mustard in it – but there was nothing. The rock was solid.

She looked back at Cantarelli, baffled.

To her surprise he was smiling – and pointing to the ceiling. She looked up and was amazed to see a small round hole cut into the rock, with iron bars inset on both sides. 'You are *kidding* me,' she whispered. The rough floor and permeating darkness meant there wasn't much scope for looking up. If she hadn't known to stop here, she would have walked straight past it.

Cantarelli laughed at her expression and she looked at him in even more surprise. She hadn't even imagined that he could smile, much less laugh, and it made him look completely different. 'You want to see?'

'I want to know how you thought the Viscontessa was

going to get up here . . .' she quipped, stepping into the cavity and peering up.

'We have a mirror. A periscope. But, if you want, you can go over and see for yourself.'

'No! How would I . . . ? I mean . . . I couldn't possibly get up there.'

Cantarelli laced his fingers together. 'You do a leg up, grab the bars and push yourself up.'

'I can't—'

'Yes. I push you.' He lowered his laced fingers and waited for her to step into them.

'But then how will you get up?'

He looked perplexed by the question. 'I will pull myself up. How else? Now come.'

Cesca stepped onto his hands, feeling wobbly as she reached for the bars, her head and shoulders going straight into the hole. But it was surprisingly easy to grab them and heave herself up and into the low tunnel that led off to the left. She was grateful that her skirt was long.

'Now on your stomach, wriggle.' Cantarelli's voice followed her, sounding echoey. 'When you see the drop hole, try to turn so you get your legs down first.'

Cesca didn't particularly like the sound of that – he hadn't seen her three-point turns – but the space was surprisingly capacious for manoeuvring and a few moments later she dropped down on the other side.

She was still gasping when Cantarelli followed seconds after.

'Incredible, no?' he asked, walking into the vast space, arms outstretched. It was almost double the width of the previous tunnel, a foot higher at least and built from the thin red bricks that characterized so many of the early Roman buildings. Further down, maybe twenty metres, the tunnel split four ways. 'My whole career I wait for moments like this.'

Cesca turned on the spot, hardly able to believe how her day had changed. Twenty minutes earlier, she'd been sipping jasmine tea and listening to an heiress reminisce about the break-up of her second marriage – exactly how many were there? she was beginning to wonder – and now here she was in an ancient and almost immaculate underground tunnel.

'I've never seen anything like it,' Cesca gasped. 'How old do you think this is?'

'We think this dates from Hadrian's era – so, nearly two thousand years old.'

Cesca paused. 'But that's significantly older than the palazzo.' By her own estimate – from what she knew from tour guiding – the building was fourteenth-century at the very earliest.

'Yes. This would have been built for the dwelling that previously occupied the site.'

'And the tunnel we were just in? Is that newer?'

'It looks like that one was built at the same time as the palace. We think when the palace was built they must either have destroyed the rest of this tunnel to allow for the east-west tunnel, or it was already ruined and they just built in front of it.'

Cesca thought about the cobbles of this tunnel poking into the other one. It couldn't have been *that* destroyed if it butted right up to the palace's planned service tunnel. 'Isn't it odd that when they built the wall for that service tunnel, they kept the access by putting in the roof tunnel? Surely they could have incorporated the two, as was done further down?' she asked, pointing to the four split-away tunnels. 'Why block it off and yet still retain an access point?'

Cantarelli shrugged. 'Possibly those tunnels would have compromised the security of the palace. The Damiani art collection is priceless. By making the tunnel look blocked up, anyone stumbling down here would see there was no way through and turn back.'

'Hmm,' Cesca murmured, beginning to walk. 'Have you gone down these yet? Do you know where they lead?'

'Not yet,' he said, catching her by the elbow and keeping her from going any further. 'And we will need to scan and map them first before we proceed. It is important to make sure they are safe.'

'They look safe.'

'You don't know that. Thousands of years of building, flooding, traffic could have weakened the structure so that one sneeze could make it all come toppling down.'

Cesca took a step back, chastened. When he put it like that . . . 'So how do you check they're safe, then?'

'We have wire-controlled robots equipped with cameras and imaging scanners.'

Cesca looked at him, impressed. And to think all this time she'd thought they'd been just pointlessly 'digging around'. 'It's incredible down here. I love it.'

Cantarelli smiled again. 'Yes. Often it is only these underground networks that can tell us how our ancestors lived. When the Empire disintegrated, all the greatest villas fell into disrepair or were plundered for their stone, whereas these networks were left intact. The more complex the network of tunnels underground, the grander the villa was above ground, keeping the slaves out of sight whilst they serviced the estate, moving firewood or food to where it was needed. At Caracalla, the tunnels were five storeys deep.'

'My God.' She nodded wonderingly, thinking now how glad she was to swap her wig for a hard hat. Then she narrowed her eyes suddenly. 'Wait a minute, does any of this have anything to do with that little tile you risked your neck for?'

'Perhaps.'

'Yes or no?'

Cantarelli stared at her for a long moment.

'Oh, for heaven's sake, if you don't tell me, Elena will,' she said exasperatedly. 'She's telling me *everything*, you know. I'm her biographer. I don't get what's so precious about one little tile.'

'Very well. But over pizza.'

If he had started tap-dancing, she couldn't have looked more stunned. '*Pizza?*'

'You don't eat pizza?'

'Of course I eat pizza. Everyone eats pizza.'

'Not if they have gluten intolerance.'

'Oh, so what are you saying? That I'm pasty?'

He watched her solemnly, but amusement flickered in those dark eyes. 'You are argumentative.'

'You can talk.'

He sighed. 'Is that a yes?'

Cesca opened her mouth – and then closed it again. 'Well, of course. I'm hungry and I'm curious.'

'About the tile?'

'About the tile.'

Chapter Twenty

The drawer came off the runners and fell to the floor with a heavy thump, narrowly missing her bare foot. 'Goddammit!' Laney hissed as clothes disgorged frothily on the carpet, joining the other cast-offs she had pulled out and discarded as she ran from room to room, stuffing the bags with whatever essentials they'd need until they were properly set up.

She had dispatched Matilda, their nanny, to collect little Stevie from kindergarten. Steve may have been in LA but she didn't underestimate him. He had sworn he'd never let her have their son and she believed him. His cold words were still scaldingly hot in her ear. Her long-withheld grenade of divorce, finally lobbed following this morning's latest headline about the baby, had exploded in her own face as he'd viciously turned the tables and confronted her with an image of herself which she didn't share – and yet could recognize. The party girl in the clubs every night and the It Girl in the papers every morning, she was no more than a rich addict, a society whore, an unfit mother, he'd hissed. No matter that it was all his doing – his idea, his plan; *he* was the one who had plied her with champagne and charlie to make her 'lively' when they went out, prescription drugs to keep her 'docile' when they stayed in. But the courts would never hear that because the papers didn't report it; it didn't make for good copy. Instead, her shame was all there, just like the old joke went: in black and white and read all over.

He had bent her to his will in front of everyone, in front of herself. The man was an actor, after all, a master manipulator, controlling her with drugs, destroying her public image and corroding her self-esteem. He was right – what judge would ever let her keep their son? She had put on a show and America had been watching. Stanley Charles could only do so much.

The pilot of their private jet had been informed and was already logging their flight path, the plane fuelled and ready to go. She ran to the safe and retrieved their passports, turning on the spot in her panic, trying to think what else she would need. It was usually Fatima who did the packing but there was no time today to call on her for help.

Her eyes fell to the newspaper, open on page six on the bed. Oh, how she longed for bed – to sleep, to escape this waking nightmare. The sheets were still warm from her exhausted body, but she hadn't rested properly in years. Food, drink, sleep: none of it nourished her.

She paused for a moment, trying to push past the panic, trying to see through his propaganda. He was making her hysterical again – he was so good at it, even from the other side of the country – but wait: what was that unborn baby going to mean for *his* reputation? His career had only got to where it was because of the profile he'd assumed from marrying her. He'd been careful with his countless affairs, only ever sleeping within their set – with her so-called friends, who would never dream of spilling the beans publicly, or with model types whose words counted for nothing.

But Steve had slipped up: that baby changed everything. What had merely been rumour before was now going to be substantiated in flesh and blood. Yet he was dragging her down with him. Their pretence of happy families was going to be exposed as the sham it really was. No amount of glossy 'At Home' features in the pages of *Harper's Bazaar* and *Cosmopolitan* were going to outshout a bawling baby.

She sank onto the bed, as further down the apartment she heard the elevator bell sound. It would be the porter, coming up to bring the bags down to the waiting car. Matilda was under instruction to wait with little Stevie down there; she hadn't wanted him coming up to this scene of devastation, nor had she wanted to lose a second as they made their escape.

She straightened her back and took a deep breath, trying to push her mind back into her body. Calm descended. First things first, she needed to call Charles. Perhaps she had more cause to hope than Steve had led her to believe. Maybe he was just playing her with his threats, exactly the way he had played her throughout their entire marriage. Divorce was different now, she knew. The Governor of California, Reagan, had brought in new laws. 'No fault' divorces, someone had told her; you didn't have to prove anything, they'd said, instead, you could cite 'irreconcilable differences' or 'irretrievable breakdown' . . . It all boiled down to the same thing: this marriage could be torn up as easily as cigarette paper.

She left the bedroom and headed down the hall – only to find three uniformed police officers walking towards her. Fatima was running after them, looking harried and upset, but Laney could see the sheet of paper in the sergeant's hand that prevented her maid from stopping them.

'Mrs Easton?' he asked, knowing full well who she was.

'Yes?' she asked, terror bolting through her.

'Sergeant Delaney of the Narcotics Division, Nineteenth Precinct, NYPD.' He held up the sheet of paper. 'We have a warrant to search these premises on suspicion of possession of Class A drugs.'

'What?' she cried. 'But that is preposterous! How dare you! What on earth makes you think—'

'I take it the bedrooms are this way?' the sergeant asked, pointing in the direction from which she had just come.

'Yes, but—'

He nodded his head to the two other police officers, who split off and disappeared into the flanking rooms. 'Excuse me, please,' the sergeant said, moving past her. He looked in at the two guest bedrooms – immaculate, untouched – pausing longer at the scene of chaos in the master suite. He looked back at her, an eyebrow arched as though the very scene confirmed her guilt. 'Going somewhere, Mrs Easton?'

Laney straightened up, determined not to show her fear. 'Is there any reason why I shouldn't?'

He didn't bother to reply – not yet. He wanted the proof he had come for. He merely turned away from her and walked down the rest of the corridor, to where little Stevie's room was located.

'Wait! Why are you going in there?' she called after him, breaking into a run as he disappeared inside. It was almost as though he'd been looking for that room specifically. 'Sergeant!'

He wasn't in the bedroom, but in the en suite. The bathroom light was on and she burst into the room to find the policeman crouched down beside the vanity unit, one arm reaching up into the cabinet. He had headed straight for it.

'You can't do this! This is my son's bathroom!' she cried, feeling hysteria begin to grip her, blanching her skin, pinching her heart. 'How could you possibly think—?'

The words died in her throat as the sergeant retracted his arm and held out a small Elizabeth Arden make-up bag she had mislaid a few weeks earlier. The masking tape hung floppy from where it had detached from the sink unit. She already knew exactly what they would find inside.

They hadn't needed to think, to search: *they knew*. To have produced this warrant this early, to have got here this fast . . . Nothing Steve ever did was accidental. He hadn't slipped up at all. He had known that headline was coming out. He wasn't the one who'd been caught unawares, and it was all going to play out exactly as he'd said it would. Party girl. Addict.

Unfit mother.

Chapter Twenty-One

Rome, July 2017

'Hey, Cesca!' Silvano cried happily as they wandered in. 'Why we no see you for so long?'

'I've been working. Hard,' she grinned, leaning on the counter as his brother, Luciano, tossed the dough behind him. 'Hey, Luciano.'

'Hey, *bella*!' Luciano smiled, throwing the dough with a little more flourish, just for her.

'You are hungry, yes?' Silvano asked, expertly spreading the passata on the dough base stretched out before him.

'Always.'

'Don't tell me, *salsiccia e friarielli*,' he said, already sprinkling fresh fennel, basil and red chilli over sausage slices and broccoli florets.

'You know me too well,' she laughed. She was nothing if not a creature of habit. 'What would you like, Signor Cantarelli?' she asked lightly, glancing over to find him looking displeased by the encounter, his customary frown back on his face.

'*Ciao*, Silvano,' he muttered. '*Margherita con bufala.*'

'*Ciao*. I did not know you two are *friends*,' Silvano said to them with a sly wink, an openly curious expression on his face as he dipped into the tubs of pre-prepared toppings and decorated the pizzas with an artisanal touch. He looked at Cantarelli. 'How did you catch the most beautiful Renaissance woman in Rome?'

'We're not friends,' he said.

'Well, we're not *not* friends . . .' Cesca stammered, embarrassed as she looked from Cantarelli back to Silvano again. 'We're . . . sort of colleagues, I gue—'

'We work in the same building,' Cantarelli said decisively. 'That is all.'

'Okay,' Silvano said, looking sorry he'd asked, using his enormous paddle to hoist the pizzas into the wood-fired oven.

An awkward silence bloomed; Cesca looked away, feeling hurt by his comment. Why had Cantarelli even asked her for lunch if he was only going to be hostile and rude? This was a bad idea. The momentary brightness between them as they'd shared the excitement and awe of the subterranean discovery had quickly dissipated when they'd returned above ground, the sunlight somehow shattering his good mood as he listened to her tell Elena about the tunnels. He had cut in, when Elena had failed to look moved by the find, stressing their potentially immense archaeological significance – but it was clear the Viscontessa simply wanted her garden back. What did she care about underground tunnels when her parterre was in bits? Cesca supposed things hadn't been improved either by some of the men on Cantarelli's team teasing them as they left to get these pizzas, wolf-whistling and making silly sounds to their backs. If they thought there was anything romantic in the lunch offer, they couldn't have been more wrong.

Silvano propped the paddle against the rough wall and

turned back to them, his hands bunched in fists on his waist. 'So, did you go to the match last night?' he asked brightly.

As the two men lapsed into sport talk, Cesca looked back out into the little square. She watched Signora Accardo, opposite in the osteria, taking a carafe and glasses over to a table. Signora Dutti, on her way to Campo de' Fiori to buy her herbs and pasta (if Cesca was predictable when it came to pizza, Signora Dutti was as reliable as the talking clock when it came to her shopping habits), stopped to talk to her over the low jasmine hedge that delineated the osteria's outdoor area, the rattan sun shade beginning to play its part as the midday shadow pulled back over the square like a sheet and the cobbles began to bake in the sun.

The two of them often put their chairs together and sat side by side in the slow hours, when the restaurant was closed and Signora Dutti had completed her chores, their chatter non-stop. Tourists always walked past without seeing them, their eyes fixed on the side end of the grand palazzo or the pretty window boxes of the houses; peering in, too, at the windows of the bakery – before inevitably going in and purchasing several paper bags of bomboloni and cannoli. But Cesca had always noticed the two women; it was people who interested her, not buildings, and she thought it must be lovely to get to live somewhere where friendships were lifelong and an entire community could be confined to a tiny square.

Three minutes later, with the signoras still going strong over the jasmine hedge, their pizzas were done – paper-thin dough perfectly charred on the pastry bubbles, mozzarella oozing.

Silvano refused payment when Cantarelli tried to hand

over the money. 'Is on the 'ouse. Cesca's blog on us makes
our takings up by five times!'

'Oh, I'm so pleased,' Cesca smiled, delighted to hear
there'd been such a positive response. 'You totally deserve
it. It doesn't make financial sense to be *too* well-kept a
secret! *Ciao*, Silvano,' she said, taking her box.

'*Ciao*, Cesca – and tell Matteo he owes me ten euros on
the match last night!'

'Will do,' she grinned, wandering out into the square.
'Shall we sit over here?' she suggested, pointing to her own
steps as Cantarelli joined her. His silence had turned up a
notch. Something appeared to have annoyed him. Again.

Cantarelli shook his head. 'No. They are private.' He
jerked his head towards the shade of the olive tree and the
low wall surrounding it.

'Well, they're my steps so—' Cantarelli looked so surprised, she felt almost sorry for him. 'But we can sit on the
wall if you prefer.'

For a moment, he looked conflicted. 'No. The steps are
fine.'

She led him up the steps past the maze of geraniums and
retrieved the key from under the closest flowerpot.

'That is terrible security,' he said, frowning.

'I know,' she replied, pulling a grimace herself and opening the door. 'But on the other hand, it's not like I've got
anything worth stealing. Half the time, I don't even bother
to close the door, much less lock it. And my landlady lets
anyone in who happens to be passing half the time, so . . .'
She shrugged as she remembered finding Elena sitting there
in the dim light. 'Beer?' she asked, heading straight for the
fridge, enjoying the immediate cool of the dark, shaded
apartment. As ever, she had left the window open but the

shutters closed so that a breeze could enter but not the heat; the curtains lifted a little every now and then.

Cantarelli, standing in the doorway but making no signs to enter, nodded. He looked like a cardboard cutout, perfectly backlit by the sun and curiously hesitant.

'If you want to come in to wash some of the dust off, you're more than welcome,' she said, running the taps and splashing water over her own face and hands. It felt good to clean up after spending time underground; she hadn't realized how dusty she was until she was back in the daylight.

Cantarelli came in and did the same, Cesca watching as his skin turned from grey to brown again. If it weren't for the ever-present frown and dust, she'd think he was actually very good-looking. 'Here,' she said, opening both bottles and handing him a beer. 'Let's eat outside.'

'I did not know you lived here.'

'Well, why would you?' she asked, stepping out into the sun and sitting down with her back against the wall, facing the little square. 'It's not as if I know where you live.' She pulled her long skirt up to expose her legs; they were almost brown (well, by her Celtic standards, anyway), the scabs from her various run-ins with him still on her knees.

'What I mean is, if I had known, I would not have suggested pizza here,' Cantarelli said, joining her on the small patch of concrete. 'There were other places we could have gone. But this was close and—'

'And Franco's are the best in the city,' she smiled, taking a huge bite of pizza and grinning as the cheese fronds refused to break, continuing to stretch even as her arms were straightened completely. 'I refuse to eat any pizza but theirs,' she grinned, her mouth full.

'He said you write a blog?' he asked, watching her with

an expression of bewilderment as she continued to grapple with the cheese as though she were winding yarn on a loom.

'That's right, it's called The Rome Affair,' she said, beginning to laugh at the tangle she was getting herself into.

'The Rome Affair,' he repeated vaguely, still watching her. She supposed Italian girls didn't eat their pizza like this.

'It's about all my favourite things here and the discoveries I make.'

He looked alarmed. 'You cannot talk about what is happening in the palazzo.'

'Well, of course I wouldn't,' she groaned. 'God, what do you take me for?'

He looked at her, his eyes darting over her face as though that was an actual question: what exactly *did* he take her for?

'You live very close to your work,' he said instead, sitting back, his eyes on the palazzo now.

'I do.' Cesca shot him a sidelong look – it was hard to differentiate between accusations and mere statements of fact with him – but he was eating and staring ahead, watching two children running ahead of their mother with the shopping bags. 'Where do you live?' she asked instead.

'Parioli.'

She raised her eyebrows. 'Fancy,' she mumbled, her mouth full.

'Not really. I grew up there. It is just home.'

'How long does it take you to get in?'

'Ten minutes on the scooter.'

She wondered how many other sites he was working on. 'Tell me more about your job. I can't quite get a handle on what exactly it is you do.'

'I could say the same about you. I do not believe you are a writer.'

'Why not?'

He shrugged. 'I don't know. I can't say why. Is just a feeling.'

'Fine. Well, let's just say I'm a writer *for the time being.*' He looked at her sceptically and she wondered why he was so certain he was right that she wasn't a writer – and whether she should be offended that her new guise didn't fit. 'Anyway, I asked first. Do you just deal with sinkholes? Are you a sinkhole bureaucrat?' she teased.

'I am an urban speleologist,' he said, seemingly missing the humour in her question. 'I attend the scene of any sinkholes that open up in the city, but I do not work on them exclusively. Any time ruins are discovered, either through building or repair work, I am called in. My role is to examine and investigate whether there is anything of archaeological significance that is exposed when a sinkhole occurs. Rome, as you know, is built on the ruins of its past.'

'I didn't know that, actually. I'm a Londoner.' In fact, she did know it. Tour guiding meant she knew more than most about her adopted city, but she didn't like him – or anyone – making assumptions about her.

'Well, it is. Did you know, for example, that there is a Greek-style stadium below the Piazza Navona?'

'No!' She really hadn't known that.

'Yes. You can trace the evolution of this city from the ground up – from bedrock to the Republic, to Empire and then the Age of Antiquities. Rome itself was built from the very rock it now stands upon. There are vast quarries beneath huge areas of the city.'

'Actually directly underneath it?' she asked, interrupting him. It didn't sound like a great idea to her.

'Yes. And whilst the first builders knew to cut narrow channels, later ones were not so careful, meaning there are multi-storey buildings out there weighing down on these over-excavated quarries. In effect, Rome is built upon a honeycomb. You know, like the bees?'

She pulled a face. 'That's not a nice thought.'

'No.'

'How many sinkholes do you see a year?'

'About eighty, but that number is rising quickly. And if we find anything of importance down there, then the sink-hole cannot be filled until our explorations are complete.'

'That explains why Elena had a face like thunder when we told her about finding the new tunnels.' Cesca had been surprised by her boss's agitated reaction, which had bordered on a tantrum and ended with her storming off. 'I think she must have been hoping you would present her with a priceless artefact, not a damp tunnel.'

He nodded. 'Her response is not unusual. People want the hole to be fixed and to get on with their lives. They see me as responsible for stopping that from happening. You will see that I shall become more and more unpopular with the Principessa, with every day that passes.'

Cesca watched him as he picked a few crumbs from the dough of his pizza and threw them for some sparrows that were hopping below the railings. The tiny gesture warmed her towards him. She loved those sparrows. 'You must need a thick skin, then.'

He glanced across at her. 'I don't care about other people's opinions of me, if that's what you mean. I have a job to do. You know the new subway planned for the city centre?'

'The one that's cost four billion euros and taken over ten years and it *still* hasn't been built?' she groaned. 'Oh yeah, I've heard about it all right. Every time I go out for dinner I hear about it. Every time they dig, they hit rui—' Cesca gasped. 'Oh God, and *you're* the guy saying no?'

He shrugged. 'It's my job.'

'It must be like being a traffic warden,' she grimaced. 'Everyone hates you.'

Cantarelli didn't reply.

'You know what I mean, though,' she added, a little more gently, hoping he did.

They both took a swig of beer, watching as tourists trickled in from the Piazza Angelica, stumbling upon this little nook of a square whose entrance was partly obscured from view by the unwieldy fig tree.

'So why is the number of sinkholes rising?' she asked, trying to get the conversation back onto firmer ground, so to speak.

'Lots of reasons – flooding from the river, heavy rainfall, seismic shocks, and then of course human actions: leaks from the water pipelines, vibrations from traffic, excavations for networks of gas or electric or phone lines . . . it all means the substance of the structures just comes off like wet plaster. Sometimes, the membrane between the underground and the city is so thin, you can stand down there and hear voices from the streets above.' He arched an eyebrow, his hooded round eyes pinned on her. 'I once heard a couple . . . well, you know,' he finished diplomatically.

'You're kidding,' she mumbled, her mouth full but forgetting to chew. 'And the . . . ?'

'Bed?'

'The bed . . . was right above a cavity?' It was a terrifying thought.

'Basically.' He softened, smiling. 'Don't look so worried. I've been advising on a project for sinkholes in Rome, collecting data so we can identify possible locations of danger and then grade them according to their . . . how you say? Likeness? Likeness to collapse?'

'Likelihood,' she nodded.

'So the authorities have got a complete 3D map of the city now, showing all the upper and lower structures at once. They know where the highest risk areas are.'

'Are there many?'

'Inside the ring road, there is about forty square kilometres of territory that has a very high probability of triggering a sinkhole event.'

Cesca shuddered. 'Well then, if you wouldn't mind giving me a copy of that map . . .'

Cantarelli chuckled before looking over at her, enquiringly. 'Actually, it is a map I have been looking for,' he said after a moment, finishing the pizza and pulling his knees up to his chest, his elbows splayed. 'The *Forma Urbis Romae*?'

'Never heard of it,' she said blankly, pulling on another cheese string.

'It is an ancient marble map from the third century, which covered an entire wall inside the Templum Pacis. It was very big, almost two hundred and fifty square metres, and was carved with the floorplan of every building and architectural feature in the city – it even showed staircases. For this reason it is incredibly important – whatever we can find and identify of the map, we can then verify through underground exploration.'

'Wait. Let me get this straight. You're telling me that you

can trace out the *original* layout of Ancient Rome by going underground?'

'With the guidance of the map, yes.'

'But that's so cool!' Cesca said excitedly. 'And you found a piece at the palazzo?'

'Yes. There are fragments all over the city but it will never be restored in its entirety. Only 10 per cent is thought to remain now.'

'Oh! What happened to the rest?' Cesca frowned, finally finishing her pizza too and sucking her fingertips clean.

'Most of it was destroyed during the Middle Ages. They burnt marble to make building materials like chalk and lime, and what little did survive was recycled by the Renaissance builders – they would turn it over and paint the other side for wallcoverings.'

Cesca looked at him. 'So you're saying it could be lining the interiors of palaces across the city?'

'It could be, but we shall never know. Just occasionally we get lucky and a shard is found. Trying to trace it is a particular passion of mine.'

'And you think there's more in the palazzo?' she asked, her eyes sliding back to the forbidding shuttered blue facade opposite. She'd been right about that place – it kept secrets. But who said they were bad ones?

'I hope so. There is a good chance, I think. The age of the building is right.' His eyes were on the palazzo too.

'And Elena knows about the tile and the map?' She remembered Elena's caustic comment as Cesca had stood at the top of the ladder.

'Yes, I have informed her, but she has asked me to keep the information confidential. Everything I have told you today is privileged.'

'Of course. But what if you find some more? Can you seize it, or is it her property?'

'In the case of the sinkhole, where I found the tile, it becomes the property of the state. But if more were to be found inside the palazzo structures, it would come down to the Principessa's generosity.'

'I'm sure she would be generous. She can afford to be.'

'We will see. People are less enthusiastic about historic conservation when it involves having their homes turned upside down.'

'Or back to front,' she quipped.

He looked at her. 'Exactly. On the plus side, we now have the new tunnels to map, which will buy me the time I need to make further explorations on the *Forma Urbis Romae*.'

'It sounds like you're going to be busy for the foreseeable,' she said, thinking how exciting it was that all this should be happening beneath the very building in which she was working. She wondered if he would let her go down to the tunnels again. She wondered if they would do *this* again.

As if reading her mind, he checked his watch suddenly. 'Yes. In fact, I should get back.'

'Oh! Really?' To her surprise, Cesca realized she was disappointed. This lunch had been . . . interesting. He had a refreshingly different perspective on the world. As a barrister – *former* barrister, she reminded herself – she was trained to see things from two sides, but she had never met someone for whom the present could be explained so thoroughly by the past, where what was visible was less important, less treasured, than what was hidden.

The same could be said of him, she supposed. Beneath the brusque exterior, deep, *deep* down he did have something of a gentle side – feeding the sparrows, hunting for treasure maps, the light in his eyes as he showed her the tunnels . . .

He rose, looking down at her. She went to stand too, but he shook his head. 'Enjoy the sun and the rest of your lunch break.'

Cesca's mouth parted, suddenly unsure of what to say. 'Well, thanks for the pizza.'

He nodded. 'It was the least I could do. You save my life? I take you for pizza.'

It was a second before she laughed, unaccustomed to this dry humour of his. She supposed it was an acknowledgement of sorts.

'—And thanks for the chat,' she called after him as he was halfway down the steps. He raised his hand in reply.

'And the tour!' she called again as he walked across the square, his shorts still dusty, a sweat patch down the back of his t-shirt, his hobnailed boots incongruous compared to everyone else's flip-flops.

He didn't look back and she didn't know what else to say, to thank him for. She was out of reasons to keep him here, out of excuses to make him stay. And in the next moment, anyway, he was out of sight.

Chapter Twenty-Two

Ischia, August 1980

The pretty white-walled, red-roofed town of Casamicciola bobbed outside the portholes of her suite, the turquoise water sparkling in the midday sun. Laney brushed her hair back from her face. It was still wet from her swim but she preferred not to blow-dry it in the heat; she wore no make-up either. Two reasons why she loved summer so much: a private rebellion against the glossy armour that was expected in her everyday life, a below-the-radar, two-fingered salute to the Park Avenue brigade.

She tossed the hairbrush onto the quilted bedspread and tugged, straightened and smoothed her strappy navy terry shortsuit down her body, admiring her recent weight loss – four pounds in three days – from the grapefruit diet everyone was on now. It wasn't for the undisciplined; very often she felt light-headed and weak, forgetful of what she was saying mid-sentence, and she frequently needed to nap. But it was still worth it to feel extra slender in her bikinis beside the famously lissom limbs of her hostess, Allegra Santi.

Chin held high, her square Chloé sunglasses on, she left her cabin and climbed the mahogany steps to the deck of their beautiful cream schooner, the *Serena*. The seating area was in shade now that the awnings had been rolled out, platters of cut fruit set out on the tables, as colourful as floral displays; everyone was already showered and changed and lounging on the padded benches, talking loudly and sipping on margaritas. At thirteen, they were a rather large crowd. Most she already knew, in varying degrees, from her various annual jaunts – the Mongiardinos from skiing in St Moritz, the Packfords from sitting on a charity committee in Palm Beach, Yves Saint Laurent and his muse, Loulou de la Falaise, from Paris, of course. The two couples she hadn't previously known she was perfectly able to tolerate for this eight-day cruise.

'Laney!' Adolfo Santi greeted her with his usual admiring visual sweep, placing a chilled glass in her hand and indicating for her to take the empty space beside him. 'I was wondering where you were. Look at you – ravishing as always. You are like a water nymph. Your hair is always wet.'

'I'm a Cancer birth sign, darling. This is my element. Besides—' She swept out her hand, indicating the green, ice-clear waters surrounding them. 'How could anyone resist this? It's heavenly.'

'Well, I am glad you have come to visit at last and experience it for yourself. You perhaps thought I was making it up.' He raised a dark eyebrow. She had turned down their invitations countless times, brushing them off with excuses of jaunts to Marrakech and Kenya instead.

Laney smiled, knowing exactly why she had repeatedly said no. Adolfo's intentions towards her were perfectly clear – one indiscretion years earlier had left him wanting more – but she had simplified her life since losing her son, as though an ascetic life could strip back the pain as well as the fripperies. It didn't seem to be working, but she was all out of other ideas. Steve had fought dirty and won, the judge's summation a character assassination of her that was now intractable and faithfully reproduced in any article, interview or even photograph that featured her. She had become hunted, forced on the run from all those strangers who recognized her without knowing her, who judged her without understanding anything of her life.

But then, they never had. She was simply an image, no more than an idea. They neither knew nor cared that her heart was frozen, that the world had become perverse in its punishments – she was always lonely in a crowd, cold in the sun, alert in her sleep, nauseous in her starvation. Losing Stevie the first time had been like being stripped of her skin, her nervous system exposed to the elements and flayed with every touch, look or sound. But losing him the second time had left her as numb and unfeeling as if it had been pulled out of her altogether, like the bones of a fish, complete and picked clean.

Was that why she was here now? To feel something? 'I would never doubt your judgement, Dolfy. You are a man of exceptional taste.'

'I hope you will come back many times. The *Serena* is at your disposal whenever you might need it. Just say the word.' His eyes locked on hers.

'You're too sweet, darling.'

'Have you swum to the octopus cove yet?'

She shook her head, sipping on the cold drink.

'Then this afternoon, I insist. We shall take the speedboat round. I'll get Carlo to prepare the tanks.'

She looked at him. We? Was it to be just the two of them then?

He clicked his fingers for more drinks to be brought over, but Laney firmly held on to hers. 'I shall have to be a good girl and have only one of these if we're going to be diving,' she said.

'There's lunch to get through first. You'll be fine. Don't worry, I'll look after you. I am very experienced.'

Laney looked away, feeling the first rush of tequila hit her; she felt weak and yearned for lunch to be brought out – more fish, pasta . . . something to bolster her even though it would be as cardboard in her mouth; she sometimes thought she might one day float away like an untethered balloon, so unconnected was she to this life.

The distant note of a boat crossing the bay rose to her ear. Theirs was the only yacht moored in the deeper waters, although further in smaller vessels dotted the sea like landed clouds. She watched as it sped into focus, a small ensign on the back fluttering wildly in the breeze. Everyone seemed excited about the imminent arrival, for there was no doubt the boat was heading straight towards them.

'Fresh meat for lunch?' Laney asked with her usual wry drawl, an eyebrow arched as she watched the others begin to clamour towards the steps.

Adolfo lit a cigarette, one tanned bare foot resting against the table, close to hers. 'An old family friend. Gianvito Damiani.' Adolfo shrugged. '*Prince* Gianvito Damiani, actually.'

'Should I curtsey?'

'No. But he'd like it if you did. He's a stickler for protocol, a Roman.'

'I see.' Laney's eyes narrowed as she waited for a first glimpse of this guest already causing such a stir among their crowd. 'Shall I like him?'

'To look at, perhaps. He's handsome, but dull. Too dull for you, Laney darling.'

'Oh, what a shame,' she sighed, pretending to give a damn. 'And I suppose you invited him to round up the numbers? I know I'm terribly inconvenient to have around without a plus-one. I must be throwing out Allegra's table plans awfully.'

'You know I would never stand between my wife and the perfect table plan,' he grinned. 'But I much prefer you that way.'

'Single and alone?'

He looked at her wolfishly, one hand discreetly squeezing her upper thigh. 'Single, but not alone, darling.'

She blinked, more than used to this game. Plenty of men wanted her as their mistress.

They watched as the boat – having cleaved a straight line through the water from shore – cut a wide sweeping arc suddenly, sending a plume of water high behind it and seemingly gliding on its side, perfectly balanced.

'Wow!' she heard Sylvia Ginsberger exclaim; it was her first time on a yacht, so she said 'wow' a lot. Sylvia's husband Tony was something big in commodities, although they both hailed from small-town Minnesota – childhood sweethearts. Not that *that* slowed down Tony on the Manhattan club circuit, according to Allegra; she'd been very forthcoming with the salacious gossip when they'd been having their massages together earlier.

The driver cut the throttle and a moment later the tender moored alongside the *Serena*, pulling out of sight from where Laney was sitting. She didn't crane her neck to see him; everyone else was doing more than enough gawping for her.

'Shouldn't you go to greet your guest?' she prompted

Adolfo, taking his cigarette from his fingers and dragging on it herself, feeling his eyes on her profile – the suck of her cheeks, the swell of her lips . . .

'I'll come back.'

She knew he would. He was going to keep coming back until she gave in. But would she? It was the easiest option, certainly.

She took another drag, and another, sinking into her own silence, receding from the clamour at the steps. The tobacco hits merged with the margarita already swirling in her bloodstream, the lack of food only making her more light-headed, so that it was several moments before she opened her eyes and saw Prince Gianvito Damiani standing there, staring down at her.

He was indeed handsome in a navy polo shirt and white shorts: strong-jawed with hooded, elongated brown eyes, a large, nobly broken nose and a wide mouth. He looked more Greek to her eye than Roman and she felt instantly, powerfully attracted to him.

'Hello,' she said simply, feeling herself wake up at last as she threw one arm lazily along the back of the banquette and looked up at him with interested eyes. 'I'm Laney.'

Water broke around the prow as the small boat chugged into the bay, smooth rocks sitting far below the surface like dimpled glass. Silver fish darted past her dangling feet as she motioned for Adolfo to continue onwards.

'Okay,' she hailed, a few minutes later, as the water's colour brightened above sand. The anchor splashed in and the chain was released, unspooling noisily.

Tucking in her legs, she stood up and walked – arms out-stretched – to the back of the boat, to where Adolfo and

Allegra, Gianvito and the Ginsbergers were sitting. They were quite a crowd now thanks to Laney's enthusiastic invitation to the others to join them and Adolfo was sporting a dark expression, his plans for a quiet seduction on hold.

The Ginsbergers didn't dive so, in the interests of sociability, it had been agreed they would all snorkel instead. Laney wriggled out of her playsuit to reveal her now even leaner frame – the sudden excitement of Gianvito's arrival had meant she'd lost her hitherto ravenous appetite for lunch – and pulled on her mask and snorkel.

She was the first in, executing a near-splashless dive and emerging a moment later with a beaming smile. 'Come in everyone, the water's lovely!'

Adolfo, Allegra and Tony dived in without hesitation, Sylvia preferring to lower herself slowly off the steps, where she bobbed in the water like a buoyancy aid as she tried to prevent her hair from getting wet.

'Prince?' Laney asked, treading water and looking back up at the boat, waiting for him. 'Are you coming?'

'Please, call me Gianvito.' His accent was gentle, hammered out by three years at Oxford and several in London. They had sat too far apart at lunch – Adolfo's table plan getting in the way this time, she suspected – to be able to pass more than pleasantries, but she had made a point of calling him by his title every time she addressed him, for she could see that it embarrassed him. Several times now, he had asked her to call him 'just Gianvito'.

'But I don't like calling you Gianvito,' she said provocatively.

'Why not?'

'It's too . . . unwieldy.'

He stared down at her, seemingly unaware of how striking he looked in his white swimming shorts, his body finely muscled and tanned, his chest covered in a thick rug of hair. 'Then call me Vito.'

She considered the idea. 'Who else calls you Vito?'

'Those closest to me.'

'Are we going to be close then?' she asked.

He stared at her and she could see he was wrong-footed by her American directness, her impudence concerning his rank. He seemed at a loss as to how to deal with her, his formal manners sliding off her as water on the proverbial duck.

He dived in, a perfect fluid motion that matched hers for precision, and surfaced half a metre away from her. Laney felt her heart quicken at his sudden proximity, excited by the athletic prowess which belied that polite reserve. Their eyes locked for a few seconds, faces dripping wet, bodies hidden yet close—

'We should swim,' he said.

Laney watched him go, his arms like circular saws as he swam a front crawl that ate up the distance between them and the others. She felt frustrated, as confused by him as he was by her. He felt the attraction between them too, she was certain, but he wasn't like the other men she knew. Her wealth didn't give her rank above his title and it was clear he was a product of upbringing rather than ambition.

They swam for most of the afternoon, the sun on their backs as they stared down through their masks at the underwater world. As Adolfo had promised, there were plenty of octopuses, as well as a swordfish, eel and several starfish.

Vito kept close but never too close, talking with Sylvia and Allegra, his eyes darting back to her whenever the group was distracted by something – which was a lot; Adolfo was showing off, free-diving ten, twelve metres to point out a tiny electric-blue fish or to pick up a shell for one of the ladies.

Laney held her fire; she could sense both men circling her, each aware of the other's as-yet-unmade threat. When the group finally swam in to the beach, she made a point of lying alone in the shallows, waiting to see which would linger with her – to her disappointment Adolfo won that battle, pretending to collect dollar shells for her, but Allegra soon called him over again.

Laney walked by herself along the sand, heading towards the shadow of the domed cliffs. Cypress and olive trees dotted the landscape, not a building in sight of the little bay – another reason why Adolfo had tried to bring her here, no doubt.

She stepped into the shade of the cliff and sank onto the sand, feeling weary and too hot. The skin on her back felt tight. Their little boat (and on it, the water bottles) was bobbing on the sea farther out than she had realized. She shouldn't have had so many margaritas at lunch; she should have stayed back for a sleep in her cabin. It had been a long day, an even longer year. A bee buzzed her and she lazily swatted it away. What was she doing anyway, toying with this man . . . ?

The buzzing suddenly clamoured, loud and insistent. *What?*

She turned, then jumped to her feet, frowning at what looked like a cloud of sand flies coming from a small cave in the cliff. Only . . . they were too large to be flies. Far too large.

One stung her. 'Ow!' She jumped and rubbed her arm,

beginning to walk backwards, just as she was stung again, this time on her shoulder.

She screamed. 'Oh my God!'

She began running, but was stung again on her thigh, the dark swarm now following her down the beach. From the corner of her eye, she could see the others looking over.

'Bees!' she screamed as loudly as she could. 'Bees! Get in the water!'

Her words carried, for they all began running for the sea too, Tony Ginsberger grabbing his little wife's hand and pulling her along behind him, Adolfo and Allegra long-leggedly leading the charge. Only Vito ran towards her.

The bees were swarming her now and stopping her from running, a black cloud stinging her over and over so that she couldn't move, couldn't see where to go. He reached her in seconds, grabbing her arm as she swatted wildly at the attacking mob and yanking her hard, so that her feet moved whether she could see or not.

Seven steps and she felt the water on her feet, Vito pulling her along so fast she could barely keep up, then his hands on her waist as he lifted and threw her into the deeper water.

She sank, ridded of the swarm instantaneously, the water cool and soothing as it wrapped around her. She blew out a little stream of bubbles and opened her eyes, looking up through the surface of the water just as Vito crashed in as if he was diving through a glass mirror. She saw him twist and turn, several livid red stings already visible on his chest and arms as he rid himself of their assailants.

When the water had settled, she could see that the sky above was now clear. Running out of breath, she burst upwards, gasping for air. A second later, Vito did the same.

'Are you okay? Let me see,' he demanded, unceremoniously taking her by the arms and inspecting her for stings.

'Th-thank you,' she stammered, her teeth chattering, even though she was so hot.

He looked at her, like a father to a child. 'We need to get you back.'

Adolfo and the others – already on the boat and hauling up the anchor – turned on the engine and brought the boat round to them. Adolfo, in heroic mode now, reached over the side and, grabbing her by the arms, lifted her clear of the water. She flopped onto the small deck like a landed salmon, everyone fussing over her, Sylvia saying 'wow' every time they discovered another sting.

Vito climbed aboard without a word and Adolfo hit the throttle, the little boat cutting through the water, their wet hair slapping their skin, faces turned into the wind as they headed back to the safety of the *Serena*.

She stared at the tiny town of Casamicciola through the round portholes, her pillow wet, ears tuned in loneliness to the sound of everyone padding on deck above her head.

She wanted to sleep but she couldn't drop off: her nervous system felt rewired, back on after all this time, her body still tingling from the 114 stings she had suffered. Everyone had been very sweet, of course. Adolfo had dispatched the tender to fetch the nearest doctor on the island, who had come to the boat and examined her, pulling out the many splinter-sized barbs still left in her skin, before administering painkillers, a powerful dose of antihistamines and a topical anaesthetic cream, and then ordering her to rest.

She closed her eyes, feeling sore, feeling humiliated. She

wanted to go home – only, she had no idea where that might be. Not Graystones – she hadn't been back there in over nineteen years – not Newport or Malibu or New York. Since losing Stevie, she had lived in a succession of hotels, moving from one city, one country, to the next, meeting up with acquaintances in a dizzying whirl of parties and balls and discos where she could hide behind a pretty dress and a martini.

The knock on the door was so soft, she didn't hear it at first – but he came in anyway. The mattress sank beneath his weight as he sat beside her, looking down with that clear gaze of his.

She went to move, to sit up, but he put a hand on her shoulder and shook his head. 'I have come to say goodbye.'

Laney stared at him, dressed in his navy top and white shorts, wondering why those words should hurt so much. 'Hello and goodbye in one day,' she said, her voice quiet. 'Funny, I thought we'd have longer.'

He looked at her, as though there was something he wished to say, then down at his own hands. Her gaze followed his, as if she could find answers there. She saw his hands were marked with stings too.

She sat up, taking his hands in hers and examining them. On the fleshy side of one, she could see the barb still caught in the skin.

'Did the doctor see you too?' she asked, frowning, inspecting his stings even more closely.

'It is fine.'

'No, it's not. Look, the stinger's still in there. You have to get it out.'

He looked at his own hand curiously but, before he could

stop her, Laney brought his hand to her mouth and sucked on it. The taste of his skin was salty, slightly tangy.

'There. See?' she asked, taking the barb from her tongue and showing it to him. But he wasn't interested in the barb. He was staring at her with an expression of open, unadulterated longing. She felt the breath leave her body – no man had ever looked at her like that before – as in the next instant he swept her into him and kissed her.

What he wouldn't – or couldn't – say out loud, was said in the kiss instead. When they finally pulled apart, she knew the world had changed again.

'Come home with me,' he said.

She smiled. *Home*. With Vito. 'Yes.'

Chapter Twenty-Three

Rome, July 2017

For the rest of the week, Cesca ate lunch on the steps outside her apartment, tanning her legs and feeding the sparrows. For the rest of the week, she worked late, hunched over the open boxes and sorting through the thousands of photographs she found in each one, transcribing interviews and beginning a timeline of the major events of Elena's life, which would serve to help with the chapters and the flow of the book, looking up through the windows whenever she heard a shout outside. But, for the rest of the week, she didn't see him.

She knew he was still working there – Elena's increasingly irritable mood as the hole in the courtyard became ever more established, with props and ladders and a winch with scanning equipment, told her as much – and she hated, no, deplored, how crushed she felt by the disappointment that he hadn't sought her out again after their lunch. Clearly, that spark she'd thought she had detected between them, albeit intermittent, had only been there for her. She felt stupid and idiotic and she couldn't understand why it bothered her so much, when most of the time she didn't even like the guy.

'You sound grumpy,' Alé said, her voice echoing on the

loudspeaker of her phone as Cesca sat cross-legged on the floor in the Victorian bloomers she liked to wear as shorts. The acoustics in the gallery were fantastic.

'I'm not grumpy,' she denied. 'I'm just . . . tired.'

'Oh, poor baby. Life in the palace too tiring?' Alé teased. 'You should spend a day in the classroom with my fourteen-year-old literature students, see how you like it then.'

'You're right. You're a saint and I'm a loser.'

There was a pause. 'Okay, that's it – we're going out.'

'I can't go out. I'm still working.'

'You know the rule – first sign of sarcasm? Tequila.'

'Alé—'

'Don't argue. It's Friday night, anyway. What the hell else did you think we were going to do? I'll be at the bar in twenty minutes.'

She hung up.

Cesca looked back out into the empty garden: the hard hats were all lined up on the grass like a row of plastic ducks. Everyone was gone for the weekend; only Elena's light shone from her apartment on the top floor, and she really didn't fancy getting into yet another discussion about her fabulous life at this time of night. Alé was right. What was she even doing here, hoping to see a guy who clearly couldn't care less about seeing her, for whom pizza had merely been thanks for a life saved, who enraged her as much as he intrigued her, whom she only knew by his last name? It was a Friday night in Rome and she was a tired, sarcastic twenty-seven-year-old. What the hell else was she going to do?

Blue light spilled out onto the streets, hot bodies cooling in the night breeze. Alé had got them a table at the back by the toilets – far from ideal, but it meant they could sit. The boys were possibly going to join them later, although the girls both knew that depended on whether they got lucky at the place they were at now.

They'd been there an hour and were on their fourth shots when Alé cut to the chase.

'There's something I have to tell you,' she said, leaning forward earnestly, her pupils beginning to dilate as the liquor danced in her bloodstream. Her wild hair was caught up in her usual messy bun, a turquoise bra strap on full show beneath her white vest, the pockets peeking through the bottom of her super-short cutoffs. Cesca was certain she must be the sexiest teacher any of her pupils had ever seen. She certainly made a decided contrast to Cesca, with her floppy plait and panama, white cotton bloomer shorts and Edwardian camisole.

'Fire away,' Cesca said, raising her shot glass and downing it, finishing with a hiccup for garnish.

Alé's mouth opened for a long time before she could say the words. '. . . I'm having an affair.'

Cesca's mouth dropped open – but not with shock at the revelation. Did Alé really think she didn't already know about it?

'Nooooo. That's not the bad bit,' Alé slurred, cutting her off before she could say a word. '. . . It's with my headmaster.'

'Oh God, Alé, *why*?' Cesca wailed, slapping her forehead with her hand and realizing at some level that her own reaction was also a very drunk one.

'Because I wanted to try an older guy. You know, to see if it's true what they say about . . .' She arched an eyebrow.

'No, I meant why *him*?'

Alé shrugged. 'Because he was there?'

Cesca curled her lip in response. 'How old is he?'

'Fifty-four.'

'Eww!' Cesca cried, half-laughing too as Alé grabbed her hand and squeezed it, collapsing into giggles. '. . . And is it true?'

'Yes!'

They both laughed wildly again, throwing their heads back. 'Well, I guess that's something!' She shook her head, looking across at her wild and free friend as she refilled their glasses with the bottle, tequila splashing over the side.

'I really love you, Alé,' she gushed, slurring her words too. 'You've been such a good friend to me this past year.'

'Aw, I love you too, baby,' Alé cooed. 'I don't know how I ever partied without you. We're a master team.'

'No, no, but it's not just that.' Cesca managed to smack the table emphatically, trying to focus. 'I so admire you, Alé. I wish I could be more like you.'

'*Why?*'

'Because you're free. You're completely true to who you are. You know what you want and you go get it. Me, I can't cross the room without changing my mind.'

'That is not true.'

'It is. It is,' she said, shaking her head. 'I can't even hold an opinion long enough to hold a grudge.'

'Well, why would you want to do that?'

Cesca's shoulders sagged. Why indeed?

The thumping bass made the floor vibrate and she looked down at it worriedly. 'Did you know that, right now, there could be just a few inches of earth between us sitting here and an ancient quarry? And that every single one of these drumbeats could be dislodging it, bit by bit, until . . .

whoosh!' She blew out through her cheeks and threw her arms up in the air.

Alé looked at her, aghast. 'No!'

'Yes!' Cesca said, shaking her head like an anxious sage. 'We could be seconds from disaster.'

'Not here,' a voice said, interrupting. 'It's only a category *one* risk here.'

Cesca looked up, finding herself almost nose to nose with a man bending down at their table.

'Cantarelli!' Cesca exclaimed, almost falling backwards off her chair. 'What are you . . . *you* doing here?' It seemed incongruous in the extreme to see him relaxing in a bar.

'Having a drink with friends,' he said, jerking his head in the direction of a group of guys by the bar, but his eyes were steady upon her, assessing her level of drunkenness and probably grading her as a category four.

'You have friends?'

'That's rude.' But he grinned. He actually *grinned*. Clearly, this was off-duty Cantarelli. 'Yes, I have friends.'

'You're . . .' She wanted to say various things. Handsome. Sexy. Interesting. Bad-tempered. Forgetful. Bossy. 'Not dusty,' she managed.

He cracked another smile, clearly amused by her altered state. 'No. I showered.'

'Oh.' She tried not to think about that too. She couldn't trust her face right now.

He looked over apologetically at Alé. 'Sorry, I didn't mean to interrupt,' he said in Italian.

'No, by all means, continue. This is fascinating. I'm Alessandra. Call me Alé.'

'Hi Alé. Nico.'

'Take a seat. Join us.'

231

'Well, just for a minute. Thanks.'

'Nico?' Cesca echoed, just about keeping up. 'Now, I didn't know *that*.'

He looked at Cesca again, then arched an eyebrow at Alé. 'Been here long?'

'Not long enough. Cesca was just about to tell me why she can't hold a grudge.'

'Huh?' Cesca hiccupped.

'Sounds interesting. Who have you got a grudge against?' he asked, looking back at her again.

She wished he wouldn't. It made it too hard to concentrate. 'No one.'

He pinned her with another one of those stares. 'I don't believe you.'

'It's just a p-person—'

'Oh yeah?' Nico grinned, more amused by the minute.

'—Who's really . . . *annoying*.' She finished with a hiccup.

'Why are they annoying?' Alé asked, leaning in closer and looking deeply sympathetic.

'Because he is mean to me. And then he's nice.' Her voice rose up on the last word, highlighting her bafflement. 'I mean, if I want to hate him, then he should just let me hate him. He can't just suddenly be all nice and sexy. He must stay hateful. For all of the time.'

'So this annoying person's a he then,' Nico said, watching her.

'They usually are,' Alé nodded earnestly. 'And if they're annoying, then they're out: that's my rule. That's what I've told my guy. I don't want any of this "falling in love with me" crap.'

'Alé's having an affair. With an older man,' Cesca said dramatically.

'Good for you,' Nico said diplomatically. 'How much older?'

'Twenty-five years.'

'Ah.'

'I wanted to see if it was true about—'

'Yeah, right, got it,' he said quickly.

'How old are *you*?' Alé asked after a pause.

'Thirty-six.'

Alé's eyes widened. '*He's* an older man,' she said to Cesca, as though Nico wasn't actually still sitting there.

'Alé!' Cesca spluttered.

'You forget that Cesca's got her annoying grudge man to deal with first,' Nico said.

'Ah yes.' Alé pouted. 'Shame. You're hot.'

He grinned. 'Thanks.' He noticed Cesca staring at him. 'What?'

She frowned, studying him intensely. 'Have I ever seen you . . . without a hard hat?'

He laughed again. 'Yes, you have. Lunch, remember?'

But Cesca didn't remember. She couldn't think straight right now. 'No, I don't think I have. I think I thought it was surgically attached to his head,' she said in wonderment to Alé.

'He looks good without it. Good hair,' Alé said, reaching up and ruffling it, before leaning back to get a better look at him. 'Good everything.'

'You look good without the hat,' Cesca said to him.

'Thank you. So do you. You have beautiful hair.'

Cesca's mouth parted. She frowned as she did remember something. 'You said I have *bright* hair.'

'It is bright. Bright and beautiful.'

'You are *very* annoying,' she sighed, resting her cheek in her hand and feeling incredibly weary.

Nico blinked at her.

'Cesca used to hide her beautiful bright hair under a wig all day. Can you believe that?' Alé asked him.

'A wig?'

'She was a barrister.'

Nico looked back at Cesca but her eyes were closed. 'Then what are you doing talking fairy tales with that foolish woman all day?' He sounded cross, he sounded like Guido. He was back to on-duty Cantarelli again. 'Why would you give something like that up?'

She didn't reply except to open her eyes reluctantly, squinting against the too-bright lights of the bar. Was that one glass in front of her? Or two?

'Because I did,' she shrugged, feeling so sleepy now.

'But why?' he asked, tapping her arm, as though to get her attention, as though to keep her awake. 'Cesca? Are you mad? Why would you do that?'

'Well, you would too if you'd killed someone,' she mumbled.

His hand fell away, his heat off her skin. '*What?*' he whispered. 'You . . . ?'

Somewhere in her mind, Cesca knew a terrible thing had just happened but she couldn't quite reach it. She felt very far away. Oblivion was claiming her.

There was a long silence. Even Alé wasn't talking.

'Come on. We need to get her to bed,' Nico said.

'I'll take her,' Alé said, swaying slightly as she tried to get up.

'No. You need to go home too.'

'What's going on here? Alé? Cesca?'

Faintly, Cesca could hear Matteo's voice.

'They're drunk. They need to get home.' It was Nico.

There was a pause. 'That's fine,' she heard Matteo say. 'We can handle it from here.'

'I'll call a cab,' Guido said, slightly further away.

'I'm happy to take Cesca back. I know where she lives,' Nico said.

'Yeah?' Matteo sounded prickly, Cesca thought. 'Well, thanks for your help but we've got this.'

'Okay. Whatever. Just trying to help.'

Cesca felt arms around her, lifting her to her feet. She opened her eyes. Matteo had his arm around her waist, her arm slung over his shoulder. 'You okay, Cesca? We're going to take you home now.'

'Matty?'

'Yeah. Looks like you started the party without us.'

He began to walk her out. 'Where's . . . where's Nico?'

'I'm here.'

She saw him standing just off to the side, his hands jammed in his pockets, that angry look in his eyes again.

She pointed at him. 'You . . .' She faltered, trying to think of the words. 'You are a very annoying man.'

He nodded. 'So you said.'

'Did I?' She pouted, unable to remember, unable to think as he followed her with his eyes until Matteo led her out of sight.

Chapter Twenty-Four

Rome, August 1980

Even by her standards, the palazzo was magnificent. Fronting onto one end of the majestic Piazza Angelica in a charming wash of baby-blue plaster dotted with ivory shutters, it was a country house in the city, a fortress amidst the cafes: somewhere she could be safe. Her father would have approved, though he would never know of it now. His death – eighteen months earlier – still stunned her. Was he really gone? Could it really be true?

For the first week, as Vito attended to business, she had walked the full length of the building with the housekeeper, Maria, trying to remember the names of each of the near-1,000 rooms: the Papal Suite, the Whispering Gallery (with walls clad entirely in onyx), the Mirrored Gallery . . . Their unapologetic baroque richness was a culture shock to her clean-cut preppy sensibilities; the fact that they remained today exactly as they had been 600 years earlier was a concept difficult to comprehend for the woman who was used to waking up every week in a different hotel and refurbishing her homes on a bi-annual basis.

Vito's private apartment was a mere ten-room suite on the top floor of the east wing. He needed no more space than that, he said. Laney loved his modesty – they both came from excess but she felt inspired by this man who wanted no more than just enough. Apart from some black-and-white photos of his parents and himself, and the white monogrammed linen envelope which held his folded pyjamas on the corner of the bed, the only evidence that the apartment was private to the rest of the palazzo was that his furniture was brown and not gilded. Standing behind the metre-thick stone walls, watching the colour and clamour of the markets outside the windows on one side of the room, and then revelling in the bucolic peace of the garden on the other, she knew she had found the refuge she had been seeking.

The garden was five acres of symmetrical perfection, beginning with a formal parterre and orange and lemon tree courtyard nestled within the colonnaded wings of the building, before opening out into terraced lawns with conical clipped box trees and mirrored ponds. Every time she looked down upon it – as she did whenever Vito was in a meeting or on the phone – she could just see herself drifting through it with a basket of cut flowers on one arm; she could see the parties they would have – just like her parents' ones at Graystones; she could see their children running through the maze . . . A new life was unfolding, she could feel it. After so many false starts and losses and tears and frog princes, the real thing had arrived and from now on, her life would be here. She would be Vito's wife, the Principessa Elena dei Damiani Pignatelli della Mirandola (Elena was so much more elegant, Vito had reasoned).

For the first time, she felt she was what she'd been told all her life: *lucky*.

September 1980

'She is my oldest friend. I promise you, you will adore her. She has a wild spirit like you. When we were children, we would run like wolves through the halls and play football in the ballroom.' He tapped her nose with his index finger. 'One time, when Maria Callas came to stay, she even sneaked into her bedroom and put a frog into her water glass beside the bed.'

Laney smiled, looping her arms around his waist. 'Well then, I like her already.'

'You will be firmest friends, you'll see. You will be so busy talking and making plans, you will have no more time for me.'

She tightened her grip around him, resting her chin on his dinner shirt and looking up at him; she knew she would never tire of looking at that handsome face. 'Never.'

'I've told her all about you; she can't wait to meet you.'

'Tell me her husband's name again.'

He smiled. 'I have told you five times already. Sigmundo. He is the Count of Carbonana.'

'I just like to hear you say it. Sigmundo, Count of Carbonana,' Laney echoed in her best Italian accent. She had been having lessons for the past month but her voice kept going down on the stresses when it should go up and she could never remember how to pronounce 'cc' and 'ch'.

'He works as a commercial attaché to the US Embassy here but it looks likely he'll be made Ambassador to Madrid.'

'Does he know about his wife's wild past?' she teased with mock horror, pulling away and seeing a smudge of her foundation left on his shirt. 'Oh dammit. Let me see if I can—'

'No. Maria will deal with it.' He rang the bell that connected to the staff quarters, and unbuttoned his shirt while he waited, reaching for a fresh one on the hanger; Maria appeared at their elbows not a minute later.

'Would you attend to this, please, Maria?' Vito asked her, holding out the shirt.

Laney crossed the room and put in the drop emerald Bulgari earrings that he had given her as an engagement gift. She went to put on the necklace too – a magnificent emerald, ruby and diamond sautoir with a suspended hexagonal emerald of almost 45 carats. 'Darling, would you?' she asked, lifting her hair off her neck in readiness.

'No, not the necklace,' Vito said, looking up from tying the laces of his dinner shoes; they were so brightly polished, she had seen foggier mirrors.

'But I chose this dress specifically. The neckline—'

'It is too much, Elena. The cuff is more discreet. You don't want to come across as ostentatious, do you?'

'No, of course not.' Laney looked back down at the emerald suite, nestled in its black velvet case. Unlike the low-key gold mesh Tiffany chains made by her friend Elsa Peretti, which she had been wearing all summer, the Bulgari jewels couldn't fail to be ostentatious, no matter how few of them were worn at once. She felt confused by this new etiquette, where more was somehow passed off as less.

Vito rose from the bed and lifted the exquisite diamond-and-emerald cuff from the case, fastening it for her. 'There,' he said, kissing the inside of her wrist and looking down at her proudly. 'They will love you, my little bird, as I do.'

*

239

Christina was everything she was not. Tall and dark-skinned, she wore her hair short and swept back, emphasizing a long neck and the kind of bone structure that had been generations in the making. Beside her, Elena felt scrawny, not delicate, and wished she had spent more time on her tan.

They had one thing in common, though: they both adored Vito, and that was bigger than any differences between them.

'I just *love* your earrings,' Elena said as they were introduced, Christina greeting her with the type of dazzling smile that belonged on a Bond Girl.

'Elena, my goodness, you are *ravishing*,' Christina gushed, holding her in outstretched arms so as to get a better look. 'When Vito told me he had fallen in love with this exquisite American, I could hardly believe it. My dear, precious friend, finding love at last? I had begun to fear it would never happen,' she smiled. 'I have been quite anxious to meet you.'

'And I you. He's told me so much about you, I feel we are friends already.'

'Wasn't it sweet of him to throw this little party in your honour?' Christina asked, gesturing to the grand Gallery of Mirrors in which they were standing and in which Elena was painfully aware of one hundred sets of eyes upon her, groups hovering in satellites around them, waiting for their moment with her.

'It is our engagement party,' Vito clarified. 'Besides, I wanted to show her off,' he said, quietly but proudly, his fingers brushing hers as they stood side by side. It was the closest he would come to any public display of affection, Elena knew now, but she understood that; after everything she'd been through with Steve, she liked the novelty of it.

A man in a ceremonial red sash came to join them and Christina linked her arm through his. 'Elena, this is my husband, Sigmundo. He's an attaché at the embassy.' She leaned in conspiratorially. 'Don't worry, he's already spoken to his contacts there. You should have no problem with your visa from now on.'

She laughed before Elena could frown, for she had indeed had a problem with her visa – Steve's allegations about her drug use had caused problems that rippled far beyond the custody of their son – but Elena realized it was merely a light-hearted jest and laughed too, albeit unnerved.

'A pleasure to meet you,' Sigmundo said, bowing his head. 'We felt quite certain that Vito must have been exaggerating when he described you but I see now, if anything, he was modest.'

'Well, thank you.' Elena smiled, relaxing. 'That's very kind of you to say.'

'Tell me again how you met,' Christina demanded, her dark eyes bright above her wine glass. 'Vito said something about killer bees?'

Elena laughed. 'It's preposterous, isn't it? The most unlikely start to a love story ever.' She looked up at her handsome fiancé and linked her arm through his. 'But he saved me. When everyone else was busy saving their own skin, he put himself in jeopardy to rescue me.'

'Your hero,' Christina beamed, looking proudly at her friend. 'He is a good man. The very best.'

'Yes, he is,' Elena agreed. 'I'm very lucky.' She looked back at Christina. 'And I would love to spend more time with you and hear all about what he was like as a boy. What stories you must be able to tell. Your childhood sounds idyllic.'

'Oh it was, it really was,' Christina replied, looking round wistfully at the hallowed gallery. 'We used to creep in at night and play ghosts in here, do you remember?'

'When they had covered the furniture with dust sheets before we decamped to Tuscany for the summer? Yes, I remember,' Vito chuckled. He looked down at Elena to explain. 'We would hide under the dust sheets and take it in turns to run the gauntlet. You never knew who was where.' He laughed. 'My poor parents, being woken by our screams.'

'Poor Maria, more like! I think she had a heart attack more than once,' Christina added. 'Although, I think your mother rather liked it. She said our noise made it a home—'

A stab of pain tore at Elena's heart as she thought of Stevie.

'—And brought this place alive. She was right. It could all too easily have been a mausoleum otherwise.'

'Where did you grow up, Elena?' Sigmundo asked.

'Newport in Rhode Island, on the East Coast. A world away from here in many ways.'

'Really? How so?'

'Well, the weight of history for one thing. Back home, if I hold onto a handbag for more than two seasons it's considered an antique.'

Christina laughed. 'So you like it here then? You will settle here?'

'Absolutely. I've always loved Rome. I just never thought I would be lucky enough to one day make it my home.'

'Well, we feel so privileged that we will get to share our beautiful city with you. I hope you'll allow me to introduce you to my dearest friends. Roman society can be . . . difficult to infiltrate sometimes. Are you involved with any charities? I believe Vito mentioned your family has a foundation?'

'Well, I'm not involved with that personally. My mother runs it now.'

Christina frowned lightly. 'You know, I think we may have met her once, at a gala in Beverly Hills for Tusk Force. Do you remember, darling?' she asked, turning to her husband. 'They had dyed the elephants' tusks bright colours. It renders the ivory worthless to poachers, you see,' she explained to Vito, who was looking alarmed by the thought. 'What is your mother's name, if you don't mind me asking—?'

'Ladies, if you will excuse us, there is someone to whom I would like to introduce Sigmundo; a business connection.' Vito squeezed her arm lightly, shooting her a private look to check she was happy to be left. She winked in reply.

'Of course, you boys go, network,' Christina smiled, shooing them away. 'Leave us girls to the important task of setting up some lunches so that we can make this beautiful bird of paradise one of our own.' She looked back at Elena. 'You were saying? Your mother's name?'

'Oh, Whitney Valentine,' Elena replied. It was soon to be Whitney Shaffer, but she wasn't going to ever call her by that name herself.

'Oh yes, Valentine. Valentine, of course.'

The men wandered off but something in her tone had caught Elena's attention – the way she'd stressed her family name, as though it carried connotations.

'I wonder that you have not returned to using the name yourself since the divorce?' Christina continued. 'After all, as the entire world is aware, it was not an amicable parting from your latest husband.'

Latest husband? Elena straightened at the barb, if that was indeed what it was. In truth, keeping Steve's name felt like wearing a crown of thorns every day – if she had her way, she would never hear or say his name again – but it was her son's name too, and keeping it felt like one of the only ways left to hold him close to her.

But surely Christina didn't mean to wound her? Elena must have misunderstood. Perhaps Christina's English wasn't as faultless as it first appeared?

'Tell me,' Christina smiled, moving in a little closer. 'How exactly did you fall to such depths that the courts saw fit to award custody of your son to a promiscuous, drug-addled actor rather than you?'

What?

'That poor, poor child. How different things might have been for him. How different they should have been. Born into everything – and yet nothing. I cried when I heard; it should never have happened and if you had been any kind of fit mother, it never *would* have.'

Elena felt as if she'd taken a blow to the head. The room began to spin – faces, strangers' faces, reflecting back at her in the mirrors, all of them watching, knowing, judging . . . Christina had put Elena's face to the lurid headlines; she knew every last detail of Elena's wretched pain and if the rest of them didn't already, they soon would.

'You don't seriously think I'm going to allow this to happen, do you? Just stand by and watch my oldest friend in the world throw his heart and good name away for *you*?'

Elena couldn't breathe. Christina was still smiling, her beautiful expression as unchanged now as it had been with the men present.

'Christina, what the papers wrote . . . it wasn't true.'

'Oh, I think it was. Sigmundo knows the judge.'

'But Steve lied. He perjured himself. He set me up.'

'I suppose you would say that. How else could you convince a good man like Vito that you're not a monster?'

'Because I'm not. I've told Vito everything; he knows the truth. He believes me.'

It was true she had told him all about Steve's lies – how he'd exaggerated her cocaine use, calling her an addict when she did no more than anyone else they knew; how he'd lied about her hiding her stash in Stevie's bathroom when it was *his* they had found. She'd described, too, how she had gone with other men because her own husband had wanted her to . . . when all it had done was enable him to flaunt his affairs in front of her and call her a whore.

But what she hadn't told Vito was that it wasn't a clear-cut picture, for she didn't know herself exactly where the truth ended and the lies began. Everything from that time was murky, the blackouts meaning anything was possible. All the very worst things Steve had said she'd done – to her shame, she couldn't be certain they *weren't* true . . .

But Vito – he was good, he had rescued her and she was different now. He had given her hope, been a guiding light when she'd been in the blackest despair after losing Stevie.

'It doesn't matter anyway,' Christina said dismissively. 'In the eyes of the world now, you're damaged goods and that's the only opinion that counts. Vito is the scion of one of the grandest families in Rome. He is born to greatness. He can't be linked to your tawdry scandals. You may have turned his head with, well, God only knows what tricks,' she said, still smiling, 'but it won't last. I'll see to that. Vito knows his obligations; his sense of duty will overrule whatever feelings he may temporarily harbour for you.'

'Christina, please, we're happy together. I make him happy.'

'No, you will destroy him and I want you to know I will not allow it to happen.' Christina tipped her head to the side, looking to all the room as if she was passing a compliment on Elena's dress. 'Well, we should mingle. But I'm pleased we were able to have this chat. It's good that we understand each other.'

Their eyes locked and Christina blinked just once before she glided off, leaving Elena alone in the room of strangers, her company suddenly less desirable now that neither Vito nor Christina was in her orbit. Backs turned to her as the tears rose to her eyes and she found herself alone in the middle of the party. She had been here before, she recalled, one night nineteen years earlier – and all the pain and all the lies of the intervening years had been for nothing.

Chapter Twenty-Five

Rome, August 2017

'I actually cannot believe this,' Cesca murmured. 'It's not a safe. It's a bank vault.'

'Yes, well, when you live in the building that houses one of the most important private art collections in the country, you can't skimp on things like insurance. I'm afraid they insist upon it,' Elena said, walking into the reinforced steel room and up to the floor-to-ceiling glass-fronted cabinets. Automatically, lights came on – 'pressure pads in the floor,' Elena explained – highlighting the dazzling jewels arranged on velvet trays.

'I would have thought something like this would need armed guards or, I don't know, a Swiss bank and a few fierce Dobermans at least,' Cesca gasped, as she saw rows of sapphires and rubies, emeralds and diamonds, pearls and aquamarines . . . It was like being inside Asprey's on Bond Street, or Tiffany on Fifth Avenue, or—

'I know, it's like Bulgari on Via Condotti in here,' Elena smiled, opening one of the cabinets and tenderly lifting a sapphire drop necklace. 'Bulgari always say I own more of their collection than they do. They're forever asking me to sell pieces back to them for their private collection.' She sighed. 'I don't know. Maybe I will. After all, I have no daughter to whom to leave them.'

'No? What about your daughter-in-law?'

'She's a liberal.' The tone in which she said this made Cesca wonder whether she had in fact meant to say 'radical'. 'She thinks it's "unethical" to spend this sort of money on jewellery. She doesn't understand – or doesn't want to understand – that it's a form of investment every bit as sound and wise as art or wine or property. But then, she's a biochemist; she'd rather look at things in her microscope than this.'

'It's a shame she thinks the two things have to be mutually exclusive,' Cesca said lightly.

'My thoughts precisely, Francesca. I've never understood this mindset of "Sunday Best". Beauty is an elevating force, don't you agree? We should try to make every day our best.'

'Well, I will make a point of remembering that, should I *ever* be given something even a fraction as lovely as any of this – which of course I won't.'

Elena glanced over at her, seeing how her eyes tripped over the shelves, absorbing the colours, longing to touch. 'Try something on.'

'What?' Cesca look alarmed. 'Oh, no, I didn't mean to . . . I couldn't.'

'Why not?'

'Because it's too precious,' Cesca laughed, clasping her hands behind her back for good measure.

Elena turned and came over to her. 'For a beautiful girl like you? Of course it isn't. Here, let me put this on you.'

She had to reach up – and Cesca had to bend her legs, keeping her plait out of the way – to fasten the criss-cross diamond torque around her neck.

'Oh my goodness, it's exquisite,' Cesca breathed, fingering it lightly, feeling the cold of the metal against her skin.

'This one's a Tiffany. Platinum with 32-carat diamonds.'

'Do you know the spec for all of these?' Cesca asked.

'Of course. Every piece tells a story for me. That one, for example, was a gift from my father to my mother on their silver wedding anniversary.' She walked over to the open cabinet and lifted an emerald, diamond and ruby necklace with a suspended diamond. 'And Vito gave me this sautoir as an engagement gift – 44.90 carats. This really was a special piece. I usually just wore the bracelet for everyday use.'

Everyday use? Like it was a string friendship bracelet?

She picked up a sapphire cuff. 'And this belonged to my dear friend Elizabeth Taylor.'

'Oh wow,' Cesca murmured, peering at it closely but not daring to touch, knowing Guido would *die* to be in her shoes right now. 'I've seen some photographs of you and Elizabeth Taylor together. We really should put those in the book.'

'Absolutely. I do agree. Everybody always loved looking at Elizabeth.'

'Which one is your favourite?' Cesca asked, reluctantly unfastening the necklace from her own neck and handing it back. It was already warming against her skin and it wouldn't do to get a taste for such things.

'Now there's a question,' Elena said, stepping back and looking around at her own jewelled vault. Cesca couldn't begin to imagine the net worth in this room alone. 'And you may think it's a hard answer to give, but actually, it's this one,' she said, walking across to a necklace that Cesca hadn't even noticed: palest pink beads simply strung to sit at the base of the neck.

'*That* one?' Cesca asked in amazement. She could see yellow diamonds, pink sapphires and black pearls, and yet that humble, almost plain, string of beads was Elena's favourite?

'It's not the most valuable. Not by a long way. In fact—' Elena considered, standing back and looking around. 'I think it may be the least valuable . . . Still, it means a great deal to me.' She lifted it from the velvet case and carried it over. 'Vito gave it to me. I wore it every day that we were married.' She handed it to Cesca. 'Would you mind . . . ?'

Cesca fastened it for her, admiring its modest simplicity in the full-length mirror. It was by far the closest piece to her own taste too.

'Opal,' Elena murmured, touching it lightly. 'It's funny. Some people are superstitious about opal. In Eastern Europe, jewellers simply won't sell it at all. People think it brings bad luck to marriage, whereas the Romans thought quite the opposite – the Caesars gave them to their wives as good-luck amulets. Some say a Roman senator called Nonius opted for exile rather than sell his opal to Mark Antony, who wanted to give it to his lover, Cleopatra.' She shrugged. 'And then the Greeks, on the other hand, believed it brought the wearer second sight.'

'Second sight?' Cesca echoed.

'I just thought it was pretty,' Elena smiled, taking it off again and kissing the beads tenderly, before replacing them on the velvet shelf.

'So which one are you going to wear tonight?' Cesca asked, sinking onto the ivory silk-velvet buttoned ottoman in the middle of the room, her elbows on her knees, her chin in her hand.

'Well, Signor Armani has been so kind as to make me an

oyster silk skirt suit, so I thought perhaps . . . this,' she said, picking up a string of large gold pearls. 'These are from the South Sea and so flattering against the skin. At my age, Francesca, less is most definitely more.'

'They're stunning,' Cesca smiled, gazing at them dreamily. Never in a million years would she ever get so close to such beauty again.

Elena stopped and stared at her. 'You should wear emeralds.'

'Me?' Cesca laughed. 'Yes, well, I don't think I'll ever have to make a choice on the matter.'

'With your hair and skin tone, they're absolutely the stone for you.'

'Well, that's nice of you to say but—'

'Try this.' Elena picked up a dramatic piece that wasn't so much jewellery as clothing – an elaborate lattice of white diamonds and emeralds that swept from a high, Victorian neckline down to the shoulders and chest, almost like a collar.

'God, no. I couldn't possibly,' Cesca cried, looking horrified.

'Why ever not?' Elena laughed, amused by her reaction. 'Come on. It won't hurt you.'

'But—'

'No excuses. I insist.'

Cesca got up, lifting her plait out of the way again and marvelling as Elena draped the necklace over her skin.

'A plait is not how we accessorize it,' she said, pulling the band from her hair and teasing out the braid. 'There, that's better.'

Cesca's hair, fanned out, looked aflame against the radiant

jewels. 'I've never . . . I've never seen . . .' she mumbled, her fingers tickling the stones.

'Me neither,' Elena said, looking thoughtful. 'It needs something simple. Strapless.'

'Black?'

'No. White.' She looked at Cesca in the mirror, their eyes meeting. 'Wait there.'

Cesca gawped as Elena left the room, leaving her standing there wearing what must be several million pounds' worth of jewellery – and her Converse.

Elena returned a few minutes later. 'It's all settled. Signor Valentino is sending it over.'

'What over?'

'Your dress for tonight.'

'*Tonight?*'

'The Bulgari party.'

'But I'm not invited.'

'Of course you are. You can be my plus-one, Francesca. It's absolutely right you should come with me. Every girl should get to wear a four-million-dollar necklace for at least one night in her life.'

'But—' Four million dollars? Worse than she'd thought, then. She'd need a guard, or an AK47, or an SAS SWAT team to leave the palace in this.

Elena smiled, taking the necklace from her. 'What are you waiting for? Go home and shower. The dress will be with you in forty minutes. I've given them your address. Get ready and come back here in an hour to put the necklace on. Insurance, I'm afraid.'

'I don't know what to say.'

'There's nothing to say,' Elena said, patting her shoulder.

'We've both been working very hard recently, Francesca. Tonight, we shall have some fun.'

The dress alone was worth more than her car back home (a battered twelve-year-old Golf that actually groaned every time she sat in it and only went into fifth gear from third). White lace and floor-length, with a black velvet bow at the waist, it gave her a shape she'd never imagined on herself before. She had blow-dried her hair for once, and gone as far as applying some grey kohl and mascara to her eyes, as well as slicking a tinted gloss across her lips.

She stood in front of the mirror in her bald little apartment, the lace hem incongruous as it kissed the terracotta tiles, and worrying whether it mattered that her toenails – which peeked through the black suede shoes that had come with the dress (all miraculously in her size) – were unpainted.

Well, there was no time to do anything about it now. With a deep breath, she closed the door of the apartment and tiptoed carefully down her steps, taking care to lift the hem of the dress so as not to trail it through the freshly watered geranium pots.

She felt conspicuous as she walked the short distance between the apartment and the palazzo, wishing it had a side door onto the piazzetta as people stopped to stare at her hurrying over the cobbles, feeling too tall in her heels, lace gathered in one hand, her hair shimmering in the fiery dusk light.

'Francesca!'

The cry made her stop in her tracks. Signora Accardo came hurrying out of the osteria towards her, abandoning her diners and making them all turn and stare. The little old lady's white bun didn't wobble as she bustled quickly in her direction, shaking her hands in the air in a gesture that could have been praising the heavens – or damning them. '*Carina, carina*, where are you going? You look like a princess.'

'I feel like one,' Cesca shrugged shyly, noticing even Signor Accardo standing by the fig tree watching them, wiping his hands on his long white apron. He'd left the kitchen? She *must* look different . . . 'I've been invited to the Bulgari party on Via Condotti tonight. They're showcasing their new collection. Or something.'

'You are a vision,' Signora Accardo said, walking around her and sighing. '*Mia cara. Mia cara.* Where is Signora Dutti?'

'I'm not su—'

'She should see you. Otto!' She called across the width of the square to her husband. 'Fetch her! Fetch her!' she cried, motioning to the closed door below Cesca's apartment.

'Actually, I should get going. I've got to—'

But Signora Dutti had been roused anyway by the shouts outside and was already hurrying towards them.

'*Mia cara, mia cara,*' she began crying, her hands fluttering above her heart as she too started praising Cesca's fairy-tale dress and the two women started gabbling in rapid-fire Italian. Cesca didn't dare tell them about the four million dollars' worth of emeralds she was about to put on with it.

'I'm sorry, but I really have to go,' Cesca said, using her thumb to indicate her direction. 'I'll be late.'

'You go with your sweetheart?' Signora Dutti asked, eyes misty with the romance of it all.

'My boss. The Principessa.'

In a flash, both women's faces changed.

254

'Pah.'

'Tuh.'

'She is wicked woman, Francesca. Bad lady. Why are you with her?' Signora Dutti demanded.

'Because it's a job. And I need a job. I really don't understand why you both don't like her. She's fine.'

But Signora Accardo shook her head stoutly. 'Is no good, Francesca. Is *problema*.'

Cesca nodded, knowing they meant well. 'Thank you for your concern, but I'm okay. It's fine. Really. It's just a job. It's fine. But thank you. I know you're only looking out for me. But I really must go. I'm sorry. Thank you . . . Okay . . .'

She took her leave, having almost to run out of the piazzetta and into the Piazza Angelica, up the steps to the palazzo. The door opened as she reached the top step, as though Alberto had been waiting for her – which, of course, he had been.

Elena, too, was waiting: on a satin bench, the necklace ready for her. Within three minutes, they were in a bullet-proof black limousine being whisked off to the party, security guards riding on motorbikes behind. Her fingers at her neck, Cesca looked out of the tinted windows as they sped through the city – past Mussolini's grand marble monuments, past the crumbling ruins of an ancient empire, past the winged angels of Castel Sant'Angelo and the colonnaded saints of Vatican City – and she knew she was part of a different Rome tonight, one where she could almost forget that beneath the pomp and the grandeur, there were quarries and holes and pitfalls which could break the ground beneath her feet at any given moment.

Chapter Twenty-Six

Venice, October 1980

The clerk's polite claps would have to pass for the ceremonial ringing of bells. The flowers in her hands were not her favourite old-fashioned Blanche de Belgique roses, but pale-pink tulips bought from the market that morning; her plain white shift dress was enlivened only by the short white lace communion veil she had borrowed from Vito's goddaughter, whose parents were officiating as their only witnesses. No one else knew. It was their secret.

It had to be.

As the clerk wound up the formalities and Elena stared lovingly at her new husband through the heavy lacework, she felt heady with relief that she had pulled it off. She had beaten Christina. True to her word, the other woman had begun an insidious whisper campaign in which smiles to her face when she was on Vito's arm turned to vicious sneers when she was alone. Christina knew exactly how to tread the line between treachery and loyalty, pleading prior commitments at her country estate whenever Vito questioned why the dinner-party invitations were not as forthcoming as he had expected. But Elena knew what was happening. They were being frozen out and, sooner or later, Vito would realize that too and have to make a choice.

She had managed to convince him that her 'past record' as thrice a bride meant a low-key wedding would be in the best interests of his family's profile. She hadn't wanted to embarrass him, she had said, and although he had replied that he could never be embarrassed by her, that he was proud to have her as his wife, he had still readily agreed to elope. It was all the proof she needed that Christina had been right – the family name mattered above all else.

So as Vito lifted the veil back and clasped her face gently with his hands, kissing her lightly on the lips, she felt the thrill of victory ripple through her. Those bitches might not like her, they might not approve of her obscene wealth and chequered romantic past, but she was safe at last. As Vito's wife, as the Principessa dei Damiani Pignatelli della Mirandola, married to the scion of one of the grandest families of Rome's Black Nobility, she was untouchable now.

Born lucky. She had won.

Rome, Christmas Eve 1980

'You agree now I was right?' Elena asked as she walked slowly through the galleries with him, the large beeswax church candles flickering at every single window.

'I agree it is still the greatest fire hazard ever to afflict the palazzo in its 800-year history,' Vito said lightly, before squeezing her hand. 'But it does look beautiful.'

'Maria and Julio worked so hard getting it just right. It's so atmospheric now, don't you think? And it must surely look so beautiful from the piazza, such a welcoming sight,' she sighed.

'An extravagant one, perhaps.'

'Well, I'm sure your mother would have agreed with me. You're always telling me how she wanted this place to feel like a home and not a museum.'

Vito stopped walking and turned to face her. 'I know what this is really about, Elena. Stop fretting. He will love it,' Vito said reassuringly. 'He will love *you*.'

But Elena took no comfort from his words – wasn't that exactly what he'd said about Christina? Wasn't Aurelio going to resent her for robbing him of a brother's greatest duty by insisting they elope? Wasn't he going to think of her the way the rest of them did? A flashy American: no class, just money? It was turning out that her victory over Christina had been a pyrrhic one. The usual invitations had started coming in for dinner and cocktail parties, balls and the opera – enough, anyway, to reassure Vito that in spite of the shock elopement, his marriage had been accepted. But Elena knew better. Women were attuned to the minutiae of each other's social behaviour – cool eyes and tight smiles, limp handshakes and slightly turned cheeks, the whispered asides and shared looks. Though to the common onlooker she held rank in their top tier, from within the enclave it had been made perfectly clear she would never be one of them.

But then . . . hadn't it ever been thus? She had been an outsider her entire life, excluded by the middle-class women in Newport on account of her wealth; by Leo's circles on account of her youth; by Steve's on account of her motherhood; and now again, here.

She would have felt more secure if she could have been

more certain of Vito's overarching affection for her. She knew he loved her – more passionately, perhaps, than he had ever loved anyone – but his feelings were still second-ary to his duty. Like her, he was a product of his upbringing, unable fully to break free. Whilst she had been taught to live in exclusion and stand apart from the masses, always perversely yearning to belong but never quite breaching the gap, Vito – as the eldest son and heir – had been trained to override his own passions and no longer recognized this sublimation as sacrifice; the need to do the 'Right Thing' had become automatic.

As a result, he often seemed distant and hard to reach. He wouldn't hold her hand in public. He insisted on follow-ing the aristocratic protocol of separate bedrooms, even though he visited her most nights. And although he was technically proficient in bed, he was very straight; playful affection was hard for him and if she was sitting on his lap or nuzzling his neck when Maria entered the room, he would gently push her off. He didn't like her in any fash-ions that were too short or too tight or too low-cut – and, of course, not too much jewellery either. Modesty was the highest virtue, it seemed.

Tonight's black velvet Yves Saint Laurent wrap dress was a daring push of the boundaries. Falling to her knee, with long sleeves, it nonetheless featured a deep V neckline that precluded the wearing of a bra. He hadn't commented – it was just a private family dinner, after all – but she would have to sit with her back ramrod straight at the table whilst entertaining the prodigal son.

In spite of what Vito assumed, it wasn't nerves that had her on edge about tonight. Aurelio was everything Vito could never afford to be and – protective of her husband –

she resented him for it. As the 'spare' and not the heir, there was none of the weight of expectation upon him to uphold the family reputation, run the estates, be the figurehead for a family held in the highest regard. Instead, he'd been spoilt, indulged by his mother to run wild and free himself from the constraints that were inevitable for her oldest son.

At seventeen, Vito had told her, Aurelio had run away from boarding school to take part in the 1957 Mille Miglia, racing a prize Alfa Romeo 750 Competizione from his father's collection and crashing it a mile outside Rimini. At nineteen, whilst playing polo in Argentina, he had been embroiled in a scandal involving one of the daughters of a cartel druglord and had to be smuggled from the country in the back of a coffee truck. He had continued in much the same mercurial vein until their aged father's death in 1974, which proved to be a sobering event for him. For a short time, he had appeared to mellow somewhat, helping Vito with the daunting task of running the estate. Until, that was, four years ago when he had packed his suitcase for a week-long safari to Kenya and simply not come back. According to Maria – who could be a useful source of infor-mation if handled lightly – Vito had been furious and dismayed in equal measure, his anger hardening with every year that passed without contact. It was little wonder Vito didn't keep a photograph of him in the apartments and Aurelio's sudden reappearance – a telegram informing them he would be 'home for Christmas' – was both unex-pected and unwelcome.

It was her and Vito's first Christmas together as man and wife, their first Christmas together full stop, and she could only hope Aurelio would remain true to wandering form and sequester himself in his (currently locked) suite of rooms, which lay directly opposite theirs in the west wing. She wanted privacy – a lot of it. She was hoping to fall pregnant this holiday, to cement this relationship by becoming a family. A new one. Vito needed an heir and she needed another Stevie, a child to cradle in her arms.

The Christmas tree in the sitting room of their private apartment was enormous. Four metres high and almost as much round, Maria had decked it with red satin ribbons tied in bows. Several large bow-topped boxes sat at the foot of it, including one which was to be opened privately, later. She had set the lamps to a low setting, creating an ambient, flickering light, and added huge bunches of mistletoe to every doorway – a tradition he didn't understand but which gave her the perfect excuse to flirt with her own husband.

The bell sounded and Vito looked across at her. She saw the tension in his face suddenly and realized it wasn't her nerves he'd been trying to calm earlier.

'Darling, stop fretting,' she laughed, running over to him and taking his face in her hands, kissing him lightly on the lips. 'He's your brother. Of course I shall love him.'

He nodded but the motion was stiff, his feelings withdrawn to a place far below the surface. She felt a rush of love for her husband. His love for his brother was deep but complicated.

'I'll give you two a few minutes alone together first. You go greet him. I'm just going to freshen up,' she said, squeezing his hand and walking to the powder room.

She appraised her reflection in the wall-to-wall mirror. She was wearing her hair – dyed dark again – in a tight, lacquered bun, red lipstick on her mouth. She touched up her bronze eyeshadow and walked through a mist of Shalimar.

With one final, approving glance, she took a deep breath and walked out.

She could hear their voices as she strode through the rooms, her stilettoes intermittently click-clacking on the parquet floors as she passed over the rugs.

The brothers were talking, drinks in hand, both of them smart in their dinner jackets. Vito, facing her, looked up as she entered, breaking into a relaxed smile at the sight of her. She felt herself loosen. The reunion had clearly been successful, Vito as forgiving and magnanimous as always. She could afford to be too.

'Aurelio,' she said to his back.

Slowly, with an almost indolent air, he turned and she came face to face with the only person in the world who could compete with her for Vito's love. He was strong-jawed, with hooded, elongated brown eyes, a large, nobly broken nose and a wide mouth. He looked more Greek, to her eye, than Roman.

And she felt instantly, powerfully attracted to him.

'Darling, you're not eating,' Vito said, noticing her food was barely touched.

'No. I'm sorry. It's . . . been a long day. I must be more tired than I realized.' She smiled, placing her knife and fork together and giving up the pretence of having any appetite.

'Lighting all those candles, no doubt,' Aurelio said wryly, spearing his *baccalà*. 'I thought the place was ablaze when I got to the piazza.'

'It's atmospheric,' Vito said loyally. 'Elena wanted to

create a festive setting that could be enjoyed by people on the other side of the walls as well.'

'Did she now?'

'Vito told me how much your mother strove to make this a family home,' she said, ignoring the undertone in his voice. 'I've heard all sorts of stories about how you two and Christina would tear about the place, playing football in the galleries.'

'Christina?' Aurelio looked at his brother. 'How is she? Still married to that boring old toad?'

'Some of us happen to like Sigmundo,' Vito said stiffly.

'Well, some of us don't,' Aurelio said crisply, putting a slice of the cod in his mouth and chewing it. 'Has Christina been a good friend to you, Elena?'

'The best. She's been incredibly welcoming.'

Aurelio stared at her, his eyes openly roaming her face as she lied. 'Uh huh,' he muttered, keeping his opinion as to whether or not he believed her a secret.

'So . . . Kenya,' Vito said after a growing pause. 'Good trip?'

Aurelio chuckled and reached for his glass of white burgundy, understanding perfectly his brother's nuanced dig. According to Maria, Aurelio had been forced to leave the country in rather a hurry, after the irate husband of his current lover had tried to kill him. With a rifle. 'Very, thank you. Interesting people, the Masai. You should visit some time.'

'Well, if I ever get the time, I will.'

'Oh, come. You must get time off for good behaviour, surely, brother?' Aurelio taunted, refusing to satisfy their curiosity with details of his life-saving surgery. 'How did you come to meet your new bride here?'

Vito sighed. 'Ischia. I paid a visit to the Santis.'

Aurelio spluttered on his drink. 'Christ, don't tell me they're still limping along? What's her name? The model.'

'Allegra. And I wouldn't call it limping, by any means,' Vito said, his eyes flitting only briefly in Elena's direction. 'They've got a new yacht, the *Serena*. Life seems very rosy for them, in fact.'

Aurelio seemed unconvinced. He looked across at Elena, a glimmer of hostility beginning to shine from his eyes. 'And you were on this yacht too, Elena?'

'Yes. I know them from New York. We share a lot of mutual acquaintances.'

'I'm sure you do,' he muttered, just below his breath. 'So, you met on the yacht and what – your eyes met over the poached lobster?'

Vito chuckled. 'Nothing so humdrum. I had to save Elena from a swarm of killer bees to get her to even notice me.'

'Darling, I *had* noticed you,' Elena protested.

'Being pursued by more than just the bees, was she?' Aurelio asked, arching an eyebrow to his brother, and Elena had a sudden flash of the connection between them. Their twin-ness. They seemed to understand more than needed to be said – like icebergs, most of what went on was hidden beneath the surface.

'You could say that,' Vito said shortly. 'But, luckily, the bees played right into my hands and she was obliged to marry me out of sheer gratitude for saving her life.'

'It was love at first sight and you know it,' Elena laughed, holding her husband's gaze.

Aurelio said nothing, reaching out of his chair slightly to grab the wine bottle and refresh everyone's glasses, especially his own.

'So what do you think of the palace? Daunted by it?'

'Not really.' Elena shrugged as lightly as she could.

'Elena's a Valentine. She grew up in a house this size.'

'Not as old, though,' Elena added lightly, looking for self-deprecation as she always did whenever her inheritance came into the frame.

'Ah, a *Valentine*. So then it really is a love match. You didn't marry him for his money after all.' Aurelio's voice was pickled with pique.

'Aurelio. That's out of order,' Vito said sharply.

'Is it? I think it's perfectly fair. It's always been the risk. We both know we're targets for a certain type.'

'Well, Elena isn't one of them. If anything, people could accuse me of marrying her for *her* money.'

'Now, wouldn't that be a thing?' Aurelio grinned, pushing his plate away and sitting back in the chair. 'Well, I'm glad to hear it's a true love story. Welcome to the family, sister dearest.'

The words fell from his lips like a taunt, his eyes steady, looking for her reaction.

'Thank you,' she replied in a quiet voice.

Maria came in to clear the plates, the three of them sitting in silence as she did so. Elena kept the smile fixed on her face, her eyes on the table, aware that Vito was beginning to glare at his brother.

Aurelio clapped his hands as Maria left the room. 'Well, you know – I'm sure – that it is tradition to open a present on Christmas Eve?' He was directing the question at her, forcing – daring – her to look at him.

'No, I didn't know.'

'You don't do that in America?'

She shook her head.

'Well, let me just—'

He left the table – Vito took the opportunity to shoot her an encouraging smile – and returned a moment later with a gift in each hand. Elena took hers.

'Thank you.'

'You must open it now. I insist. Both of you.'

He sat down again and watched as she tugged on the ribbon. She lifted the lid to find a card on the top nestled in tissue paper: *For darling Elena, with love always, Vito.*

'It's from Vito?' she asked in astonishment. 'I assumed it was from—'

'Me?' Aurelio finished for her. 'No, I'm afraid I haven't been able to get round to presents yet. Besides, I needed to meet you first. I couldn't very well buy for my new sister, without ever having met her.'

Elena looked away, unable to hold his gaze, which seemed to be deliberately pushing her. She opened the tissue and lifted out a silver musical carousel.

'Oh Vito! It's beautiful.'

'It plays "Mockingbird" – you said that your parents always used to sing it to you. So if you ever get home-sick . . .'

'Darling, I love it. How thoughtful,' she said warmly, determined to exclude Aurelio from the moment and blank out his biting cynicism.

'Now open yours, brother,' Aurelio said as she carefully replaced the carousel in the box and set it on the floor.

She looked up. And gasped. 'Wait. No!—' she cried, as she saw the wrapping paper already peeled open.

But it was too late. Parting the many layers of blush-pink tissue paper, Vito pulled out a black lace negligee so skimpy, most of it appeared to be missing. Both brothers' jaws dropped open.

'That was supposed to be given *privately*,' Elena stammered, feeling her cheeks burn as she looked over at Vito, pleading with him to understand that it had not been intended for public display. Aurelio didn't move, his eyes fixed upon her as Vito hurriedly replaced it, trying to hide it below the tissue again.

'For God's sake, Aurelio,' Vito snapped. 'Why did you have to interfere?'

'How was I supposed to know?'

'You should have just left it. Everything was arranged.'

'Well, I can see that, now,' he drawled, a white heat beginning to emanate from him.

Maria came back in with the *dolci*, the three of them sitting in silence again, waiting until she left the room.

'So, is this just a flying visit or are you back . . . for good?' Elena asked, trying to keep her tone light as she dug a spoon into the *struffoli*.

'Why? Would I be in the way if I were?'

'Aurelio. That is enough,' Vito snapped. 'Elena is merely being polite. Besides, it's not unreasonable to know what your plans are.'

'Isn't this place big enough for the three of us then?' There was a silence before he suddenly laughed. 'Brother, relax. The answer is, I don't know. I thought I might stay for a while but, if things are . . . busy here, or something comes up . . .' He shrugged.

Elena stared at him. He was a nomad, as rootless as a leaf that travelled wherever the wind blew it, and she didn't know which alarmed her more: the thought of him staying here. Or the thought of him leaving.

Chapter Twenty-Seven

Rome, August 2017

The colours were kaleidoscopic – not just the jewels, but the women's dresses: red chiffon and midnight silk, peacock velvet and primrose satin. In the company of Elena in Armani minimalism, Cesca had feared her outfit would be *de trop* but, to her amazement, she simply fitted in. Seemingly it was normal to these people to wear couture and house-price jewels on a Tuesday night.

Flashbulbs popped as they walked the short distance between the car and the boutique, glimpsing the Spanish Steps at the end of the street, the security staff waving them past the red ropes without asking for either their names or invitations. Even without partnering one of the most high-profile socialites in the city, Cesca suspected her necklace did all the talking necessary to get into something like this.

Champagne flutes were placed in their hands and Cesca followed as Elena made a stately procession through the centre of the room, people swooping to kiss her and talk quickly in low voices as they passed.

Cesca didn't listen to their pleasantries. At almost a head taller than most of them, she had a good view of the room and scanned it with interest – noting Carla Bruni, Carine

Roitfeld, Monica Bellucci . . . God, was that *Sophia Loren*? – not expecting in the least to recognize anyone *not* from a magazine.

But she did.

Nico Cantarelli was standing in a small group by a ceiling-suspended glass cabinet. Were it not for his mop of hair – still unruly – and his somewhat disapproving expression, she wouldn't have recognized him, for he was wearing an unbelievably well-cut dinner suit. (All the men were; perhaps it was an Italian citizenship requirement?) He looked more like a screen actor than a . . . speleologist, was it?

She turned away quickly, not wanting him to see her. She didn't recall much about Friday night – in fact, she wasn't 100 per cent sure she'd actually seen him, so it could have been a dream – but she had a bad feeling that *something* had happened, and it was strong enough that she had hidden from him since then. Arriving early on Monday morning, pleading distraction from the workers' noise outside, she had hurriedly relocated from her 'office' in the west wing to the library on the second floor of the central north wing. There were almost a thousand rooms in the palace. Unless he was going to spend the four hours it took to stride through each and every one looking for her – which, she knew, he wasn't – then she was safe.

But not here.

What was he doing here? By day, he looked like any other construction worker! Why was he here looking handsome and holding a champagne glass the correct way? And, more to the point, who was the brunette beside him?

She snuck another glance over – and found herself staring straight at him. His expression changed as he saw her face.

She quickly turned back to Elena again, closing her eyes and berating herself. Why had she done that? Why? *Why?*

'Are you okay, Francesca?' Elena asked, looking concerned.

Cesca opened her eyes again. 'Oh yes. Fine, thank you.'

'You look pale.'

'Maybe just a little hot,' she faltered.

'Viscontessa. Signorina Hackett.'

He was here and as his presence settled over her like a warm coat, she felt that strange, new tug towards him that she couldn't comprehend. She couldn't understand why this was happening, although she'd seen it happen to other people. As a barrister, she had come across enough people – victims – women who had fallen for the wrong men, bad boys who treated them mean and kept them keen, throwing out just enough affection or attention to keep them hanging like a dog waiting for scraps. My God, she thought to herself in horror. Was this what was happening to her? A pizza slice and a smile and that was it?

'Signor Cantarelli,' Elena greeted him brightly, allowing two light kisses on her cheeks as though they were warm acquaintances and he was not, in fact, the man currently infuriating her by making bigger the already enormous hole in her exquisite garden. 'Is your mother here?'

'I'm afraid not. She's in Tuscany for the week. I've come in her place.'

'That is very good of you.'

'Francesca,' he said, turning his attention – those direct eyes – on her. Cesca copied her boss, allowing two light kisses on her cheeks as though they were warm acquaintances and he was not, in fact, the reason she had spent the last few days hiding out in a 1,000-room palace.

'What do you think of our Cinderella?' Elena asked, one eyebrow arched lightly. 'Quite the belle of the ball, wouldn't you agree?'

Nico's eyes travelled over her. 'I did not believe it could be Francesca at first,' he said. 'But, of course, the hair – who else could it be? No one else in Rome has hair that—'

Cesca tensed, waiting for the word 'bright'.

'—Colour,' he said, watching her.

'And do you like the dress?' Elena asked.

Cesca inwardly cringed. Every question enabled Nico to look at her – examine her, almost – when all she wanted to do was hide from him. What had she done last Friday? Why couldn't she remember and yet it rustled her peace of mind like a foraging beast?

'It's Valentino,' Elena continued. 'The atelier very kindly loaned it to us for the night. I remembered seeing it at the couture shows the other week and, luckily, this beautiful creature is a sample size. I think she looks exquisite, don't you? So lovely to see her in something new, and that fits.'

'Yes,' Nico agreed, nodding with Elena before looking back at her. 'I do not understand your clothes.'

'Well, I don't understand . . . yours,' she shot back, faltering as she took in the impeccable cut of his suit. He should change jobs. He needed to find a reason to look like that every day.

He watched her, seeing how she squirmed. 'You look very beautiful, is what I meant. Everyone is looking at you.'

'Yes, well, maybe I don't want everyone looking at me,' she mumbled, bending her head down and tucking her hair behind her ear.

There was a short pause. 'Well, if you'll excuse me, I can

see Paolo Bulgari over there and I really must speak to him.' Elena glided away, disappearing into the crowd.

Cesca looked after her, in panic. How could she leave her alone? With *him*.

'Are you enjoying the party?' he asked after a moment.

'It's fine.' Cesca looked out at the sea of famous faces. Why had she let Elena talk her into this? She would far rather have been sitting on her steps, eating pizza and drinking a beer with Guido. 'How come you're here?'

He blinked, looking offended. 'Because I was invited.'

Vaguely, Cesca remembered him saying he'd grown up in one of the city's smartest districts. It was just so incongruous seeing him here, looking like that, when she was accustomed to seeing him dangling from ropes, covered in mud and dust and looking more like a builder.

'Cesca, about the other night—'

Oh God, here it was. She half turned away. 'Look, I'd had too much to drink. I'm sorry if I embarrassed you in some way.'

'No, you didn't—'

'I was just blowing off some steam.'

'It wasn't that. It was something you said.'

It came to her! *Annoying*. She'd told him he was annoying. It was the last thing she remembered doing as Matteo had practically carried her out. God, she'd been so rude.

'I'm so sorry. You should never pay any attention to what I say after I've had tequila. I'll try to convince you I'm the Pope.'

'No—'

A woman came over – the brunette she'd seen with him earlier – and rested one hand lightly on his shoulder. He turned.

'Oh. Isabella, this is Francesca. We . . . work in the same building.'

'Pleased to meet you,' Cesca said, feeling nothing of the sort. Isabella's was the kind of smouldering Italian beauty that left her Celtic looks seeming wan and insipid by comparison.

'What a beautiful necklace,' Isabella smiled, looking rather radiant in a diamond collar of her own. 'I've been admiring it.'

'I'm afraid it's not mine. I've just borrowed it for the evening.'

'Haven't we all?' Isabella laughed delicately. 'I'm sorry to interrupt.' She looked at Cantarelli. 'I just need the keys,' she said in a low voice.

'Sure,' he replied, reaching into his jacket pocket and fishing for them.

Cesca felt her stomach clench as she stood witness to the low-key intimacy, trying to catch sight of Isabella's left hand for signs of an engagement or wedding ring. But from where she was standing, she couldn't get a clear view, not without moving and pointedly staring.

'If you'll excuse me, I should catch up with Elena. She may be feeling tired,' she said quietly.

'But—' Cantarelli began.

'It was good seeing you,' she said quickly. 'Lovely to meet you, Isabella.'

'And you,' Isabella nodded, looking surprised as Cesca hurried away.

She could feel their – his? – eyes on her back as she slipped past the other guests, her heart banging loudly against her ribs, neck craned as she looked for Elena. She wanted to leave; ordinarily she would, but the necklace

273

kept her here like a prisoner. She couldn't just leave with four million dollars hanging around her neck.

She found her boss standing in a small, select group in the next gallery beside some brightly coloured fine jewels. A grouping of narrow sofas were clustered on the lacquered parquet floors, and the walls were hung with several large black-and-white portraits of some of the most beautiful and recognizable women in the world – including Elizabeth Taylor as Cleopatra and, next to her, Elena, in what appeared to be a white lynx fur coat and diamonds. It was a striking image, cementing Elena's reputation as a top-flight socialite, and Cesca wondered whether they should request permission to reproduce the image in the book.

'Ah, here she is, the very same. Francesca, do come over and meet Signor Bulgari. I've just been explaining what marvellous work you've been doing,' Elena said with the same bright tone she'd used to greet Nico.

'*Piacere*,' Paolo Bulgari said, kissing the back of her hand lightly. 'You look stunning, Signorina. I'm very glad your necklace is by our own craftsmen. All eyes are upon you tonight. We shall boast about you for weeks.'

'Thank you, but I can't take the credit for any of it. Everything you see is down to the Principessa's generosity and wonderful eye.'

'We were just saying how excited we are about the existence of this book, for it shall surely prove – inadvertently – to be a most wonderful showcase for Bulgari too.'

'I know. Just this afternoon I was lucky enough to visit the Principessa's collection. I'm still dazzled, even now,' Cesca said brightly, playing the game.

'We are very lucky; the Principessa is one of our most devoted clients.'

'Well, me and Elizabeth. What was it her husband said?'

Signor Bulgari looked at Cesca, already in on the joke, and Cesca suspected they had repeated these words many times before. 'Richard Burton said, "The only word Elizabeth knows in Italian is Bulgari."'

They all laughed, Cesca too, but hers was hollow, her eyes flitting around the gallery and looking for Nico, but he was still in the next room. *With Isabella.*

'Well, if there was only one Italian word *to* know . . .' Cesca smiled. 'Your creations really are incredible.' She pointed to a glittering sky-blue sapphire ring. 'I mean, that colour. It's just sensational.'

'Yes. That is known as a Vivid Blue Diamond. One of the crowns of our jewels,' he quipped.

'That's a *diamond*?'

'Indeed. The Vivid Blue is one of the most coveted colours, but incredibly rare to find these days, especially in a size such as this. It's almost impossible now to get anything over ten carats.' He looked at Elena. 'You still, to my mind, possess the most beautiful of them all. The Bulgari Blue.'

Out of the corner of her eye, Cesca saw Nico enter the room. Isabella was with him, talking to him, but his eyes found hers again as though he'd been looking for her, too. Following her.

'I'd love to hear about it,' Cesca said quickly, giving their host her full attention.

'Well, quite simply, the Bulgari Blue is one of the most famous diamonds in the world. The GIA graded it a Fancy Vivid, which is the highest of all honours. Only one in ten million qualify for the grading.'

'The GIA?' Cesca queried, sensing Nico drawing closer as

he and Isabella admired more of the displays, stopping to chat and shake hands with people intermittently.

'The Gemological Institute of America. The Principessa's ring is actually made of two diamonds – one flawless, colourless diamond at 9.87 carats and the blue at 10.95. Your husband bought it for you to celebrate the happy occasion of the birth of your son, I believe.'

'That's right,' Elena sighed. 'I was so lucky to have married such a romantic man. He was so sweet with those little gestures.'

Sweet? Little gestures? Cesca doubted there had been anything little at all about that gesture. Forget a house-worth of jewels, that one ring sounded akin to a yacht's worth.

Nico was across the room from her now. She knew if she were to look straight ahead, their eyes would meet.

'Do you wear it often?' she asked, determinedly turning away to Elena at her side, trying to look engrossed in the small talk. 'Perhaps you should have worn it tonight.'

'Gracious, no,' Elena replied. 'I would have had to bring the entire Swiss Guard with me. No, sadly I have to keep it in a safe in Switzerland. That one really is too precious to risk.'

Cesca thought back to the safe – vault – in the palace, with its reinforced triple-layered steel walls, 14-ton doors, humidity controls and weight-sensitive pressure pads in the floor. It was fireproof and, with its direct line to the *carabinieri* and two-way CCTV, Elena had said it could also double as a panic room; not that it had been, nor ever would be, needed as such. But if that wasn't enough security for one little (admittedly priceless) ring, she didn't know what was.

'Oh.' Elena fluttered suddenly, as though her muscles had been tweaked or weakened.

'Elena? Are you okay?' Cesca asked, reaching forward to offer a hand. Elena looked as though she was about to slip to the floor.

'I'm fine. Absolutely fine. Just a little tired, perhaps. I ought not to have flown to London and back in a day yesterday, but I did so want to see the Lesedi La Rona before it goes to auction.' Elena straightened, expertly deflecting the attention away from herself. 'What are your thoughts on it, Paolo?'

Cesca had read about it – the world's second-largest uncut diamond in history, about to go to auction at Sotheby's.

'Well, we have seen it, of course,' he said with discreet understatement. 'It is *magnifico*.'

'Shall you bid?' Elena enquired.

He smiled. 'If you tell me there is something special you would like us to create for you, then most certainly.'

Elena laughed. 'Oh, you are wicked. Sadly, I'm afraid my fancy diamond-buying days are over. A woman should only be bought such things by a man who loves her.' She smiled sadly. 'Darling Vito.'

Signor Bulgari patted her hand affectionately. 'We too miss him. He was a splendid man.'

'The very best.'

Elena paled again, her body seeming to tremor, and Cesca reached out once more. 'Should we get you home?' she asked quietly.

'You may be right,' Elena agreed. 'Paolo, do you mind terribly if we make an early exit?'

'On the contrary, it was an honour to see you here tonight, Principessa. Let us have lunch together soon.'

'Yes, let's.'

Signor Bulgari turned to Cesca. 'And it has been a pleasure to make your acquaintance, young lady. I wish you could have stayed longer so that we might have enjoyed the sight of such riches against such beauty.'

Cesca demurred. 'Oh, I think I've worn them long enough. It's almost midnight for this Cinderella – time to get back to my pumpkin and ashes.'

With Elena leaning her arm lightly on Cesca's, they walked slowly through the crowd, Elena nodding her goodbyes regally.

'We'll see you tomorrow, Signor Cantarelli,' Elena said as they passed by Nico and Isabella, her tone a little less warm than before.

'You shall, Signora,' he replied, but his eyes were on Cesca – and from the way they searched hers, she knew she was going to need more than a thousand rooms if she wanted to hide from this man.

Chapter Twenty-Eight

Rome, New Year's Eve, 1980

The room was alive, pulsing with energy. Vibrant. Exotic. Teasing. Men in white tie and women in extravagant, daring dresses that had seemingly been hanging ready for just such a night as this. From behind her feathered mask, Elena watched from the sides. This was her greatest triumph – a ball that would be talked about for generations to come. Even those not invited were muscling in on the event, as crowds gathered outside, people stopping to admire the procession of guests making their way up the steps, others craning to snatch glimpses of the ball within as dancers and revellers whirled past the windows. Christina was vanquished once and for all. Aurelio's return had quickened Rome's blood, the women – the wives – sweeping aside their queen's diktats to shun Elena's occasions for a night of flirting, of being held in his arms, if only for a while, on the dance floor.

There had been less than a week's planning for it, Aurelio carelessly dropping the suggestion at breakfast on Christmas morning – he was the kind of man who assumed such things could be thrown together in under a week – but such was his draw, the city made it possible. Prior commitments were revised, apologies to jilted hosts submitted and the RSVPs rushed in like the floodwaters of the Tiber.

Vito had been reluctant, of course. It was hasty, rash; these things needed to be organized. But the pulse in the palace was up, everyone could feel it; the staff too, all of them rushing to polish the mirrors, buff the gold, scour the steps and dust the marble busts, for the mania had been exactly the thing – the only thing – to make this familial arrangement work. No sooner had the words dropped from Aurelio's mouth than she knew he had given her the means for them all to remain within the palace walls and not have war – or something worse – break out.

She had never worked so hard – up with the sun and in bed after the moon – overseeing every last detail so that Vito couldn't keep track of her, much less his brother. Every day, she walked miles as she swept through the corridors issuing commands to Maria – move those chairs, lower that chandelier, roll back the rugs – so that every night she fell alone into her bed and into dreamless sleeps, out of reach of her husband's arms and his brother's shadow.

It had worked for a week. But what now?

She watched Christina dance, taking perhaps the most joy in that. She had had no choice but to accept. Everyone was here and she knew as well as Elena that her absence would have raised too many direct questions, and theirs wasn't a war that could be waged in the open air.

'See how she bends at your knee,' a voice murmured in her ear, the scent of leather and cinnamon drifting over her like a mist.

Elena straightened, holding the mask even closer to her face as she turned. Those hooded, elongated eyes she knew so well blinked back at her from behind black velvet. It was no disguise. She would have known him anywhere. In any lifetime.

'I don't know what you're talking about,' she demurred.

'Of course you don't. She's been nothing but a charm since you got here, opening doors, taking you under her wing.'

Elena didn't reply. How did he know? Christina hadn't been in the palace since he'd arrived. Unless . . . he'd heard the things Christina was saying about her . . . ?

'Bravo, sister. She is vanquished.'

'Don't call me that.'

'It's what you are, though.'

She felt her heart thrash, like a trapped bird caught in a cage. 'I am your brother's wife,' she said carefully. Determinedly.

He stared at her, his expression hardening before he looked away suddenly, standing beside her in a frigid silence as they watched the party swing. 'Where is Vito anyway? I haven't seen him all night.'

'Glad-handing, I expect. He's always the consummate host.'

Did he hear the edge of bitterness in her voice? From the corner of her eye, she saw him look back at her sharply. 'Has he danced with you?'

'Not yet.' She glanced at him. 'I'm fine with it . . . We don't go in for public displays.'

'No. You like to keep things *private*, don't you?' he said, harking back to the embarrassment of Christmas Eve.

'Stop it,' she hissed, feeling her throat constrict. She had yet to wear the negligee. Her intended plan of nightly seductions to fall pregnant with immediate effect had yet to materialize. Tonight, perhaps? She couldn't keep putting

Vito off, even though the thought of putting it on, when Aurelio was in his rooms across the courtyard, the lights on . . .

'Well, it's quite the success,' he said eventually, backing off. 'Your legacy. They'll be talking about it for years. Far better than Capote's in New York.'

'The Black and White Ball? I was there.' She turned her head to him, feeling her breath catch, her heart on hold. Nothing was safe. She could scarcely bring herself to ask the question. 'Were you?'

'Yes.' She saw the flare of his nostrils, the pulse in his jaw, the intense blaze behind those chocolate-brown irises. 'It's a wonder we didn't meet then.'

His voice was cruelly sardonic, the thought haunting. What if they had met that night, fourteen years earlier? Before Vito. Steve. Just before she had married Leo. What if he had been the brother she'd met first? How very different might her life have been? 'Yes,' she said, looking away quickly, aiming for the same bored carelessness. 'A wonder.'

He reached for her hand suddenly. 'Elena—'

'Aurelio!' A woman in a dramatically feathered red mask sashayed up to them, her bosom all but on display in a deeply corseted dress. Elena inclined her head in greeting, as Aurelio dropped her hand.

'Aurelio, dance with me,' she said brightly, coquettishly holding out a hand.

'That wouldn't be a good idea. We have already danced, Signora Bertorelli . . . What would your husband say?'

The woman's hand dropped, the mask – though obscuring her identity effectively – still not large enough to hide her dismay as she gathered her skirts and hurried away with a sob.

'You bastard,' Elena said under her breath. 'There was no reason to humiliate her like that.'

She heard his intake of breath and glanced to find him looking at her with glittering eyes. 'On the contrary, I'd argue she's the one doing the humiliating. I'm single. She's not. Her husband would have me duelling in the courtyard by dawn.'

'Well, I doubt he'd be the only one. You've certainly cut a swathe through their wives tonight.'

She couldn't keep the edge from her voice. Since the very first dance, he had flirted with every woman in the palace, making them laugh and tremble with an intensity that bordered on savagery. Was it any wonder they were all lining up for more?

'I'm surprised you noticed.'

'I didn't,' she replied with deliberate lightness. 'I overheard some of the ladies in the powder room. You're the talk of the town.'

He stared at her with a look that threw heat on her cheeks, but she refused to meet his eyes. 'Well, I guess you'd know all about that.'

She gasped and whirled to face him. 'What did you say?'

In one fluid movement, he had grabbed her by the wrist and pulled her round to the back of the column, into a deep, shadowy niche. The music fell away, silence wrapping around them, fastening them to one another. His eyes were only inches from hers, their faces obscured, but the truth, somehow, plainly written. Time slowed, worlds clashed.

'He's my husband, Aurelio,' she said, her voice breaking. 'I love him.'

'I know,' he said, his gaze on her mouth. 'So do I.'

*

She sat at the table in the courtyard in the shade of the orange tree, the blanket wrapped tightly around her, deep moons cradled beneath her eyes. She hadn't slept, lying on top of the sheets all night, locking the door to Vito and keeping him out as she turned over the options in her mind. But, really, there was only one.

A movement behind the glass caught her eye and she saw Vito – already dressed – behind the run of windows, striding through the galleries and assessing the morning-after detritus of the night before. The party had continued until three, the legend already begun: Aurelio had been right – they would talk about this ball for years. Christina couldn't reach her now.

Christina. How long ago it seemed now, when she had been her biggest concern.

She watched as Vito picked up a sequinned mask that had been left on the immobile face of a bust of Nero. She could see him tutting: glittery fragments peppered the marble and his long, elegant hands brushed them away.

He was a good man. Steadfast and honourable. Loyal and principled.

He deserved better.

She looked away, back at the garden, the grass hard and tipped white with frost, the topiaries silhouetted and emerging from the mists. A loud caw sent her gaze up to the rooks nesting in the cloud pines on the distant boundaries. The birds were free. They could fly away, just leave.

Couldn't she? She could go anywhere. She had the means. She had the houses.

A plane crossed the sky, its vapour trail slicing through the last of the bruised night clouds. She could go anywhere. Begin again and pick up the life she'd left before she'd stepped onto that boat. It wasn't as though she hadn't done it before. Another call – to Mr Charles's successor – and a plane ticket; that was how it usually went. Where this time? Paris? Berlin? St Moritz? London?

But she thought of Vito and of what she would say; she thought of the expression on his face as she told him . . . he wouldn't understand because how could he, when the truth wasn't an option?

Somewhere inside the palace a door slammed and a sudden shout made her look up. Vito was on the top floor of the west wing, wrestling open a window.

'I cannot believe it!' he shouted, with an anger she'd never glimpsed in him before, his face red even from this distance. 'He's done it again!'

Elena straightened up, the blanket falling off her shoulders. 'Done what, Vito? Whatever is the matter?'

But dismay was already arrowing through her. Because she knew.

'He's gone.'

Chapter Twenty-Nine

Rome, August 2017

There was something faintly ridiculous about walking through a marble gallery with a mug of tea. It was the kind of space that called for last night's Krug and Jimmy Choos, not English Breakfast and yellow Converse with a hole in the left sole under the big toe. Nonetheless, here she was, back to her usual self: Cinderella back in her second-hand rags, last night but a dream. Albeit a bad one. The open windows allowed the breeze in and she shivered slightly as it blew on her skin, pushing her hair off her neck and moulding her long floaty patchwork 1970s 'Holly Hobbie' dress to her frame. She had bought it only the other weekend from her favourite vintage boutique off the Piazza Navona, Alé urging her to get it on account of the 'sexy' straps which criss-crossed at the back.

Elena would no doubt struggle to suppress her usual look of bafflement at Cesca's outfit when they met up this afternoon for the next interview. As for Cantarelli – what was it he'd said last night? *'I do not understand your clothes.'* What did that even mean? Why did they need to be understood? She bet he didn't have any problems understanding

Isabella's clothes. She was the kind of 'matching bra and knickers' woman who dressed for men.

Not that she had any intention of seeing him anyway, she thought to herself, banishing him from her mind *again* and closing her eyes as another cooling gust of wind swept over her. She wouldn't be troubling him with the bother of trying to 'understand' today's outfit. This place was plenty big enough for the both of them, she would personally see to—

'Oh!' Tea slopped over her hands, splashing the floor, as she found herself suddenly travelling backwards, rebounding off something hard. 'Bugger!' she cried, setting the mug down quickly and rubbing the tea off her skin with her dress before it scalded her.

Nico, doing the same and holding his polo shirt away from his stomach, watched. 'Are you okay?'

She looked up at him in disbelief. Seriously? Of all the people . . . ? 'Yes. Thank you,' she said tightly.

'You weren't looking where you were going.'

She stopped rubbing her arm and glared at him. 'Oh well, just so long as we've established who's at fault,' she said sarcastically, picking up the mug and striding past him.

'I didn't mean . . . Cesca!'

She didn't stop, the sound of her own blood rushing through her ears. What *was* it with that man?

'Cesca, wait.' His hand was on her arm.

'*What?* I've got work to do.'

'I thought we could talk.'

'We talked last night. You, me and Isabella, remember?'

Oh, why had she said that? She saw the confusion in his eyes – and then the clarity. 'That is right,' he said, jamming his hand in his trouser pocket. 'And my sister very much enjoyed meeting you.'

'Your sis—?'

He stared at her, his eyes hard and probing, as if trying to see into her, but she could tell he couldn't gauge her at all. She was a riddle he could not read. 'Of course, it was a shame your boyfriend could not have joined us. We could have made a four.'

Now it was her turn to look baffled. 'My boyfriend?'

'Yes, Matteo, is that not his name? He took you home on Friday. Did you pass on Silvano's message to him, by the way?'

'Matteo's not my boyfriend!' she scoffed. 'He's the most terrible tart. He's just a friend.'

'I see.' Nico nodded but bemusement danced through his eyes and she realized it had been a trick question. An ambush of sorts. His eyes still danced. Were they . . . *flirting?*

'Well, I can introduce him to your sister if you li—'

'No.' Nico shook his head, firmly, his eyes still dancing.

Cesca felt her muscles tighten under his stare. What was going on here?

'I was coming to find you—' he said finally.

She tensed, remembering what he'd tried to start last night – a conversation about Friday, digging away at whatever it was she'd said, the memory still hidden from her, yet somehow grinding in the pit of her stomach.

'—We've mapped the first tunnel.'

'Oh!'

'Would you like to see?'

'I-I . . .' she stammered. The thought of being alone with him in the dark both excited and terrified her.

'It cannot be now. The area is restricted, naturally. It would have to be this evening.'

'I'm not sure.' She looked down at her now-tea-splashed dress. 'I'm not dressed for it.'

He looked at her dress too. 'No.' A puzzled silence passed before he added, 'We could give you a suit to wear.'

He meant a boilersuit; not a grey flannel one of the single-breasted variety. She had seen some of the men in them – navy, rugged all-in-ones – but she was remembering how good he had looked in his dinner suit last night.

'You will like it . . .'

The suit or the tunnel?

'Meet me outside at 6 p.m. Everyone will be gone by then.'

He didn't wait for an answer, turning and disappearing around the corner before she could say either yes or no.

'I guess it's a date, then,' she murmured, listening to the sound of his heavy boots receding on the marble, every bit as incongruous in this place as she.

'. . . What people need to understand, Francesca, is that I never saw them as a "string" of husbands. I never, ever thought I would divorce once, much less three times. I was just a young woman, making mistakes like anyone else. I can see there's almost a pattern to it, when I look back: I married too young, so then I swung the other way and married someone too old. And when that didn't work, I stopped looking for ways *out* of the life I knew and tried marrying within it to someone who was just like me – famous and rich, but also isolated, marginalized. Steve and I would have been a match made in heaven but for one crucial aspect. Although we moved in the same circles when we met, he hadn't been *born* to that life and that made all the difference in the world; I can see that now. I was jaded and tired – I wanted to settle down, have a family and make a home, but he wanted even *more* of it; he couldn't get enough. Fame, money – it was like a drug to him. He wanted to be seen with all the right people at all the right parties. God forbid we should spend a night at home on our own. Right from the start, we were pulling in different directions.'

Elena, standing by the bookcase, looked back at her. She looked older, somehow, today, her eyes pale and rheumy. She shook her head sadly. 'I was desperate to make it work. I tried everything I could. The shame I felt that my third marriage was breaking up was immense. My father had recently died, I felt alone and such a failure.'

She inhaled, filling herself up with air – energy – and beginning to pace again as Cesca watched from her perch on the sofa. 'But looking at the positives – and there were many – Steve was . . . he was a sweet man. Ferociously talented, of course, but that was often overlooked; Redford had the same problem. He had just won Best Supporting Actor for his role in *City Lights* when we got together, but he kept getting offered the same parts – the lover, the sexy waiter – and he wanted to be known for more than just his looks. It frustrated him enormously and, even back then, he was already beginning to talk about getting behind the camera. It was the only way he could be taken seriously.'

Cesca had spent a long time looking over his photographs. Steve Easton was a name that she recognized, although she couldn't necessarily have put a face to the name as, in her lifetime, he'd worked only as a director. The camera loved him, though, and he was perhaps the most handsome of all of Elena's husbands to date. Yet he seemed to have a hard-edged arrogance in his demeanour. His eye met the lens in almost every image, challenging it (or the person taking it) somehow.

'Did you live in Hollywood?'

'Not really. It was never my scene. Besides, Steve signed up to a long stint on Broadway, so most of our marriage was spent living in New York. It was the place to be back then, anyway. Studio 54, all the biggest names playing at Madison Square Garden . . . our marriage may have been falling apart but we were having a ball. Ironic, isn't it?'

Cesca had to agree. Marriage and divorce number three brought with them perhaps the most exciting collection of images yet. Cesca had known immediately upon delving into the box scrawled with '*New York 1975–79*' that it contained exactly the kind of thing the publishers would want. Every big name of the era was in there in one frame or another: the Studio 54 set – Andy Warhol, Mick and Bianca Jagger, Liza Minnelli, Calvin Klein and Halston; rock giants the Rolling Stones, the Eagles and Fleetwood Mac (some taken backstage on tour), as well as some studio shots with John Lennon and Yoko; Manhattan royalty with Jackie Onassis in her iconic sunglasses, Truman Capote and Rudolf Nureyev; and Hollywood stars Barbra Streisand, John Travolta, Jane Fonda, Robert Redford . . .

'What was Warhol like?' Cesca asked, more out of genuine curiosity than mere professional diligence. Their routine was well rehearsed by now: a pot of tea, some judiciously chosen pictures and the anecdotes and stories came rushing out. But Elena had surprised her today with her frankness, revealing some vulnerability for once instead of simply pushing an image of heady happiness. She felt Elena was beginning to trust her, that they were beginning to understand one another. Hell, they'd even started socializing together! Elena had been right that first day in Cesca's apartment when she'd said she could see them as friends.

'Rather spooky. He once came to a dinner and sat in the corner all night. He didn't say a word.'

Cesca gasped and giggled at once. 'That's so rude!'

Elena shrugged. 'He was an artist. I've always found it best to be tolerant of their sensitive moods.'

A sudden terrible crash outside made them both jump.

'Oh my God, what was that?' Cesca gasped, rushing to the window.

A small spider crane, which had been lowering the building props into the sinkhole, had toppled onto its side, the hydraulic arm still moving, cutting deeper and deeper grooves into what remained of the courtyard.

'Oh *no*! My garden!' Elena cried, her hands to her mouth as they watched the driver emerge tentatively from the upturned cab. 'Do you think he's all right?'

'He looks okay. Just a bit shaken,' Cesca said, watching as Nico climbed into the cab himself to turn off the ignition and stop the arm from swinging dangerously, before ordering the team to help the driver to sit down, get water . . .

'This will mean yet another delay, no doubt,' Elena tutted, moving away from the glass. 'Honestly, why can't they just be *done* with it? If it weren't for my friendship with his mother, I'd have put my foot down weeks ago. They can't remain camped out there for the rest of the summer.'

'He said it's for your own safety. The city's effectively sitting on a honeycomb and with the discovery of these tunnels running beneath your garden and possibly the palace too, he said they need to check they're stable before they close up the sinkhole again.'

Elena looked bemused. 'You seem to know an awful lot

about it, Francesca. Have you been spending much time with Signor Cantarelli?'

Cesca blushed. 'No. Of course not. It was just what he said the other day when I went down there on your behalf.'

'Oh, I see,' Elena said, seeming to see much more as she turned away from the window and walked back to the chairs.

'Nic— Signor Cantarelli,' Cesca corrected herself, 'said you already knew about the service tunnel.'

'Of course. Vito loved to regale me with stories of how he and his brother would play in it as children. It was one of their favourite games, hiding from their parents at bedtime, scooting down the east wing and popping up in the west wing moments later. It infuriated their father, apparently. He was a rather strict figure by all accounts.'

'Victorian Dad,' Cesca smiled.

'I'm sorry?' Elena appeared not to have heard her.

'It's a saying – referring to strict fathers.' She shrugged. 'Maybe it's a British thing.'

'Oh. I see.' She seemed distracted.

'Did you ever meet him? Vito's father?'

'No. He died when the boys were teenagers. Poor man, I get the impression he was as shackled by the responsibilities upon him as Vito came to be.'

'What do you mean, "shackled"?' Cesca probed. It was a strong word to use.

'People think having a title and owning something like this is all glamour but it comes with a huge amount of responsibility – when Vito took over the running of the palace, it employed over a hundred staff. You become a fig-urehead, not a person. When I first got here, I thought the best thing about marrying into the *Nobiltà nera* was having a parking permit for the Vatican City,' she quipped drily. 'But social standing underwrites everything in this city. Its importance cannot be underestimated – even now, when so many of the noble families have lost their fortunes and had to sell their estates. The obligation remains: charity, duty, discretion above all else.' She sighed, sounding weary now. 'I used to think duty was a mild concept – rather boring, almost, and held against one's own will – but as I have got older, I see it as a form of love, a passionate, raging thing.'

'Could you give me an example of what you mean?'

'Well, take Vito's father. He worked with the Italian Resistance, first against Mussolini, who tried to plunder the art collection here, and later the Waffen-SS, who commandeered the palazzo as their headquarters in 1943. For two years, the Nazi flag hung from those windows looking onto the piazza, bringing shame onto the Damiani name. But Vito's father crafted a plan, running bombs into that very service tunnel. Such was his sense of duty, he was prepared to sacrifice himself and blow up his family home, this awe-inspiring building, just to rid his city of those German invaders. Can you imagine possessing such conviction, such love for something, that you would put a bomb under your own life to preserve it?' Elena stared, unseeing, at the piazza on the other side of the far windows. She stared for so long that Cesca even began to wonder if something was the matter. 'That is what I mean when I say duty can be love and it can be a passionate, raging thing.'

'What happened?'

But Elena didn't reply; she didn't seem to hear her, still lost in her thoughts. '. . . I'm sorry, what?'

'Well, it can't have worked – the plan. I mean, the palazzo's still standing. Was Vito's father caught?'

'Oh. No.' She shook her head and slowly wandered back to the small armchair, lowering herself into it gingerly. 'I'm afraid it was far more boring than that. The Allies won. His father's plan wasn't needed in the end.' She closed her eyes, looking depleted. 'Aurelio always said he thought it was the greatest tragedy of his father's life, to have been robbed of his moment in history and instead have to settle down as a dutiful father and husband.'

'Aurelio?'

'Vito's twin,' Elena murmured, leaning her head back and closing her eyes for a moment.

'Oh, right,' Cesca said in surprise. 'Were they identical?'

'As exactly as it's possible to be.'

'Could you tell them apart?' Cesca asked. She'd always been fascinated by the concept of twins, ever since – as a left-hander – reading that left-handed people were likely to be the surviving twin of an early miscarriage. '. . . Elena?'

But to her astonishment, she saw that Elena was asleep. That interview – and all the answers to her questions – would have to wait.

'One size fits all, huh?' Cesca asked, rolling up the arms and legs of the boilersuit. Aside from being enormous, it was also incredibly hot to wear. 'I think I'd prefer to wear my own clothes, thanks.'

'No. You must wear it. To protect your skin.'

Cesca glanced at him as she put on the hard hat he handed to her. *Now* he cared about her skin? After two accidents and countless grazes?

Somehow, the crane had been righted again and was standing motionless in the dusk.

'You had an accident today – I saw,' she said.

He looked up; he'd been checking the ladder was stable. 'You saw?'

'Yes. It was very brave of you to jump into the cab when the arm was still moving about like that.'

He looked away disapprovingly and she sighed, flopping her arms down to her sides. Whatever she had daydreamed this evening might be, she already knew this wasn't it. Nico was in a distant mood, barely looking at her, even seeming surprised when she'd turned up, and so far he had spent more time examining images on his beloved computer than talking to her. 'Okay. Shall we get this over with, then?' she asked.

Her words made him stare but she headed for the ladder, knowing this part of the drill at least. At the bottom, she waited for him, turning on her head torch herself this time, and let him lead her the short distance through the make-shift shaft into the service tunnel.

They crept through the narrow, low cavity in silence, apart from the occasional warning from Nico to 'mind' something. He gave her a leg up again into the overhead tunnel and she waited for him on the other side, marvelling once more at the vast space that opened up. It was almost like a subway station down there. How could it be thousands of years old?

'Ready?' Nico asked, dropping down beside her. That grin was back on his face again now that they were down here, the one that rarely seemed to surface above ground. He was like a little boy in a sweet shop.

'As I'll ever be,' she replied, following after him with a bemused smile in spite of herself. He made her emotions bounce like a yo-yo.

'See this?' he asked as they got to the delta of the tunnels, pointing out a taut length of string drawn over with blue chalk, which stretched out of sight down one of the tunnels. He pinged it, and she saw the chalk make a line along the brick wall. 'It is a backup for getting out, in case the string should fail.'

'Why should it fail?'

He shrugged. 'Rats.'

She shuddered. 'Wish I hadn't asked,' she mumbled as he headed on again.

'See how wide this is?' he said from ahead, arms out-stretched to the sides yet unable to reach either wall. 'It is to allow carts through. Probably for carrying firewood along here.'

It could easily have accommodated a family-sized saloon, Cesca found herself thinking.

They continued walking – Nico just ahead, even though it was wide enough to walk side by side. It was so dark, only what fell within the scope of her head-torch beam could be seen at all. 'Are you okay?' he called back intermittently.

'Uh huh,' she replied, thinking it was lucky she wasn't afraid of the dark, or confined spaces, or being metres underground with a grumpy man she barely knew.

A sudden rumble made her shriek; it sounded as though the tunnel itself was moving, heaving itself up and shifting. 'Sorry,' she squeaked, covering her mouth with her hand and feeling embarrassed as it subsided again within a few seconds. 'That . . . that really startled me.'

Nico, who had rushed back, stared down at her, blinding her with his torch. 'It is the subway.'

'Right. I wasn't expecting it, that's all.'

'No.'

He hesitated, before turning and continuing down the tunnel.

'So, where does this lead to then?' she asked.

'It is a surprise.' She thought she could hear a grin – suppressed excitement, even – in his voice.

'What's down there?' she asked, stopping and pointing her beam in the direction of a new tunnel that led off sharply to the right.

'We don't know yet. It has not been mapped.'

'It's almost curving back on itself.'

'Cesca, you must come this way. This is the tunnel which has been investigated. You will be pleasantly surprised, I think. I have—'

'But I think—' She turned off the beam of her headlight and squinted. 'Yes, look. There's light over there.' She pointed towards a faint haze, almost indistinct even in this pitch blackness. It would have been all but impossible to spot in daylight.

Nico, still standing where he had stopped, shook his head. 'Cesca, we cannot go there. It may not be safe.'

'But why not? The parts of the tunnel we've been through so far have been in excellent condition. Relatively speaking.'

'That is not to say they all are. I already told you – the damage or weakness cannot necessarily be seen by the eye. We need to bring down the 3D scanners first. Now come,' Nico said, sounding impatient and beginning to walk again.

'But it's literally just coming from around that bend there. It's not far and I can clearly see there's nothing in the way – no rockfalls, no cracks . . . I don't think.'

'*This* way.' Nico's voice was firm and he was still walking, clearly thinking she would follow. Clearly not knowing her at all.

She was almost at the bend before he realized she wasn't behind him.

'Cesca!' His footsteps echoed loudly as he ran, the beam of his torch bouncing up and down with every bound as he charged furiously back towards her. 'What the hell do you think you are doing?' he demanded, taking hold of her arm. 'Do you have any idea of how reckless this is? This entire structure could come down at any moment.'

'Well, it will if you keep shouting like that,' Cesca said, defiant. 'Besides, if it's stood here for two millennia, it hardly seems likely it's going to collapse right now.'

'It has stood here for two millennia because it was *undisturbed*. You have no right to charge about down here as you like. You are not even supposed to be here. I only brought you because—' He stopped suddenly, his breathing heavy.

'What? Why *did* you bring me down here, Nico?'

He stared at her, at a loss for words. After another moment, he shook his head. 'This was a mistake. We will go back.' He turned to walk away.

'It's not been undisturbed,' she said to his back.

He stopped again and looked back at her, frowning, almost scowling now. 'What?'

She pointed to a space in the roof, just ahead. 'I think there's some sort of access point there . . . I can hear voices.'

'What? Where? Let me see.' He ran past her, angling his beam upwards. A round hole squirrelled a short distance upwards towards a primitive sort of manhole cover, iron handholds in the walls as before. He reached up for one and swung on it, testing its strength against his weight. It groaned weakly in its bracket, tiny stones skittering down the surface. He looked back at her. 'You must get back.'

'But—'

'Cesca, I am not asking you. Get back.'

The tone of his voice dissuaded her from arguing this time and she did as she was told.

'Further.'

She stepped right back, at least ten metres away from him now, the blackness wrapping its damp arms around her. 'What are you going to do?'

'Check it out, of course. But if it starts to give way, you must run back the way we have come. Follow the string. You understand?'

'Look, maybe this isn't a good idea,' she said, not liking the way she could hear more stones falling. They were only tiny, but what was it he had said about them sloughing off like plaster? That train had sounded as if it was just behind the next wall and all those years of vibrations . . . Surely that was what had instigated the sinkhole to open up in the first place. The walls of this tunnel could be paper-thin . . . He'd been right. What the hell had she been thinking, charging around down here as though she was in the Famous Five? 'I'm sorry, all right? Let's just—'

But a grunt of effort told her he had already lifted himself up, his beam of light swinging upwards and now boxed in the overhead cavity so that only a faint glow showered down. She could hear the dull clang of his boots on the iron bars of the steps as he slowly, carefully, climbed, testing every bar first before he committed his weight to it.

'Nico?' she asked.

There was no reply. He was out of sight. The footsteps had stopped now and she could hear more grunting, a faint pounding. She looked behind her, swinging the beam of her torch around, checking she was alone. She knew it was stupid to think otherwise. Of course she was. It was a secret underground tunnel. Aloneness was the one thing you could guarantee down here. Still, it felt more forbidding to be standing here alone in the dark.

When she looked back again, the glow from his torch had gone. 'Nico, are you okay?' she asked, walking forwards a few steps. 'Nico—?'

'I'm right here.'

Cesca stopped below the access hole and looked up. He was lying on his stomach, somewhere dark, one arm reaching down to her. 'Come up.'

Allowing him to grab her by the wrist, she managed to get her feet on the first rung.

'Mind the second one. It is very loose,' he cautioned, just as another stream of stones slid away.

She climbed as lightly as she could, her heart beating as fast as a brigadier's drum. Nico helped to pull her up through the manhole, which she could see now had been covered by half-rotten planks of wood nailed to an iron frame. With just her head and shoulders through, she looked around curiously. They were in a dark room. A cellar, perhaps. It smelled damp, with stacked wine bottles gleaming like nocturnal creatures' eyes. Overhead, footsteps sounded thunderous, muffled voices falling through the cracks of the floorboards, a door rattling lightly on its lock.

Nico was already prowling the room. He picked up a bottle of chianti, appraising the label.

'Where are we?' she marvelled, just as there was a sudden shout, very close, coming from behind the door. She gasped and looked up as in the next instant it swung open, a body silhouetted in the frame. Startled, Nico dropped the bottle, glass shattering on the stone floor, and there was an ear-splitting scream. A light was switched on, flooding the room and dazzling them both.

'*Francesca?*'

Hurriedly, Cesca turned off the beam on her head torch and looked up.

'*Signora Accardo?*'

Dinner hadn't been on the cards for this evening, but then neither had breaking and entering into the basement of the osteria. Besides, Signora Accardo wasn't going to take 'no' for an answer.

They had to sit at a table indoors; the osteria was busy with the first sittings of the evening and every table outside had already been taken. Cesca watched the ceiling fan rotate, trying to feel some relief from the oppressive heat; she was baking in the boilersuit and wished she could take it off. Her apartment was only a few metres from here. She could be home, changed and back again in minutes . . .

Nico – having insisted on paying for the bottle he had dropped – had ordered another bottle for them, his finger tapping on the stem of his glass, his eyes roaming the dark room. He didn't speak and she knew he was angry with her for wandering off. She could see that he was also restless, wanting to talk further to Signora Accardo but, as ever, she was manning the front-of-house operations of the restaurant. She kept bustling past every few minutes, nodding in their direction to indicate that she would be over any moment, any moment now . . .

'Well, that was a turn-up for the books,' Cesca said,

trying to break the ice. 'Who'd have thought the tunnel would have led here?'

He looked at her, his eyes coal-black and inscrutable. 'It had to lead somewhere.'

'Well, yes, but . . .' She faltered. 'I wonder if Signora Accardo knew about it?'

'How could she not? It was in the middle of her cellar floor.'

'I suppose lots of people don't bother investigating things like that, though, do they? They just assume it's to provide access to the sewer or something and leave it. After a while, they probably don't even notice it and then, after another while, they forget—' She was wittering, she knew.

'Yes, yes, I get the picture,' he snapped.

Cesca's shoulders slumped. 'Look, I'm sorry. I shouldn't have gone off like that.'

'No. You shouldn't,' he shot back, his dark eyes shining.

'But it turned out okay, didn't it?'

'Luckily for you,' he said hotly. 'It easily could not have been the case. You were *lucky*.'

'Okay, I said I'm sorry. I get it.' She looked away, hating that his anger upset her.

'No, I don't think you do. Do you think those protocols are there for no reason? Do you think I have not lost people before because they too thought they knew better? You could easily have been killed, Cesca. We both could.'

'Okay, Nico! You've made your point. How many times can I say it? I'm sorry. I'm sorry, I'm sorry, I'm sorry!' She sat back, chastened, feeling like she'd just been pummelled. 'Jesus, you're always so mad at me.'

'Yes! Because—' He stopped, looking away. His finger began tapping faster on the glass.

'Because what?' She arched an eyebrow. 'It's sport to you?'

Signora Accardo appeared, a steaming plate in each hand.

'Here,' she said, setting them down and pulling out the spare chair. 'Osso bucco.'

Cesca smiled weakly. Nico's anger had completely taken away her appetite, not to mention she was already over-heating in this damned boilersuit. Couldn't she just have had a salad?

'Thank you, Signora. It smells incredible,' Nico replied, his eyes bright again. 'Please – I know you are busy, but what can you tell us about the tunnel? Did you know about it?'

'Of course! It was used as a bomb shelter in the war.'

'Did you ever go down into it?'

'Me? No. Umberto, though . . . for a while he grew the mushrooms.' Signora Accardo had dropped her voice, her eyes cautioning.

Nico looked across at Cesca, anticipating he needed to explain. 'The mushroom farms were illegal, set up in the disused underground tunnels; not only in the old quarries here in Rome, but also in other cities across Europe, such as the catacombs in Paris. The dark, damp conditions are per-fect for cultivation and the farms difficult for the authorities to find. But there was a big crackdown in the 1980s and most of them were closed down.'

'Since then . . .' Signora Accardo shrugged. 'Why go down there? Dark, dirty, cold.'

'When was the last time your husband accessed the tunnel?' Nico asked, cutting the meat on his plate.

'It was not for him to go down; it was for others to come up.'

'Which others?'

Signora Accardo's eyes flickered towards the piazzetta.

'From the palazzo?' Nico asked.

'The princes. They would always be chasing down there as children. We could hear them from the cellar sometimes.' She smiled, shaking her head indulgently at the memories. 'They would sneak out from here, knowing we would not tell.'

'So Vito knew about it?' Cesca murmured. 'That's interesting. Elena says she only knew about the service tunnel.'

'That is correct. *This* tunnel—' Signora Accardo said, lightly stamping her foot on the floor. '—Was blocked up from the private palazzo tunnel twenty-eight years ago by the Visconti, after his brother died.'

Nico frowned. 'Why?'

She shrugged. 'To stop the memories.'

'There must have been a security risk to the palace too,' Cesca said thoughtfully. 'If the princes could get out, surely thieves could get in? They have one of the most important art collections in Europe behind those walls,' she remembered.

'Where do the tunnels lead to, do you know?' Nico asked.

'All over. Some to the garden—'

Nico's eyes slid across to Cesca.

'—Some to the piazzetta here too.'

'You mean there are other buildings with access points like yours?' Cesca asked.

'Of course.' Signora Accardo looked at Cesca, her expression darkening. 'Yours, for example.'

'Mine?' The access point would lead out into Signora Dutti's apartment, then, as she occupied the ground floor.

'The Damiani estate still owns all the properties in the Piazzetta Palombella.'

'I didn't know that,' Cesca said.

Signora Accardo shrugged, wiping her hands on her apron and making to stand. She could see a couple outside looking for her. 'Eat. I bring you *secondi*.' She left again.

'Well, that was interesting,' Cesca said, watching her go.

'Yes.'

'But you look disappointed.'

'Only in that the tunnels are not as new to find as we had hoped.'

'You mean in terms of archaeological treasures?'

He shrugged.

'Well, at least you still get to map them. That's got to be worth something. You can add them to your big 3D underground map and fill in the gaps – so to speak.' She laughed at her own joke.

Nico watched her, observing how she lifted her hair up to cool her neck.

'What?' She felt self-conscious.

He looked away, shaking his head, his eyes back on the palazzo. 'Nothing.'

She sighed, frustrated. 'There's obviously something. You keep looking at me as if . . . as if you hate me.'

'I do not hate you,' he refuted. 'I just don't . . .' His voice tailed off again. 'I don't understand you.'

'Like you don't understand my clothes, you mean?'

He leaned in towards her suddenly. 'You cannot say what you said and not expect it to make a difference,' he hissed. 'What am I *supposed* to think?'

She groaned. 'Look, I already apologized for calling you annoying. I told you I was drunk.'

'Not that.'

'Then *what*?' The way he looked at her . . . Cesca went very still, feeling cold fingers begin to creep on her skin. 'What did I say, Nico?'

'You said . . .' He inhaled and held his breath, his eyes probing hers. 'You said you killed someone.'

The air sucked out of the room as though on vacuum, the ceiling fan as loud as an aeroplane. Her eyes dropped from his to the floor, the walls, outside – anywhere so that she didn't have to look at him and see the expression in his eyes.

'Cesca? It does not make sense. I do not believe it. But why would you say it?'

She felt herself tremble, tears filling her eyes. It had been a long day. She was tired. This was all too much. 'I didn't. I never said such a thing.'

'Cesca, you did.'

'No, I didn't. I know I didn't,' she said, getting up and pushing the chair away so forcefully that it clattered to the floor. She ran from the restaurant, but she didn't go to the haven of her apartment, not to fifty metres from here where he could simply follow her. Instead, she rounded the corner and dived into the warren of tiny streets, running as fast as she could, trying to get lost.

She knew she hadn't said that thing, because it was wrong, a lie. She hadn't killed some*one*.

It had been two.

Chapter Thirty

Rome, May 1982

'Isn't that Phillipe Santana in the third row?' Vito murmured in her ear.

Elena didn't need to turn her head to get a good look. The Damiani family box gave them a bird's-eye view from which no one could escape their scrutiny. Not that she bothered to look. The point of sitting up here was to be looked at. 'Is it?'

'I think so.' He paused. 'I thought they were in Verona.'

'How so?'

'The hostile takeover I told you about.'

She shifted in her seat. 'Oh yes. Of course.'

'We should try to speak to them afterwards.'

'Mmm.'

The lights dimmed and the hum of conversation dwindled to silence at the first stray touch of bows on strings as the velvet curtain rose.

'Do you want the programme?' he asked, leaning forwards again.

'It's *Così fan tutte*, Vito,' she sighed. 'I've seen it a thousand times. I know it better than that soprano.'

The stage lights rose and she inclined her head as she

always did when something had to be endured. She had perfected the art of sitting like a statue. She could still every part of her body so that the only part of her moving was her heart – which was ironic, given it was her heart that felt so completely dead these days. Sometimes she thought she was like a black bear, able to lower her heart rate so that it barely beat at all, drifting into a sort of hibernating state, alive but not awake.

Behind her, the door opened and closed again: Vito making the toilet break he couldn't during the interval when everyone clamoured to talk to them; a blade of light falling over her seat and the front of the balcony.

She let her mind drift, blocking out Despina's mischief on stage and thinking of what needed to be done tomorrow. There was a meeting with the Red Cross scheduled to discuss fundraising initiatives for the growing Ethiopia crisis, as well as lunch with her publisher friend Max Everstein, who was in town for three days – a lunch at which he would no doubt beg her to agree to that book idea of his, even though they both knew the answer would be no. Then she had a fitting with Mr Armani at 3 p.m. for an AIDS benefit next month; drinks with Christina and Sigmundo at 7 p.m., followed by dinner at the embassy with the new American ambassador to Rome. She hoped Maria had brought out her white pantsuit for the lunch – it always needed a good few hours to hang before she wore it; she would need to check when they got in.

She tipped her head to the other side and wondered whether Vito would come to her tonight. She hoped not. It was a Thursday. He didn't usually visit her bed on a Thursday – Tuesday, Friday and Sunday was his preferred pattern – but he'd been growing concerned about her continuing inability to fall pregnant and had surprised her recently with some ad hoc visits, surprising her yet further with some new positions, claiming it was perhaps the fact that she didn't climax that was hindering conception. Nothing to do with the fact that she was now almost thirty-seven.

Had Vito chosen the wines yet for the dinner they were hosting a week Saturday? she wondered. The cook couldn't prepare a menu without knowing the wines they'd be serving and the food would need to be ordered by tomorrow. Seventy-two for dinner couldn't be done off the hoof.

And how had they left it about Cannes? If they couldn't get the yacht round in time from Mustique, then really what was the poin—?

Like a dog sniffing the wind, she suddenly caught a trace of something. She turned her head fractionally. What was it?

On stage, the silly girls flirted with their suitors, but she couldn't hear them. It was as though silence had been turned on to max and was blasting around the auditorium. All her other senses dialled up – colour became almost painfully intense to her eyes, she could feel the individual fibres of the velvet pile of her chair against her leg, the appley tang of the prosecco still lingered on her tongue, she could smell Shalimar and Poison, cigarettes; dual notes of leather and cinnamon drifted to her nose.

She stiffened, understanding immediately, her body responding sightlessly, wordlessly. She could feel his stare as though it was a hundred fingers on her skin, in her hair.

The door opened again, Vito quietly shuffling into his seat, which was set slightly behind her, coughing discreetly into his fist. Always so proper. Always so considerate.

She didn't move her head, her eyes raking the crowd in

the dim light for the face that she dreamed of seeing again, even though she saw it every day. The face she had loved at first sight and then second.

He was sitting in the dress circle, not quite opposite them, his eyes burning into her. She saw it all – his anger, his lust, his despair that even now, a year and a half later, it was quite clearly exactly the same as it had been then. Nothing had changed. The sacrifice had been worthless.

He was deeply tanned, Elena noticed. A blonde woman in navy chiffon sat to his right. She leaned over, whispering something in his ear, forcing him to break eye contact, and to Elena the sudden release felt like being dropped from a great height; her stomach felt hollow, panic gripping her. They were at an impasse, the two of them simultaneously held together and forced apart by a gravity that would not ever let them go.

Because she was the reason he'd left.

And he was the reason she'd stayed.

'Darling, you're burning up.' Vito's hand was cool against her skin.

'I know, I'm . . . I'm sorry.'

'Don't be silly.' He leant down and kissed her tenderly on her parched lips. 'It's not your fault. We can go anytime. I'll call and rearrange. They'll understand.'

'No!' She smiled apologetically. 'I mean, you go. There's no need for both of us to miss out on the fun. I'm sure he's got plenty of stories to tell. And it's been so long since you saw each other. You know Aurelio, there's no telling when he might disappear again. See him while you've got the chance.'

Vito sank onto the edge of the bed. 'But I hate leaving you like this.'

'I'm fine. I've got Maria to look after me.'

'Well . . .' He looked uncertain. 'If you're sure.'

'I am.' She squeezed his hand. 'Besides, you need to report back on his sexy new girlfriend. Although don't you go falling in love with her too,' she joked.

He chuckled. 'As if I could ever have eyes for anyone but you.' He kissed her forehead again.

'Do you think it's serious between them?'

Vito sighed. 'Perhaps. He's certainly never been bothered about introducing any of his women to me before. Who knows? Maybe she's tamed him. I guess it had to happen at some time or other.'

'Can tigers be tamed?' she quipped.

He patted her hand and rose, looking as elegant as ever in his pale-grey Zegna jacket and navy trousers, a navy spotted handkerchief tucked in the breast pocket. 'I won't be late.'

'Take your time. I'll be asleep within the hour anyway.'

'It's no wonder you're exhausted. You've taken on far too much lately. You've been a woman possessed.'

'Yes, well . . . Lesson learnt.'

The door clicked behind him and she listened to the sound of his footsteps retreating down the long, long corridors. She could tell from the number of silences as he crossed the rugs exactly which gallery he was in, until eventually the extended silence told her he was gone.

She stared up at the ceiling – a fresco of cherubim frolicking on pink clouds. She'd always hated it.

She turned away onto her side, facing the windows that gave onto the courtyard and the blank windows of the west wing, which had remained defiantly dark for three long days now. He had kept his presence at the opera a secret from Vito, disappearing straight after the performance and making no contact, no sign he was in town at all, until he had breezily telephoned yesterday to suggest dinner at the Aventine Hill apartment of his new love, Milana Novelli. She was a twenty-something starlet currently riding high on the back of a well-received supporting role in the latest Fellini film.

Elena closed her eyes, a single tear dropping from her lashes onto the Frette sheets. Did he really think she would have gone there tonight, to sit across from them at the table as new love shone in their eyes, Milana's slim, unlined hand on his thigh?

Probably not. She knew what it was as well as he – a glove on the ground, a statement of intent. Milana was the most beautiful of diversions, a buffer, there to enforce the necessary distance between them. And he was right. He had to do it. She wanted him to do it. They both needed him to do it.

But that didn't mean she had to like it.

Chapter Thirty-One

Rome, August 2017

Slowly but surely, Cesca was working her way through the thousand rooms of the palace. Today's interview was taking place in a hitherto unknown space – Elena's private sitting room. It was set just off from the grand space of the white sitting room, which, she now learned, was merely for 'entertaining'.

It was clear they were in the inner sanctum here. The room led directly to Elena's bedroom – an exquisite dome-tented Napoleon bed was just visible through the crack in the door – with views of the courtyard and the west wing. It had been decorated in a discreet, restful chinoiserie with duck-egg-blue silk walls, pale-grey curtains and blush sofas. Cesca thought it was like sitting in a dream. Old-fashioned roses from the garden sat in a Lalique crystal bowl, black-and-white photos were arranged in dense clusters in silver frames and a large round tasselled ottoman was carefully stacked with coffee-table books on Richard Avedon, the Royal Gardens of England, Bulgari jewels, Delft stoneware, modern apartments of Paris . . . The room stood as apart from the palazzo as the white room did: more a statement of Elena's personality than the building in which it was contained. It was a room that could just as easily have been found in London's Chelsea or Manhattan's Upper East Side – tasteful, discreet, gentle, it lacked the almost brutal lavishness of the rest of the palazzo. Cesca felt she could breathe more easily in here – that the secrets she felt pulsating behind every tapestry, every statue, every portrait, had been stopped at the door.

Elena was arranged on the sofa in cream slacks and a soft jumper, a cashmere blanket draped over her legs, even though it was almost thirty degrees outside. She had come down with a heavy cold – 'one of the great bores of getting older, this falling ill at the drop of a hat,' she had muttered as Alberto served the tea.

'So, where are we?' she asked, glancing only vaguely at the photographs Cesca had fanned out for her.

Cesca smiled. 'Vito.'

Elena inhaled deeply and sank back into the cushions, a radiant smile on her face. 'Oh, my darling Vito. *Finally.* When my life began in earnest. Everything that preceded it was just a dress rehearsal.'

Cesca sank back into her chair, too. She could hardly believe she was getting paid for this – tea and a chat. It felt almost wrong to accept the money. 'Tell me about how the two of you met.'

'Well, formally, it was on Christmas Eve, 1980, at a drinks reception here. I know it was 1980 because Yves had just shown his Diaghilev collection and I bought pretty much the entire thing.' She shook her head disdainfully. 'I'm not usually so extravagant.'

'You always talk about him as the love of your life.'

'Who? Yves?' Elena laughed, enjoying her little joke.

'Vito,' Cesca grinned. 'Was there an immediate connection between you?'

'Oh my dear, it was love at first sight! We were married within weeks. We eloped to Venice, you know; we just couldn't wait to be man and wife.'

'You eloped? Wow. He really did sweep you off your feet! Where did you honeymoon?'

'On Mustique. Lord Snowdon was a friend and very generously lent us his villa as a wedding present. So sweet.'

Cesca frowned a little. 'Hmm, I don't recall having come across any of those photos, though, and I think I'm up to about 1985, 1986 now.'

'That is odd. I'll ask Alberto to do another search.' Elena frowned. 'The archivist may have filed them separately for some reason, although I can't really think why . . . Oh, I do hope they're not mislaid.'

'I'm sure not. And I'll double-check the boxes again. I could have overlooked a file. Your archivist really was incredibly thorough. Everything's dated in separate envelopes.'

'Well, he was certainly paid enough for it.' Elena closed her eyes. 'Honestly, Francesca, it was exhausting. I had to give him lists of every place we'd been, every year. Can you imagine?'

For a globetrotter like Elena? No! 'How on earth did you manage it?'

'I had to go through *all* my old diaries. Mother used to be very particular about it, it was one of the few things she insisted upon – that I simply *had* to record my day on paper. She said it would be a historical record one day, although I fear she was rather overstating our family's importance.'

Cesca's ears had pricked up. 'You've got diaries? But that's brilliant—'

'Oh heavens, no, you can't use those!' Elena said, heading her off at the pass. 'You'd die of boredom, they're just the scribblings of a lucky little rich girl who became a princess.'

'Precisely!'

'No, no, you flatter me, but people don't want to hear me moan about whatever mundane trivialities I may have had going on. People like me aren't allowed to complain, Francesca. We've already got the lion's share of luck. It's poor form to be ungrateful.'

Cesca could see she had a point – no one was going to feel sympathy if they ran out of milk on the yacht. Nonetheless, they needed some sort of balance, the text was going to need some *body*, otherwise it was going to read like a puff piece, stroking Elena's ego and with no credibility whatsoever. Once they were through with the photographic interviews and she had established this preliminary timeline of Elena's life, she intended to knuckle down to the next stage of some serious fact-checking and research, and those diaries could be invaluable for providing a bit more tone for the events as they happened. The problem with hindsight and recollecting events in posterity was that everything tended to be viewed through rose-tinted spectacles.

'I really do think it would be worthwhile me having a quick scan of them, at least. I'm sure there must be all sorts of anecdotes you've forgotten, which could really add colour to the book.'

'Trust me, I'm doing you a kindness, Francesca. They wouldn't add anything of note.'

She was smiling – but there was steel in her eyes, and

Cesca knew better now than to try to force the issue. Still, the kernel of another idea began to present itself in her mind. If they couldn't use the diaries for the book, could this be the exclusive for her blog she'd been looking for? She had no doubt her readers would love nothing more than the edited diary extracts of one of Rome's most noted socialites.

Biting her tongue, knowing now wasn't the time to moot the suggestion, she pointed instead to a photo of Elena and Vito sitting on the bonnet of a silver Ferrari. Elena was sitting slightly behind her husband, her chin nestled in his neck as they both looked to the camera. She was wearing flared jeans and a navy t-shirt, a headscarf covering her long hair. She did indeed look truly happy, her eyes shining. Vito was more relaxed, one foot propped up on the fender, and a hand clasping the arm that she had slung lovingly around his neck. They looked as if they couldn't keep their hands off each other.

'You made such a beautiful couple.'

Elena reached forwards for it, staring at it with misted eyes. 'Thank you. Love does that, doesn't it? You just . . . *glow*, from the inside out. We were travelling to Positano that day. He'd just picked up the car from Maranello. Always such a little boy at heart.'

'Oh, talking of little boys,' Cesca said, suddenly remembering something. Their interview had been cut short the other day. 'You said Vito was a twin?'

'That's right. His brother was called Aurelio. Younger by fourteen minutes.' She tutted, shaking her head. 'Extraordinary, isn't it? They spent nine months together in the womb, yet by dint of Vito coming out first, he inherited the titles, the estates . . . just everything. Those fourteen minutes changed the entire direction of both their lives.'

'What did Aurelio do? I assume he didn't need to work?'

'No, but it rarely benefits those who don't. Ah, now there's a question. What did he do? Well, let me see – latterly he worked as a banker in Hong Kong, but before I met Vito, he had spent some time as a racing driver for Alfa Romeo, and then he worked as a stunt man on a film set. Vito had employed him to run the vineyards up in Chianti for a while but he took off after a year or so. And by the time I met Vito, his brother was running a safari business in Kenya, although by all accounts that mainly involved sitting on a deck drinking gin and having affairs with his friends' wives.'

'Nice,' Cesca said, thinking precisely the opposite.

'Oh, they were all at it; you know what it's like in the colonies. He ended up leaving when one particularly irate husband shot him in the chest.'

'Good God.'

'Yes,' Elena sighed. 'He was lucky to survive.'

'Was the husband who shot him prosecuted?'

'Heavens, no. Reli understood the poor man was perfectly within his rights.'

'To shoot him in the chest?'

'Of course. He'd been having it off with his wife, what did he expect? It was par for the course. That was Reli all over, really – he had that sort of dangerous glamour.'

'So, it wasn't a one-off then?'

'Lord, no. He'd been smuggled over the Argentinian border by the time he was nineteen for getting involved with the daughter of one of the druglords. Potato van, I think they used; he never ate another potato again.' Elena smiled affectionately. 'He somehow lived a larger life than other people.'

'Did you get on with him?'

'On the whole, although he could drive me crazy; well, me and Vito. He was arrogant and selfish. I guess that's the problem with people like that – the usual rules don't apply. Poor Maria, our housekeeper at the time, he drove her around the bend. He was incapable of hanging up a shirt; she said his bedroom always looked like a scene of mass destruction.'

'Were he and Vito close?'

'They didn't live in each other's pockets or finish each other's sentences, if that's what you mean. In fact, they were like chalk and cheese in many ways. Vito had to *become* himself, if you see what I mean; he wasn't in a position to choose the direction of his life, whereas Aurelio had the freedom to live as he chose. It didn't seem very fair to me. Their mother always used to say they were one face but two hearts. But for all that, you could sense the bond between them: it was like a velvet rope, connecting them. There was no question they loved each other more than anyone on the planet.'

Cesca arched an eyebrow. 'Even more than you?'

'Oh, absolutely. I was a distant second.'

'Was that hard for you?'

'Well now, coming third I would have taken issue with,' she laughed, retrieving a handkerchief from her sleeve and gently dabbing her nose with it. 'But no, that's twins for you. You could say you almost have to love them both. They come as a package, really.'

Cesca stared down at the only photograph she had seen of both the twins together. There were two scooters – Elena riding pillion on an aqua one with Vito in front, a blonde girl straddling the red one beside it. Aurelio stood to the side, ankles crossed as he leaned against a bollard. The girls and Vito had ice creams; Aurelio was smoking and not looking to the camera, glancing over at his brother and Elena instead.

Even after scrutinizing it, Cesca couldn't find any discernible difference between the twins – both seemed to be the same height and build, their hair worn in a traditional barber's cut. Perhaps, at a push, Vito's eyes were slightly more elongated? But then, that could have just been because he was laughing. Aurelio, possibly, had a slightly more louche air? But then, that could just have been because of the cigarette dangling from his fingers.

'Tell me about this photo,' she said, tapping the photograph.

'Oh.' Elena paled at the sight of it, reaching for it with a visibly trembling hand. 'Well now, that day . . . that day, I seem to recall Vito and I had the most terrible argument.'

'Oh, I'm sorry,' Cesca said sympathetically, but inwardly she was groaning. It was a great picture but she could already see what was going to happen.

The silence lengthened as Elena continued to stare at it. She looked . . . haunted, almost.

'Was the argument after the photo was taken, do you remember?' Cesca asked. Elena's eyes in the image looked distant, as though she hadn't heard the command to 'say "cheese"'.

'. . . What? Oh, yes. I think so.'

Cesca wondered what the argument could have been about to upset her so much all these years later. 'The thing is, it would be lovely to use it if we could; it's the only photo I've been able to find so far of Vito and his brother together.'

Elena's eyes flickered to hers. 'Well, it's not like that is crucial to the book. I don't think anyone cares one way or the other that my fourth husband had a twin.'

'No. I guess not,' Cesca agreed reluctantly. 'But it is a great image. Quintessentially Italian. And you look so glamorous. It really encapsulates the spirit of your life in the Eternal City. We've got the yacht pictures in Newport, shots of the surfing scene and beaches in Malibu, snaps of the discos in New York, and this is—'

'I don't think so.'

That was it? The topic was closed? Cesca felt a pulse of anger that there would be no further discussion on the subject. As with the diaries, there was no collaboration here and she felt her professional pride needled, springing back to life just for a moment. She wasn't used to being a 'yes person'.

'Well, perhaps we could put it in the "maybe" pile?' she persevered, digging her own heels in.

'There is no maybe pile, Francesca, just what makes the cut – and I don't wish to include, in a book about my life, a photograph that is painful to me.'

'I'm sorry, but I just th—'

There was a sudden commotion outside the door – they heard Alberto's voice raised in anger – and in the next moment it flew open and Nico fell into the room, physically wrestling Alberto off him. For one second, as the butler backed off and Nico was still bent double, his clothes awry, his eyes met Cesca's and the disaster of their dinner at the osteria, three days earlier, mushroomed between them. She had hidden herself away since then, and she had been both relieved and devastated that he had made no attempts to find her. His expression darkened at the sight of her. *You killed someone.*

'Signor Cantarelli!' Elena exclaimed in alarm. 'What on *earth* is going on?'

Nico tore his eyes off Cesca, seeming surprised to find Elena sitting there too, even though it was she who he had fought his way in to see. 'I am sorry for the intrusion, but I had to see you.'

'It couldn't wait?' she demanded, looking displeased.

'No.' He straightened up, practically swatting away the butler, who could only send his employer a disapproving but helpless stare.

Elena in turn glared at Nico, but eventually sighed, defeated in the end by sheer curiosity. 'Very well. It's fine, Alberto.' She waited for the door to close behind him. 'What is it you needed to see me about so very urgently?'

Nico glanced at Cesca, his scowl deeper than ever. 'You may wish for us to continue this discussion in private.'

Cesca bridled, straightening in her chair. Seriously? He was going to be petty about this?

'Oh, for heaven's sake,' Elena tutted, obviously of the same mind. 'Francesca is my biographer. Isn't it implicit I keep nothing from her?'

The irony that she had been doing exactly that just before Nico had disturbed them seemed to pass her by.

Nico's eyes slid between the two women. He looked especially displeased today, Cesca thought. 'Very well. Then I thought you would want to know . . . we found this.' And from the deep cargo pocket on his right thigh, he pulled out something small and wrapped in cloth. He let the cloth fall open.

'Holy shit!' Cesca cried, her hands flying to her mouth at

the sight of an absolutely enormous ring comprised of two triangular stones: one a diamond, the other a pale sapphire. She had never seen anything like it: not the scale of it, nor the brightness. Even dirty, as it clearly was, it was more dazzling than anything she had ever seen.

Nico held it up to the light, watching Elena closely. 'I assume it is yours?'

Elena was already on her feet, her legs shaky, her face ashen. '*Where* did you get this? I demand to know.'

'As I said, it was in the tunnel, Principessa. It must have been there for many years.'

'Yes,' Elena whispered, looking as if she might pass out. Cesca had never seen someone go that pale before. Elena took the ring from him and slipped it on. It was slightly loose but the stones were too big to let it slide around her finger.

'If this is your ring then there is something I do not understand, Principessa – and it is a question I must ask. If you did not know about the tunnels, as you told me you did not, then how did your ring come to be down there?'

It was a good question, Cesca thought, her eyes sliding over to her employer.

'Well, *clearly* someone must have tried to rob me,' Elena replied tersely.

'Rob you?'

'Yes. They must have wanted to use the tunnel as an escape route and . . . accidentally dropped it somewhere down there.'

'And then turned back when they could find no other way out?' Nico suggested.

'Exactly.'

'No.'

'No?'

'There *is* a way out. We know now that one of the tunnels leads to the basement of the osteria in Piazzetta Palombella.' His eyes slid across to Cesca and she felt herself hold her breath.

Elena arched an eyebrow. 'Oh, I see.' She was quiet for a moment before seeming to become aware of Cesca's presence again. 'On second thought, I say we continue this privately, Signor Cantarelli. Francesca, you will excuse us? We can pick this up later.'

'O-of course,' Cesca murmured, staring after them as Elena rose to her feet and led Nico to another room. Nico's dark gaze was the last thing Cesca saw before he closed the door softly behind them.

What the hell? Irritated by both her burning curiosity and her restlessness at Nico's new indifference towards her, she scooped the photographs into a pile and returned them to the envelope, switching off the digital recorder. The photograph of the four of them on the scooters was still on Elena's chair where she had dropped it when Nico had barged in and Cesca walked over to retrieve it, her eyes falling upon the framed black-and-white photos arranged on the side table beside the chair. From where she had been sitting, she had been able to see only the backs of them.

That wasn't the case any more. Cesca stopped dead at the sight of one, knowing that to examine it further was going beyond her professional remit. This wasn't research, it was snooping. The photographs in the boxes she'd been *invited* to see, but that one there . . . Was she *ever* supposed to have seen it? This was Elena's private space; Cesca was here only because Elena felt too sick to move about much today.

Hands trembling, she picked up the heavy silver Tiffany

frame. The black-and-white image was backlit, light streaming in through a window in the background, lending a celestial aura to the picture. In it, Elena was holding a newborn baby, its skin still creased, eyes slitted against the light. Elena's lips were in a tender pucker on the baby's cheek, her eyes closed. The frame had been engraved with an inscription: *Stevie Easton, 14 March 1974.*

Cesca sank into the chair as she realized what it meant. Elena had had a child, with her previous husband – and she had said nothing about him. She was writing a book on her life but hadn't thought to mention *having a child*?

She looked around the beautiful room again, realizing she'd got everything the wrong way round: the secrets didn't stop at that door there – they started at it. The lies were all in here.

Chapter Thirty-Two

Rome, June 1982

'. . . called my agent. They want me to go in for a part in the new Scorsese,' Milana said, her cigarette tip glowing brightly. She sucked hard on it again, leaving pink lipstick marks on the paper. 'I don't know, though.'

Vito looked up at her incredulously. 'You don't *know* about working with Scorsese?'

'I don't know about upping sticks and moving to New York for six months. Your brother here can't be trusted.'

Vito and Elena looked at Aurelio, anticipating his stock outraged expression. He was dipping his bread in the olive oil. 'What?' he asked, seeing their stares, seeing how they waited. 'You want me to respond to that?' Aurelio glanced at his lover. 'You gotta do what you think is right, baby.'

Milana arched an eyebrow. 'See what I'm saying?' She shifted in her seat to face him more squarely. 'You never reassure me, Reli. You never say that I can trust you. Which means that I *can't*.'

'Not this again,' he sighed, dropping the rest of the bread back in the basket and reaching for his own cigarettes on the table. His eyes flickered towards Elena and back off her again. It had become almost like a tic.

'Why do you do that?' Milana demanded, beginning to sound shrill. 'Fob me off. You always—'

A young girl, maybe thirteen or fourteen years of age, came over to their table, a square piece of paper in her hands. 'Excuse me, Signorita. I'm sorry to interrupt but I'm a huge fan of yours. Could I get your autograph?'

Milana smiled, blowing the cigarette smoke away from the girl's face and taking her pen. 'Sure. What's your name, sweetie?'

'Domenica.'

'Domenica? That's a pretty name.' Milana smiled again, signing the paper with an elaborate yet easy flourish that suggested hours spent perfecting a suitable signature.

Elena looked away, sensing the end was in sight. Milana and Aurelio were on the brink of another of their fights; she gave it less than five minutes before they would leave the table in their usual high passion and it would be up to Vito to pick up the bill, the two of them left sitting in muted, companionable silence.

The horizon was black, the sky beyond the parasols billowing and restless, great bruised clouds roiling and jostling for space. Rain was coming – Rome's urgent heavy pelting rain that made a mockery of London's drizzle and New York's sleet. Here, it really was as though the heavens opened, the raindrops like bullets. Elena welcomed it; anything to break the heat. The rain was one of the things she loved most about this city.

The teenager departed and the mega-watt smile left Milana's beautiful face as she sat back in her chair and pinned Aurelio with one of her stares.

'Don't start up again,' Aurelio said in a low growl, not even looking at her.

Four minutes.

Vito cleared his throat. 'We should think about getting up to Pienza next weekend,' he said to his wife.

Elena looked at him. 'Why?'

'There's the *Cacio al Fuso*. The cheese-rolling competition.'

It was another moment before Milana could respond. She looked as though she had never heard of such a thing. 'Really?' she asked Elena. 'You want to watch *cheese* being rolled?'

'It is a tradition,' Vito said stiffly. 'Someone in our family always judges.'

'Not Aurelio, I bet,' Milana smirked.

Elena felt another tiny piece of her begin to die. 'Of course we must go.'

'Good girl, Elena. We can't break with tradition,' Aurelio said, tapping his cigarette in the ashtray. 'What would people say?'

'It is more fun than it sounds,' Vito smiled, taking his wife's hand and squeezing it. 'Isn't it?'

She managed a nod, knowing Aurelio was staring again. She didn't need to look at him to know it. The weight of his gaze was almost like something she wore now – a scarf in the summer months, making her too hot, fidgety, restless. She kept her eyes down on the green-checked tablecloth. She had quickly become accomplished at avoiding his presence, even when she was in it. Avoiding him – them – wasn't a viable long-term option, for Vito would become suspicious, but she had become adept at minimizing her presence. She didn't say much; she didn't look at anyone.

Milana stretched like a cat. 'I want an ice cream.'

'Really?' Aurelio sighed. 'You are not a child—'

'It's too hot! I can't breathe!' Milana panted, pulling her flimsy off-the-shoulder top away from her skin.

Aurelio rolled his eyes but stubbed out the cigarette.

Two minutes. This would be over soon; soon, he would be gone. Elena kept still.

Vito's arm went up, signalling the waiter.

Aurelio scraped his chair back and reached for the scooter helmet dangling off the back of his chair. He fastened the chin strap and reached into his pocket for the keys to his red Vespa. Milana stood too.

One minute.

'Hold on, we'll join you,' Vito said unexpectedly, rising too. 'And I believe this meal's on you, Reli?'

What? Elena looked in alarm between her husband and his brother.

'Milana's right. It's so muggy,' Vito explained, putting on his own helmet. 'I fancy an ice cream. Giolitti?'

Aurelio shrugged but he was looking at Elena as he handed his credit card to the waiter. 'You're the boss, big brother.'

Strawberry and hazelnut for Milana; pistachio for Vito; lemon sorbet for Elena . . . another cigarette for Aurelio. They ate the ice creams on the kerb, all sitting on the bikes, Vito insisting on a photograph and flagging down a passing girl who looked delighted to have been both noticed and asked.

'You know, there's one thing that you haven't said to me, Aurelio,' Milana said, eating her ice cream alluringly and attracting the admiring glances of several more passers-by.

'Jesus, Milana, you think now is the time?'

Milana glowered at him. 'I was going to say, you could

have said you'd come to New York with me. But yeah, seeing as you brought it up, there's that too—'

Aurelio got off the bike and started pacing. 'Enough, woman. Jesus!' He flicked ash on the pavement and scowled.

Milana watched him. 'It's an idea, though, isn't it? You, me and Manhattan?'

'I don't know. Maybe.'

'It's only six months,' she laughed, but her eyes were pinned on him, anxiously watching as he paced. 'It's not like I'm asking you to give all this up. I'm not asking you to fucking marry me.'

Aurelio stopped pacing and walked over to her, kissing her on the lips. 'Okay, we can talk about it. Six months . . . six months is possible.'

Elena felt her gut twist.

'Thank God I wasn't after a proposal,' Milana said wryly, watching as he grabbed the bike helmet from the handlebars.

'What are you doing, huh?' Aurelio snapped, tetchily. 'I never promised you anything. Not marriage, not babies.'

'No, it looks like I got the wrong brother for that,' Milana retorted, casting a look at Elena and Vito. 'Hey, you don't want to swap, do you, Elena?'

Elena felt his eyes again. What would he – any of them – do if she actually said it? *Yes.*

'Sorry. Can't help you there,' she said, managing to sound bored.

'That's right. Elena married the man and not the face, isn't that right?' Aurelio said, scorn in his voice.

Elena looked into the crowd, refusing to meet his eyes again, noticing how people turned to stare as they passed. Once, she would have feared it was because they knew she was a Valentine, or they recognized her from paparazzi pictures of the Broadway parties with Steve, but now she knew their wattage as a four didn't come from her background or Milana's bit part in a film at all. It was the brothers – both of them tall and commanding, oozing glamour with their dark looks and easy style, their shared handsome brooding face remarkable enough just once over, much less twice. She saw how people tried to scrutinize them, looking for a defining difference that simply wasn't there, wondering which one was the elder, which one more attractive (because there always was one that edged it, even in identical cases); looking at her and wondering why she had chosen Vito and not Aurelio, and then wondering the same of Milana. Did any of them ever wonder that perhaps it had never been a choice? That it had come down to circumstance, fortune, sheer rotten bad luck to have met one first and not the other. Could any of them see it in her eyes, the awful shocking truth that she had married the wrong brother?

The sorbet dropped from her hand as the scales fell finally away. *Oh God.* There was never going to be an escape from this anguish; no remedy. She had thought that staying would be enough – that just seeing him was better than nothing at all – but she'd been wrong. It was like pouring vinegar on an open wound, having to suffer him parading his girlfriend in front of her, flaunting their passion and everything they had that she and Vito didn't. She couldn't eat. Couldn't sleep. Recently, she'd taken to going to bed with her shutters open in case the lights should come on in the private apartment of the west wing, telling her he was back, he was near. And yet still too far.

And now he was going to go again. But it didn't matter how many times or how long he left for – six months in

New York, two years in Paris – he would always come back, for this was his home, and that would mean they'd go through this all again. It would never stop.

'Elena?' Vito asked, turning around to see what had happened, just as the first heavy raindrops smacked the ground.

'Shit,' Aurelio muttered, grinding out the cigarette beneath his heel and throwing his leg over the bike as Milana made room for him. He turned on the ignition. Nothing happened.

'I . . .' Elena stared past Vito blindly. She was beginning to tremble, to shake. She couldn't do this any more. She had thought it would kill her to leave but it was destroying her to stay. She suddenly got off the bike and took off the helmet, the rain slickening her hair almost immediately.

'Darling, what are you doing? Get back on the bike. We need to get back before the roads are too wet.'

'I don't feel well.' Her voice sounded odd.

'Again?' Milana asked under her breath.

A thunderclap in the distance made the others turn to the sky. It was glowing violet. Vito threw the remains of his cone in the bin and turned on the scooter. 'Elena, come. There's no time. It's dangerous driving this thing in the wet. Let's get you back. You look pale.'

'No—' She shook her head.

'What the fuck is wrong with this bike?' Aurelio demanded, turning the ignition over, again and again, but it failed to spark.

'Reli, I'm getting wet,' Milana whined.

'What is it?' Vito asked his wife, as the rain began to drip off the bottom of his helmet and down his shirt collar.

'I want to walk,' Elena said.

'But it's raining!' Vito cried, pointing out the obvious.

The pavements were already glistening darkly, the street hawkers out in force, running up to the tourists and offering them cheap umbrellas.

'I need . . . I just need to . . . to be on my own for a while,' she said, beginning to walk off.

'Elena!' he called after her, just as a sudden bolt of lightning cracked open the sky; seconds later, thunder rumbled.

'I have to *think*, Vito!' she cried, wheeling round, her hands clenched into fists, tears twisting with the rain on her wet face. 'Leave me alone!'

Aurelio stopped trying the bike.

'What the hell . . . ?' Milana muttered.

Vito went to turn off the engine of his scooter to chase after her.

'No,' Aurelio said, shooting out an arm and catching him. 'I'll go after her.'

'You? She's *my* wife!' Vito scoffed furiously.

'Yes, but she clearly doesn't want to talk to you at the moment, does she? Perhaps I can help.'

'I doubt that.'

'Vito.' Aurelio put his hand on his brother's shoulder. 'Let me talk to her. She's obviously upset.'

'It's about the baby,' Vito murmured, watching as she turned the corner and disappeared from sight. 'We've been trying for so long now and . . . I think she's depressed.'

'I'll talk to her,' Aurelio said. 'Just get Milana home.' And then he ran through the rain towards the lightning that was trying, with every jagged stab, to split open the earth.

Chapter Thirty-Three

Rome, August 2017

Cesca dropped her head in her hands, trying to be objective about what she had just read. As a barrister, she knew she had to see everything in the round before she took the side she was being paid to take and formulated the argument that best supported it. But there was only one side to this. What could *possibly* support an argument against what these photos clearly showed? she wondered, her eyes falling again to the grainy black-and-white photographs on the screen. There was no plausible explanation that she could see.

Getting up, she began to pace. Focus, Cesca, she told herself. Slow down. Look at the facts. Keep calm.

But that was easier said than done when almost every search she entered came back with a substantially altered story to the one she had been told. Jack Montgomery? He'd been the very definition of *not sweet*, with a rap sheet providing compelling evidence of an abusive nature towards women, including a lengthy custodial term for the aggravated assault and battery of his second wife. Elena's parents' idyllic marriage, meanwhile, was – according to the tabloid headlines – a sham, rocked by numerous affairs on both sides and ending only when George Valentine took his own life after his wife ran off with a Hollywood director. Elena's beloved Winnie had died destitute and alone in a women's shelter in Brooklyn; and as for little Stevie . . . she had thought it couldn't get any worse than that.

And it wouldn't have done, if she had stopped looking. If she had just stopped right there and allowed herself to believe everything Elena had told her from that point on, she could have pretended that losing Stevie was her rock bottom, the nadir of her life. But it hadn't been; there was yet further to fall. And as Cesca stared at the lightly dented Alfa Romeo sports car, the bollard not so much crashed into as gently nudged, she understood exactly why – as the newspapers put it – 'mystery surrounded' the death of Aurelio Damiani. That crash simply couldn't have killed him.

But, if the papers were to be believed, *someone* had.

Chapter Thirty-Four

Rome, June 1982

The streets hissed with the sluice of rubber tyres in the wet. People were running, pushing past her, jackets and newspapers held over their heads. She didn't know where she was going and it didn't matter. From here on in, all roads led from Rome. She was leaving. Vito wouldn't understand and she couldn't tell him, and she knew, in the absence of explanation, he would have to hate her.

She sobbed as she ran, her clothes clinging to her, her shoes slipping off her heels and making her stumble. People stared, moving out of the way as she fell against them. She pushed them away, continuing blindly onwards.

The narrow streets wove in a lacy dance, winding back on themselves in decorative loops, disorienting all but the locals who stood under cover of their doorways, watching the masses run. The air was singing now, the scent of jasmine thronging the alleys as the rain woke everything up. She was awake now too. The dream – the nightmare – was over.

The little road opened up and suddenly the Pantheon stood before her, as fat and round as Ella Fitzgerald's Santa Claus in the chimney, the ancient stacked wafer-bricks resolute against the storm. The piazza, usually teeming with

tourists in entrance queues that snaked in coils, was empty-
ing out, people looking for cosy cafes in which to sit out the
rain. In contrast, she headed straight for the historic church,
darting under the cover of the colonnaded marketplace and
through the massive doors.

Immediately, the acoustics changed: the storm not locked
out from here, but locked in, the torrents gushing through
the open oculus, down, down the thirteen storeys to the
marble floor below. High splashes kept people back but she
didn't care – she was soaked to the bone already. She turned
her face to the sky, panting hard and letting the rain mist
spritz her skin. She wanted to be washed clean, set free.

'Elena.'

The word was like the strike of a bell, chiming to the very
heart of her.

She didn't turn. She didn't have to. He was right behind
her, his voice a heat that warmed her neck. 'Leave me alone,
Aurelio.'

She felt his hand on her arm, turning her. 'I tried that,' he
said, his intense gaze holding her up.

She blinked up at him, at that face which was to be her
undoing. 'What are you doing here?' she whispered, feeling
the tears begin to fall again. She could see only desolation
on the one hand, ruin on the other.

'Stopping you. You can't go.'

'I can't stay!' she wept, shaking her head.

He held her upper arms with both his hands, gripping
her tightly lest she should break away. 'Leaving achieves
nothing. I should know.'

'But Vito—'

'I know! Don't you think I know? He is my brother. My
mirror. My shadow. My soul. He is the better half of me. I

338

am my brother – and I am not. You were right to marry *him*.' She looked away, crying harder, but he caught her chin with his hand and she felt the universe click into alignment, propelling him to her. 'But I wish every day that you had not.'

His eyes probed hers – everything that couldn't be said swimming between them. This was bigger than the two of them and they had no more fight left.

'Reli,' she whispered, letting the truth write itself all over her face. She felt his grip on her loosen as his own will crumbled at the sight of it, and his breath hitched. They were powerless against it.

'No!' The word was violent. He let go of her, trembling with the force. 'Do you think this is what I *want*? To betray the person I love most in this world? You make me hate myself, Elena.'

'I-I'm sorry,' she sobbed.

'Are you? Or do you like what you have done?' His tone was angry, disgusted.

'What?' she whispered, her eyes black with shock.

'Maybe . . . maybe you just want what you cannot have.' His lip curled. 'Maybe I am the only thing you cannot buy.'

She smacked his cheek, the slap resounding over the rain. She gasped, shocked and stunned by her own action as she saw fury burn in his eyes, but it was done before she had even known it, instinct overriding everything now. The mask hadn't just slipped; it was on the floor. They were fully exposed.

He caught her by the wrist and kissed her hard. Angry. Resentful. Yearning . . . She felt it all as her mouth finally met his, their wet skin on fire.

He pulled away, almost throwing her arms down, panting

from the effort it took to stay there, the effort it took not to leave. 'Are you happy now? You've got what you wanted. Is it worth it? Is it enough?'

His words were a sneer, and he was already walking away from her – but she'd seen the answer in his eyes.

It would never be enough.

The lights blazed in the west wing. Elena sat on her bed in the dark, watching him pace past the windows. A tumbler of whisky in one hand, he was dragging on cigarette after cigarette. He had arrived home late – too late for dinner. That was just as well, for it had been a disaster, Vito attentive and loving as she had simply stared at the plate of food, unable to swallow any of it down. Elena knew that Milana had thrown Aurelio out of her place after another of their rows – the one that had been brewing all day – but she also knew Milana would already be regretting it, plotting ways to get him back, bring him round again. No woman threw away a man like Aurelio. He was addictive. A drug.

He was at the window now, staring straight across at the darkened windows on her side of the courtyard. Did he know she was watching him? Could he sense her stare?

He hadn't looked at her once upon his return and she had excused herself early, leaving them to a game of backgammon. Her door was unlocked, yet Vito knew better than to knock on it tonight. She was out of reach to him now. He sensed it, even if he didn't know why.

Eventually, the lights went off opposite, darkness shrouding the building so that the bats could be glimpsed flitting in the moonlight. She remained where she was, her mind replaying every last moment of the afternoon's interlude – the tautness of every sinew in his body as he fought both to

340

pull her closer and push her away, the hunger of his tongue invading and claiming her . . .

It wasn't enough.

She threw back the covers and crept from the room. Shadows leapt in the ghost light, her bare feet warm on the cool floor as she ran through the galleries, past the eyes of the cardinals and kings, popes and dukes, her hand on the bannister as she curved down through the palace. At the ground floor, she ran the length of the east wing to the Papal Suite and to the secret door hidden behind an enormous tapestry of the Last Supper. Without even glancing at the back-to-front throne, she slipped from the room, flying down the stone staircase and into the service tunnel. Ironically, Maria and the rest of the staff never used it.

The unremitting blackness was shocking – there were no windows, no lights at all down here – and she felt the damp chill her bones with every step. She walked with her arms outstretched, using the rough face of each wall to guide her in the dark, though she stumbled as she trod on loose rocks, her pedicured feet too soft for this hostile environment. She cursed that she hadn't thought to put on slippers at the very least, but then, if she'd allowed herself to think, would she be down here now?

A small sound ahead made her stop, her heart jackhammering. What was that? A rat? Rats? She froze. It was as far now to go back as to carry on. And in this darkness, she couldn't run. If she screamed, no one would hear. She scarcely dared to breathe, waiting to hear it again. If only she could see something, but it was so dark, she couldn't see her own hand in front of her face.

When the hairs on the back of her neck rose, she knew she wasn't alone.

She knew he was here. And he was right beside her.

'Aurelio.' She felt his hand on her right hip, turning her, pushing her back to the wall, his mouth on her neck, grazing her skin with his teeth. She moaned, arching into him, away from the rough surface that stippled her skin as his grip on her tightened. The strap of her nightgown fell off her shoulder and his head fell to her breast, his lips teasing her nipple and making her gasp. She wrapped one thigh around him, wanting more now, unable to wait. This had to be done; it wouldn't be denied. He pushed the silk nightdress up and grabbed her other leg, lifting her up and onto him.

By the time her feet touched the ground once more, she was lost. And nothing could ever be the same again.

Chapter Thirty-Five

Rome, August 2017

Her eyes hurt. Almost eighteen hours spent looking at the screen had left her with a headache and she stretched out her stiff neck as she stirred the arrabbiata. Guido came back down the stairs that led to the roof terrace.

'We're out of ice,' he said, walking to the fridge and filling a small bowl from the icebox.

'Well timed, this is ready,' she told him, beginning to spoon out their dinners. 'Help me with these?'

They took up two bowls each to the roof terrace. Alé and Matteo were already settled at the small table there, chattering away as sparrows hopped hopefully at their feet.

'Cesca, you become more Italian by the day,' Alé grinned, pinching a basil leaf between her fingers and sniffing it appreciatively.

'Not with those freckles,' Matteo quipped.

'Hey, if you two had kids together, I wonder what they'd look like?' Alé mused curiously, looking between them both.

'Alé! Don't give him material to work with, Jesus,' Cesca sighed, tutting.

'That's easy. They would be dark, like me,' Matteo said in a smooth voice, sliding into his seat opposite her. 'My genes

would overwhelm hers, dominating her into complete sub-
mission.'

'Regression,' Guido corrected, but he was laughing as he
said it.

'Urgh,' Cesca groaned as they fell about. 'I can't believe
you can ever get any girl to go out with you.'

He shrugged happily. 'And yet, somehow, they are lining
up . . .'

'Shame it didn't work out with the hot dentist, huh?' Alé
asked him, pouring them all another Aperol spritz.

'For her, maybe.'

'Matty!' Cesca chided, chucking a paper napkin at him.
'God, I can't believe Nico thought you were my boyfriend.'

Everyone looked at her.

'What?' she asked, wide-eyed.

'Nico? That's the guy from the bar?' Matteo asked.

'The guy from the sinkhole?' Guido asked at the same
time.

'Sorry? Did you say the guy's an arsehole? Yes, that's
him,' she said, voice dripping with sarcasm.

Eyebrows were raised.

'I didn't know you two had a thing,' Alé said, her fork
poised in mid-air.

'We didn't. We don't.'

The eyebrows went higher.

'So then . . . why are you calling him an *arsehole*?' Alé
probed, echoing Cesca's English accent.

'And if he's such an arsehole, why are you bringing him
up?' Matteo added.

'He's older, right?' Guido asked.

'That's the one. He was pushy as fuck at the bar. Wanting
to take you home himself . . .' Matty added.

'Ooh,' Alé giggled flirtatiously.

'Exactly,' Matteo said, chewing quickly. 'Which was why *I* was having none of it.'

'He was hot – from what I remember.' Alé frowned. '*Am I remembering it right? He was hot?*'

'Yeah, he's hot,' Cesca mumbled. 'It doesn't mean he's not an arsehole, though.'

'What's so bad about him, then?' Alé asked.

'He's always so bloody grumpy, for one thing. And he *always* thinks he's right. About everything. And he never lets anything go. Plus, he just barges in whenever he feels like it. He's a total nightmare to work with.'

'*Do* you work with him?' Guido questioned.

'Well, same difference – it's the same building, it's hard to escape him.'

'Yeah, of course – one of the largest private buildings in the city, you must be constantly stepping on each other's toes.' Matty winked at her.

'Don't laugh at me! I'm beginning to get seriously claustrophobic in that place,' she muttered. 'It feels as if there are eyes everywhere.'

Guido glanced up from his food. 'That's because there are – Velázquez, Caravaggio, Raphael, Leonardo . . .'

'I mean it,' she snapped. 'The place is creepy.'

'Well, just remember what she's paying you,' Alé said, eyebrows hitched up at the others at Cesca's sharp tone, warning them off the topic.

'Oh, trust me, it's not enough for this shit,' Cesca said viciously, sinking back into the black mood that had been snapping at her heels all evening.

'What do you mean?' Guido asked, reaching over to

cover her hand with his. 'What's wrong, babe? You're not yourself tonight.'

Cesca groaned, sliding her arm along the table and dropping her head onto it. 'Urgh, I'm sorry, I'm just . . . hacked off.'

'Why?' Alé asked.

Cesca gave an enormous sigh, as though even breathing was exhausting. 'Because I don't like being lied to and it turns out Elena's basically been feeding me a fairy tale that bears practically no resemblance whatsoever to how her life really was.'

'How do you know?'

'Because I've just spent the past day and a half reading up everything I possibly can on her and, let me tell you, there's a reason why she was the tabloids' favourite. Throughout her entire childhood, any time she appeared in public she was on the front page with the headline: "The luckiest little girl in America." Then she was voted Best Dressed Woman in 1970, 1971 and 1973.'

'What happened to 1972?' Guido asked wryly.

'Bad hair days?' Alé grinned. 'Can happen to the best of us.'

'Then in 1980 she did a Grace Kelly and became a bona fide princess. I swear, there's scarcely been a month in her life when she hasn't featured in one headline or another.'

'What's so bad about that?'

'Oh, no, that's all fine. That's the good stuff, the fluff. But you don't even want to know what else has been written about her.'

'Oh, I think we do,' Alé breathed, looking excited.

'Listen, you know you can't believe half of what's in the papers,' Guido said. 'I bet most of it is hype or myth, rumour, tittle-tattle or downright perjurous slurs. She's far more likely to be telling you the truth than they are.'

'Oh, you think? Then why did she forget to mention having a child with her third husband, then?'

'What?' Matteo asked with a shocked laugh.

'Yes. Not a word about it. Nothing. Zip. Great biography this is turning out to be.'

'But she can't just *ignore* something like that!' Alé said, indignant. 'If nothing else, it's a matter of public record.'

'*Exactly*. But she had a baby with her third husband and hasn't mentioned it to me, not once. I only know about it because I happened to see a photo of him in her private sitting room when she left me in there. She had very conveniently turned the photo away from me, so that I wouldn't see it.'

'But why? Why would she do something like that?' Alé asked, looking appalled.

Cesca's expression changed. 'Well, having done my research, I imagine it's because she lost custody of him when he was four. The court awarded full custody to the father.'

'Seriously? Why? Why would they take a child away from its mother?'

'According to the judge's summation, she was an "unreliable witness whose erratic behaviour could only be considered a danger to the child". He also went on to call her an alcoholic and "drug-addicted dilettante".'

'A "drug-addicted dilettante"?' Matteo said, delighted by the description. 'Your viscontessa has gone up in my estimation!'

But Cesca wasn't smiling. 'Don't . . .' She swallowed. 'The little boy died when he was six. He drowned in a pool at the father's house in Bel Air when there was a party going on. Drugs paraphernalia was found; it looks like the father wasn't whiter-than-white either.'

There was an appalled silence.

'Shit,' Guido muttered.

'Oh my God,' Alé frowned, her hands pressed to her mouth.

'Elena hadn't seen him for over two years by then. She was denied access. The custody battle was pretty nasty.'

'Damn, that's fucked up,' Matteo said, shaking his head.

'And she never mentioned any of this?' Guido asked, disbelieving.

'Nope. Although I guess I can kind of see why,' Cesca admitted. 'It must have been so incredibly painful.'

'Yeah,' Alé whispered. 'I mean, how do you get over something like that?'

They were all quiet for a moment, passing round the balsamic vinegar and olive oil.

'Has she kept anything else from you?' Alé asked.

'Yes – every time I fact-check something it's different. Honestly, it's like stepping into an alternative reality to hers. I mean, I'm supposed to be writing the only authorized record of the life of one of the most recognized women of the twentieth century. If this book is to have any credibility, her life needs to be seen and judged in its totality. I can't believe she doesn't realize that to do anything less would make her a laughing stock. The public are not stupid. Patronize them at your cost.'

'So what are you going to do?' Alé asked.

Cesca shrugged. 'I'll have to confront her about it. I can't *unknow* what I've read.' She wrinkled her nose, baffled by something. 'Frankly, I just don't get why she's tried to hide it from me. She must surely have known that I would come across this stuff. It's all out there, just waiting for anyone who's interested to have a look.'

'Exactly!' Guido agreed. 'And especially given your past career, she must know that you, more than anyone, are trained in knowing how to separate the truth from the lies. After all, you're vastly overqualified for this project; she must realize how lucky she is even to have you doing it for her.'

Cesca shrugged.

'How do you think she'll take it? We already know she doesn't like to be challenged,' Matteo said.

'Well, she either wants to write a book about her life or she doesn't,' Cesca sighed. 'But there's no point in only doing half a job.'

'I don't envy you that conversation,' Alé said, her eyes narrowing as she caught sight of the time on Matteo's watch. 'Shoot. Come on, guys, eat faster or we'll be late.' She looked at Cesca. 'I wish you were coming with us tonight.'

'Oh, I'm rather glad I'm not, actually,' Cesca admitted. 'I need a quiet night in to let this settle in my mind.'

She stared past the terrace to the church towers and domes reaching into the blushing sky, clay peg-tiled roofs and tiny terraces cluttered with washing lines, bikes and geraniums spreading all the way back to the horizon. But she didn't *see* any of it – because something wasn't smelling right about this.

Guido had been right. Elena *must* have known she would find all this out about her past. Unless Cesca was negligent in her professional duties, she couldn't fail to. She was troubled, too – now she knew the truth – as to why Elena had even pursued the project in the first place. Elena was a fully paid-up member of the *Nobiltà nera*, for whom discretion was the better part of valour, so why would she embark on a course of action that guaranteed exactly the opposite? Why, when she was now a princess and highly regarded philanthropist, did she actively want to rake up a past littered with failed marriages and hard-partying antics, a dead child and even the hushed whisper of murder?

Cesca couldn't understand it. This book would be akin to social suicide. It was almost as though Elena was dousing herself in gasoline – and simply waiting for Cesca to strike a match.

Cesca sat on the small square at the top of her steps, legs outstretched and the last of the wine in her hand as she caught the final rays from the fast-melting sun, which was oozing from the sky. The others had gone on to the Coldplay concert, which – when they'd booked, five months earlier – she couldn't make, having been scheduled to lead a night tour.

Not that she minded. She wasn't in the mood to spend her night waving her arms in the air with 60,000 strangers. Her brain was overloaded with truths and counter-truths and she felt distracted by the new facts thrown up by her research. The more she uncovered, the more shaky Elena's own account of her life seemed to become – not just historically, but now, too; the memory of that magnificent ring in Nico's palm yesterday morning still lingered. Something wasn't right. The way Elena had suddenly become furtive about it, taking the meeting privately once Nico had unwrapped it . . . Didn't she trust Cesca? But then, if so, why had she invited her into her private vault? Let her wear a priceless necklace from her own collection? No, it couldn't be a trust issue.

The image of the ring shimmered in her mind. She'd never seen anything like it – not even at the Bulgari store at the party the other week. How could something like that have been lost in a disused tunnel and not even be known to be lost?

She tilted her head back against the wall, feeling the gentle heat on her pale throat and listening to the soundtrack of the square: the rattle of the metal shutters as the bakery closed for another day; the low murmur of conversation building up as the osteria's first sittings began to arrive; scooters zipping past and parking outside the pizzeria.

And voices. Close by.

In fact – below.

Signora Dutti was standing at her door, talking animatedly to someone.

'. . . *Sì, sì*. It is Maria. Maria Dutti.'

'Thank you, Signora Dutti. You have been very helpful. I apologize for interrupting you at the weekend—'

Cesca's eyes opened at the voice and she scrabbled forwards on her hands and knees to look through the railings. She saw the top of a curly, dark-haired dusty head, powerful climber's shoulders, hobnailed boots.

Nico?

'It makes no difference to me,' Signora Dutti said, with an almost-girlish, dismissive laugh. 'Saturday. Thursday. They are all the same to me.'

'—We will be in touch if we have any further questions.'

He stepped back, nodding adieu and reflexively glancing up.

Their eyes met in mutual astonishment. Cesca blinked back at him, open-mouthed, embarrassed to have been caught prying.

He looked away immediately. *'Buona notte*, Signora.' He turned and began to walk in the direction of the north-west corner of the square, between the bakery and Franco's.

'Nico?' The word was out before she could stop herself. Sheer curiosity impelled her to make him stay. (Was it only curiosity . . . ?)

He stopped and turned around. 'What?' His manner was cold and closed.

'What are you doing here?' she asked, a half-laugh in her voice that he should be coming out of her elderly landlady's apartment at 9 p.m. on a Saturday evening.

'That's none of your business.'

'Oh.' She sank back onto her heels, the smile slipping from her face as she took in the outright hostility on his. They were no longer friends – or whatever it was that they had been, or might have been. Her poor behaviour at the osteria had well and truly slammed the door shut on that. 'Sorry.'

Inexplicably, she felt tears spring to her eyes as he turned around and walked away again. It seemed they were destined to be at loggerheads with one another, never quite falling into step. But he'd gone only ten paces before he stopped suddenly and dropped his head, his hands on his hips. She watched, feeling frozen herself as she sensed conflict in his pose. Then he wheeled around again and marched back, somehow looking furious and helpless at once as he stood there, staring up at her – just staring, unwilling or unable to say what was running through his head and behind his eyes.

Cesca felt her stomach drop and she got to her feet, swallowing nervously as he bounded up the steps to her left. She turned to face him as, suddenly, he was there – as though he always should have been, as though he always was going to be – standing just a metre from her, his eyes burning.

'Would you . . . like a glass of wine?' she managed, her voice barely above a whisper.

'No.'

'Oh.' She didn't dare ask what he did want then. She didn't have time, for in the next moment he had stepped forward and breached the gap between them, his hands clasping her face and kissing her. Her hands covered his, her body arching towards him. She could taste the dust on his lips, feel his hunger for her.

He pulled back and stared down at her, seeing his own urgency reflected in her eyes and then his mouth was on hers again. And as they stumbled, locked together, through the open door of the apartment, they didn't notice the shocked expression of Signora Dutti, sweeping brush in hand, downstairs; nor did they see the movement behind the glass of the ice-blue palace opposite, where all the window shutters were closed . . . apart from one.

She looked down at their long bodies intertwined on the sheets, hers vanilla, his mocha. Nico was dozing, one hand clasped behind his head, the other wrapped round her waist. Her head was on his chest, one hand gently ruffling the hair that tapered down to his navel. She wanted to sleep too but she couldn't. What had just happened?

She felt ecstatically happy, but more than a little flummoxed. The way they'd left things at the osteria the other

353

night . . . and then the way he'd glowered at her in Elena's room afterwards. She thought he hated her. She thought he thought she was ridiculous. He thought she was a killer.

She flinched at the memory of it and his hand automatically tightened its grip on her, as though she was a toddler about to fall out of bed. She sank into him again, lifting her head to look at him better; it felt like such a luxury to get to rest her eyes on him for once, without having to look away for fear of his scorn or rejection.

'What?' His voice was heavy, drowsy with sleep, but a small smile curved on his lips, his stubble thick on his cheeks.

'What just happened here?' she whispered, twirling a curl of chest hair around her right index finger. 'I had no idea you liked me like that.'

'Then you are blind.'

Cesca smiled. True to form, then? Even post-coital, he was as direct as a line.

His hand tightened again, squeezing her to him gently, and she felt her heart leap at the subtle gesture.

'It's lucky for you you're as handsome as you are or I would have been entirely successful in managing to hate you,' she murmured. 'I was quite determined, you know.'

He opened one eye and stared at her with it. 'I know.'

'In fact, it's only because you look so good in a suit. I mean, like, *so* good. I think it's an Italian thing.'

'You look really good naked.' His hand reached down and clasped her buttock, before gently smacking it and making her jump.

'Ow!' she laughed, squirming against him.

'Hmm,' he grinned, smacking her again, making her writhe.

She chuckled, kissing his chest above his heart, before laying her head down again.

'I'm so glad Isabella is your sister,' she sighed. 'I felt sick when I saw her. She's so gorgeous and the complete opposite of me. I knew I couldn't compare to her.'

'No.' And when he felt her stiffen, he added. 'I mean, you are not like anyone else, Cesca. There is no one like you.' He kissed the top of her head tenderly. 'Besides, I am very glad that Matteo is a . . . what did you say? Terrible tart.'

'I told you. He's just a friend.'

'He likes you.'

'He doesn't.'

'Trust me. Men know. It's an instinct.'

She felt butterflies in her stomach. 'Were you wildly jealous?' When he didn't reply, she looked up at him, resting her chin on his chest. 'Were you?'

His eyes burned again. 'You know I was.'

She sighed, gratified, staring at him with coquettish eyes, marvelling that he was here. 'So what was the deal earlier? Are you cheating on Signora Dutti with me?'

He gave a low laugh. 'Oh, I see. This was just your way of getting me to talk.'

'On the contrary, you jumped me. I thought this was your way to *stop* me talking,' she replied with an arch tone.

He laughed again, the sound magnificent against her ear, and she watched him, revelling in his beauty. He met her gaze, the look in his eyes soft and indulgent for once. 'One of the tunnels leads out to her apartment,' he said, smoothing her hair back from her face, his eyes falling to her temples, cheeks, freckles . . .

'You didn't find the crown jewels down there, did you?'

'Sadly not,' he grinned. 'Although next time I'll know

better than to hand the goods over. I'll just pack my bag and head for the border.'

'Throwing me over your shoulder first, I hope.'

'Of course.' His eyes danced.

'So the ring was definitely Elena's?'

'Who else's? It is a very famous piece, called the Bulgari Blue.'

'The Bul . . . ?' Cesca frowned, pushing herself up on one elbow. She had heard that name before. 'But it can't be.'

'Why not?'

Cesca thought back. 'Because she said it was in a safe in Switzerland. She was talking about it with Signor Bulgari himself at the party the other week. I was standing right there.'

'Well, unless it's a fake, there's no question it's the Blue.' Nico's eyes flashed. 'But she told *me* it had been lost many years before.'

Cesca was quiet. 'Why would she lie about it to the head of Bulgari? You can't *forget* losing something like that and think you've stored it in a foreign bank vault instead.' She bit her lip. 'Perhaps she didn't want to admit it was lost? Insurance . . . ?'

He watched her. 'Still the barrister.' Cesca stiffened but he caught her head with his hands, making her look at him. 'It is not a bad thing, Cesca. Why do you act as if it is a dirty word?'

She just blinked, her heart rate accelerating – there was so much she wanted to say, but couldn't. After a minute, seeing she wouldn't break her silence, he curled up and kissed her lightly on the mouth.

With determination, she changed the subject. 'So two of

the tunnels lead under the little square to the osteria and this building, and the third . . . ?' she asked.

He arched an eyebrow, not fooled for a moment by her desire to switch subjects, but indulging her anyway. 'And the third one leads to the water garden at the south-east aspect of the garden.'

'A water garden?' she smiled. 'I'd love to see that.'

'You were supposed to. There was wine chilling, olives . . .'

She heard the wry note in his voice and thought back to Wednesday evening. He'd been so edgy, and she'd taken it as disinterest – but was it nerves? He'd been so adamant they could only follow one route, but if he had set up a picnic for them . . . 'Oh, God. It was supposed to be a *date*?'

'A first step, at least. I wasn't sure whether you felt the same. But instead—'

'I made a detour,' she cringed, remembering how she'd refused to listen, and then the angry way they'd parted. 'I really messed up,' she whispered.

'Yes.' He tried to be stern but the look in his eyes told her otherwise.

Her hand began to travel downwards under the sheet as her eyes danced. 'Is there any way I can make it up to you . . . ?'

Chapter Thirty-Six

Rome, August 1982

The thrum of the engine vibrated through her bones, the wind whipping her ponytail as the car gripped the winding coast road and, below them, pretty pastel-coloured villages clung to the cliffs like barnacles above the bright blue sea. She sighed, knowing that this was true happiness at last. Even though Aurelio had gone again. Even though she'd heard not a word from him since. Even though he'd said not a word apart from her name – angry, despairing – as he'd slumped against her, his face buried in her neck, her legs still wrapped around him. Even though he'd left her there in the dark, his breathing ragged as he'd stumbled back to the west wing. 'You make me hate myself, Elena.' Wasn't that what he'd told her, standing in the rain in the Pantheon?

But if Aurelio couldn't forgive himself, she didn't regret a thing. How could she be sorry for something that was so right? It had been inevitable from the start and they'd both known it. They had done everything in their power to fight and resist, to push back and keep away, but it had been an unwinnable war. It wasn't just chemistry that locked them together, but gravity: they had been destined for one another.

Beside her, Vito's arms were outstretched, his fingers unconsciously stroking the leather wheel. He was wearing sunglasses and a blue linen shirt, navy shorts, his Tod's car shoes. He looked incredible. He looked like *him*.

She smiled as he glanced across at her, his hand reaching for and squeezing her thigh. If anything, her seduction by Aurelio had improved things between her and her husband. She felt alive again; Aurelio's touch – passionate, hungry and intense – had awakened her to Vito's. They laughed, talked once more. She felt able to take on the role of a Damiani wife which had previously felt so stifling, and she was throwing herself into the charity circuit with a zeal that made Christina's appear positively anaemic.

She could do all this because, one day, Aurelio would come back – to Vito, to her – and it would happen all over again. The pattern had been set. He would resist her and fail; he would leave her and return. He would resist her and fail and leave . . . But he would always come back because their love had a physical shape now, one that was growing day by day. Her hands fluttered to her stomach again, her newfound sense of peace like a sedative in her bloodstream. He didn't know it yet, but seven months from now, she was bringing a baby into this world – one that would look just like its father.

Chapter Thirty-Seven

Rome, August 2017

Cesca knocked on the door, not even sure if Elena was behind it. She had walked through the palace looking for her and the private sitting room of the private apartment was the only suite left.

'Yes?'

The voice was faint but distinct and Cesca popped her head around the door. Elena was sitting on the sofa, a blanket wrapped around her as it had been the previous week, when Nico had interrupted them with his discovery of the ring.

'I'm sorry to disturb you. I just wondered whether you were free to talk? We didn't get a chance to finish our interview the other day.'

Elena was quiet and very still. 'The other day . . . ?'

'On Friday. Signor Cantarelli interrupted,' Cesca prompted.

'Ah yes.' Her eyes seemed to sharpen at the mention of his name. 'Come in. I am in fact waiting for Signor Cantarelli. I am expecting him to tell me they are finally finished with their wretched explorations and I can reclaim my privacy again.'

Cesca was puzzled as to why she should think that. Only

three days ago, Nico had returned to her a priceless ring. If that could have been found down there, surely there might be other items of interest or value, too? What if a burglary had gone wrong? What if a burglary had been *missed*? What was the rush to seal it all up again?

'He will be here any minute, but we can talk while we wait. This won't take long, will it? I recall we had almost finished our discussion anyway.'

'Uh, well, however long you've got,' Cesca said, though she still had plenty of questions to ask – such as why Elena had failed to mention the small matter of having had a son? She could well understand the subject was too painful to *want* to discuss it, but they couldn't just ignore something like that. Today's was going to have to be a tough conversation. An interrogation, for once.

She crossed the room, feeling Elena's eyes on her 1920s high-waisted cream bags and black vest. 'How are you feeling today?'

'Not as tired as you, I suspect.'

'I'm sorry?' Cesca asked, not sure if she'd heard correctly.

'You look pale this morning, Francesca,' Elena said, her grey eyes steady upon her. 'Did you not sleep well?'

Cesca swallowed. 'I slept very well, thank you.'

'Ah.'

The thought of Nico, of last night and the night before that, of all Sunday spent in bed, flustered her, and she fussed with the digital recorder and the photographs in the envelope, trying to buy some time to compose herself. He had left ten minutes before her this morning so that they could stagger their arrivals at work, and even that separation had felt hard to bear. Things were moving fast and she was falling for him, hard. 'So, I thought we could continue our conversation about Vito,' she said, her eyes flicking up as she laid out the photographs on the ottoman again.

Elena nodded, without looking at them.

'So we . . . uh . . . we'd been talking about his relationship with his brother – Aurelio – and how that impacted upon you.'

'Indeed.'

Cesca's eyes flittered towards the photo frame beside Elena's left arm – the picture within it, of her first son, was out of sight from where she sat.

'Is he still alive?'

'Reli? No. He died in November 1989.'

'Can I ask how?'

Elena looked surprised, no doubt wondering at its relevance to the book. 'He was in a car crash,' she said simply.

Cesca nodded, knowing perfectly well now that that crash hadn't killed anyone. 'It must have been a terrible loss for Vito,' she said, watching Elena's expression closely, noticing it was a long time before Elena answered.

'Yes. He might even have been destroyed by it, had it not been for Giotto . . .' Her voice faded into silence.

Cesca nodded understandingly. 'Destroyed' was a strong word, almost violent, but she knew, herself, what guilt did to a person. 'Giotto is your son?'

'Correct.'

Cesca fell into silence, deciding to let Elena guide the conversation for once – an old tactic she'd used when interviewing witnesses – but her heart was racing and she felt sure her colour was high. Could Elena see it – the inquisition in her eyes? She felt as though she might as well have been sitting there in her wig and gown.

But Elena wasn't even looking at her. 'Vito changed after

362

Reli's death. He became more like his brother – a little more reckless and unpredictable. He had lost the person he loved most in the world and all bets were off. In some ways, I think being the *only* son freed him from the straitjacket of being the *older* son.'

'I've noticed that whenever you talk about Vito, it's always sadly. As though he was somehow a tragic figure.'

Elena's stare sharpened at Cesca's more direct line of questioning. 'Well, it is not so easy being good in this world, is it?'

Cesca shook her head. 'Did it place a strain on your marriage? If he changed so much, I mean.'

Elena considered the question. 'You'd think so, but actually, in a curious way, I think it strengthened it. We all had to learn to adapt. It brought us closer together, somehow. We realized how short life really is, how fragile. After all, we never know when we awaken into our final day.'

'May I ask when Vito died?'

Elena pinned her with a cool stare. '13 November 2002. A heart attack. Do you need a time of death?'

Cesca didn't look down from those icy eyes. 'I'm just trying to establish a timeline of the major events in your life, that's all,' she said, equally coolly, leading into the first big question, the one that was going to lead to all the other questions she knew Elena didn't want asked. 'So you didn't have any other children?'

The photograph of Stevie – only the back of it visible to Cesca from her seat – was just a metre away.

Elena's gaze flickered over her. 'No. Giotto was our only child.'

Cesca picked up on the sleight of hand. *Our* only child. Not an outright lie, then, but still not the whole truth.

'I was really very sorry to read about Stevie,' Cesca said, deploying her own sleight of hand – she had read about him, not heard, clearly implying that she knew Elena was choosing which truths to share and which not.

Elena didn't move, the expression on her face becoming almost frozen, and Cesca felt herself paralysed in Elena's spectral stare. A full minute passed before she stirred.

'Not that we needed another child. Giotto cemented us as a family.'

It was as though Elena hadn't heard her, or couldn't allow herself to hear the expression of sympathy. Cesca swallowed, wondering whether she had gone too far, but she had needed to throw down a marker of sorts, something that showed Elena they needed to be open and honest. They couldn't dance around the facts – facts that were out there for anyone to see.

'Elena, look, if this book is to be at all credible, I need you to be honest with me. And I mean that in the fullest sense; half-truths are no good. I need full disclosure, do you see? Elena?'

Elena blinked back at her, that curiously impassive expression on her face that made it so impossible to read her feelings. She could have been absolutely furious or utterly despairing and there would have been no way of knowing which it was.

She tried again. 'Elena, I know the truth. I know about everything. Little Stevie. The questions around your brother-in-law's death—'

There was a knock at the door. 'Ah. That will be Signor Cantarelli for our appointment. Come in,' she called, looking almost triumphant that their interview would be terminated early again.

The door opened and Nico walked in, faltering a step as he saw Cesca sitting there. Vignettes of last night and this morning bloomed between them and he looked away from her quickly, his expression closing up again as she felt her own cheeks burn. 'Principessa? If this is not a good time—'

Elena held up a hand. 'It is fine. Francesca and I were just finishing up.' She looked back at Cesca with cold eyes. 'You were just leaving, weren't you, Francesca?'

Cesca exhaled. So that was it, then? Elena was going with a bare-faced denial of the facts, like a Holocaust denier, refusing to see a truth that was clearly documented for anyone who cared to look. 'Yes,' she said wearily, gathering herself to stand.

'I've been thinking, Francesca,' Elena said, watching closely as she stooped to pick up the photographs. 'I would like to see a first draft of what you've written so far.'

'Excuse me?' Cesca asked in shock. She had barely written anything so far. She was still interviewing and compiling notes.

'Yes. Giotto is coming over for the gala next weekend and I should like him to cast an eye over what you've done so far, to make sure we're on the right track. I'm sure you understand. If you could get it to me by then?'

Cesca raised an eyebrow. That was five days from now. In five days she wanted a manuscript for the first forty years of her life, when, just seconds ago, she had literally closed her ears to Cesca's pleas for the whole truth?

'I very much hope you will have been rigorous in your research and application of the facts. My son is a stickler for the truth.'

'So you want me to put down everything I know so far? *Everything?*'

Elena nodded. 'Indeed.'

Cesca blinked at her, realizing this was a test: Elena wanted to know if she had her loyalty. She wanted to see with her own eyes exactly what she was going to put in – and what she intended to leave out. Cesca was in no doubt that if she were to literally do as Elena asked, and include the less savoury chapters about which she had just questioned her boss, she'd be fired on the spot. Elena was clearly of the mind that there was no point wasting time continuing with the book if they were going to fight over the content. Was this what had happened with the archivist? Cesca wondered. Had he got too close to the truth too? It was obvious Elena had no intention of opening up about Stevie and Jack and all the rest of it.

'Okay,' she said, benignly. 'I'll do my best.'

'Do.' Elena's eyes slid smoothly towards Nico, brightening considerably. 'Tell me, Signor, shall you be going to the gala on Saturday night?'

'I'm not sure,' he said noncommittally. Cesca could tell by his guarded expression that he had picked up on the tension between her and Elena.

'Oh, but you must. Giotto would be pleased to see you; he would find your work deeply interesting. And you must bring your beautiful fiancée.'

There was a frigid silence before Nico replied. 'Thank you, Principessa, but—'

'I insist. After all your work here safeguarding the palazzo's structures, it would be a fitting end to our interlude this summer.'

Cesca didn't move her eyes off the roses on the console table immediately behind Elena's head, but though she was still and silent she felt sure the furious drumming of her heart could be heard by every single one of them. Nico kept glancing over at her but his and Elena's voices sounded distant. There was too much to take in, but only one word echoed in her head. *Fiancée?*

'I'll leave you to your meeting,' Cesca said quietly, slipping from the room, Nico's eyes pinned to her back. She could sense his sudden desperation, but she wouldn't look at him, not at either of them, and with shaking hands she closed the door behind her. It looked as though Elena wasn't the only one to have played her for a fool.

'I'm a damned idiot; I never even *liked* the guy. Well, not before now, anyway,' she sobbed, as Alé handed over another tissue.

'He's contemptible,' Alé spat. 'Treating you like that. Just because he's hot, he thinks he can do what he likes. Guys like him are the worst.'

Cesca sniffed, shaking her head. 'No. It's my own fault. I should have seen it coming.'

'*How?*'

'. . . I don't know,' Cesca wailed. 'But I should have done. Of course he's bloody engaged! He's thirty-six. Why would he still be single?'

'He's thirty-six, not a hundred and six. He is not old. *Ish.* You weren't to know.' Alé rubbed her arm consolingly as Cesca dabbed at her eyes for the thousandth time. 'But you deserve better than this, Cesca.'

'I-I know.'

'You've just got to put him out of your mind.'

Cesca nodded. Out of her mind. Yes. She could do that.

'And think of it this way – at least you found out early, before you got really involved.'

'Uh huh.' It had felt pretty involved in the shower that morning.

'Not to mention, pity the poor fiancée! She probably has no idea of who she's really marrying, and by the time she does find out . . . ?' Alé drew a line across her throat. 'Christ, who'd be a wife?'

Cesca sniffed again, looking across at her friend, detecting a particularly poignant note in her voice. 'What's happened with you and the headmaster?'

'Oh. We broke up.'

Cesca's hand fell down into her lap. '*When?*'

'Few days ago.'

'But why? I mean, apart from the obvious that he's your boss and he's too old for you . . .'

Alé gave a deep sigh. 'Because he's got a family, that's why.'

'Oh, Alé.'

'I know. And before you say how terrible it is he deceived me – he didn't. I knew.' She bit her lip, shaking her head disgustedly. 'I knew, but as far as I was concerned, it was all just supposed to be a bit of a laugh. A learning curve. Until he started talking about leaving them, walking out on them – for me. *Me!*' Alé's eyes were wide with horror. 'It was never supposed to be that.'

'So we're both the "other woman" then,' Cesca sniffed.

'No. You were in the dark about it. Me? I knew and I didn't care. I'm the shit here.'

It was Cesca's turn to put her hand on Alé's arm. 'Well, you're doing the right thing now. At least it's not too late.'

'I hope so. I've handed in my notice.'

'Alé! Why should you be the one to leave? He's the cheater!'

Alé shrugged. 'Less fuss this way. He's got a family, remember. I can work anywhere. I've still got my freedom.'

'Freedom,' Cesca echoed, remembering how wonderful it had felt wrapped in Nico's arms last night, the weight of his leg over hers. 'Well, I may be getting mine back sooner than I thought.'

'What do you mean?'

'Elena has asked me to write up the first draft of everything we've covered so far – i.e. the first forty years of her life. Supposedly her son's coming over at the weekend and she wants him to read it.'

'Supposedly?'

'It's not about her son coming over. She's testing me, daring me to see whether I've got the nerve to defy her version of events and present the truth.'

Alé looked worried. 'And do you?'

Cesca stared into the distance, remembering Elena's scathing treatment of her that morning, how she'd brought Nico's fiancée into the mix, almost as if she'd known. *'Have you been spending much time with Signor Cantarelli?'* Elena had once asked. *'You look tired.'*

Cesca's eyes narrowed. 'Yeah, actually. I think I do.'

'What about Nico, though? Can you work if he's around?'

'He's pretty much finished now. They've mapped the tunnels and completed all their examinations – there's nothing more to do down there so they're going to start filling in the sinkhole. Supposedly he'll be done by the end of the week. And I need never see him again!' She was aiming for brightness, but it came out as a monotonous chant instead.

'Good riddance!'

'Yeah.'

'Well, I guess it should be easy enough to avoid him between now and then.'

Cesca thought of the thousand-room palace. 'You'd be surprised,' she muttered. 'I might have to start using the tunnels myself, just to avoid seeing him. Did I tell you there's one that goes into my building?'

'No!' Alé exclaimed, delighted by the idea.

'Well, there is. Straight from the palazzo to Signora Dutti's sitting room.'

'Could be useful when it's raining,' Alé grinned.

Cesca straightened up suddenly – remembering something. 'Signora Dutti.'

'What about her?'

She squinted, thinking hard, thinking back. 'On Saturday night, Nico called her Maria.'

'What was he doing with your landlady on Saturday night?' Alé asked with a cocked eyebrow and a half smile.

Cesca rolled her eyes. 'He was getting her to sign off the paperwork for the tunnel, but it's not that . . .' She looked at Alé. 'Elena's old housekeeper was a woman called Maria.'

Alé squawked in amusement. 'Listen, I hate to break it to you, but there are a lot of women in Rome called Maria.'

'I know that, but . . . she lives right across the square from the palace. And she's been so vociferous about Elena – well, her and Signora Accardo – telling me to stay away from her, calling her a wicked woman and all sorts of things. I mean, why do they care so much?' Her eyes narrowed in deep thought. 'Unless Signora Dutti *is* the Maria who worked there, and something happened?'

'Like what?'

'I don't know. But it must have been pretty bad. You

should hear how she goes on about her. It's as if she thinks I'm going to be contaminated.'

Alé looked sceptical. 'It's a long shot.'

'Is it, though? It seems to make perfect sense to me the more I think about it. Maybe she knows something. After all, Elena is clearly lying about her past.'

'Did you confront her?'

'I tried, today.'

'How did that go?'

'A total disaster. She blanked me. Literally. I could have been a wall. But you can be sure that's why she's got me jumping through hoops. I told her outright that I know everything: about her little boy, about her brother-in-law's mysterious death—'

'Wait, what's so mysterious about it?'

'The official line is he died in a car crash – but I saw the photos, Alé. It was just a knock; a prang, really. *No one* could have died in that accident. They'd barely have been bruised.'

'So then, what happened to him?'

'I don't know.' She shrugged. 'But maybe Maria does. There's definitely a secret Elena is trying to keep and if you ask me, as the former housekeeper, she will know something.'

'But how can you tell?'

'Because I'm a barrister, hon. Getting to the truth is what I do.'

Chapter Thirty-Eight

Rome, November 1989

The air was sharp, burning the back of her throat and making her ears ache, the ground covered in a thick blanket of crisp brown leaves, which rustled as she walked. Giotto was running ahead on the path, arms outstretched, kicking great plumes of them into the sky. The heavy, pecking pigeons struggled to escape in time, wings flapping wildly as the little boy careered towards them, the string of his woollen gloves disappearing up his sleeves, the bobble on his hat wobbling madly. Like most six-year-old boys, he was both an innocent and a tyrant at once.

Elena's stride, behind, was slow. She was tired from another morning of outdoor activities. Her cheeks felt pink from their exertions around the estate, her sheepskin coat bulky and heavy on her shoulders. She had lost weight again recently – losing heart, beginning to give up hope.

She watched Giotto disappear into the garden room in the west wing, the French door banging dangerously against the wall as he tore into the palace, ready for the hot chocolate Maria had promised on their return.

She pulled off her gloves and unbuttoned her coat as she stepped through the doors and into the room. Vito was sitting there, the newspaper littering the floor in open spreads at his feet, as though it had drifted there, as though he had stood up without realizing he was still holding it. As though he'd been surprised.

'Darling! There you are!' Vito said, his eyes enlivened. 'Look who's back.'

As though in slow motion, her eyes slid over to the dark head that was turning to face her. 'Elena,' Aurelio said, getting up and staring at her. 'We've been waiting for you.'

He had a command of understatement that bordered on mastery.

'Yes, I'm afraid you'd gone out of sight,' Vito said as Aurelio picked his way past the Lego still on the floor from where Giotto had been playing earlier, coming towards her. 'We weren't exactly sure where you were in the garden or we'd have come to find you.'

Aurelio was in front of her now and he stopped, appraising her flushed cheeks, their colour heightened against the white fur of her hat. 'You look radiant, sister,' he said lightly but his eyes burned her, as they always did, as they always would. 'Motherhood suits you.' He bent down and gently planted a kiss on each cheek and, as he did, she clasped her hands on his arms, her fingers digging into his flesh.

Two seconds and it was done. Space settled between them again.

'It's a shame you've waited so long to meet your nephew. He's a young boy now.' Her voice sounded brittle and tremulous. Was he really here? She'd waited so long, prayed for this moment, and now, on a quiet Monday lunchtime in November, he was back. And it was as though he'd never been away.

'I hear he's the image of his father,' Aurelio laughed. Joked.

Vito laughed too. 'Come sit, Elena. You must be exhausted. You've been out for well over an hour. Maria's bringing coffee once she's dealt with Gio. He was through the room before we could stop him. He doesn't even know Reli's here yet, he didn't see him sitting here.'

'It will be odd for him, to see someone who looks exactly like his father,' Elena said, taking a seat beside her husband – all the better for gazing at his brother.

'But you must have told him about me, surely?' Aurelio asked, making himself comfortable again.

'Of course, but the idea of you and the reality are quite different,' Elena said.

Aurelio's gaze snapped over to her. She smiled but an unspoken conversation crackled between them. There was so much to say.

'So. How's Hong Kong?' she asked politely. God, but not this. She didn't want to talk about this.

'Bright. Busy.' Clearly he didn't want to talk about it either.

'Why Hong Kong?' Vito questioned, puzzlement in his eyes. 'Did you really have to go so far? You could have worked in London, Frankfurt. Places much closer to here.'

'Maybe that was the point?' Elena smiled, her tone slightly mocking. 'He wants to escape us, darling.'

Aurelio studied a fleck on his knee before inhaling sharply. 'Oh, you know me, big brother, forever restless. I needed a change of scene. Can't stay anywhere too long.'

'Well, you've stayed there long enough,' Vito said warmly. 'I think seven years is the longest you've ever spent anywhere.'

'Is it? Yes, perhaps,' he said dismissively, stretching his

arms out across the back of the sofa, one ankle over one knee, taking up space, taking up the room. 'Still, it's taken that long to build up the company.'

'Why did you even set up a company? It's not like you need to work,' Elena said sniffily. Getting over the initial shock, now, of his return, she was beginning to feel angry. Resentful. Seven years!

Aurelio fixed her with a hard stare. 'A man could go mad, Elena, if he doesn't fill his days.'

'So that's what you've been doing for the past seven years,' she murmured. 'Filling your days.' She wanted to scream at him. To tell him she'd spent the last six of those raising his son, waiting for the moment he'd come back through the door so she could lay him in his arms. But he'd missed it – he'd missed it all: the baby years, the toddler years; and now Gio was six, almost seven, and he was becoming every day more like Vito, losing his little-boy wildness to the importance of standing up straight and remembering his table manners, greeting adults with a handshake and a proper look in the eye. He was being groomed to become the new heir. History was repeating itself. 'Well, I'm glad it's gone so brilliantly for you,' she said icily. 'You are quite the banking tycoon. We've never had one of those in the family before, have we, Vito?'

'Popes. Cardinals. Farmers. Vineyard owners. But no, never a banker.' Vito shrugged. 'You're a first, Reli.'

'Oh, no, I'm very definitely a *second*,' Aurelio quipped. 'You beat me every time. I'm always just slightly too late to every party.'

'Fourteen minutes late?' Vito chuckled.

But Aurelio looked at Elena. No, four months. That was how late he'd been to *their* party.

Elena felt her desperation build. She couldn't play this game. She wanted to hate him, to rail at him, to punish him for making her wait so long. It was pushing her to breaking point having to sit opposite him, making jokes and talking about nothing, when all she wanted was to run into his arms, to feel his lips upon hers again and to hear him say her name into her hair.

'Still, we'll have another banker in the family soon enough and then there'll be two of us,' Aurelio continued. 'Safety in numbers, I say.'

Elena blinked. 'What?'

'Aurelio is engaged,' Vito said, patting her thigh. 'Can you believe it? Finally, he settles down!' He laughed as he saw the stunned expression on her face. 'Oh darling, just look at you!' He looked across at Aurelio. 'See what you've done? She can't believe that you've been tamed at last.'

But Elena wasn't laughing. Words were stuck in her chest. Her heart refused to beat. Her brain stopped processing, her nervous system fading to black like a computer switching off.

'Her name's Ling,' Vito continued, oblivious. 'She works with Reli. In the mergers and acquisitions division, wasn't it?'

Aurelio nodded, fiddling again with that fleck on his knee. 'That's right.'

'When will we get to meet her?' Vito pressed. 'Finally, I get to have a sister too!'

'Soon. She wanted to come with me now but she's leading a deal and couldn't get away.'

Vito cleared his throat. 'And the wedding will be . . . here, I hope?'

'Hong Kong. Her family live there. We were thinking February time.'

'Well, I can't say I'm not disappointed that we're not having a wedding in the palazzo, but your timing's perfect – just after the couture shows,' Vito said, squeezing Elena's thigh affectionately. 'You must be delighted, darling.'

She felt as if she was falling off a house, a cliff, a cloud. '. . . Congratulations.'

'Thank you. We're very happy.' Aurelio's eyes flickered up to meet hers.

But it was a statement of intent. Not fact.

'Elena.' Her whispered name carried down the onyx hall as if on a zephyr, like a fairy on a snowflake. 'Elena, stop.' She ran, but his words were faster here, travelling down the gallery with a speed she could not match. It was called the whispering gallery for a reason.

'Elena, wait.' His hand on her elbow, and then she was spun around, into the chest that should have been hers to lay her head on at night.

'What? What do you want me to say?' she hissed, angry tears skimming down her cheeks. 'Seven years you've been gone and now you're back to tell me that?'

'Sssh,' he said angrily. 'Do you want him to hear?'

'He's on the phone, he can't hear anything. He *never* hears anything. He can't even see what's right in front of him!'

Aurelio looked up and down the length of the gallery. 'I'm doing what's best, Elena,' he whispered, pleading with her to understand.

'Best for whom?'

'For all of us. You know that. You know there's no other way.'

A sob escaped her. 'How can you *say* that?'

He held her upper arms, the fingers almost closing round her biceps. 'Because we can't keep doing this, Elena. We have to find a way to stop it once and for all. It doesn't matter what I do, how long I go for, whenever I see you . . .' His eyes raked her face. 'I forget myself. I forget about Vito. And I can't allow that to happen. I won't.'

'So you're just going to keep living on the other side of the world? That's your plan?'

He nodded, a pulse in his jaw. 'It's easier when you're not there. I can almost believe . . .'

'What? That it never happened? That I don't exist?'

'Yes.'

The word drew blood and she shook in his arms. 'Do you know – every day, when I have looked in Gio's eyes, all I have seen is you. He's the image of you.'

'He's the image of Vito too.'

'No. You. He's got your spirit.' She looked up at him blindly, his face obscured in her vision by tears, her hands spreading on his chest. 'Reli, I've missed you so much. There's another way. I know there is,' she said, the sobs coming hard now and hitching up her shoulders. 'We can leave here. Together. Start a new life for ourselves some-where – wherever you want. Just say it and we can go. Tonight.'

'Elena, no.' The word was firm but his face was tense, his own eyes filmy. 'For once in my life, I am trying to do the right thing.'

'Then I hate you for it.' She tried to step away from him,

beginning to tremble, feeling herself lose control, but he gripped her harder, almost lifting her onto her tiptoes.

'Don't say that.'

'I do. I hate you. I hate you. I hate you.' His eyes fell to her mouth. 'I love you.'

What happened next was entirely reflexive – his mouth on hers, their arms wrapped so tightly around each other she thought her ribs might crack, her heart burst. And for years afterwards, Elena reflected that one moment had been like a crystal glass falling to the floor, something whole – beautiful and perfect – spinning in the air for several final moments before it smashed into obliteration. Destroying itself.

He pulled apart from her. 'Elena,' he whispered.

'—Mama?'

Gio ran down the long gallery and took her hand, blinking up at her, a rim of hot chocolate encircling his upper lip.

'D-darling,' she laughed, an edge of hysteria in her voice as the shock of being discovered made her tremble. 'Just look at you! You're covered in chocolate!' She rubbed her thumb against his velvety skin but the chocolate had dried already. 'Oh, look. It's all dried.'

'Who's he?' Gio asked in a small voice, his eyes staying on her the whole time as he took her other hand, as though pulling her away.

'W-why, that's Papa,' she stammered.

'No.' Gio looked away from her towards Aurelio, but the boy would not – or could not – make eye contact, his gaze stuck shyly on his uncle's hand, directly in his eyeline.

'But of course it is.' She felt her heart leap almost clear of her chest. 'Oh! You big meanie! Are you teasing me?'

He looked up at her again, big eyes blinking. 'Why were you crying?'

'Oh, darling. I wasn't.'

'You were. I heard you.'

'They were happy tears, darling. There's some wonderful news – Daddy's brother has come back after all these years and he's so excited to meet you.'

Gio's eyes slid over to Aurelio again, this time looking up to take in the face he knew so well, the hair, the clothes . . .

'But you must run along quickly and get cleaned up before you meet him,' Elena said hurriedly, turning him around by the shoulders and pushing him gently in the opposite direction. 'We don't want Uncle Reli thinking you're a vagabond. Hurry now.'

The little boy ran down the corridor, his shoes squeaking on the floor.

Elena waited till he was out of sight and then turned back to Aurelio, wiping her cheeks dry frantically. 'You need to get changed. Right now.'

Chapter Thirty-Nine

Rome, August 2017

It was only the second time Cesca had ever been in the downstairs apartment, the first time being to collect the keys when she moved in. There was no doubt her rooms upstairs were superior – brighter, more open, and of course with access to the tiny roof terrace at the back – but the narrow steps weren't going to become any easier for a woman of Signora Dutti's age to navigate.

Cesca was sitting at the small, square, dark wood table, over which was draped a hand-worked lace cloth. A bowl of oranges sat in the middle beside a stubby red candle, the wax coagulating in beaded drips down the sides. Signora Dutti was hand-grinding the coffee beans, the rich aroma perfuming the dim room, as a light breeze drifted in through the open front door.

'I saw Signor Cantarelli the other day,' Cesca said, wishing she didn't even have to say his name. She didn't want to think about him. Not at all. Ever.

Signora Dutti glanced over. 'Yes?' she said in a meaningful tone, a knowing smile on her lips. 'So did I. He has been here, looking for you. Last night and again this morning. I told him I did not know where you were.'

'Oh.' Cesca stalled, wondering why her landlady had such a crafty look on her face. 'Well, I've been staying over with my friend, Alessandra.'

Signora Dutti nodded, but her eyes danced. 'He was quite persistent. I had to show him your room was empty.'

Cesca suppressed a groan of annoyance that her landlady had yet again just opened up her home to seemingly casual passers-by. First Elena, now him?

'He is a handsome man.'

'Uh, is he? I hadn't really—'

'Should smile more, though.' Signora Dutti pulled a stern face. 'He is always so serious.'

Cesca, determined not to envisage him smiling, or glowering, or naked, tried to pull the conversation back to the reason she'd come here. 'Yes, well, anyway . . . he, uh, he said one of the tunnels from the palazzo leads to this room.'

'That is correct.'

'Did you know about it, before?'

'Of course!'

She blinked. So Freda Accardo had been familiar with them, and now Maria Dutti too. Had Elena been the only person who *hadn't* known about them? 'Had you been down there?'

'Once, but not for a long time. They're cold and dark. They went only into the palazzo, and what did I want to go in there for?' She pulled a face, her mouth in a down-turned U.

'Signora Dutti – did you ever work at the palazzo?'

The old lady stopped grinding the coffee beans. 'Why do you ask that?'

'Because—' She swallowed, deciding to show her hand.

'Because I think something terrible may have happened there. And I thought you might know something about it?'

There was a long silence as Signora Dutti turned away and bustled about the worktops, making the coffee and fishing out biscotti from a tin on a high shelf, which she could access only by standing on a footstool. But eventually she came back to the table. The coffees were short, dark and so thick Cesca thought she could probably stand a spoon in hers.

'You were the housekeeper, weren't you?' Cesca prompted, wrapping her hand around the cup, even though it was another hot night. A minute ago, it had only been a hunch but she knew from the way the old lady was behaving that she had hit upon the truth. 'I already know you were.'

Signora Dutti stared at her and then out through the door, towards the ice-blue facade of the building that had come to dominate all their lives. 'It was all a long time ago now.'

What was? 'Can I ask why you hate the Principessa so much?'

Signora Dutti's eyes slid over to her. 'Does she know you are here?'

'No. She's in Florence.' She mentioned it casually, but in fact Elena's flight to the renaissance city had come as a complete surprise; Elena had said nothing of her trip in their conversation on Monday and Alberto had told Cesca she wasn't expected back until Friday evening.

'But does she know you are talking to *me*?'

'No. And I don't want her to.' Cesca bit her lip. 'But I've read some things which don't make sense and I already know she's been lying to me. It's about her brother-in—'

'Aurelio!' Signora Dutti's lips flattened into a grim line.

'She is a wicked woman!' she said forcefully. 'She is the very devil!'

'That's exactly what Signora Accardo said. *Why* do you think that?' Cesca pushed.

'What other word is there for a woman who destroys a family, especially one as noble as the Damianis?'

'How did she destroy them?' Cesca probed – but even as she asked the question, the answer suddenly came to her. They were identical twins. *He had a dangerous glamour.* How could Elena – the former party girl trying to reinvent herself as a princess of the *Nobiltà nera* – have resisted *him*? 'Oh God.' Her hands flew to her mouth as she realized; it was so obvious. 'Elena had an affair with Vito's brother.'

'She turned them against one another, brothers who shared one blood, one shadow. They could never be separated until *she* came along.' Signora Dutti's voice was almost a rasp, such was her anger.

'Do you know this for certain?'

Signora Dutti straightened up, her back ramrod straight. 'I saw it with my own eyes.'

Cesca felt every fibre in her body tense. A witness? 'Please. Tell me what happened. It's really important.'

Signora Dutti's fingers drummed the table in consideration and there was a long silence before she finally spoke. 'This building still belonged to the family back then,' she said eventually. 'Many in the square still do. Originally, this used to be a stable and the bedroom upstairs – in what is now your apartment – was for visitors' grooms. There was a staircase in that corner there,' she said, pointing to where a small, red-painted housekeeper's cupboard now sat. 'But it had not been used as a stable for many years. Instead, after the war, it was well known that the old Visconte would use the tunnels to meet his mistresses here.'

'Okay.' Cesca tried to keep the shock from her expression. 'Go on.'

'As children, the twins would play in them all the time. They knew them inside out. They would always be disappearing down them when it was time for their bath or their schoolwork. So perhaps it was no surprise they chose to meet up here.'

Cesca was half a beat behind. 'Elena and Aurelio, you mean?'

A look of disgust deepened the lines on the old lady's face. 'Aurelio would have known they would be safe here. No one would see them coming or going – they did not need to worry about the staff walking in on them; nor the Visconte.'

'But *you* saw them?'

Signora Dutti's expression hardened. 'I would like to come here to sit sometimes during my time off. I lived in the palazzo, of course, but it can be – how you say?' She made a compressing action around her head.

'Claustrophobic?'

Signora Dutti shrugged. 'You might be wondering how such a big building can feel so little. But it did. Sometimes I felt the walls had eyes.' She gave a shudder.

Cesca could imagine it only too well. She felt exactly the same herself.

'So I would come here to do the reading, or if I was very tired, some sleeping. I could be sure that no one would disturb me here.'

'So that's what you were doing, when . . . ?' Cesca prompted, hardly able to hold back. She had a sense now of how this was all going to hang together.

'I was reading when suddenly the door there opened.' She smacked the access hole in the ground with her foot, clapping a hand over her chest, remembering the fright. 'It was the Visconte. He was . . . he was wild! I had never seen him in such a state before. He was frantic. A crazy man.'

'Why? What had happened?'

'It was what he thought was happening. No – what he *knew*! He kept asking, "Where are they? Where are they?" I did not know of who he was talking. Then he ran straight for the stairs.' She pointed to the corner where they no longer stood, her eyes no longer seeing the present but sunk back into the past. Into that night. 'He broke open the door. And then I heard a scream. Shouts.' Her fingers worried at the edge of the lace cloth. 'I ran up after him. I did not even know there was anyone up there.'

'Maybe they had heard you?'

She shrugged. 'Perhaps. They were standing there, *together*. And Aurelio, he—' She shook her head. 'It was terrible. They began to fight, Vito swinging at his brother, Aurelio pleading with him. The Viscontessa could not stop screaming. I tried to stop them and Vito catched me with his fist. It was an accident – he did not mean to.' She shook her head sadly. 'He was such a good man, he cried. Then he apologized to me and left. Aurelio ran after him – and I never saw him again.'

'What happened?'

'Vito drove away. Aurelio tried to catch up with him, but there was a car crash.'

Cesca swallowed, disappointed that her witness had

bowed out at this point in the story. She already knew the rest – that the crash *hadn't* been what had killed Aurelio, in spite of what the headlines had said. Something more *must* have happened – Signora Dutti's account proved it was no mere accident but a crime of passion; there was a motive now, but still no witnesses at the crucial moment . . . Had they continued the fight outside, after the crash . . . ?

'Aurelio was killed.' Signora Dutti sighed, the sound so heavy and weary, it was as though her life force itself was leaving her body. 'And it was all *her* fault. She is responsible and she knows it. Why else would she do what she did? It was the behaviour of a guilty woman.'

'What do you mean?'

'Immediately afterwards, she had the tunnel bricked up. She gave me money and this—' Signora Dutti held her hands up in the air, indicating the little building '—if I would not speak of what I saw that night.'

'So she bribed you.'

'I suppose that is the word. What else could I do but accept? If I spoke of what I had seen, it would have brought disgrace on the family – they would have been ruined – and I could not do that to the Visconte. I took the money, but I would not step foot in that building again; I would not work for her. She disgusted me.'

'Does anyone else know about this?'

Signora Dutti crossed her arms and pursed her lips together.

'Signora Accardo, I'm guessing?' Cesca pressed.

'Of course. She is my oldest friend. It was no surprise to her. She knew about the tunnels too. She knew what used to go on.'

Cesca nodded. The twins had been cleaved apart, destroyed by their love for the same woman. What their mother always said about them had been wrong: they had been one face, *one* heart, after all.

Chapter Forty

Rome, November 1989

Elena stood by the window, watching him pace through his private rooms on the far side of the courtyard. He was on the phone, the coiled line stretching and contracting as he gesticulated angrily. She knew who he was speaking to, but what were they saying? Was he telling her he couldn't go through with it? Was she crying, begging him, just as she herself had done, only this morning?

This poor girl didn't stand a chance. She was just another Milana.

She turned away and sank back onto her bed, unfolding and rereading the note, which had been slipped under her door: *'Palombella stable in one hour. I need to see you.'*

Her stomach fluttered again as she checked her appearance – she had changed into a silky wrap dress by her friend Diane (it was easy to get out of and, crucially, to get back into before dinner) and she was wearing the divine new champagne satin Janet Reger bra and cami knickers she hadn't had the heart to wear for Vito. Her cheeks were flushed, her eyes bright. She looked almost as if she was coming down with a fever.

Her pulse was certainly high, she thought, placing two fingers over her wrist.

Her eyes fell to the dazzling ring on her left hand – the one Vito had given to her the day Gio had been born. An eternity ring of the highest order, he'd had it made especially – the white diamond for their love, the blue one for Gio – as a commemoration of the day they had 'become a family', Vito had said. She hadn't taken it off in six and a half years, but every day she felt its weight on her hand, a physical emblem of the secret she must carry.

But not tonight. Tonight she was free to tell the truth, to live it. She slipped it off and left it on the dressing table, hiding the note beneath the grey Baccarat crystal ring dish.

She checked across the courtyard. Aurelio was still on the phone, still shouting.

She smiled and stole from the room anyway. It wouldn't hurt to be a few minutes early. She wanted to be ready for him. They had both waited long enough.

Restless, she paced the room, before sitting on the bed, before getting up and pacing again. The place was primitive to say the least – the mattress was lumpen and the building still smelled of horses. It wasn't what she was used to, but then what she was used to didn't thrill her like this and she would take him any way she could get him. In a dark tunnel, in an old stable . . . She would give up everything for him: she knew that now. She would choose poverty and disgrace over living another day without him. She had lost enough love in this life to know it was the only thing that made life worth living.

She heard his footsteps coming up the wooden treads and she stood, scarcely able to wait for the extra moments before the door opened and she could rest her eyes upon him again.

When the door did open, he didn't move – as though he'd almost convinced himself she wouldn't come. He was holding something.

'Won't you come in?' she asked.

He closed the door behind him.

'What's that?' she asked, her eyes on the forest-green box.

'It's for you.'

Her eyes sparkled as he walked towards her, opening the box for her to see inside. A simple string of pale-pink beads nestled on a velvet cushion. She gasped. As a woman used to fine jewellery of the very highest order, she could see that, though striking, it was modest to the point of neglect. But it came from *him* and that made it the most precious necklace she had ever seen in her very privileged life.

'Oh, Reli,' she whispered. 'It's so beautiful.'

'They are opals.'

'Opals?'

'Here, let me put it on for you.'

She turned, lifting her hair up, feeling how her skin flickered at the brush of his hands against her skin.

He turned her back to face him, his eyes focused on the way the necklace nestled at her throat. 'According to tradition, they represent second sight.'

'Second sight?'

'Love at second sight,' he murmured, his eyes lifting to hers, and a black hole opened up between them, swallowing time. 'If you had only met me first . . .' His voice broke.

'Oh, I know, darling,' she cried, throwing her arms around him, feeling the warmth of his body against hers as she kissed his neck. 'I know.'

He pulled her back and kissed her then. It was the kiss of her life, touching the very soul of her, claiming her and making her his even more than that night in the tunnel.

But when he pulled away, there was a shadow in his eyes. 'I hope that when you wear this, you will remember me, and what you are to me. And how I wish things could have been different.'

'Different?' she echoed, feeling confused. 'But Reli—'

He walked away, crossing the room, his hands on his hips, his shoulders up by his ears. 'I brought you here to tell you I'm leaving tomorrow. I'm booked on the first flight out.'

'What? No!' He'd only just got here. Seven years he'd been gone and he was back for only one day? No. It didn't make sense. 'You've got to stop doing this! You can't keep running away! It's killing me!'

He stared back at her, desperate, defeated. Resolute. 'I thought it would work this time. I thought it had been long enough. God knows I've tried everything I could think of to stay away from you. But I have to face the truth – if I can't have you, then I can't see you.'

'Reli, no—' she protested, feeling panic begin to flood her limbs. 'You don't mean that. You'll come back. You always do.'

'I know – which is why I'm telling you this face to face. I'm not running out this time. You need to know not to wait for me, because when I leave here tomorrow, I'm never coming back.'

'No!' The word was a bark, short and furious, the shock like a bullet ricocheting through her bones.

'Yes. Yes, Elena.' He winced at the sight of her pain.

'But I love you. And you love me.'

'Yes,' he admitted. 'I do. But I love Vito more.'

'No.' Her face crumpled as the fight left her, enormous sobs surging up through her body with volcanic force. She fell to the bed, feeling the pain might rip her in two.

He rushed over to her. 'Elena—'

She kissed him, grabbing his face, his arms, feeling like an animal. Feral. He kissed her back, just as desperate, just as—

A sudden sound downstairs made them both stop. Aurelio froze. 'What was that?' he whispered, their bodies still gripping one another. It had sounded like a chair leg on the floor. Someone was down there. He looked back at her, their noses almost touching, his eyes soaking her up.

She kissed him again, pressing herself to him so that she almost couldn't tell where she ended and he began. She could change his mind. She could stop this.

She put his hands on her body, and he groaned at the touch of her, his defences crumbling.

Yes, she—

There was another sound now. More of a . . . more of a crash. They both froze again.

Voices.

Aurelio looked at her in horror as Vito's shouts burst through the draughty floorboards like grenades. 'Where are they? Where are they?' he roared.

Maria's cries sounded weak and frightened as in the very next moment his footsteps were on the staircase and they could only look on in frozen horror as the door burst open.

Vito stared back at them, anguish on his face, fury in his eyes, as the secret they had kept for the best part of ten years fell into the world and stopped at his feet.

Chapter Forty-One

Rome, September 2017

'Her Grace is indisposed,' Alberto said, standing in the middle of the doorway to the white apartment as though he was a bodyguard and not a middle-aged, rather portly butler.

'But you said she was getting back from Florence last night.'

'Yes.'

'And that I could see her today.' Aware that she was sounding almost whiny, she drew herself up to her full height. 'It really is very important I speak to her before I hand this over.' She held up the weighty ream of papers in her hands. 'There are some matters which I do need to discuss with her as a matter of urgency.' Cesca stared beyond him into the large, empty space. The door leading to the private sitting room was ajar. Was Elena in there? Could she hear her?

She had spent the past five days and nights at Alessandra's kitchen table, writing around the clock and putting down what she knew, the best way she knew how: in the round. The truth, the whole truth and nothing but the truth. It was all in there – the gritty lows as well as the pink-tinted gloss that made the headlines of Elena's life. The publishers wanted the woman behind the enigma? Well, she'd given them that. Hell, yes she had! She had researched and fact-checked every last movement of Elena's life, bringing to bear all her barristerial knowledge, experience and instinct, compiling the narrative of Elena's history as though it was a case about to go to trial. She had pulled no punches. She wasn't interested – any longer – in painting a pretty picture. This had become about the truth; when she was confronted with lies, she simply couldn't help herself.

But there was no dramatic summing up, no great sur-mises of Elena's life story, for there was still one thing – something vital – which she didn't yet know. The copy of Aurelio's death certificate that she had requested had come through: heart failure, it had read; not a broken neck or head injury, not blood loss or any of the other likely causes of death from a car crash, as the papers had reported. Only Elena really knew the full truth of what went on that night.

'I'm afraid it will have to wait,' Alberto insisted. 'Her Grace is resting after the journey. She wants to be prepared for when she meets with her son later this afternoon.'

Cesca looked past him, through to that open sitting-room door again. She could do with a rest herself. This project had been the perfect distraction from Nico's betrayal; com-pletely immersing herself in Elena's life meant she hadn't had to confront her own. But the heartbreak that came with his treachery was still there, waiting for her, and as the adrenaline of her deadline ebbed away, exhaustion was claiming her. Her body felt as shattered as her heart.

'Fine,' she said loudly. 'Well, could you please pass on to her that I need to see her *urgently*? Tell her . . . tell her I spoke with Signora Dutti.' That would surely flush her out.

The butler's brow puckered at the mention of his predecessor's name. 'I shall pass on your message. *And* this,' he said, lifting the manuscript from her hands before she could object. 'Good morning.'

And the door closed in her face.

Cesca stared at it for a few moments, knowing she was out of a job. Once Elena set eyes on what she'd written, she'd fire her for . . . insubordination. Or . . . or treason.

Well, she wouldn't have changed any of it, Cesca reassured herself as she walked slowly back through the galleries of gold, feeling all those eyes on her back and secrets snapping at her heels. Because she had to live with herself. She knew better than anyone that sometimes it was silence that was the lie. That sometimes it was silence that could kill.

Cesca kept her eyes right as she walked, watching through the galleried windows the men pulling out all the equipment which had stabilized the sinkhole for the past six weeks. Struts, joists and boards were being piled up on the gravel in neat piles, ready to be carried through the palace and loaded onto the lorries which had special temporary permits to park outside in the piazza. It was strange to think that probably this time next week, none of them would be here – not them, not her, not Nico.

She was grateful to see there was no sign of him – was he underground, making last desperate recces for any sign of his beloved ancient map that was now scattered in buildings and lost in ruins around the city? Or had he moved on to the next job, the memory of her fading already?

'—it's not an option. You know what she's like!'

The violence of the whisper made her stop in her tracks.

Fifty metres ahead, at the far end of the gallery, was a man she had never seen before. He was suited, dark-haired, his back to her. And he was arguing with someone on the phone.

She knew he must be Elena's son, Giotto – the way he was leaning one arm outstretched on the pillar suggested intimate familiarity with his surroundings – but from the tension radiating off him, this clearly wasn't the time to make his acquaintance. Discreetly, grateful for her stealthy Stan Smiths, she turned and went to leave. There were other ways out of this labyrinthine palazzo.

'Christina, I don't care—'

She stopped dead again. *Christina?*

'I already told you what I heard . . . No, it'll be too late.'

'Cesca.' The hand on her arm made her jump and she flew around, coming face to face with the one – the very – person she desperately didn't want to see. 'Can we talk?'

'No,' she said, wresting her arm free, her heart pounding at double time because it was him, because he'd found her eavesdropping. 'I have nothing to say to you.'

'I have things to say to you.'

'Tough.' She heard footsteps and saw Giotto walking away towards the garden room, the phone still clamped to his ear. 'Dammit, now look what you've done!'

'Where have you been? I've been looking for you all week.'

'I've been staying with a friend; not that it's any of your business.'

'With Matteo?'

'*What?*'

He shook his head, as though trying to push the word away. 'Look, we have to talk about the other day.'

397

'No, we don't. I don't care.'

'I'm not engaged.'

'I don't c—' she insisted. '. . . What?'

'She broke it off after the party.'

'Wait – *what* party?' The man was mad. She hadn't been at any parties where he'd—

The penny dropped. Bulgari.

The other penny dropped. 'Isabella?' she whispered. 'She's *not* your sister?'

He shook his head.

'She was your fiancée?'

He nodded.

'So you lied!' she gasped, fresh and even more righteous indignation billowing up inside her.

'Yes. I didn't want to tell you the truth. Not then.'

'Oh, I bet you didn't!' she raged.

'No, I don't mean it like that.' He looked impatient. Frustrated. 'I thought it would scare you off if I told you she was – or, rather, *had* been – my fiancée.'

'Damn right it would!' she blustered, hardly able to get the words out. 'You're practically a married man.'

'No. I'm not.' His voice was calm, his face impassive as ever and she wished she could read what went on behind those dark eyes. She wished, too, that they weren't so beautiful . . .

She straightened up, determined not to fall for his act again. 'Well, I'm . . . I'm glad she saw you for what you are. Good on her. She can do better.' She paused, running out of indignation. 'Good riddance,' she muttered, beginning to wilt under his continuing stare as he waited for her to finish. Did the man never blink? Was no situation ever awkward for him? Finally, she asked curiously, '*Why* did she break it off with you?'

'Because she said she saw how I looked at you.'

Oh crap. 'Really?'

He shrugged. 'I didn't know. Not back then. She knew before I did.'

'Knew what?' But the twitch of his right eyebrow was all the answer she needed.

'But you hardly know me,' she whispered. 'And you knew me even less *then*.'

'I know, and I told her that. I told her there was nothing going on between us; she said that was obvious. She said you were like the cat on the hot roof trying to get away from me. She doesn't think I stand a chance with you.'

Cesca sighed. 'Look, that's all very flattering but I'm not going to be the other woman in this—'

'You're not,' he said bluntly. 'And you're not why we broke up. You are just the reason why we had the conversation. It wasn't right – or not right *enough* – between me and her.'

Cesca frowned, flummoxed. 'But she's so beautiful.'

He shrugged again, as if to say, 'So?' All he said aloud was simple acknowledgement of the fact of it: 'Yes.'

'God, I'd marry her,' she mumbled. Nico looked baffled again.

'Do you love her?'

'Yes. But we were always more friends than lovers. We have known each other a long time. We're very comfortable together.'

'Comfortable? What, like a mattress?' She arched an eyebrow. 'Perhaps that was the problem.'

'Well, *you*, on the other hand, are *not* comfortable for me.'

She allowed a wry smile and indicated her Annie Hall-inspired wide-legged cream trousers and braces, with shirt and panama. 'I hope you're not being rude about my dress sense again.'

He shook his head despairingly, but his eyes had come alive and she could read him now. Tentatively, he hooked an arm around her waist, pulling her into him, and he stared into her eyes. 'I don't know what it is about you,' he murmured. 'But you are the single most frustrating and fascinating woman I have ever met.'

'Likewise. Man version, I mean.'

He bent to kiss her – but a sudden round of applause and cheers outside the window made them spring apart again.

'Oh God,' they both murmured, yet they were not quite able to stop their own grins as they saw the team were all watching and clapping. Pulling down a frown, Nico waved his arm to get them back to work. He winked at her as they dispersed, still laughing.

'Will you be my date tonight?' he asked, putting back on the hard hat she had grown to know and love on him.

'Hmm?' she smiled, feeling dreamy and light again after five days of alternating tears and rages. 'Oh, wait. No.'

'What?'

'Do you mean the gala thing?'

'Yes.'

'I can't go to that.'

'Why not?'

'Well, because for one thing, it's Elena's bash and I'm going to be officially *persona non grata*.'

'Why?'

She grimaced. 'I may have just presented her with some cold, hard truths.'

He looked baffled.

'Just trust me when I say she will not want to see me there.'

'Well, I do. Listen, I know the organizers. You are coming as my guest.'

'But—'

He shook his head, pressing his finger against her lips to silence her. 'No. No "but"s this time. No more waiting. We are going together. I will pick you up tonight at eight.'

'Well, if you're going to be bossy about it . . . fine,' she grinned, happy to give in for once as she watched him go, her stomach flipping over at the sight of him.

'And dress up tonight. It will be smart,' he called, walking backwards.

'Says the guy in the boilersuit,' she quipped just before he turned out of sight, his eyes on her till the last.

She settled on a vintage white swiss-dot cotton nightdress that fell to her feet; it had a low scoop behind, a gently billowing skirt and frilled straps that criss-crossed at the back. She usually wore it as a sundress, cinched in with a tan belt and worn with roman sandals, but Alé had loaned her a pair of strappy red suede heels and she wore a string of large turquoise beads at her throat to take it up a level. She had blow-dried her hair, too, tonging it into soft curls and pulling up the side sections, letting the rest hang down her back.

Nico arrived at ten to eight.

'Don't you know it's rude to arrive early?' she asked, styling the last section of hair.

'Actually, I was hoping to catch you before you were dressed,' he said with dancing eyes as he leaned in the doorway. He had pulled off another of his transformations – showering, shaving and changing into a dinner suit. He looked *so* handsome, it was just rude.

She giggled, putting down the curlers as he crossed the room to her, his eyes all over her.

'You look beautiful,' he said, before grinning. 'But that's a nightdress, isn't it?'

She laughed. 'Yes.'

He laughed too, his arms reaching for her. 'Then it's no wonder all I want to do is take you to bed.'

They walked hand in hand across Piazzetta Palombella and Piazza Angelica, to the public parking area at the bottom. Only Elena's cars had special permits for parking at the top of the square. Cesca saw tourists looking at them as they walked past the fountain in their finery, the sky aglow with a celestial light, the statues on the buildings beginning to darken against the horizon, slowly becoming shadows of the night.

'Here she is.' He stopped at an old Fiat 500, pillar-box red and gleaming.

'Do you fit in that?' she asked, astonished.

'Yes. But I'm a little worried about you. You're so long,' he grinned, picking up one of her arms and waggling it playfully, as though she was Mr Tickle.

He opened the passenger door for her.

'I hope I won't have to stick my feet out the window,' she laughed, gathering her skirt and showing off her red shoes and dainty ankles as she tucked herself in.

'Hmm. I hope you do!' He winked.

The little car gave a groan as he got in too and they rumbled over the cobbles. It was slow-going through the back streets, tourists and pedestrians walking in the middle of the roads, their eyes on the dinner menus or shop windows or the spectacular molten sky. As a former tour guide, she knew the city well but, as a local, Nico knew every shortcut, every turn. They zipped through the streets, glimpsing the Pantheon at the end of an alley, merging with the city and its tired commuters at Corso Vittorio, passing the crowds still queuing outside the Bocca della Verità, awaiting their own Audrey Hepburn and Gregory Peck moment.

They stopped at some traffic lights, rooks cawing in the cloud pines, Mussolini's grand monuments looking mighty in marble. A heat haze made the city shimmer as they whizzed past the illuminated flower stalls and ancient churches, the magnificent fountains that were more intricately worked than most cathedrals.

The Colosseum hove into view, patched up and half-covered in scaffolding but still standing, as much a surviving warrior now as the gladiators who had once fought for their lives within her. Cesca kept her eyes on the stadium as Nico sped them past, merging with the sea of scooters on the peripheral road. This city would never stop being awe-inspiring to her; she could never grow bored of it.

Or of this, she thought, glancing at Nico in the driver's seat, both their knees tucked comically high on the tiny seats of the dinky red car. The night felt sparkling, somehow; she couldn't quite put her finger on it, but she had a feeling of being on the cusp of something momentous, as though, tonight, their lives were about to change.

Chapter Forty-Two

Massimo's Forum lay in the foothills of the Colosseum and the encircling ruins were duly colossal, huge and ancient slabs that were eight storeys high, lit up in red and purple lights. Cesca noted there were no signs of any scaffolding anywhere and she wondered whether Christina had been as successful in rectifying the truffle shortage. Tables had been set up in the grassy area in the middle and a small podium was set off to the front, behind which stood a vast screen showing a black-and-white image of Vito in a suit and tie. He looked older in it than in any of the photos Cesca had so far examined in the boxes.

At a glance, she guessed there must be 500 people there. Naturally, she was the only redhead. 'I feel conspicuous,' she mumbled to Nico as heads began to turn at their entrance.

'That's because you are.'

'You're not one for sugar-coating things, are you?'

'No,' he said, but his eyes were gleaming as they looked down at her. She couldn't wait till this was over and they were alone again. The first time they had got together it had happened so unexpectedly – sheer animal instinct, no reasoning, no logic involved – but this time, the anticipation was almost more than she could bear.

Elena, the guest of honour, was already there, making her way through the crowd with her son, Giotto. The likeness to his father (and, ergo, uncle) was staggering; he was like a third twin, with deep-set elongated brown eyes, a broken nose and wide mouth. It was an aristocratic face that had surely been painted and cast many times over the generations; Cesca felt sure she'd seen marble statues of his ancestors in the British Museum. Or the Louvre, perhaps.

'You know an awful lot of people,' Cesca said through another smile as Nico was greeted by almost everyone they passed. He solicitously introduced her, names and faces fast becoming a blur as they waltzed through the crowd. Cesca wanted to hold his hand but didn't dare, for how many of these people knew him with Isabella? And how many knew that the engagement was off? Not many, she could tell, as she sensed them regarding her with quizzical eyes.

'Friends of my family.'

They mingled, making small talk with everyone, but, inevitably, the point of the gala was soon reached and everyone was invited to take their seats at their tables.

Nico led them through the crowds to a centrally positioned table that—

'Oh God,' Cesca mumbled, as she saw Elena's distinctive tiny back. Even from behind, she looked impossibly chic in a teal silk belted kaftan with ostrich feathers at the neck and cuffs.

'Stop worrying,' Nico said, squeezing her hand. 'You're with me.'

The man she had seen in the whispering gallery earlier that day greeted Nico at the table with a friendly, though formal, handshake. 'Nico. It has been a long time,' he said.

'Too long. You look very well.'

'Thank you. And you likewise.'

'Giotto, may I introduce you to Francesca Hackett?'

Giotto's expression changed slightly at the mention of her name. 'Signorina Hackett?'

'Hello. Please, call me Cesca,' she said, shaking his hand.

'You, if I am not mistaken, are the writer of my mother's biography?'

She swallowed. *Present tense.* She wasn't fired yet, then? 'Yes, that's right.'

'And how have you found the endeavour?'

'Fascinating,' she said diplomatically. 'Your mother has led a quite remarkable life.'

'Indeed she has.' There was a coolness to Giotto's demeanour. His manner was relaxed and she guessed he was a consummate host, but he emitted no personal warmth. She felt he had stood at a thousand of such evenings as these – a drink in his hand, small talk on his lips. 'I must admit, I was very surprised when I first heard about the project. I have always considered my mother to be discreet to the point of evasive when it comes to talking about her life. She has certainly never been forthcoming about the events of her life before meeting my father.'

'Well, it's . . . it's a hard thing to do, actually – examining your own past with an almost forensic eye. I'm not sure I'd rush to do it myself and my life isn't a fraction as long or as interesting as your mother's. It can throw you into the path of memories or experiences that you might prefer to forget.' She wondered how much he knew about his own big brother, dead before he was born.

'Yes, I suppose so.'

'It's cathartic, though, too. You get to admit to mistakes, forgive yourself and others, wipe the slate clean.'

'Well, my mother is in the winter of her life,' Giotto said, glancing over at her diminutive form. 'I imagine the decision to greenlight this project was not undertaken lightly. She must feel she has a good reason for doing it.' His gaze flickered back to her and she could see a shade of distrust in his eyes. Did he worry she would compromise his family? Had his mother already shown him the manuscript?

'And it appears rather a lot more has happened at Palazzo Mirandola besides books,' Giotto said, turning his attention to Nico. 'Sinkholes, landslides, hidden underground tunnels. It has an almost apocalyptic undertone to it, don't you think? As though the past is beginning to swallow up the present?'

'Yes, I suppose so,' Nico agreed.

'Of course, it's been lucky for us that you were leading the investigation. At least you are sensitive to the history of the place. I had no idea you'd moved into spe—?' he tailed off, the word eluding him.

'Speleology,' Nico offered. 'It's a specialized field.'

'Was your interest in all things underground and ancient prompted by your family's time in Athens?'

'In part, yes. Papa would take me on expeditions with him.'

'Athens?' Cesca asked.

Giotto looked at Cesca, seeing the bafflement on her face. 'Nico's father was a diplomat.'

'Oh,' Cesca said, genuinely surprised. She had guessed he came from a well-to-do family, but the diplomatic world was another step beyond. She vowed to interrogate him later; she wanted to know every last thing about him. He was a tall glass of water in the desert and the desire to know him was like a thirst. 'I didn't know that.'

'My father was posted there when I was four and we stayed until I was seventeen,' Nico explained.

'Which was a great shame for me,' Giotto said. 'We used to be partners in crime as toddlers.'

'Giotto, darling—' Elena's voice swept over them all, halting as she saw to whom her son was talking, her eyes scanning over their select group. It took her only a fraction of a second to recover. 'Well, Francesca, how lovely to see you here. You look radiant. I don't know how you do it – that gown would look like a nightdress on me.'

Cesca gave a nervous laugh as Elena swooped in for an air kiss. She wouldn't have been surprised if she had slapped her instead. But, of course, such a response was out of the question – it would never do to make a fuss. That wasn't how these people operated.

'And Nico, is Isabella not coming?' Elena asked brightly.

'Isabella and I are no longer together,' Nico said simply.

'Oh?' Elena said, glancing at Cesca and, seeing how Nico was holding her hand, realizing the truth. 'Oh, I see. Well, I have to say I'm sorry to hear that. She's such a charming young woman and so beautiful too. Your mother must be terribly disappointed. You seemed very well matched.'

If Nico wondered at Elena's unusual personal interest in his private life, he didn't show it. In fact, he didn't respond at all and an awkward silence developed, the conversation seemingly stalled on the disappointment of his broken engagement.

Cesca swallowed, knowing this was how Elena exacted her revenge – words as razor blades, hidden behind smiles. It didn't matter whether Elena had started reading the manuscript yet, she already knew Cesca had spoken to Maria Dutti; she already knew from the way Cesca had used her name earlier – calling it through to her in the bedroom – that the old woman had spoken, revealing her darkest secret: the one that couldn't be researched or googled, the one that had left no paper trail, just a single eyewitness. It was the old housekeeper alone who had the power to dismantle the myth about Elena's relationship with her beloved Vito, the man they were all assembled to honour here tonight. With one sentence from her, the fantasies Elena had worked so hard to spin about their love story could be torn in the breeze and left hanging in rags.

'Well, shall we?' Giotto asked, gesturing for them all to take their places. Cesca saw that she was sitting between Nico and Christina—

'Mother,' Nico said, lightly kissing on the cheek the tall handsome woman with whom Cesca had had lunch all those weeks ago. She was wearing a grey silk mousseline gown, with her hair combed back into a chignon and held in place with diamond clips. 'I'd like you to meet Francesca Hackett.'

'Ah! But we've already met,' Christina smiled, greeting her too.

'You have?' he asked.

'Yes. Francesca interviewed me for this book of Elena's. We were discussing her charity work over the years.' She looked at Cesca and Cesca immediately recognized in her face Nico's penetrating gaze and warm smile. 'Come, you are sitting beside me. I am afraid I always throw out the seating plans; I am a widow but I refuse to bring a companion. What do they call them? "Walkers"?' She gave a disapproving tut. 'I may be old but I am perfectly capable of conducting myself on my own at a dinner.'

Nico had turned away and begun talking to someone at

the next table as Cesca took her seat beside his mother. She made a mental note to kill him when they got home. She needed advance notice of this kind of thing. Meeting his mother on their first date was enough to tip her over the edge.

'I imagine you must be very used to these types of events? I understand your husband was a diplomat,' Cesca said, reaching for what little information she had about his family. It had been one thing talking to Christina as an interview subject, quite another as her boyfriend's mother.

'Yes. We've lived in Costa Rica, Oslo, Madrid and finally Athens. We've been very fortunate – we have spent most of our adult lives living in the most wonderful places, places we might never have had the chance to visit had Sigmundo not been in such a privileged position.'

'But you are from Rome originally?'

'Originally and always. In my heart, this is where I belong.'

Cesca nodded, still more than a little stunned to discover that Nico was from a family every bit as noble as the Damianis – a cousin, in fact – and yet he spent his days working, getting mucky, being a normal person. 'I guess that's the thing about Rome – it's almost impossible to leave. I wasn't born here but I love it as if I were. And clearly Elena feels the same way too. One might have thought she would return to the States after the death of her husband.'

'Yes. One might.'

'I . . . I hadn't realized that Nico is your son. It's quite extraordinary, isn't it, that he has been working in the very tunnels you used to play in as a child? There's something almost poetic about it,' she said, trying not to look over her shoulder at all the striking, well-to-do people thronging past them on their way to their own tables. There were a lot of jewel-coloured silks and taffetas passing by, yet more serious jewellery.

'Oh, absolutely. But then, I'm a great fatalist. I believe everything happens for a reason, even the sinkhole opening up like that. If you ask me, the ground at Elena's feet has split open because it is *literally* trying to push a truth back to the surface.'

Cesca blinked, not quite sure what to say to that. 'Well, it looks like you pulled out all the stops for tonight,' she said, changing the subject. 'No scaffolding, I see.'

'Thank God! Though if you'd been here at eleven o'clock this morning, you wouldn't have thought I was quite so on top of things.'

'Well, you've done Vito proud,' she said, her gaze on the huge image of him on the screen again. His body was slightly turned away, but his eyes – guarded, reserved and gentle – were to camera.

'I do hope so. We were so close. I always sensed he needed me, somehow.' Her eyes flickered towards Elena as she spoke and Cesca glanced over too, to see whether Elena – on the opposite side of the table – had overheard. She had a feeling Christina's comment wouldn't be well received; Elena's devotion to her late husband had a decidedly territorial bent to it.

'But not Aurelio?'

'Oh no, Reli could handle himself. He had a freedom Vito could only have dreamed about. There was no pressure on him as the second son. He just travelled, drank, caroused with women . . .' She looked thoughtful. 'Although that isn't to say he wasn't vulnerable in his own way. He'd always had a certain resilience, but after the shooting in

Kenya, I think it made him reckless, angry even. He pushed people away. I don't think he believed he would live to old age.'

Cesca felt confused; she vaguely remembered Elena telling her about the vengeful husband. 'But he . . . survived the shooting?'

'Yes, but the bullet had to stay where it was. It was too close to his heart for the surgeons to remove.'

'Oh! My goodness,' Cesca said. Elena hadn't mentioned that. Or perhaps she simply hadn't known. 'But how did you ever tell them apart? There's only one photo I've seen of them both in Elena's archives and it doesn't matter how much I look at it, there is nothing I can see to distinguish one from the other.'

'It's true, the differences between them were fractional, but – perhaps because I knew them from childhood – it was easier for me. I have a photograph of them in my purse,' Christina murmured, reaching for the yellow satin clutch on the table. 'Yes, see here? I take it everywhere. I took this of them at their twenty-firsts.'

Cesca took the black-and-white photograph from her and stared at it. If it was their twenty-firsts, then it would have been 1961, but it could have been taken at any time in the past fifty years – there was nothing to date it. The twins were in classic black tie, their dark hair short and swept back, each holding a glass of wine. They were standing side by side in what Cesca knew at a glance was the mirrored gallery. A deliberate pun? she wondered.

'And so, which one is Vito?' Cesca asked after a moment, for she was still completely unable to make a judgement call.

Christina smiled at her and pointed to the twin on the right of the photograph. 'That's him there.'

Cesca squinted at it. 'But how can you tell?'

'Well, for one thing, if you look closely, you can see Vito had a freckle immediately below his left eye.'

'*One* freckle?'

'One freckle.'

'But surely that could change in the summer, if he had a tan?'

'Precisely. So if ever I wasn't sure, I'd just throw a ball at them and see which hand they caught it with.' She gave a shrug. 'Vito was right-handed, Aurelio left-handed.'

Cesca looked at the photograph and saw now how they were holding the wine glasses in opposite hands. 'Wow, so they really were mirrors of each other.'

'Yes. Going on physicality alone, it was almost impossible to tell them apart, but in terms of temperament? You couldn't mistake them: they were completely opposite to one another. Vito was calm. An old soul, my mother used to call him. Aurelio, on the other hand, was like a whirl-wind.' She tutted.

'Yes, Elena said the same,' Cesca murmured, wondering if Christina had any idea of what had gone on between Vito and his brother and his wife.

'Did I hear my name?' Elena enquired and Cesca looked up with alarm to find she had the full attention of Giotto and Elena, both of whom were looking at her avidly.

Cesca wondered just how long they had been listening in on the conversation.

'We were just talking about how impossible it was to tell the twins apart,' Christina said.

413

'Well, to those who didn't know them, perhaps,' Elena replied crisply, straightening up.

'Of course. And now Giotto is the image of them, too,' Christina smiled, looking across at him fondly. 'Looking at you is like stepping back in time, darling.'

'Do I look like one more than the other, would you say?' Giotto asked with interest.

Christina tipped her head to the side as she studied him. 'I could not say. There's really nothing in it. But you have your father's manners, that's for certain.'

Giotto nodded. 'Did you know, in a standard paternity test, there need only be fifteen matching genetic markers to link a father and his son, but when dealing with identical twins, the number of genetic markers required for a match jumps to six billion?'

'Really?' Christina asked, looking fascinated.

'Why would you know such a thing?' Elena asked, looking ashen.

Giotto shrugged his eyebrows, then his shoulders. 'I'm not sure. I just do.'

Cesca watched the exchange, a growing unease blooming in her mind as something shocking occurred to her – she wondered if the same thing had occurred to Giotto. She knew that Elena and Aurelio had been having an affair, yes, but she only knew the day on which the affair ended – which was the day it was discovered, the same day Aurelio had been killed in the car crash. But she didn't know when it had begun. Was it possible Elena and Aurelio had been carrying on for months – even *years* – beforehand? Who would ever have known if Elena had had her husband's brother's child? They were identical. The boy would be like his father, regardless of which one that might actually prove to be.

'Tell me, could *you* tell them apart when you were a child?' Christina asked Giotto.

'Yes, of course.'

Elena straightened in her chair. 'How?'

'It was easy. I just looked at their signet rings.'

'Their signet rings?' Elena echoed, with a note of incredulity, as though he'd just said nose rings instead.

'Yes. Papa's had a V, obviously, and Uncle Reli's an A.' He chuckled. 'You tried to trick me when I met Uncle Reli for the first time, do you remember? He'd been off somewhere, travelling I think, and you both tried to pretend he was Papa. I couldn't have been more than six at the time. I wasn't sure if it was a joke or not, because you were telling me one thing but I was looking straight at his ring and it clearly told me another – I was the perfect height at the time, you see.' He blinked, his gaze steady upon his mother. 'Do you remember?'

Elena was immobile. 'I'm sorry, darling. I have no recollection of that at all.'

Giotto was silent for a moment. 'Well, why would you?' he said finally. 'It was just you teasing me. Hardly memorable. I don't know why it even stuck in my mind. I suppose I just remember staring at that ring. But after that, I would always check Papa's ring, just to be sure it was him.'

'But Uncle Reli died that same day, darling,' Elena said, gently reaching for his hand and squeezing it, as though he was still a young boy. 'Why would you have needed to keep checking it?'

Giotto gave a blank smile. 'The irrational insecurity of a

child, I suppose. Although it's good to see you remember some things about that day, at least.'

Elena withdrew her hand. 'It's not a day I would ever be likely to forget,' she said quietly, looking stung.

Christina straightened up briskly. 'Well, I just used to tell people to check which hand they wore the rings on. Vito wore his on the left hand and Reli wore his on the right.'

'Did he?' Elena asked, looking stricken as she gazed at the giant black-and-white image of her husband on the screen, behind Giotto's head. Sure enough, the signet ring could be seen on the little finger of his left hand, a faint, swirling 'V' etched into the gold.

Cesca watched Elena closely, seeing how tiny, almost microscopically small spasms of pain twitched at her mouth at the mention of Reli's name. Even looking for it, the response was hard to spot. But then, Elena had had years of practice, half a lifetime of hiding her love for one brother, whilst being married to the other.

'And I can certainly share some choice memories of your father and uncle switching places when they were young – it wasn't just you they teased, darling,' Christina said, smiling fondly at Giotto. 'They did it at school, with the nannies. It was one of their favourite things to do.'

'I bet all identical twins do it,' Cesca said.

'Oh, I'm certain they do. To just what extent, though?' Christina arched an eyebrow mischievously. 'Is it something they ever fully grow out of, do you think? Surely the temptation to . . . switch lives, even for a day, would be irresistible? It would be like having a superpower, wouldn't it? Like being invisible.'

Cesca nodded, smiling benignly, but she was one of two

people at this table who knew perfectly well just how much Aurelio had crossed over into his brother's life.

'Do you think they ever tricked you, Elena, dear?' Christina asked teasingly, looking at her from above the rim of her wine glass.

Elena didn't appear to hear. Her eyes were still on the image of her husband. She seemed lost to the past.

'Elena!'

'Hmm? What?' Elena asked, pulling herself back.

'I said, do you think the twins ever tricked you? Switching places?'

Elena looked scandalized. 'Absolutely not! Why on earth—'

'But how can you be so certain?' Christina was smiling. Teasing.

'Because I can. Vito was my husband. It surely goes without saying how well I knew him.' Elena's voice was brittle as the joke fell flat.

Christina smiled beatifically, giving a shrug at Elena's sense-of-humour failure.

Elena looked back at her son, reaching for Giotto's hand suddenly. 'Darling, did I ever tell you about your grandfather during the war?'

Giotto suppressed a sigh. 'Running bombs into the tunnels? Yes, Mama, you've told me,' he said wearily. 'Many times.'

'But can you just *imagine* a love like that? One so great that you would put a bomb under your own life to protect it? That's how I love you, my boy. And it's how your father loved—'

'Mother, have some water,' he said quietly, handing her a glass. He looked embarrassed by her suddenly vehement ramblings. 'You're going to be on stage shortly. Have you brought your speech?'

'Oh! Look! You're wearing your beautiful ring again, Elena,' Christina trilled. 'How did I not notice it before now? Oh, you must let me see it. You haven't worn it in such a long time.' Christina reached her hand across the table and Elena was obliged to extend her arm to allow her to admire the Bulgari Blue. 'Do you know, I feared you'd mislaid it?' Christina smiled, looking up at her old friend. 'Silly, I know. Obviously there's no way something as valuable as this could go missing and the world not know about it. The insurance industry would have gone into meltdown.'

Cesca held her breath at Christina's disingenuous words. Surely she knew that the ring had indeed been lost? It was her own son who had found it!

'It's not an everyday piece, Christina.'

'Oh, but on the contrary, you used to wear it daily when Giotto was a child. Vito gave it to you to celebrate Giotto's birth, don't you remember?'

'As if I'd be likely to forget,' Elena snipped.

Christina smiled at Giotto. 'Of course, *I* remember. I was with your father when he commissioned it. We chose the diamonds together.'

'You—?' Elena looked thunderstruck.

'Naturally. Vito wanted it to be a surprise for you so he couldn't very well ask you to assist, but he needed a feminine perspective, so I went along. It was a very happy experience. I cherish the memories still.'

'I'm sure you do,' Elena said tartly.

Cesca sat in alert silence, her antennae buzzing at these verbal drive-bys – *what exactly was going on here?* – as the sudden whine of a microphone being switched on made them all turn towards the stage. A grey-haired man climbed the podium and asked for their attention.

Nico turned back to the table, straightening his napkin on his lap. 'Sorry, I got caught. Have I missed much?' It was a question to the table, but he was looking at her, checking she was okay, checking she was still there. Still his. She smiled back but she felt distracted by the undercurrents sparking between the older women.

'We've just been reminiscing,' Christina replied in a loud whisper, leaning slightly across Cesca. 'You timed it well; they're just about ready to start the presentation.' She turned to her old friend. 'Your moment has come, Elena,' she said in a louder voice.

Elena didn't reply. She was now looking quite imperious in her chair, her gaze yet again on the enormous black-and-white photograph of Vito projected onto the screen behind the podium. Tears misted her eyes as the man spoke at length about Vito's life and the achievements of the foundation, prompting spontaneous little outbreaks of applause, coos and laughter.

'Giotto, you must be so proud,' Christina said to him. 'This honour is not before time. When I think of how your father devoted his life to good works for this city . . . Long before Fendi restored the Trevi, long before Tod's got involved with the Colosseum, or Bulgari with the Spanish Steps, it was Vito who was paving the way for privately funding the historic monuments which make this city so eternal.'

'Really, Christina, sometimes I think people would confuse *you* for his wife,' Elena said in an arch tone, breaking off momentarily from her gracious widow scene. 'Perhaps you should get up there and speak tonight?'

'Well, I should be more than happy to step in if you're not feeling up to it, dear. We're old friends, after all. Just say the word.' Christina was smiling as though to a newborn – utter gentleness on her face – even though there was steel in her words.

Cesca slid her eyes nervously from one to the other, wondering exactly how much love was lost between them. Was this really a friendship? Every conversation seemed loaded, tension crackling across the table.

They all clapped as Elena was introduced and Giotto jumped up to help his mother to the stage, giving her his arm as they climbed the steps together. Cesca heard some people on a nearby table commenting on his likeness to his father as Elena pulled some notes for her speech from her bag. A small, tatty blue envelope fluttered out too and Giotto stepped forwards to pick it up, his eyes falling to the name written in brown ink on the front. He handed it back to her without a word.

Cesca blinked, recognizing it immediately – there was no doubt it was the one that had been in the bag she had found in her bin. The letter Vito had supposedly written on his deathbed, the letter that remained unread fifteen years later. Cesca frowned. She had completely forgotten about it, but now the same questions she'd had that first night rushed back at her. Why couldn't Elena bring herself to read it? What could it possibly say that was so hard for her to face? But Cesca thought she could guess – it was guilt; guilt over what she and Aurelio had done. Elena was too frightened to face up to Vito's final word on the matter.

Elena began to speak, her American-accented Italian rolling over the people sitting rapt at their tables, their eyes falling continually to the Bulgari Blue on her left hand. It was impossible to ignore. Had Giotto known his father had bought it to commemorate his birth? It had been lost for most of his life, after all.

'Oh, what I wouldn't give to know what is in that letter,' Christina murmured, sitting back in her chair towards Cesca, her lips scarcely moving.

'The letter?' Cesca asked, surprised, not entirely sure at first that Christina was directing the comment to her.

'Yes. Giotto, too. It would give him great peace to know, but she will not let it out of her sight. Not for a second. She even sleeps with it under her pillow.' Christina was silent for a few moments before she glanced over at her. 'You do realize you have been the only person in fifteen years to have had any opportunity to see what is inside it?'

Cesca blinked, feeling her heart rate accelerate. Why on earth would she have done that – read a stranger's unopened old letter? And more to the point, why was Christina talking to *her* about it? 'Sorry, I don't follow . . . It would give Giotto great peace to know what, exactly?'

Christina's chin tipped up, her gaze remaining on the diminutive figure on the stage. Elena's voice was wavering with emotion as images of Vito flicked behind her in a slide-show, his love token, the Bulgari Blue, flashing with every movement of her hand. 'Haven't you guessed yet?'

Cesca's stomach clenched. *Oh God*. Did Christina know about the affair? Worse – did Giotto?

Cesca leaned forwards in her seat to be closer to Christina, who was smiling and nodding graciously as Elena mentioned her name, bringing admiring glances their way. She showed no sign of having just rolled a grenade into Cesca's lap. 'Why doesn't he just confront her directly?' she whispered, being careful not to put anything in concrete terms. If she was wrong about this and Christina didn't know about the affair, she couldn't afford to be the one to tell her.

'You ask me that, even after you've spent an entire summer in her company?'

Cesca knew Christina was right. Cesca wasn't sure Elena even knew what was truth and what was fantasy any more. She had deceived her husband – and her son – to the extent that Cesca was sure she believed her own lies. Appearance was all.

'Poor boy,' Christina tutted, her eyes on Giotto standing stiffly at his mother's shoulder, there for her lest she should stumble, trip or collapse. She did look incredibly frail. 'He's been lied to for all these years and still he has no answers. And now she is declining fast.'

'Declining? She's—'

'Dying. Progressive supranuclear palsy, or PSP as it's more commonly called. It's a rare form of Alzheimer's – tremors, difficulty walking, personality changes, that kind of thing. She's been getting treatment in Florence but the prognosis is poor.'

Florence? *That* was why she'd gone up there this week? Cesca felt as if she was being beaten about the head, these new facts coming too fast.

'In spite of that – or perhaps because of it – Giotto deserves to know the truth, but Elena is the only person still alive who can tell him what really went on.' She turned to face Cesca suddenly. 'Or you, of course.'

'Me?'

'Yes. I've tried telling him to talk to you about it but . . .' She shrugged. 'He is a very private person. It's hard for him, which I understand; I felt the same way myself.' Cesca remembered the phone conversation she had overheard in the whispering gallery. 'But it makes perfect sense. You've been Elena's confidante all summer; you have access to all her material – photographs, diaries.'

'But she hasn't said anything to me that isn't already in the public domain. In fact, quite the opposite. She's been very guarded.'

'*Really?*' Christina pressed, looking highly sceptical. 'Well, if she's that concerned about her privacy, why is she even writing this book?'

Why indeed? Cesca didn't argue the point but, in actual fact, it wasn't an unfamiliar dichotomy. As a barrister she'd had a similar issue with witnesses, who could be known to pour forth in the initial interviews, only to retract their testimonies when they got to the courtroom. Elena's skittish dance with the truth over this biography wasn't much different. She wanted it to present the realities of her life, but when actually faced with them, she turned away; full disclosure was easier said than done, and it begged the question – what did Elena want to admit to, but couldn't?

Did Christina even know the truth Cesca had stumbled upon, or was all this a bluff? She knew it was time to speak plainly – and one of them had to go first.

'You know about the affair,' Cesca said quietly, barely moving her lips lest anyone should be watching them.

Christina nodded. 'Yes.'

'And you think that Aurelio is Giotto's father.'

'Yes.'

'Giotto thinks so too?'

'Yes.'

Cesca took a deep breath, hesitating to say the words. As far as she was aware, no one else had ever requested to see the death certificate – everyone had bought the official line that Aurelio had been killed in the car crash. '. . . And you think Vito killed his brother because of it.'

'No.'

Wait, what?

'What?' Cesca whispered, feeling bewildered. 'What exactly do you think is in that letter, then?'

Christina looked straight at her, giving up any pretence of looking at the action on the stage. The real story of the night was happening right here. 'Giotto has told me that after the accident, several times over the years he overheard his mother speaking to his father behind closed doors.'

'So?'

'She called him Reli . . .'

Cesca blinked, looking back up at the little old lady on the stage – still beautiful, still formidable, as she held the cream of Rome's elite in her palm.

'It wasn't Aurelio who died in the car accident that night,' Christina said intensely as Cesca's eyes flickered to the too-handsome face on the screen behind Elena. 'It was Vito.'

Chapter Forty-Three

She was silent on the journey back, her face turned towards the window, his jacket over her shoulders to shield her from the plummeting night temperatures. She felt so angry she didn't know what to do with herself.

'Can I come up?' Nico asked, seeing how she wouldn't meet his eye as he parked in the tiny street off the west side of the piazzetta.

'Oh, I don't think so. "Dinner with your mother" has left me rather worn out,' she said with her best sarcasm, hauling herself out of the tiny car before he could stop her.

'Cesca!'

But she strode away, refusing to look back. Thirty seconds later, just as she got to the bottom of the steps, he grabbed her by the hand, pulling her up the stairs. 'I'm coming up,' he insisted. 'We're going to talk.'

'No. Nico!' she protested as he retrieved the key from under the geranium by the door.

'In.' He opened the door and she stumbled in, feeling how he took up the space in the small room, in her head.

She whirled around to face him, refusing to let him boss her, to let him dictate how this went. 'You knew!' she accused.

He nodded. 'Yes.'

She gawped at the blunt response. Did he not even have the decency to lie? 'And you never thought to tell me? Your mother just ambushed me, Nico! Did you know what she was going to do tonight?'

'No. But there are often problems between her and Elena. Their relationship has always been . . . difficult.'

'Yeah, I got that, thanks. It was just great to be caught up in the middle of them.'

'Look, whatever she has said is not some sort of action against you, but her trying to do her best by Giotto – she is his godmother. She doesn't even know about us yet. As far as she is aware, you are just working for Elena.'

'Oh! So you think she'd have been a bit more diplomatic if she'd known I was sleeping with her son?'

'Probably not.'

'You know she effectively wants me to *spy* on Elena? She wants me to get hold of that letter and read it.' But even if she did, Cesca thought, was it really going to tell them what Giotto needed to know – to confirm which of them was his father? To confirm Vito's death, and not Aurelio's?

Cesca couldn't imagine what reserves it must have taken the two of them to get through each day – Aurelio passing himself off in public as his own brother, pretending to be Elena's husband as he quietened his voice and toned down his jokes, swapping the playboy lifestyle for opening fetes and judging at cheese festivals. How had he done it without anyone ever knowing? Had there really been no slip-ups in all those years? They'd even managed to push out Christina, the one person who could have unmasked them.

He shrugged. 'My mother is a woman of strong principles. She loved Vito like a sister and she believes it is her duty to protect his son.'

'Really? She loved him as a sister? That's what you think?'

A pulse beat in his jaw as he looked away and she realized the implications – for him – of what she had said. 'Nico—'

'None of this is anything to do with me, okay? It's between my mother and Elena. I don't get involved with it.'

'But you are involved! You're working there! You're down there in those—' She stopped suddenly.

'What?' he asked. 'What is it?'

'You're in the tunnels. You knew about the tunnels.'

'. . . What?'

'Your mother said she told you stories about how she used to play in the tunnels. They weren't a discovery at all. You already knew they were there.' Her eyes widened as the facts began to shuffle into the slots in her mind. She gasped. '*That's* why you extended through from the sink-hole into the service tunnel. You knew it would connect to the other tunnels that had been bricked off.'

'Ces—'

But she cut him off by holding up a hand, her eyes narrowed as she began to pace. Pace and think. 'At the time I couldn't understand why you looked beyond the sinkhole itself; it was like you *knew* there was something extra down there.' She looked at him again. 'And you did. It's why you were down there on your own that Friday night; it's why you were so cross with me for getting you out.'

He sighed, raking a hand through his hair. 'Yes, I'm sorry.'

She stared at him, not wanting his apology. 'Why, though? Why were you trying to find the tunnels?'

He sighed, a look of resignation dawning on his face as he saw the intensity on hers. It was clear she wasn't going to let this drop. 'Because of the ring. My mother knew it was down there.'

Cesca's eyebrows shot up. 'Your mother knew the Bulgari Blue was in that tunnel?' So she *had* known it was lost! She had been deliberately provoking Elena at dinner, pushing her.

'Yes.'

'And she sent you down there to find it for her?'

'She didn't *send* me anywhere,' he said shortly. 'But when I told her about the sinkhole, she saw an opportunity to see if it could be retrieved and I agreed to help. I knew how important it was to her to try to help Giotto.'

'And you too, I'm sure,' she added drily. 'It bought you time to look for more pieces of your map?'

He nodded. 'Yes. But you have to under—'

Cesca held up a finger again, as though trying to halt the too-fast thoughts racing through her mind. 'Why would finding the ring help Giotto?'

'Oh my God,' he groaned, becoming exasperated. 'Now I see who you used to be! Look, I don't know for sure; I didn't ask for details. She thought it had something to do with the night of the crash when Aurelio died.'

'You mean, Vito.'

He shrugged. 'Yes.'

Cesca tore her eyes away from him and stared at the wall again, her antennae quivering. What was it? What did that ring have to do with the crash? She was reaching towards something, but . . . but she couldn't see it yet. She squinted, biting her lip. 'Why didn't your mother just go into the tunnels herself to look for the ring?'

'You mean, apart from the fact she is a woman in her late seventies?'

She ignored the sarcasm. 'That ring was lost almost thirty years ago, Nico. Why has she waited all this time?'

He sighed. 'Look, why are we even talking about this? We are not working now. It's supposed to be our night!'

'Tell me.'

He turned away, his hands on his hips, frustrated. 'She only found out about the affair recently – Easter, I think. She ran into Maria Dutti and they had coffee – they had always been close. Signora Dutti had never been fond of Elena either. Apparently she found her to be imperious.'

'But why did Maria only tell your mother about the affair now? Years had passed.'

'Because they had not seen each other since Aurelio's funeral.'

'Vito's,' she corrected, rather pedantically.

He shrugged and sighed. 'Yes. Whatever.'

'Why hadn't they seen each other? If they were close, surely your mother would have run into her when she was visiting at the Palazzo Mirandola? She lives just across the square.'

'Because after he – *Vito* – died, my mother was pretty much cut out of their lives. She continued to see Elena "socially",' he said, making speech marks in the air with his fingers. 'But she almost never went back to Mirandola. I think she had lunch with Vito – I mean, *Aurelio*—' He rolled his eyes, frustrated. '—Just once, immediately after the funeral. But after that, she practically never visited them at home again.'

'Why not?'

'She said he was very distant with her – he had just buried his twin, after all – but she said it was more than grief. Something in him had changed. She was devastated. It was only when Giotto came to her and confided what he had heard that it all made sense.'

'So she was pushed away because Aurelio knew she'd see straight through him and would realize that he wasn't Vito?' Cesca blinked, trying to absorb this new truth: Vito had died that night and Aurelio had assumed his identity; Elena had pretended he was her husband . . . But it didn't matter how many times she repeated the facts, she couldn't accept them. 'No, it's just monstrous!' she cried, shaking her head and turning away, pacing the small room.

Nico watched her. 'Yes.'

'How could they do it?'

He shrugged. 'Desperation? Maybe it really was true love.'

True love. Cesca's eyes narrowed to slits as she remembered something. '. . . You know, I asked Elena recently whether her marriage suffered after Aurelio died. She'd been married so many times by then, I kind of assumed marriage was like handbags for her – something to change with the seasons. I'd thought that Vito would surely have been broken by the loss of his twin, and I found it surprising they had managed to weather it. But she said a really odd thing. She said, if anything, they were strengthened by it. It brought them closer together.'

'And now you know why – it meant she was able to be with the brother she really wanted.'

'My God, that car crash turned out to be the perfect solution, didn't it?' she murmured. 'They got to live as man and wife without any of the scandal that would have ensued if the world had caught scent of the fact that Aurelio was having an affair with his dead brother's wife.' She clicked her tongue against the roof of her mouth. 'And if that *was* the solution to their problem, then it's also a cast-iron motive behind Vito's death.'

Nico frowned. 'Motive? But it was an accident.'

'No. I've got a copy of the death certificate. He died of heart failure.'

'Heart failure,' Nico repeated.

'Exactly. Not from the crash. I've examined the photographs and there's no way that's what killed him. Something else *must* have happened.' She slapped a palm to her forehead, frustrated. 'Ugh, I've been looking at it all the wrong way round.'

Nico frowned. 'I am lost.'

'When I thought it was Aurelio who had died, I assumed it was Vito who had killed him in a crime of passion – he'd just found his wife in bed with his brother; at most it was manslaughter.' She drew a breath, trying to steady her thoughts. 'But with Vito dead, it's different again. If Aurelio killed Vito to be with his wife . . . then that's murder.'

Nico stared at her, watching the way her expression changed with every thought, her mind racing, her body tense. 'Why did you stop, Cesca?'

She blinked, looking over at him, but still deep in contemplation. 'Huh?'

'You are good, you know that? I can see it in you, how you must have been.'

'Been where? Sorry, I wasn't listening. What are you talking about?'

'Your old job. Why did you stop?'

Her expression folded down. 'No. I'm not talking about that.'

'Why? Why do you always shut it out?'

'Because that's my prerogative. It's in the past. It was a mistake. I've moved on.'

'Have you? Then what are we doing here?' He held his arms out questioningly. 'Is this *writing*? Or are you constructing a case?'

Cesca felt the blood begin to rush to her cheeks. 'It's about getting to the truth. Something terrible has happened, Nico – can't you see that? We have to talk about it.'

'Yeah? Well, what about the fact you told me *you* killed someone, Cesca?' he said, losing his temper suddenly. 'When are we going to talk about that?'

She felt as though the air had been punched from her lungs. Hot tears sprang to her eyes as she stared back at him, yet she refused to let them fall. 'We're not – this isn't about me. Don't twist this . . .'

He turned away, taking a few deep breaths before he turned back again. 'Listen, I don't care what you said, okay? I don't believe it. I know you – you are not capable of something like that.' He walked over to her, taking her hands in his. 'But you have to tell me what happened.'

'No.' She looked up at him, feeling the guilt, the shame, rushing through her blood again, her head shaking from side to side. 'I can't.'

'You can.'

She shook her head harder. The tears were beginning to splash onto her cheeks, in spite of her best efforts.

'*Yes*,' he insisted. 'And if we're going to have any sort of future at all, you have to.'

He let go of her then, stepping back, giving her space, giving her hope. She watched as he moved across to the window, looking out across the square. It was shrouded in darkness, everywhere shut up for the night. He leaned against the ledge of the open window and waited patiently, the ends of his bow tie hanging at his neck, the top button undone, moonlight catching on the satin stripe down his trouser leg. His silhouette, his stillness, his calm – everything about him was strong.

And in that moment, she knew he was right. To do otherwise would be to live like Elena: dodging the truth, living a lie. She had to tell him. Somehow, she had to put a voice to the shadows that stalked like wolves in her heart. She could feel the secret straining to be let out, but to say those words, to admit to what she had done . . . After all, who was she to judge Elena for her weaknesses and indiscretions, when she herself had done something just as bad, if not worse?

She held her breath, feeling the memories assault her from within as she put her mind back there, back in a past she had been determined to outrun. 'I was legal counsel for a man charged with aggravated assault and battery against his wife,' she began finally, her voice halting. 'It was . . . it was a tough case; he had a rap sheet as long as this room. But I was known in my chambers for having an eye for detail. I was getting a reputation for being able to find the one anomaly that could make or break a case and I did it with him. I found a technicality and got him off; I had him returned to society a free man.' She stared down at her own toes, knowing she once would have said these words with pride, not shame.

'There's a big difference between "not guilty" and "innocent", you know,' she said more quietly, as he stayed silent. 'People think they're one and the same, but they're not. I had a friend who once asked me how I could defend people when I knew they were guilty and I told her it was because justice is a process that is based upon the assertion that a defendant is innocent *until proven guilty*. It was for the prosecution to prove guilt, not for me to prove innocence, and I believed in that system. No matter what I may have thought about someone privately, when I stood up in court and addressed the jury, I was defending a person who was considered innocent until the moment that verdict was delivered – and it was my responsibility to defend them to the fullest of my abilities.'

'And that's what you did.'

She shook her head. 'No, because if it's a process, it's also a game. Like anything, you learn to keep an eye on the stakes and if I wanted to progress in my career, I couldn't afford to lose. It stopped becoming about seeing that justice was served and instead became about getting the right result, getting the win.'

She glanced up to see if he was still listening; still there, even. She wouldn't have blamed him if he'd turned on his heel and left. 'Ten days later, I had a call from a colleague at the CPS. The police had a man in custody, charged with murder.'

A sob escaped her, bringing her hands flying to her mouth, tears streaming in an unstoppable torrent as the memories – the full horror – broke through in a rush. 'H-his wife had moved with their daughter to a new part of town. They had changed their names, their hair, *everything*. They were starting over; they wanted a new life away from him. But he found them. He f-found them and broke in while they were sleeping. He—' She covered her face, not wanting to see it, not wanting to say it. '—He s-s-stabbed the little girl in her bed. Then h-he tortured his wife for six hours before h-he killed her too.'

Nico was across the room in a heartbeat, his arms around her. 'Oh *mia cara*,' he whispered as the tears choked her, making her shake. 'Cesca, I am so sorry.'

'I-I think about them every day. Every hour, every day. I see them when I close my eyes at night, w-when I wake up in the morning.'

'Oh no. No. No.'

'*Yes*,' she argued, refusing to take comfort, to be consoled. 'It's only right. It's something I have to live with, because *I* put him back out on the streets. I sent him straight back to them. *I* am as responsible for their deaths as if I'd had that knife in my hand myself.'

He clasped her head between his hands, forcing her to look at him, though she couldn't see a thing past her tears. 'Cesca, no! You have to forgive yourself.'

'No. It's my fault. It's on *me*. It is. I could have ignored the technicality. We would have lost the case without it and I could have let him go down. I *should* have done that. I knew what he was.' Her mouth twisted into a sneer of repugnance. 'But I wanted the win: it's that simple. I wanted the win and to hell with the human cost.'

He wiped her tears with his thumbs but they were no sooner gone than replaced. 'You have more than paid the price, Cesca. Punishing yourself will not change the past. You have to let it go now.'

'I c-can't.'

'You must. Right or wrong, you did your job. Maybe too well.' He kissed her forehead gently, his lips lingering on her skin, making her eyes close and her soul relax. He pulled back and she looked up at him. He didn't hate her? She didn't disgust him?

435

'But you're doing it again now,' he said. 'You have to learn to step back.'

'I tried. I thought I *was* stepping back,' she protested, remembering how lightly she'd taken her duties in the first few weeks, sorting through photographs, sipping tea . . . 'Well, initially.'

'Initially?'

'Until I realized Elena was lying to me,' she sniffed. She rubbed her cheeks hard, dragging away the tears, knowing and not caring that she probably looked a state. 'Oh God, what am I supposed to do this time? Going public with this would destroy the family.'

'Yes. It would,' he said sombrely.

'But what about Vito – doesn't he deserve justice? Doesn't Giotto?'

Nico looked at her. 'You need to confront Elena. Tell her what you know.'

Cesca shook her head. 'I've already tried that. She just stonewalls me. And besides, I need proof. Actual evidence. An overheard conversation proves nothing.'

He stepped towards her, his eyes on one of her shoulder straps that had become twisted. He lifted and corrected it, his fingers brushing against her bare skin. The action made her shiver, her body reacting automatically to his touch.

He saw it.

'Well, you have unlimited access in the palazzo. Alberto does not question where you go, what you do, does he?'

She shook her head.

'There must be something in that building that gives them away,' he murmured. 'They can't have not made a single mistake in all those years,' he said, combing his fingers under her hair and tipping her head back so that she looked up at him.

The diaries? she wondered, as she felt that current of electricity dart through her stomach again, as it did every time their eyes met. 'Okay. I'll look into it,' she murmured, knowing it was the blue letter she really needed. Christina had been right. Everything would be in there.

'But not yet,' he murmured, his other hand sweeping down her neck and, this time, brushing the strap *off* her shoulder.

'No,' she whispered. 'Not just yet.'

Chapter Forty-Four

Alberto's expression as he had opened the door to her just after 6 a.m. had been priceless. It would have sent most people running. Her too, once. But not now, not today. She had to re-examine Elena's life with forensic detail. She had a mission, an opportunity, to right a terrible wrong and nothing was going to put her off.

She was sitting in the middle of the floor in the library – still her latest office, even though there was no hiding from Nico any more; there were only so many times she could move – boxes upturned and photographs scattered all around her. She had grabbed everything from 1980 – from when Elena had first met Vito – and separated it into two piles: photographs taken up until 1989, the year of the car crash; and those taken from then until 2002, when 'Vito', ergo Aurelio, had died.

At first, she had just let her eyes drift over the images almost as in a stream of consciousness, getting a sense of the brothers' and Elena's body language over the years and hoping to find any glaring errors that might be lying in wait, now she knew what she was looking for. But, of course, there were none. By the time Nico's team arrived outside at 8.30 a.m., and the cement mixers began to roll, filling in the sinkhole, she was working through the images more methodically. She was now picking the photos up one by one, checking the date that the archivist had written on the back, and then looking for something, anything, that would tell her Vito was really Aurelio.

It was a nice thought, but so far – futile.

She saw the photo she had liked so much of the four of them having ice creams. It was surely the quintessential *dolce vita* image – gelato and cigarettes, brooding boys and pouting girls, scooters and sunglasses . . . She bit her lip. Elena had been adamant they couldn't use it – something about a fight.

She picked up one beside it and checked the date on the back: *Positano, 1990*. Aurelio, then. Aurelio masquerading as Vito. He was sitting on an old stone wall, the sea behind him and the wind blowing his hair, a cigarette between his fingers, camel Tod's on his feet. His mouth was curled in a half-smile but his eyes . . . she couldn't decipher the expression in his eyes. It was guarded. No, more than that – haunted. No, she shook her head, wrong again – it was the very opposite of haunted: he was there in body, but not in spirit. Was that hollowness the price he had paid for what he had done?

Good, she thought bitterly, letting the pictures drop and picking up another photograph. She hoped they had suf—

The hairs on her arms rose up and she gasped as something suddenly occurred to her. She picked up the two pictures again, her eyes sliding quickly between one, then the other. Then back to the first one again. Her hackles were up, her senses on full alert as she checked and double-checked the images. But it was there in plain sight, the one detail that belied the outward pretence and unravelled the entire charade; it was obvious now that she knew what to look for.

Her heart pounded at double time as she mentally worked through the ramifications, the facts beginning to shuffle into place like a deck of cards as threads of conversations, snippets of chat, rushed to the front of her mind, confirming the truth. *'Bulgari Blue . . .' 'Truly mirror images . . .' 'Dangerous glamour . . .' 'A love so great you'd put a bomb . . .'*

'Oh my God!' Grabbing her phone, she punched in Nico's number and ran to the window. She could see him down there, talking with someone. She saw him reach for the phone in his pocket, see her name on the screen and make his apologies. He walked away towards the garden, wanting some privacy.

'Cesca?' There was a smile in his voice.

'Nico, how did your mother know the ring was in the tunnels?'

From her vantage point, she saw him frown. One hand went to his hip. 'What?'

'Your mother. Who told her about the ring?'

'. . . I don't know. I assume Vito.'

'Vito?'

He tutted. 'I mean Aurelio. You know what I mean. Why?'

'Turn around.' She waved at him as he turned and looked back at the building, his gaze automatically rising up and scanning the windows. His face broke into a smile as he raised a hand. 'Meet me by the top of the north wing stairs,' she said, hanging up and picking up the two photos from the floor.

She heard Nico's boots on the marble treads as he ran up, dressed in his overalls again; last night's hand-stitched dinner suit already a memory. He kissed her as he reached her, but his eyes were questioning. They were at work.

'It couldn't have been Aurelio who told your mother about the ring,' she said, getting straight to the point. She had to say the words out loud, to hear how they sounded, to check she wasn't going completely mad.

'Huh . . . ?'

'There's no reason why he would have had the ring in his possession, for one thing, right? And the accident happened straight after Vito confronted Aurelio in the stable with Elena; they didn't go back into the tunnels but out into the streets to the cars, so Aurelio could never have known the ring was down there. Agree?'

'Yes,' he said slowly.

'And it was patently clear from Elena's response when you showed it to her that *she* didn't know it was down there, either; if she had lost it on her way over, she would surely have had those tunnels searched until the ring was found, not had them blocked up.'

'Okay.'

'Which means the only person who could have lost the ring was Vito. He must have dropped it on his way to confront them. Signora Dutti said he came up through the tunnel, right?'

'Right,' he said, still slowly, still trying to keep up. 'But I don't understand your point.'

'Well, if it was Vito who dropped the ring but the others had no idea he even had it, then it had to have been—'

She stopped talking. Suddenly the question of who had told Christina the ring was in the tunnel wasn't important. She was remembering something else from last night, something more troubling. It had hit a dud note at the time,

Elena's behaviour abruptly and uncharacteristically emotional and erratic. Giotto had been embarrassed. *'Imagine a love so great that you'd put a bomb under your own life to protect it . . .'*

Was that what Vito had done? Cesca fell still . . . and Elena too?

'What is it? You've gone white,' Nico said, alarmed.

She looked at him, her eyes wide. 'Oh my God! No!' she exclaimed, beginning to run.

Alberto was carrying the breakfast tray, his back erect in a white jacket, the day's edition of *Corriere della Sera* ironed and folded under one arm. He was moving through the galleries, one ahead of her.

Cesca sprinted, grateful for the floaty cotton skirt that didn't hinder her legs, for the trainers that were silent on the marble. She overtook him in the *imperiali* suite, Alberto dropping the tray in shock as she streaked past.

'Stop!' he hollered.

'Alberto! Get help!' she called back, over the sound of china smashing. His shouts were the least of their worries right now.

She burst through the doors into the white apartment, racing past the blossom tree and the pure white sofas to the gentle calm of the private sitting room behind it. Beyond that was the silence of Elena's bedroom. Cesca knew that Alberto woke her every morning at nine.

Cesca stopped at the door, breathless and scared to enter, Nico right on her heels. *'What are you doing?'* he hissed, grabbing her elbow too late as she knocked loudly.

She looked up at him, fear on her face. 'Please God let me

be wrong,' she whispered, as she didn't wait for a reply but simply opened the door.

Alberto arrived not two seconds later – but it was already obvious that she was heartbreakingly right.

Giotto was lying on the bed beside her, his face streaked. Elena was lying under the sheet, tucked in as if by Winnie, her hair perfectly brushed, the Bulgari Blue on her bedside cabinet. The brown pill bottle was still on the bedside table, half full. It wouldn't have taken much, Cesca supposed; she had weighed almost nothing.

'Oh Giotto,' she whispered, rushing over and gently holding one of Elena's cool hands, double-checking for a pulse. There was none and her heart plunged to her feet. 'I'm so sorry.'

'Oh God,' Nico mumbled. 'Gio.'

Cesca looked across at Alberto, who was standing like one of the palazzo's many marble statues, frozen in the doorway. 'Alberto, could you notify the authorities, please?'

She knew he would feel better to be doing something. His eyes slid over to her, unseeing at first, before he nodded and slipped from the room.

'I got up in the night and saw her light was on; I thought something might be wrong. She's been so frail lately.' Giotto swallowed. 'She was already gone.' He looked up at them both. 'Why would she do this? The doctors had given her another good year, at least.'

Cesca took in the look of peace on Elena's face. Was she free now – free from the lies, the pretence? Had it been worth it? she wondered. 'She must have felt it was time.'

'To leave me?' he asked, his voice sharp.

Gently, Cesca met his eyes. 'To face up to things.'

There was a pause as Giotto tried to read her, this stranger in the heart of his home. 'How much do you know – about us?' he asked finally.

'I think pretty much everything,' she admitted.

Giotto stared at her, then back at his mother, before pushing himself up to a seated position, shoulders slumped, his head hanging as though it was too heavy for his neck to bear. He was wearing navy monogrammed pyjamas, the front crease in the trousers still pressed even after a night's sleep.

'I think your mother made her decision last night, at the dinner.'

'What?' Giotto asked, frowning as he looked up again. 'How do you know that? Did she tell you what she was planning?' Horror shone from his eyes.

'No, she didn't. Not directly,' Cesca replied calmly. 'But do you remember last night when she asked you if you remembered what your father used to say about your grandfather?'

'. . . Yes.' He exhaled impatiently. 'As if I could ever forget it. My father used to quote it to us all the time. It was like a family motto, almost.'

'It's because that was what he had done too – for her, and for you. And I think last night was when she finally realized it.'

Giotto blinked, his expression desolate and angry all at once. 'I don't understand.'

Cesca reached into the waistband of her skirt and pulled out the two photographs: the one taken of the four of them eating ice creams, the other from years later – after the accident – with 'Vito' sitting on the wall in Positano.

'Look at these. See how in this one Vito is wearing the

444

signet ring on his left hand?' she said, pointing to the ice-cream shot. 'I started thinking about what you said last night about using the rings to identify them: a signet ring is worn on the non-dominant hand and your father was right-handed, so we know that in this picture, he is Vito; clearly that means the one with the cigarette is Aurelio. See? Aurelio's ring is on his right hand.'

He nodded and she held up the other, later photo from Positano.

'Now see, in *this* photo – which was taken in 1990, a year after the accident – the ring is still on his left hand. That means this is *Vito*. Not Aurelio. It was Aurelio who died in the crash.'

Giotto looked at her. 'I know what I heard, Signorina. My mother called him Reli. *He*—' he said, angrily stabbing the Positano picture with his finger '—is Reli. Not Vito. He . . . he probably just switched the ring to his left hand because he knew that's where Vito wore it.'

Cesca nodded. 'I know and I thought of that. But if you look in this picture here,' she said, holding up the earlier ice-cream image again. 'See how he's holding the cigarette in his left hand? We know for a fact that's Aurelio there. Left-handed. Smoking with his dominant hand. But in this one—' She brought up the Positano picture again. '—The cigarette's in his right hand.' She looked at Giotto, hoping he was able to understand. 'Do you see what I'm saying? It would have been one thing to change elements of his appearance, but it would have been much harder to change a habit or a behaviour. Vito probably wouldn't have even thought about the fact that he smoked with his right hand.'

Nico stepped forward, a look of utter disbelief on his

face. 'You're saying it was Vito who survived after all? *Not* Aurelio?'

'Yes. It was what I was saying to you earlier about the ring – if Vito lost the ring in the tunnel and then died almost immediately afterwards without going back in, who could have told your mother it was in there? Not Aurelio; he knew nothing about it. Not Elena. It *had* to have been Vito. You said your mother saw him for lunch just once after the funeral? He must have told her the ring had been lost then.'

'But then why did he push her away?'

'Because she knew him better than anyone, and he was about to start living a lie. He couldn't have kept it up in front of your moth—'

'This doesn't explain what I heard,' Giotto said, cutting in. 'I know what I heard.'

'That's right. You did overhear your mother calling him Reli – because that was what Vito *wanted* her to believe. He wanted her to believe he had died and his brother had lived.' There was a stunned silence.

'. . . But it *was* Aurelio who was killed in the car crash,' she finished, quietly.

'But you said that crash wouldn't have killed anyone,' Nico argued. They were both arguing with her now.

'And it wouldn't have killed anyone – ordinarily. But Aurelio wasn't ordinary. He had been shot years earlier in Kenya and your mother told me last night the bullet was lodged too close to his heart for the surgeons to be able to remove it. The impact of the crash was just enough—'

'To move it,' Nico murmured, looking ashen. 'Oh my God.'

'Exactly. That's why the official cause of death was heart failure.'

Everyone was quiet, trying to digest this new version of the truth. There were so many . . .

'So . . . my father *lied* about his own death?' Giotto clarified.

'To your mother, yes,' Cesca nodded. 'To the world he was still Vito Damiani, but he wanted her to believe he was his brother.'

'By pretending he was dead?' Giotto asked incredulously. 'Why? Why would he do that?'

Cesca blinked. 'Because he knew she was in love with Aurelio. And he probably guessed that if she thought Aurelio was dead, she would leave him. And take you too.'

Giotto fell silent, looking back down at the still form of his mother on the bed. 'And you think my mother . . . realized this, last night?'

'I do. I think she realized it when you talked about the rings. The talk of which rings were on which hands was just enough to highlight the anomaly for her – Vito wouldn't have been able to hide that he was right-handed. When you live with someone, their behaviours are so familiar as to become invisible, but as soon as they're pointed out, they become glaringly obvious.'

Giotto was quiet for a long time, trying to digest this twisted truth. 'But she got up on that stage last night and said all those wonderful things about Vito. You're telling me she could do that, even though she had just learnt he had lied to her for all those years?'

'Yes, because I think she understood *why* he had done it. She realized your father had put a bomb under his own life to protect his love for her and you. It was what he felt he had to do to keep you both.'

Giotto dropped his head again, hiding his face in his

hands as the sobs began to heave his shoulders. Cesca felt her own heart break for him. She couldn't imagine the pain of this – to have lost his mother, to learn the full torment of his father's love.

His eyes were red when he finally looked back at her. 'He did all that, even though . . .' His voice cracked. '. . . E-even though he may well not have been my father. You realize there's every possibility it was Aurelio?'

She swallowed and nodded. 'Yes. I'm so sorry,' she said, giving a helpless shrug. It was the one thing she didn't know, couldn't help him with.

A sound escaped him – low and urgent, like a wounded animal's acceptance of defeat, of the end. He got up and began to pace the room restlessly, his hands in his hair as he shook his head. What was he supposed to process first? Cesca wondered sadly.

Nico squeezed her shoulder, giving her a quietly proud look as he walked back towards the window and saw his team all standing in a group in the courtyard, hard hats off. The news was spreading . . .

Cesca wondered how long it would be before the authorities got here, and then, of course, the press. 'Giotto – I'm sorry to ask this. But did your mother leave a note?' she asked, twisting to see him as he walked.

He stopped, as if the realization was a wall. 'No.' His tone was flat. 'Well, I . . . I haven't looked. When I saw her on the bed, I just—' His voice cracked and he turned away quickly again.

'It's okay,' Cesca soothed, just as Nico moved suddenly in the corner of her eye.

'Wait. There's something here,' Nico said, his eyes on a stack of papers on the dressing table. It took Cesca only

a split-second to realize it was the manuscript. She and
Giotto crossed the room as Nico picked up the topmost
sheet. He handed it to Giotto but they all read it together in
silence, frowns puckering their brows.

My darling boy,
Forgive me for leaving you to learn the truth in this way. I
simply was not strong enough to face it myself, until tonight. My
life has not been what I thought it would be, and even less what
others assumed it to be. I have known great sorrows and made such
terrible mistakes that it has felt impossible to try to describe how I
came to make them.

What you find on the pages that follow is my best attempt to
explain. It will not be easy for you to read, as it was not easy for me
to tell, nor, I know, for Francesca to write, but it is my final gift to
you – from a mother to her son, this is my account of my life, of
who I am.

There are so many things I wish I could have done differently,
but you are the one thing I would never change. I could not ever
regret anything that brought you to me, for you were always my
truest love, my every consolation.

So don't be sad, my darling. This day was coming anyway – too
fast, then too slow. I have made my peace. Just keep in your heart
that everything that was done, was done out of love – for me, for
you, for our family. Love is the bomb under all our lives, as it
should be.

Your loving Mama x

Cesca put down the note, her heart clattering as she took
in what it all meant. She hadn't written a book – not in the
commercial sense, anyway – so much as a confession: a 200-

page apology, a salutary tale of money, love and luck. It had never been intended to see the light of day.

She thought back to the day she had found Elena sitting in her apartment, waiting with her proposal, the very morning after they had first met. A coincidence? Christina had made it clear at their lunch that she thought not, and Cesca was now inclined to agree. In all probability, Elena had settled upon her as her biographer at that very first meeting; she had probably set her course before Cesca had even woken from her sleep, late and panicking and about to be very nearly run over by a handsome man on a scooter. Elena had probably only had to pay Giovanni a small bribe to get him to sack her and if she hadn't conveniently overslept, they'd have found some other reason. Elena would have got her way because she had recognized that Cesca was the girl for the job – for what would she have found if she had googled Cesca's name, the way Cesca had googled hers? Headlines of a tragic case in which the defence counsel was too good at her job, a blog by a former barrister searching for pleasure in the small things, a girl overseas building a new life, a graduate with a brain and a restless need to dig out the truth.

Cesca paced, feeling the urge to move. The circle had been squared at last, but she had been manipulated in the doing of it. Elena had mined her barristerial instincts to present a case to her son. It was not up to Cesca to prove her innocence and Elena had known she wouldn't try to; Elena was innocent until proven guilty, after all, and the decision on that would be Giotto's in the end. His was the only verdict that counted. He was the legacy of a love affair that had consumed every one of them, for Aurelio, Vito and Elena had – in the end – all died for each other.

She looked back at Elena, peaceful in death, tiny in body but formidable in spirit. It was hard to believe she had once been considered the luckiest little girl in America.

But as Cesca stared at her, she saw something – a slip of a shadow beneath the pillow.

'Giotto?'

The word drew both men's attention from the manuscript and they turned to find her standing by the bed, holding out the little blue letter.

It had been opened, finally – and just as Elena had predicted – on the last day of her life. After fifteen years, she had found the courage to face her reckoning, to give Vito the last word on a love affair that had blown up all their lives.

It was like a homing pigeon, this letter, Cesca reflected as she held it in her hand: forever returning to her as though she was supposed to read it too. Would anything have been different if, that first night by the bins, she had? For by returning it unopened, she had become woven into the tapestry of this extraordinary family's history.

But it was a hypothetical question, of course. She was a woman of principle; she would never have read a stranger's letter – and that was precisely why Elena had chosen her in the first place. Anyway, she hadn't needed to. Christina had been right when she'd said the ground had opened itself up to push an old secret to the surface – that sinkhole had led to tunnels, which had led to a ring that was a token for a love beyond measure.

Events were unveiling exactly the way they were supposed to. The process had begun not fifteen years earlier, when the letter had been written, nor even twenty-two years before that, when Aurelio had returned home on Christmas Eve, nor even fourteen years before *that* when

Laney had thrown her head back in laughter at Truman Capote's Black and White masked ball . . . and missed the dashing Italian who passed right by. No, this moment had been a lifetime in the making and everything that had gone before – all the passion and the pain, the good luck and the bad – had led them to here.

Giotto – their son, heir and future – took the letter from her and, with a deep breath and tears in his eyes, he began to read.

Epilogue I

13 November 2002

My darling Elena,

My road is run. This world and our wonderful life in it have become too much for my heart to bear. I have tried my best to be what you needed and who you wanted, but even this love is no longer enough, for I miss him with an ache that folds me in half and tears me apart.

From the day of that shooting in Kenya, I always knew I would lose him too soon – he knew it too; it was why he lived so hard, knowing a sneeze, a clap on the back, could be all it took – but I would never be ready for it and I find I am still not.

Are you surprised that I am not he? Sometimes I wondered if you sensed it. I admit there have been many times I regretted what I had done, but I hope you will come to see that on the day he died, I made the only decision I could to persuade me to continue too: preserving your happiness ensured my own. I would get to keep you and our son – yes, our son.

That day – do you remember it? – we went for ice cream after lunch. I followed you both to the Pantheon. I saw you kiss in the rain, your passion and despair written over both your faces, and I knew what was going to happen between you, if it had not happened already. I waited in the tunnel that night, expecting to see him on his way to your rooms, never thinking it would be you down there. Your hunger was like a heat in the dark and though you said his name, I could not restrain myself. And so, my darling, I deceived you, even as you deceived me.

I am not sorry. How can I be when it gave us our boy? He is the one from whom we must beg forgiveness, for he is the only innocent in this affair. Perhaps one day, many years from now when he is a man, he will look into his heart and see what a high price we have paid for our love. His forgiveness may yet come, as I hope will yours.

Love strong and protect him,
Your loving husband, Vito

Epilogue II

Rome, October 2017

'You call that a carbonara?' Guido asked in outrage as Cesca set down the piping hot dish.

'I most certainly do,' she said defiantly.

'But it has onions in it! And where is the egg?'

'Egg?' Cesca cried. 'Don't be crazy, man. I'm not putting a fried egg on top of this. It's not breakfast, you know.'

'Fried?' Guido almost fell off his chair as the others fell about laughing at her joke.

'This is how we do it in England, which as you well know is not only the birthplace to chicken tikka masala but also the *home* of carbonara.' Even Guido laughed as she plated it up and set his down in front of him, kissing his cheek.

'Actually, it tastes good,' Matteo said, practically falling into his, as ever. 'I mean, even though it is not authentic.'

'Talking of authentic, what's going on with you and the gallery assistant with the fake boobs?' Alé asked, passing him the pepper.

Matteo rolled his eyes and shook his head, twirling his index finger next to his temple. 'Crazy.'

'She couldn't be as crazy as Cesca's outfit, surely?' Guido asked.

'Hey! You leave my outfit out of this,' Cesca chided. 'I'll have you know dungarees are perfectly legitimate items of clothing.'

'Not when they are yellow cord and worn by anyone out of diapers, they're not,' he quipped.

Everyone laughed and she flicked a pea at him.

'Exactly!' Matteo grinned. 'She was *that* crazy! I had to get out of there. Next!'

'You have got commitment issues, Matteo,' Alé tutted. 'Honestly, you worry me. You need to settle down.'

'Like you, you mean?'

'Excuse me. I am down to the bartender at Zoo and the geography teacher.'

'How will you choose?' Guido asked, pulling a pained expression. 'Toss a coin?'

Alé shrugged. 'That is definitely an option,' she winked as Cesca handed her a heaped plate.

'The geography teacher? Wow!' Cesca grinned. 'You didn't waste any time in the new job then.'

'Well, unlike you, some of us don't live to work,' Alé quipped. 'We work to date.'

Cesca nodded. 'Ah. So *that's* where I've been going wrong. Silly me!'

It was true, though, she reflected: she had been working almost flat out for the past month. Her fledgling consultancy – offering online *pro bono* legal advice to UK families below a certain income threshold, and taking a commission from the lawyers she referred them on to – was already beginning to make small ripples in the legal pool back home, with the number of enquiries growing every week. And the blog had been demanding more of her attention ever since the photo of her with Elena at the Bulgari party had been published. Several publications had featured it in their acres of coverage devoted to Elena's death, and as a result the number of her subscribers had sky-rocketed to 200,000, almost overnight. She hadn't needed the diary extracts for her exclusive after all, which was probably just as well, in hindsight.

The past month had been a whole heap of madness. Elena's death had been a major international news story, with hordes of reporters camping out at the steps of the palace, all desperate for a quote from Giotto about his extraordinary mother and her incredible, at one time scandalous life. Naturally, he gave them nothing of use – a *Romano di Roma*, discretion was in his blood. Although several people (Christina and Signora Dutti, for example) knew some of Elena's secrets, they had no context for her actions, which otherwise appeared iniquitous, and she remained as much an enigma to them as to the world at large. Cesca, though, had found the singular artery that had defined Elena's life – a love so great, all three of its players had put bombs under their own lives to protect it – and only she and Giotto knew Elena's story in the round. And that was how it would remain: Cesca's silence assured with a simple handshake, the manuscript already burnt.

Giotto had read it through twice before putting it in the flames. It had been a shock for him to come to terms with the fact that – after almost a lifetime of questions about his father – it had turned out to be his mother that he'd never really known. Every evening for two weeks, Cesca and Giotto had sat together, talking over his mother's final months, listening to her taped interviews and going through those same photographs she had discussed in their many meetings over the summer.

457

Before Cesca had left Palazzo Mirandola for the final time, Giotto had led her into Elena's vault and, as per the wishes in Elena's will, invited her to choose a piece of jewellery, any one at all. Although shocked, Cesca hadn't hesitated, selecting the pale-pink opal necklace. Of course, it was by far the most modest of the jewels, but it had also been Elena's favourite – and not to mention, it was the only piece Cesca would ever be likely to wear for, like Elena, she didn't believe in 'Sunday Best' either.

'Actually, strictly speaking, *your* relationship started as a work romance too,' Guido pointed out, pulling her back to the present again, just as the church bells in the distance rang out of time with one another, a flock of starlings swooping in the darkening sky. Though it was a clear evening, there was a distinct chill in the air and it would soon be too cold for evening suppers on the terrace. The world was continuing to turn. 'Wouldn't you agree, Nico?'

Nico, sitting beside her, amused as ever by the banter around the table, swept her up in his gaze as his eyes rose to meet hers. 'Well, of course. It is the classic love story,' he deadpanned. 'Boy goes to work. Boy meets girl in mad clothes. Boy falls for girl in mad clothes.'

'Oi.' Everyone guffawed as Cesca punched him lightly on the arm, and he pulled her down onto his lap, kissing her to their cheers.

'Ah, poor Cesca, it must be terrible to be such a cliché,' Guido teased her.

'I am not a cliché!' she gasped in mock-indignation.

'Oh, but you are. You used to love this city for its . . . what was it? "Amber light and sparrows"? You had poetry in your soul!' His eyes danced. 'But now look – you are like

458

all the other girls who come to Rome and fall for our tall, dark, handsome men.'

Cesca couldn't think of a rejoinder. She'd been busted. It was the truth, the whole truth and nothing but.

'Yes, well,' she grinned, staring into Nico's dark, direct, dancing eyes. '. . . Have you *seen* him in a suit?'

Acknowledgements

Often, the biggest dilemma for a writer isn't actually coming up with what the story is about, but deciding how to tell it. I'd been wanting to write a split-narrative book for a couple of years but the format didn't particularly lend itself to the plots I had in my head at the time and when I set out to write this book, I still didn't think I could tell a 'past and present' story – I initially thought it would have a four-way perspective, but I found myself so drawn in by Elena and her extraordinary life that I didn't want to lose pages to other characters when I could focus on her.

I had read widely on the pre-eminent socialites of her age – Marella Agnelli, Lee Radziwill and Gloria Vanderbilt, among others – and even though they were all from different backgrounds and cultures (although all born into money), I was struck by the parallels in their interests, concerns, tone and social circles, and wrote lists identifying the overlaps. By the time I'd finished reading, Elena was fully-fleshed in my mind; so when I found myself at a dinner party talking to a friend who's an identical twin, I hit upon the one thing that her money could not buy, and knew I had my 'past/present' story at last.

I travelled to Rome for a glorious research recce – any excuse! – with the express intention of finding the palazzo

460

and piazza that were in my head. I knew what I needed logistically speaking – an enormous palazzo fronting onto a principal square, with a smaller one off to the side – but even though I walked and walked and walked, I actually couldn't find exactly what I wanted, so I'm afraid the Palazzo Damiani, Piazza Angelica and Piazzetta Palombella are fictitious. However, if you're interested in the real-life elements, the bakery 'next door' is based upon the wonderfully old-world Biscottificio Innocenti in Trastevere and the front of Cesca's apartment, with the steps and flowers, is inspired by the lovely little house just up the road from that (you can't miss it). Piazza Angelica is very loosely based on Piazza Navona, but given that I stole the flower and food market from Campo de' Fiori and plonked it in there, it's hardly a literal representation; more an indicator of set-up and scale. I read up on various palaces in Rome but it was the Doria Pamphilj that really caught my attention – this is the palace with the papal throne facing the wall, and which has 1,000 rooms. It's open to the public if you are ever in the city and interested in visiting. And the ice cream store where the four characters sit outside on Vespas is based on Giolitti in Via del Vicario, near the Pantheon.

So: for this story I researched top-flight socialites and Roman palaces, the Black Nobility and speleology, and just how cunning identical twins can be (thanks Justin and Nuala!). I had a super time and writing this book was a joy, but the fact that it's sitting in your hands right now doesn't just come down to my input. There are so many other people who have helped get this story to you, principally my super-agent Amanda Preston, who always knows within two sentences whether or not an idea's a book, and my unflappable editor Caroline Hogg, who gets briefs from me on everything from romantic astronauts to bad-tempered speleologists and never gets spooked!

There's such a huge operation in full swing behind the scenes and I owe a debt of thanks and gratitude to Jeremy Trevathan, Wayne Brookes, James Annal, Katie James, Jonathan Atkins, Stuart Dwyer, Daniel Jenkins, Anna Bond, Alex Saunders, Amy Lines, Phoebe Taylor, Claire Gatzen; and particularly my copy-editor, Kate Moore, and proof-readers, Camilla Rockwood and Mary Chamberlain, who I think probably have the trickiest jobs of all – making me make sense!

And of course, nothing would ever get written if it weren't for my gorgeous family coming to find me in the study when I go MIA under deadline. They bring me chocolate, tea and champagne (sometimes all at once) – but all I will ever need is them.

PLAYERS

by

Karen Swan

Friendships are strong. Lust is stronger.

Harry Hunter is the new golden boy of the literary
scene. With his books selling by the millions, the
paparazzi on his tail and a supermodel on each arm,
he seems to have the world at his feet. Women all over
the globe adore him but few suspect that his angelic
looks hide a darker side, a side that conceals a lifetime
of lies and deceit.

Tor, Cress and Kate have been best friends for as long
as they can remember. Through all the challenges of
marriage, raising children and maintaining their
high-flying careers, they have stuck together as a
powerful and loyal force to be reckoned with – living
proof that twenty-first-century women can have it all,
and do. It is only when the captivating Harry comes
into their lives that things begin to get complicated,
as the friends are drawn into Harry's dangerous games.

Prima DONNA

by
Karen Swan

*Breaking the rules was what she liked best.
That was her sport.*

Renegade, rebel, bad girl. Getting away with it.

Pia Soto is the sexy and glamorous prima ballerina,
the Brazilian bombshell who's shaking up the
ballet world with her outrageous behaviour.
She's wild and precocious, and she's a survivor.
She's determined that no man will ever control her
destiny. But ruthless financier Will Silk has Pia in
his sights, and has other ideas . . .

Sophie O'Farrell is Pia's hapless, gawky assistant,
the girl-next-door to Pia's prima donna, always either
falling in love with the wrong man or just falling over.
Sophie sets her own dreams aside to pick up the debris
in Pia's wake, but she's no angel. When a devastating
accident threatens to cut short Pia's illustrious career,
Sophie has to step out of the shadows and face up to
the demons in her own life.

Christmas at TIFFANY'S

by
Karen Swan

Three cities, three seasons, one chance to find the life that fits.

Cassie settled down too young, marrying her first serious boyfriend. Now, ten years later, she is betrayed and broken. With her marriage in tatters and no career or home of her own, she needs to work out where she belongs in the world and who she really is.

So begins a year-long trial as Cassie leaves her sheltered life in rural Scotland to stay with each of her best friends in the most glamorous cities in the world: New York, Paris and London. Exchanging grouse moor and mousy hair for low-carb diets and high-end highlights, Cassie tries on each city for size as she attempts to track down the life she was supposed to have been leading, and with it, the man who was supposed to love her all along.

The Perfect PRESENT

by
Karen Swan

Memories are a gift . . .

Haunted by a past she can't escape, Laura Cunningham
desires nothing more than to keep her world small
and precise – her quiet relationship and growing
jewellery business are all she needs to get by. Until
the day when Rob Blake walks into her studio and
commissions a necklace that will tell his enigmatic
wife Cat's life in charms.

As Laura interviews Cat's family, friends and former
lovers, she steps out of her world and into theirs – a
charmed world where weekends are spent in Verbier
and the air is lavender-scented, where friends are wild,
extravagant and jealous, and a big love has to
compete with grand passions.

Hearts are opened, secrets revealed and as the necklace
begins to fill up with trinkets, Cat's intoxicating life
envelops Laura's own. By the time she has to identify the
final charm, Laura's metamorphosis is almost complete.
But the last story left to tell has the power to change all
of their lives forever, and Laura is forced to choose
between who she really is and who it is she wants to be.

Christmas at
CLARIDGE'S
by
Karen Swan

The best presents can't be wrapped . . .

This was where her dreams drifted to if she didn't blot her nights out with drink; this was where her thoughts settled if she didn't fill her days with chat. She remembered this tiny, remote foreign village on a molecular level and the sight of it soaked into her like water into sand, because this was where her old life had ended and her new one had begun.

Portobello – home to the world-famous street market, Notting Hill Carnival and Clem Alderton. She's the queen of the scene, the girl everyone wants to be or be with. But beneath the morning-after make-up, Clem is keeping a secret, and when she goes too far one reckless night she endangers everything – her home, her job and even her adored brother's love.

Portofino – a place of wild beauty and old-school glamour. Clem has been here once before and vowed never to return. But when a handsome stranger asks Clem to restore a neglected villa, it seems like the answer to her problems – if she can just face up to her past.

Claridge's – at Christmas. Clem is back in London working on a special commission for London's grandest hotel. But is this really where her heart lies?

The SUMMER WITHOUT YOU

by
Karen Swan

Everything will change . . .

Rowena Tipton isn't looking for a new life, just a new adventure; something to while away the months as her long-term boyfriend presses pause on their relationship before they become engaged. But when a chance encounter at a New York wedding leads to an audition for a coveted house share in the Hamptons – Manhattan's elite beach scene – suddenly a new life is exactly what she's got.

Stretching before her is a summer with three eclectic housemates, long days on white-sand ocean beaches and parties on gilded tennis courts. But high rewards bring high stakes and Rowena soon finds herself caught in the crossfire of a vicious intimidation campaign. Alone for the first time in her adult life, she has no one to turn to but a stranger who is everything she doesn't want – but possibly everything she needs.

Christmas in
THE SNOW
by
Karen Swan

In London, the snow is falling and Christmas is just around the corner – but Allegra Fisher barely has time to notice. She's pitching for the biggest deal of her career and can't afford to fail. When she meets attractive stranger Sam Kemp on the plane to the meeting, she can't afford to lose her focus. But when Allegra finds herself up against Sam for the bid, their passion quickly turns sour.

In Zermatt in the Swiss Alps, a long-lost mountain hut is discovered in the snow after sixty years. The last person expecting to become involved is Allegra – she hasn't even heard of the woman they found inside. It soon becomes clear the two women are linked and, as she and her best friend Isobel travel out to make sense of the mystery, hearts thaw and dark secrets are uncovered . . .

Summer at
TIFFANY'S
by
Karen Swan

A wedding to plan. A wedding to stop.
What could go wrong?

Cassie loves Henry. Henry loves Cassie. With a Tiffany ring on her finger, all that Cassie has left to do is plan the wedding. It should be so simple but when Henry pushes for a date, Cassie pulls back.

Henry's wild, young cousin, Gem, has no such hesitations and is racing to the aisle at a sprint, determined to marry in the Cornish church where her parents were wed. But the family is set against it, and Cassie resolves to stop the wedding from going ahead.

When Henry lands an expedition sailing the Pacific for the summer, Cassie decamps to Cornwall, hoping to find the peace of mind she needs to move forwards. But in the dunes and coves of the northern Cornish coast, she soon discovers that the past isn't finished with her yet.

Christmas on
PRIMROSE HILL

by
Karen Swan

On Primrose Hill . . .

Twinkling lights brighten London's Primrose Hill as
Christmas nears – but for Nettie Watson, it's not parties
and presents that she wants.

Promises are made

For Nettie, Christmas only serves as a stark reminder
of the life she used to have . . . One day she made
a promise to never leave home, and so far she's
stayed true to her word.

Promises are broken

Under the glaring spotlight of the world's media, Nettie
is unexpectedly caught up in a twenty-first-century
storm . . . Her exploits have made her a global name and
attracted the attention of one of the world's most eligible
men – famous front man, Jamie Westlake. But now she
has his attention, does she want to keep it?

The Paris Secret

by
Karen Swan

Down a cobbled street in Paris, a long-forgotten apartment is found. Thick with dust and secrets, it is full of priceless artworks that have been hidden away for decades.

When high-flying Fine Art Agent Flora Sykes is called in to assess the collection, she is thrown into the very heart of the glamorous Vermeil family – and into the path of the terse and brooding Xavier.

Shying away from the instant attraction between them and reeling from a devasting family shock back home, Flora focuses on tracing the history of the paintings, delving deep into the Vermeil family's past. But as she moves between London and Paris, Vienna and Antibes, she finds herself with more questions than answers. Xavier seems intent on forcing her out, but just what is he hiding? And will uncovering the truth heal the past – or destroy her future?

Christmas
UNDER THE STARS
by
Karen Swan

Worlds apart. A love without limit.

In the snow-topped mountains of the Canadian Rockies, Meg and Mitch are living their dream. Just weeks away from their wedding, they work and play with Tuck and Lucy, their closest and oldest friends. Meg and Lucy are as close as sisters – much to Meg's real sister's dismay – and Tuck and Mitch have successfully turned their passion for snowboarding into a booming business.

But when a polar storm hits, tragedy strikes. Alone in the tiny mountain log cabin she shares with Mitch, Meg desperately tries to radio for help – and it comes from the most unexpected quarter, a lone voice across the airwaves that sees what she cannot.

As the snow melts and the friends try to live with their loss, the relationships Meg thought were forever are buckled by tensions, rivalries and devastating secrets. Nothing is as she thought and only her radio contact understands what it is to be truly alone. As they share confidences in the dark, witnessed only by the stars, Meg feels her future begin to pull away from her past and is forced to consider a strange truth – is it her friends who are the strangers? And a stranger who really knows her best?

It's time to relax with your next good book

THE**WINDOW**SEAT.CO.UK

If you've enjoyed this book, but don't know what
to read next, then we can help. The Window Seat is
a site that's all about making it easier to discover your
next good book. We feature recommendations,
behind-the-scenes tales from the world of publishing,
creative writing tips, competitions, and, if we're honest,
quite a lot of lists based on our favourite reads.

You'll find stories and features
by authors including Lucinda Riley, Karen Swan,
Diane Chamberlain, Jane Green, Lucy Diamond
and many more. We showcase brand-new talent
as well as classic favourites, so you'll never be
stuck for what to read again.

We'd love to know what you think of the site, our books,
and what you'd like us to feature, so do let us know.

🐦 @panmacmillan.com

f facebook.com/panmacmillan

WWW.THEWINDOWSEAT.CO.UK